Liza Marklund's crime novels featuring the relentless reporter Annika Bengtzon instantly became an international hit, and Marklund's books have sold over 15 million copies in 30 languages to date. She has achieved the unique feat of being a number one bestseller in all five Nordic countries, as well as the USA.

She has been awarded numerous prizes, including the inaugural Petrona award for best Scandinavian crime novel of the year 2013 for *Last Will*, as well as a nomination for the Glass Key for best Scandinavian crime novel.

Visit her website at www.lizamarklund.com

Neil Smith studied Scandinavian Studies at University College London, and lived in Stockholm for several years. He now lives in Norfolk.

WITHOUT A TRACE

Liza Marklund

Translated from the Swedish by Neil Smith

CORGI BOOKS

TRANSWORLD PUBLISHERS
61–63 Uxbridge Road, London W5 5SA
www.transworldbooks.co.uk

Transworld is part of the Penguin Random House group of companies
whose addresses can be found at global.penguinrandomhouse.com

Penguin
Random House
UK

Originally published in Swedish by Piratförlaget in 2013
as *Lyckliga gatan*
First published in Great Britain in 2015 by Corgi Books
an imprint of Transworld Publishers

A CIP catalogue record for this book
is available from the British Library.

ISBN
9780552170963

Typeset in 10½/13pt Sabon by Kestrel Data, Exeter, Devon.
Printed and bound by CPI Group (UK) Ltd, Croydon, CR0 4YY.

Penguin Random House is committed to a sustainable
future for our business, our readers and our planet. This book is
made from Forest Stewardship Council® certified paper.

MIX
Paper from
responsible sources
FSC® C018179

1 3 5 7 9 10 8 6 4 2

WITHOUT A TRACE

PROLOGUE

Human beings can only comprehend a certain level of pain. Then they pass out. Their consciousness protests, like the trip-switch of an overloaded electrical circuit.

Staying on the right side of that boundary required sensitivity and judgement.

The man with the hammer looked at the person on the bed with stoical resignation. 'It's your decision,' he said. 'We can stop whenever you want.'

There was no response, but the man was in no doubt. The words had been understood. This particular client (he always thought of them like that, as clients he'd been asked to work with) was a rather impressive example of *Homo sapiens*: well-developed musculature, healthy skin-tone, a fairly thin layer of subcutaneous fat. And driven by ideology and conviction, a sure indication that the job was likely to be of the more complicated sort. The struggling and squirming had stopped now, and the individual was lying quietly on the bed in his trousers and shirt. The duct tape round his wrists and ankles was no longer needed; only the piece over his mouth remained.

The man looked at his twin brother, his mirror-image on the other side of the bed, and they nodded to each other. His brother bent down over the toolbox and made

9

his selection, then took out an awl with his gloved hand. The man with the hammer nodded approval at his choice.

He shut his eyes briefly to focus on his breathing and raise his awareness of the moment, of being in the here and now, in his own body, the way the soles of his feet felt against his rubber-soled shoes, the weight of the tool in his hand.

For a fleeting but intense moment he missed his Magnum.

They had actually moved away from using firearms as tools. They made such a terrible noise, even with silencers, and he wasn't thinking primarily about the damage they had done to their hearing. (Wearing ear-defenders had been one option, but that idea had been rejected as lacking subtlety.) The public tended to react badly to the sight of firearms, but ropes and toolboxes were completely unobtrusive.

He realized that his mind was wandering, and brought it firmly but gently back to focus on his breathing again. Then he opened his eyes and looked at the client. 'I'm going to give you an opportunity to answer now,' he said softly. 'If you shout or do anything silly, it will hurt.'

The client didn't answer. His eyes were closed and he was breathing through his nose in a laboured, rasping way.

He pulled the duct tape back a few centimetres, just enough to uncover the corner of the man's mouth. 'Are you ready?' he asked. 'All the unpleasantness can stop here.'

He drew the tape back a little further.

The man breathed in through his mouth, and there was a gurgling sound in his throat. He coughed, spraying saliva.

He leaned close to the client's ear, his voice a silky whisper. 'Where is she?'

The client's breathing was irregular, and his eyes were

still closed. But the question had gone in: the movement of his eyes under the lids became more rapid and his body tensed.

The man leaned even further forward. 'What did you say?' he whispered. 'I didn't quite hear you . . .'

The client attempted to speak, and his Adam's apple bobbed. The sounds that emerged were more gasps than words. 'Don't . . . know . . .'

The man sighed, and saw his mirror-image do the same. 'Such a shame,' he said, replacing the duct tape. The underside was wet with saliva and wouldn't stick properly: next time they'd have to replace it with a fresh piece. 'Well, let's see how things look under this shirt,' he said, undoing the buttons once more.

Two tears appeared below the client's closed eyelids.

'Try not to cry,' the mirror-image said. 'The nasal passages swell up, making it hard to breathe.'

He could see the client struggling to do as they said: he really did want to be amenable. That was a good sign. Carefully he felt the client's ribs, and the man groaned. The bruising had crept down the side of his torso towards his navel, and he could feel the fractures clearly beneath the skin.

'Let's take number three,' he said, and raised the hammer. His mirror-image pulled one of the client's eyelids open, and his pupil contracted as the light hit his eye. Good: the reflexes were working. He felt with his fingers across the client's ribcage, carefully took aim, then administered a firm and precisely measured blow with the hammer. The rib broke with a dull, muffled click, and the body shook in a brief convulsion. The man's breathing became quicker and shallower: he was on the verge of losing consciousness again.

His twin brother leaned over the client. 'You just have to tell us. Then it will be over.'

His eyes rolled back until only the whites were visible.

His brother took a firmer grip on the awl.

'Where is Nora?'

*

We were standing under one of the apple trees in the garden. It was spring and the tree was in full blossom – I remember the sound of bumble-bees among the petals, the sun's flickering light through the crown. It had rained that morning; glistening drops still clung to the bark and in the forks of the branches. I was holding my little boy in my arms – he was five days old, Isak, my first. I'd wrapped a blanket round him to keep the wind off, and Ingemar was holding me – he was holding us both. I remember how soft my son felt against my cheek, the way he smelt, my husband's arms round my shoulders. We stood there close together, the three of us, a unit that was greater than everything else.

That memory often comes back to me. When I need to conjure up an image of perfect happiness, that's the feeling that comes back to me, that moment with Isak and Ingemar under the apple tree: intoxication, perfection.

MONDAY, 13 MAY

The first thing she noticed was the silence. The dog wasn't barking. Usually he stood by the garage door, howling so hard that he frothed at the mouth, tugging at his leash until the pressure of the collar against his throat turned his yapping into breathless gasps.

There was something wrong with that dog – she'd always thought so. If he'd been a person, she was sure he'd have been diagnosed with one of those syndromes. He was quite a handsome creature, shiny black coat and big paws, but he was wall-eyed and his teeth were too big. He always seemed a bit out of control, unstable. That he wasn't barking gave her a brief and indefinable feeling of relief.

It vanished the instant she reached the back door and found it unlocked. She opened it without a sound and stood in the doorway, as the dry indoor heat hit her face.

The emptiness seemed to echo. Then she noticed the smell. Not offensive, just different. Sort of sweet and sharp at the same time. It didn't belong there.

She stepped quickly into the utility room and pulled the door shut behind her as quietly as she could. The feeling of unease was stronger. She could hear her own heartbeat rushing inside her head.

Slowly she bent down and took off her boots without a

15

sound. A little puddle of water had already formed around them. Without thinking she reached for a dishcloth on the worktop and wiped it up. Her slippers were by the washing-machine, but for some reason she didn't put them on. She put her gloves into her coat pockets, then took off her coat, hat and scarf and hung them on the hook next to the back door, along with her handbag. Then she walked towards the kitchen in her stockinged feet. The smell was more intense.

The light was on above the kitchen worktop. The third thing that's wrong, she thought.

The dog. The back door. The light.

Environmental awareness, she remembered. Be aware of the environment. Save electricity. Credibility is important to a politician. You have to set a good example to the voters.

She turned the light off, then walked past the worktop and into the hall.

The dog was lying there.

At first she thought it was a different dog. He seemed so small. Lifelessness had shrunk him. The untamed energy he exuded in life had dissipated and left him looking like a rag on the hall rug, the fake one with the Persian pattern. It was impossible to get it clean with the vacuum – she always had to use a roller afterwards. The dog's blood hadn't soaked into the plasticky acrylic material, just lay on top where it had dried into a brown pancake.

Her breathing became laboured. She felt her armpits start to sweat, as they usually did when things got out of hand, when the students in her old school lost concentration and stared, scraping their shoes on the cement floor. She tried to pull herself together. After all, she'd never really liked the dog. Stefan, that was its name. How could anyone give a name like that to a dog?

Keeping close to the wall she made her way into the living room. The curtains were closed. She blinked a few times in the gloom. The air was warm and stuffy. She swallowed. She ought to get out of there. At once.

Someone must have killed the dog. That had been no accident. Why would anyone want to kill it?

There was a noise. Someone groaning. Or coughing, maybe. A low voice, male.

She stiffened.

It had come from upstairs, from the bedrooms.

She looked at the staircase.

The husband mustn't see her. How could she explain what she was doing there? Mind you, the door had been open, unlocked. Anyone could have walked in.

She looked at the dog again.

He must have killed the dog. Why? Had anything happened to the children? What if they were upstairs?

She thought she could make out more sounds from upstairs, but she wasn't sure.

What should she do? The house ought to be empty. Locked, shut up.

She stood still in the hall for several minutes, but perhaps it wasn't actually that long.

Then she wiped her hands on her trousers and, before she had time to change her mind, stepped quickly past the dog and hurried breathlessly up the stairs. She made sure she didn't tread on the fifth and seventh steps, the ones that creaked.

The door to the children's room was closed. She opened it cautiously, knew it didn't squeak. It was only a few weeks since she'd oiled the hinges. The roller-blind with the rabbit pattern was pulled down. The stuffed toys were there but otherwise the room was empty. The children's beds were made, Isak's, Samuel's, and little Elisabeth's over by the window. She breathed a sigh of relief and closed the door behind her. She walked to the main bedroom.

He was lying in the double bed, if it was actually him. She'd only seen him in the wedding photograph, and his face was unrecognizable. His mouth was wide open, his front teeth missing. His body was in an unnatural position – she hadn't known that arms and legs could point in those directions. He was wearing trousers and a shirt. No socks. The soles of his feet had been lacerated.

She stared at the man and felt her body filling with something heavy and warm, making it hard to breathe.

Someone had done this to him. What if they were still in the house?

A gurgling noise came from the man's throat. She found that she could move her legs again, and stumbled backwards onto the landing, regained her balance and walked past the children's room, down the stairs, past the dog's body, into the kitchen, then the utility room.

Sweat was trickling down her sides as she fumbled with the buttons of her coat. She was crying as she locked the back door behind her, tears burning with loss and, perhaps, a little guilt.

The lift pinged and came to a stop. Its doors opened with a sucking sound. Nina Hoffman looked uncertainly at the digital numbers: was this right?

She stepped out onto the red-painted landing and the doors closed behind her. A low, muffled sound told her that the lift was disappearing, deep inside the hermetically sealed building.

Yes, this was it, the right stairwell, and the right floor.

To her left was a glass door with an alarm and a coded lock. She walked over and pressed a button that she assumed was a bell. She couldn't hear anything. She stood and waited, her mouth and throat dry. One of the lifts swept past – she couldn't tell if it was going up or down. For a moment she felt a pang of dark, giddy uncertainty: what was she doing? Was she really going to put herself through this *again*?

Then came the muffled sound of heels approaching. A face suddenly appeared on the other side of the glass door. Nina took an involuntary step back.

'Nina Hoffman?'

The woman was short and blonde, curvy and wearing high heels. *Barbie doll.*

'Welcome to National Crime! Come in.'

Nina stepped into the corridor. The ceiling was very low. There was a faint rumbling sound from somewhere. The floor was polished to a high sheen.

'I'm here for the induction course,' Nina said, by way of explanation. 'Perhaps you could tell me where . . .'

'The head of CIS says he'd like to see you straight away. You know where to find him?'

How could she? 'No,' she replied.

The Barbie doll explained.

Nina's footsteps plodded dully on the plastic floor; there was no echo. She walked past open doors, fragments of voices dancing past, light from small windows up by the ceiling. At the end of the corridor she turned left and found herself at a corner room with a view of Bergsgatan.

'Nina, come in.'

Commissioner Q had risen through the ranks. He'd left Stockholm's Violent Crime Unit to become head of

19

CIS, the Criminal Intelligence Unit at National Crime.

She stepped into the room and unbuttoned her jacket.

'Welcome to National Crime,' he said.

That must be the usual greeting for new recruits. 'Thanks.'

She studied the man behind the desk, without being too obvious about it. His garish Hawaiian shirt clashed badly with the municipal furnishings. They'd had dealings with each other before, when David Lindholm, a police officer, had been found murdered (when *she* had found David Lindholm murdered), and she wondered if he was going to mention that. His desk was empty, except for a coffee mug, a laptop and two thin folders. He stood up, walked round the desk and greeted her with a firm handshake.

'Have you found your way around the labyrinth yet?' he asked, as he gestured towards a visitor's chair.

How was she supposed to have done that? She'd arrived just five minutes ago. 'Not yet.'

She hung her jacket over the back of the chair and sat down. It was hard and uncomfortable. He returned to his chair, leaned back and looked at her intently. 'I understand you're doing the induction course today. Is that right?'

All week, she'd been told. 'Yes.'

He reached for one of the folders, put on a pair of reading glasses, opened the first page and read through her CV.

'Police Academy,' he said. 'Then Katarina Police District on Södermalm, trainee, constable and sergeant. Then more studies, Stockholm University, courses in behavioural science, criminology, social psychology and ethnology.'

He looked at her over his glasses. 'Why behavioural science?'

Because I was lost. Because I wanted to understand people.

20

'It seemed . . . interesting.'

'You speak Spanish, I understand? As well as German and Portuguese?'

'I grew up in Tenerife. My dad was German. I understand Portuguese, but I'm not fluent.'

'English?'

'Of course.'

He closed the file. 'When I took this job, I insisted on being allowed to bring in some of my own people. I want you here.'

She didn't answer, just studied him carefully. What did he mean? Why was he bringing up her education?

Q pushed his glasses up onto his forehead. 'Why did you leave Katarina and start studying again?'

Because my entire family has been criminal for generations. Because I chose the same path, but from the other side. Because I shot and killed my brother on a hash plantation in Morocco.

'I felt I needed to develop . . . that I had more to give.'

He nodded again, and regarded her calmly. 'We don't do police jargon here,' he said. 'We're looking for unusual people. Abnormalities are an asset. We want women, gays, ethnic minorities, lesbians, academics . . .'

Was he trying to shock her? If he was, he'd have to try harder. Or was he fishing?

She didn't answer.

He smiled. 'Because you're a trained police officer, you're still authorized to carry out police business, so you can conduct interrogations, and so on, in so far as you deem it necessary, but your post here will be as an operational analyst. How important is it for you to go on that induction course?'

She didn't respond.

'I mean, you know about timesheets, Lamia can sort out a pass-card, computer and a login ID, and you can go round saying hello to people later, can't you?'

Presumably Lamia was the blonde. She would have been happy to do the course – she wasn't sure she remembered how to fill in a timesheet. The system had probably been updated during the four years that had passed since she'd left the force.

The head of CIS took her silence as agreement. 'Do you know who Ingemar Lerberg is?' he asked.

Nina searched her memory: a politician, forced to resign. 'Of course.'

Superintendent Q opened the second file and pulled his glasses onto his nose. 'Lerberg has been found assaulted in his home in Solsidan, out in Saltsjöbaden, it's not yet clear if he's going to make it. We've received a request for assistance from Nacka Police. Do you have any contacts out there?'

Solsidan? Wasn't that a comedy series on television?

'Not that I can think of.'

He held the folder across the desk. 'We're putting together an investigative team today, two or three people to start with. I'd like you to go out and take a look. Don't be afraid to ask if there's anything you're not sure about . . . See it as an introduction to working here.'

The superintendent leaned back in his chair. 'We'll get together in the meeting room at nine o'clock sharp tomorrow morning. Bring whatever you've been able to find. Lamia will sort out a car for you.'

*

The house was on its own at the end of the road, not too far from the little station.

Annika Bengtzon switched off the wipers, then leaned forward and tried to peer through the windscreen. The heater was spewing hot, stuffy air into her face, and she turned it down, then glanced up the road.

Nacka Police had cordoned off the turning circle and the far end of the road, the whole of the property and parts of the neighbours' lawn. Several other journalists had already parked their cars at the side of the road and were either sitting in the warm, behind misted-up windows, or standing about by the cordon. The first news-agency report had claimed that Ingemar Lerberg was dead. Then it had been changed to 'very seriously injured'. The initial mistake was probably the reason for the remarkably large media interest. A murdered politician was always a murdered politician even if he'd only been a member of Nacka's social-services committee. But in the past Lerberg had also been a controversial Member of Parliament, someone of whom there were plenty of pictures in the archives.

Annika took a deep breath. Violence still made her feel uneasy, as did hordes of journalists. She decided to stay in the car as long as she could.

The house was situated towards the back of the plot, partially concealed by a thin lilac hedge and a few apple trees, all dripping with water. A rocky outcrop rose up behind it, greyish-yellow from the remnants of last year's grass. There was nothing remarkable about the building: painted red, white gables, hipped roof, probably built in the 1920s and renovated in the 1970s, when a new façade and large picture windows had been put in. The result was a mishmash, a strained attempt at modernity. It would be difficult to make it live up to its billing as the luxury

23

villa the head of news had said it was, but everything was relative. It was a question of how you phrased things. For her mum at home in Hälleforsnäs, a renovated wooden house in Saltsjöbaden was definitely a luxury villa.

Lerberg had been taken to hospital, she knew that much. There was already some mobile-phone footage on YouTube of him being driven off in the ambulance. Picture-Pelle had spoken to the man who'd shot the footage and offered to buy the rights to post it on the *Evening Post* website, but had lost out to their wealthier competitors.

The rain wasn't showing any sign of letting up. A television van turned into the narrow road and parked in front of her, blocking her view of the house. She switched off the engine, pulled up the hood of her raincoat, slung her bag over her shoulder, grabbed the tripod and got out of the car. The wind tugged at her coat. It really was bloody cold. She said a brief hello to TV4 and the prestigious morning paper, but pretended not to notice Bosse, from the other evening paper, who was standing by the turning circle, talking far too loudly into his mobile. She looked at her watch. She hadn't got the children that week, but she wanted to get away as quickly as possible. Jimmy, her partner, was cooking that night and she'd promised to be home in time for dinner. And there was no exclusive here, nothing to dig out, just routine coverage. Fast and efficient. Get some clips for the website and some quotes from a police officer, then try to embroider a story with fragments of fact.

Assaulted in his home. Very seriously injured.

She set up the tripod in the road in front of the cordon, just a couple of metres from a local radio reporter, then pulled the video-camera out of her bag and fixed it to the stand.

'Do you want me to hold an umbrella over that?' the reporter offered. He was tall and thin – she recognized him but didn't know his name. He was carrying a radio transmitter, with four aerials and a little flashing light, on his back. It made him look like an insect.

She smiled tentatively at him. 'That would be great. Mind you, by now my camera's got its own swimming badge, and can ski down black runs . . .'

'It's ridiculous, isn't it?' Insect Man agreed. 'Where does all this snow and rain come from? It's got to stop at some point . . .'

She plugged the microphone cable into the audio socket, cleared her throat, pressed play and stood in front of the camera. 'Here,' she said, looking hard into the lens, 'in the middle of the idyllic residential area of Solsidan in Saltsjöbaden, politician Ingemar Lerberg was found seriously assaulted earlier this morning. He has been taken to Södermalm Hospital in Stockholm, where he remains in a critical condition.' She looked at the radio reporter. 'That was fifteen seconds, wasn't it?'

'Maybe fourteen.'

She lowered the microphone, went to the camera and let it pan across the scene: the dripping cordon, the media scrum, the figures visible behind the closed curtains up in the house. She would use the pictures as a backdrop to a voiceover once she knew more about the case. The reporter was still holding the umbrella above her.

'It's not quite as smart as I thought it would be out here,' he said.

'It's probably only the address that's smart, not the houses,' Annika said.

She pressed stop, then put the camera back into her bag. The reporter lowered the umbrella.

'Do you know who first reported it?' Annika asked.

'No, just that the alarm was sounded at nine thirty-six.'

Annika looked at the house. The radio reporter and head of news weren't the only ones who had expected something more. Ingemar Lerberg was the sort of politician who expressed himself through grand gestures and seemingly infinite pomposity. He called himself a businessman, and often had himself photographed on impressive yachts.

'Why did he resign? From Parliament, I mean.'

'Something to do with tax,' Annika said. 'One of his companies, I think.' She gestured towards some unmarked cars inside the cordon. 'National Crime?'

'I think so,' the reporter said.

Annika looked up at the house again. Another floodlight was switched on upstairs, and the acid bluish-white light made the dampness outside the window seem to crackle. 'If National Crime are here, things must be pretty terrible inside,' she said.

'Unless the Nacka Police are just covering their backs,' Insect Man said.

Recent graduates weren't stupid these days, she thought.

'Annika Bengtzon,' a voice said behind her.

Her heart sank. 'Hello, Bosse,' she said. She couldn't understand why she'd once found the idiot attractive.

'Changing the world at this time in the morning?'

She could either ignore him, which would amount to a declaration of war, or talk to him – he really wasn't worth getting upset about. She turned and smiled. 'It's all food on the table, Bosse. We can't all live off the dividends from our investments.'

Bosse was fond of holding court at the Press Club, where he would bang on about his risky investments, often made with borrowed money. But the joys of hunting in the stock-

26

market jungle were seldom long-lived. Now his smile became rather more strained. 'Well,' he said, 'here you are, still trudging about in the mud with the rest of us mere mortals.'

Annika raised her eyebrows quizzically.

'You should be sitting in some state-owned palace in Norrköping, shouldn't you, now that Jimmy Halenius – your new boyfriend – is about to take charge of the Migration Authority?' Bosse went on.

Annika had heard Jimmy had been offered the post. She sighed theatrically. 'Bosse,' she said, 'you disappoint me. I thought you were a man with his eye on the ball.'

'Something's happening up there,' the radio reporter said.

Annika pulled out the video-camera and focused on the house. A group of police officers, two in uniform and three in plain clothes, were standing on the porch steps. One of the detectives was a young woman, broad shoulders, slim legs and a long, poker-straight brown ponytail. Annika's breath caught – could it be . . . ?

'That's Nina Hoffman,' Bosse said, nodding at the woman. 'She was involved in the David Lindholm murder case. I thought she'd been pensioned off.'

The two reporters went on talking, but Annika didn't hear what they said. Nina Hoffman had lost weight since she and Annika had last met. Now she was pulling off pale blue plastic bootees and walking towards one of the unmarked police cars, ignoring the media.

The officers on the steps were still talking, and one of the detectives was gesticulating wildly. Then he headed towards the reporters. He stopped a metre or so from the cordon and Annika aimed her camera at him as, beside her, the radio reporter held out his microphone.

'Well, I can confirm that Ingemar Lerberg was found unconscious in the property behind me,' the police officer said. 'We have decided to make this information public, even though some of his family have not yet been informed.'

'Who hasn't been informed?' a woman from the local television station shouted.

The policeman ignored her. A trickle of rainwater ran down his forehead. 'Ingemar Lerberg has been taken to Södermalm Hospital, where he is currently being operated on. We've been told that the outcome is uncertain.'

'Who made the emergency call?' The television journalist again.

The policeman rocked on his heels. 'A full investigation is now under way,' he said. 'The chief prosecutor in Nacka, Diana Rosenberg, has been appointed head of the preliminary stages. We will issue further information when—'

'Who made the call?' The woman wasn't about to give up.

'It was an anonymous tip-off,' the police officer said.

'Man or woman?'

'I can't answer that.'

'Can't or won't?'

The policeman had had enough. He turned to go back to the house. His hair was plastered to his head, and his jacket was streaked dark with rain.

'Are you aware of any possible motives for the assault?' the woman yelled after him. 'Had Lerberg received any threats? Are there any signs of a break-in?'

The policeman stopped and looked at her over his shoulder. 'The answer to all your questions is no,' he said, then hunched his shoulders and hurried towards the house.

Annika put the camera down again and turned back to

the group of people gathered by the police cars. There was no sign of Nina Hoffman.

'Do you want a lift into the city?' she asked the radio reporter.

'Thanks, but I've got to do a live broadcast at two o'clock.'

'Have you heard about Schyman?' Bosse said.

Annika gave him a quizzical look. Bosse looked like a cat that had just caught a canary.

'He faked his way to the Award for Excellence in Journalism – the series of articles about the billionairess who disappeared?'

Annika raised her eyebrows. 'Says who?'

'New information on the internet.'

Dear God, she thought. 'It was a television documentary,' she said, getting out her car keys.

Bosse blinked several times.

'Schyman got the award for a documentary on television,' she repeated. 'On both occasions.'

She went to her car, gave Insect Man a wave and got in. While the fan dealt with the condensation on the windscreen, Nina Hoffman drove past and disappeared into the rain.

Editor-in-chief Anders Schyman studied Ingemar Lerberg's familiar smiling face on the computer screen: chalk-white teeth, dimples, neon-blue eyes. He was standing on a quayside in front of a large oil-tanker wearing an open sports jacket, his shirt unbuttoned at the neck, wind in his hair.

They had known each other for ten years, possibly more. Fifteen? For a couple of years they had both been on the

Rotary Club's committee, but since the revelations about Lerberg's tax affairs, contact between them had been sporadic. Schyman liked him, though, and wondered who on earth could have wanted to beat the crap out of him.

He refreshed the page to read the latest news on the attack. Annika Bengtzon had posted a picture of the crime scene on Twitter: media coverage of the case seemed to be pretty extensive. There was no motive, no acknowledged threat and no sign of a break-in.

He went back to Lerberg's website – or, rather, his company's, International Transport Consultancy. Lerberg was a smart businessman, active in shipping and sea transport, something to do with digital systems for the co-ordination of maritime shipments. He was also pushing for the development of a new marina in Saltsjöbaden, a luxury harbour for yachts and cruisers. But, of course, he was best known as a politician.

Schyman typed in a search for 'lerberg politician saltsjöbaden'. A number of articles in the *Evening Post* came up – always a source of satisfaction to him, even if he knew that the search results were adapted to suit his own preferences. He glanced down the page, and found a thread on a discussion forum that made him lean forward: Gossip about powerful people in Saltsjöbaden. With Lerberg's and several others, he found his own name: Anders Schyman, Crusader for Truth.

What was this? He didn't usually Google himself, not often, anyway, but he'd never seen this before. Curious, he clicked on the link. A short video appeared on the screen, a lit candle and a picture of him taken at some party. He was standing with a glass in his hand, smiling broadly at the camera, his eyes and forehead glowing slightly. Could it have been taken after some debate at the Publicists' Club?

We know him, everyone knows him, our hero, the defender of reality, the Man Who Saves Us from Corruption and Abuses of Power, the great editor and legally accountable publisher of the *Evening Post.*

He leaned even closer to the screen. What the hell was this?

Admittedly, there are those who claim he sacrificed his ethics and morals on the altars of the paper's proprietors and capitalism when he left state-funded television and took charge of the most frivolous, attention-seeking tabloid in Sweden, but the Light of Truth judges no one without giving them a fair hearing. We value tolerance and openness here, and we stick to verifiable facts.

Schyman glanced up at the top of the screen: yes, the blogger had evidently called the site 'The Light of Truth'. It sounded ominous.

We're all aware of his magnificent past achievements, his personal appeal, his considerable background in journalism: a university lecturer, chair of the Newspaper Publishers Association, the editor who made the *Evening Post* 'Sweden's Biggest Daily Paper' – as well as winning the Award for Excellence in Journalism twice! What an achievement! What a triumph! An (almost) unparalleled accomplishment! Let us all break out into a heartfelt chorus of hallelujahs!

Well, it was hardly that remarkable. Several other journalists had won the prize twice.

But the Light of Truth didn't acquire that name for nothing. This is the home of the Light that illuminates Reality and What Really Matters. This is a haven for Critical Thinking and Counterintuitive Thought, Opposition to the ghastly Political Correctness of the Media Establishment. Feel free to call me the Scourge of Hypocrisy and Cant.

Let us take a closer look at Anders Schyman's great journalistic achievements. Let us take a step closer to the Light, and examine these triumphs carefully . . .

What on earth was going on?

No one remembers the first time Our Hero was accorded the extraordinary honour known as the Award for Excellence in Journalism.

It is Anders Schyman's second journalistic triumph that warrants proper illumination, his true media breakthrough, the documentary that led him to step out of the concrete grey shadows of state-funded television and into our cosily furnished living rooms. Ladies and gentlemen, dear friends, let us shine the Light on Viola Söderland.

'He's still alive.'

Anders Schyman started. The head of news, Patrik Nilsson, was standing, legs apart, on the other side of the desk, his voice full of disappointment. Schyman clicked away from the blog with a quick, embarrassed gesture. He hadn't heard the glass door slide open and was still seeing Viola Söderland before him in all her surgically enhanced elegance. 'I was as certain as anyone could be,' he said. 'She disappeared of her own volition.'

Nilsson looked at him blankly. 'Södermalm Hospital

has just issued a new statement,' he said. 'Lerberg suffered a cardiac arrest during the operation and the staff had to use a defibrillator to get him going again. He's being kept sedated because of the extent of his injuries.'

Schyman's thoughts were running like lava through his head, but he tried to maintain a neutral expression. He cleared his throat and looked at the empty screen in front of him. The blog post had shaken him, and he felt as if its insinuations were written on his face.

'Do you remember Viola Söderland?' he asked.

Nilsson's face shifted from expressionless to confused. 'Who?'

Schyman stood up and went to the sofa. 'The billionairess. Golden Spire.' He sank down on the worn cushions.

Nilsson hitched up his jeans under his burgeoning beergut and glanced out at the newsroom on the other side of the glass wall. 'The woman who disappeared? The one with the massive tax debt?'

At first Schyman was offended, then relieved. The Light of Truth had evidently over-estimated the level of general awareness of his journalistic triumph. No one cared any more. It wasn't an issue. 'The woman who disappeared,' he confirmed.

'What about her? Has she turned up?'

'In a way. Is Lerberg going to make it?' he asked.

'What about the billionairess? Have I missed something.'

Schyman stood up again. Why could he never learn to keep his mouth shut? 'So we're not dealing with a murdered politician?'

'He might die before we go to print,' Nilsson said hopefully. 'We'll hold the front page for the time being.'

A somewhat premature front page on which the man was

declared dead was evidently ready to print. Well, it wasn't up for debate: meeting the deadline was the only thing that mattered.

'We'll just have to hope we need a new one,' Schyman said, which Nilsson took as a sign that it was time to go back to work. He slid the door open and left, failing to close it properly behind him. The sounds of the newsroom flowed in through the narrow gap: a discordant jumble of voices, keyboards, the jingles of television news channels, the dull whirr of the ventilation system.

And soon it would be over, at least for him. The newspaper's board had been informed and had accepted his resignation. In little more than a week his departure would be made public, and the hunt for his successor would roll into action.

He wasn't leaving things in a bad state. The figures from the past year had remained strong, confirming the *Evening Post* as the biggest newspaper in Sweden. He'd beaten off the competition and now it was time to relax.

Schyman went back to his computer and looked at the screen-saver, a black-and-white photograph taken by his wife of the rocks on their island out in Rödlöga archipelago. It wasn't much more than an outcrop. No water or drainage, electricity supplied from a generator at the back of the house, but for them it was Paradise.

Maybe a wind turbine down by the shore, he mused. Then they could live there all year round. A satellite dish to keep in touch with the rest of the world. A jetty for a larger boat. A few solar panels on the roof to heat water, and a satellite phone for emergencies.

He decided to look into planning permission for a wind turbine.

*

Nina parked the car in a reserved space next to the main entrance to Södermalm Hospital. It was pouring with rain. The hospital was the largest emergency medical centre in Scandinavia, and during her time as a sergeant on Södermalm she had been there several times each month, sometimes several times a week – everything tended to blur together, with the exception of the morning of 3 June almost five years ago. The morning when David Lindholm, the most famous police officer in Sweden, had been found dead (*when she had found David dead*), and his wife Julia was admitted to intensive care in a catatonic state.

She got out of the car and walked through the vast foyer, with its glass roof and polished stone floor, showed her ID at Reception, explained why she was there, and was referred to a Dr Kararei, the senior consultant in the intensive-care unit. Fourth floor, lift B.

It smelt as it always did. The corridors were scrubbed clean and poorly lit. She passed medics in rustling coats and patients shuffling along in slippers.

She rang the bell outside ICU and had to wait several minutes before it was opened by Dr Kararei himself. He turned out to be a large man with short fingers and only a trace of an accent.

Nina introduced herself. It felt odd saying she was from National Crime – the words didn't seem to sit right in her mouth. 'Is it possible to conduct a short interview with the victim?' she asked.

'Perhaps we should discuss this in private,' the doctor said, and ushered her into an empty consulting room. It was cool, almost cold. The doctor didn't switch the lights on. The light from the window was heavy and grey.

'The patient is still in the operating theatre,' he said,

sitting heavily on a small desk. He gestured to Nina to take the patient's chair.

'How is he?'

'I'd say his chances of survival are extremely uncertain.'

If Lerberg died, the police would have the murder of a politician to deal with. Not a prime minister or foreign minister, admittedly, but a high-profile violent crime. She mustn't mess up. She shifted on the chair, cleared her throat, took out the brand new mobile, provided by Lamia, and searched for the recording function. Her fingers seemed to swell above the screen and she did something wrong. She went back to the start menu and began again.

'So his injuries are life-threatening?' she said, once the timer indicated that the phone was recording properly.

'Possibly not in themselves. But it's the combination that makes his condition so complicated, along with severe dehydration.'

He reached for a chart containing the patient's notes.

'So the victim had gone without food and water for some time?' Nina said, glancing at her phone's screen. 'How long?' She put the phone on the desk beside the doctor.

He turned a page and studied the information, then read some out quietly to himself: 'Severe metabolic disruption, principally electrolytes and salts, sodium and potassium, as well as erratic base oxygen values . . . At least three days, I'd say.'

Nina counted backwards in her head. So the assault had taken place late on Thursday or early on Friday. 'How much longer would he have lasted if he hadn't been found?'

'Difficult to say. Another hour or so. He wouldn't have survived the morning.'

She glanced at the phone and hoped their voices were

being stored on the memory chip. She'd have to make sure afterwards that she'd saved the recording properly. 'What injuries have you managed to identify?'

The doctor carried on reading. 'The patient had extensive bleeding and tissue damage to his groin and the surrounding musculature, as well as multiple torn ligaments . . .' He looked up at her over his glasses. 'We've had to open him up to drain the blood and reduce the risk of compartment syndrome.'

Nina looked at him, wide-eyed. 'I don't understand,' she said.

'The bleeding in his groin was extensive, but confined, which leads to increased pressure and the risk of tissue death. The surgeon's doing her best to reconnect his torn muscles and ligaments, but it's a very sensitive job . . .'

'So his legs had been pulled apart until the muscles ruptured?' Nina said.

The doctor looked down at the notes again and read in silence for a few moments. The room smelt of fresh disinfectant. When he spoke again, he described how the victim's shoulders had been dislocated bilaterally, with extensive swelling in the surrounding tissue, rotator cuffs and joints, which needed to be brought down. 'That means his shoulders have had to be put back in place,' he said. 'We're also having to reconnect torn muscles and ligaments there as well.'

'Does he have any injuries around his wrists?'

The doctor looked down at his notes, and read out, 'Circular ulceration and laceration, approximately one centimetre across.'

Nina checked that the recording was still working. 'So they tied his hands behind his back, then strung him up by his wrists,' she said.

Dr Kararei looked at the window for a moment, as if he were trying to imagine the scene. Then he returned to the notes. 'The tissue of the plantar fascia in his feet has been dislodged, and exhibits centimetre-wide haematomas in various stages of discoloration.'

Repeated blows to the soles of his feet with a blunt instrument, over a protracted period of time, Nina thought.

'We've found pinprick bleeding in the whites of his eyes, as well as in his mouth, inside his cheeks and under his tongue.'

Nina nodded. 'Attempted strangulation?'

'Probably not,' the doctor said. 'There's no bruising on his neck, no marks from fingers or a noose.'

'But it does suggest suffocation?'

'Yes.'

Nina took a few deep breaths. 'There was a plastic bag at the crime scene,' she said. 'On the floor in the children's room. I saw it.'

'His face exhibits both haematomas and red oedemas.'

'So he was beaten, which resulted in bleeding and swelling,' Nina said.

'Five ribs in the lower right-hand side of his ribcage have been broken, and his lung collapsed. His left eyeball was punctured with a pointed instrument . . .'

Nina's hands lay motionless on her lap. The air felt ice-cold on the back of her throat as she breathed in.

The doctor put the notes down.

Nina raised her chin and tried to keep her voice steady. 'These are means of torture,' she said. 'Classics, tried and tested. These methods have names.'

His face was calm but serious as he gazed at her. 'I've seen them in other parts of the world,' he said, 'but never before in Sweden.'

She said nothing for a while. Then: 'If he does survive, will he ever make a full recovery?'

'The soles of his feet will heal, even if it takes a few weeks. His groin will be extremely painful for a month or so, and he'll probably be left with some degree of chronic aching and weakness. We've stitched his eye back together, and the fluid will gradually build up again, but there's a risk of permanent sight impairment. There's also a risk of limited function in his shoulders, besides ongoing pain . . . The unknown factor is really the shortage of oxygen. We don't yet know if he's suffered any brain damage.'

Nina sat where she was, unable to move. 'And mentally?'

'Long-term rehabilitation,' the doctor said, getting to his feet.

Nina reached for her mobile, switched off the recording, then saved the file. She seemed to be moving slightly awkwardly, as if the chair had made her stiff. 'Thanks,' she said. 'Can I see him? Just through the door of the operating theatre?'

The doctor shook his head.

'When will he regain consciousness, to the point at which he can be questioned?'

He gave her his card, with the direct number of his mobile, and said she was welcome to call at any time. 'I keep expecting the patient's wife to get in touch,' he said, as they left the room. 'Do you know where she is?'

Nina glanced at him. How much did he know? How much could she tell him?

She stepped out into the dimly lit corridor. The door of the consulting room slid shut with a hiss. Dr Kararei gave the impression that he was the sort of man you could trust.

'This must stay between us for the time being,' she said, 'but Nora Lerberg is missing.'

The doctor started to head towards the exit, and Nina walked alongside him. 'We've located the three children,' she went on. 'They're with an aunt in Vikingshill, but we haven't managed to track down his wife. No one knows where she is.'

They reached the entrance to the department.

'Could she have been responsible for this?' Nina asked.

'If she had help, then theoretically it's possible,' the doctor said. 'But I'd say it's extremely unlikely.'

They shook hands.

She clutched her mobile all the way through the building. Images danced before her eyes: bound hands, strung up, suffocated, beaten . . . *These methods have names.*

She walked quickly through the wide entrance hall, past the information desk, the flower shop and the cafeteria, past the patients' toilets and taxi phones.

When her mobile rang she jumped, as if it had burned her.

'Nina? Nina Hoffman?'

'Annika Bengtzon. What can I do for you?' She walked out into the rain, not bothered that she was getting wet.

'I just wanted to say hi. That was you I saw outside Lerberg's house earlier today, wasn't it? Out in Solsidan?'

Nina unlocked her car with the remote and slid into the driver's seat. 'I can't tell you anything about the case, I hope you understand that,' she said, and shut her eyes.

Shoulders dislocated bilaterally, with extensive swelling in the surrounding tissue.

'Nothing at all?'

Nina opened her eyes and looked up at the façade of the main hospital building.

Hands tied behind his back, then strung up by the wrists.

'I thought you were in Washington,' she said.

Annika Bengtzon laughed – unless it was a sigh? 'The paper can't afford that sort of thing any more. I'm back on the shop-floor, these days. A news reporter for the print and online editions. The police at the scene said that Lerberg might not survive. Do you know what the situation is?'

Nina didn't answer.

She started the car. 'Now isn't a good time,' she said.

'When did you start at National Crime?' Annika asked.

Nina put the car into reverse and turned to look out of the rear windscreen. It was smeared with wet and grime. 'Goodbye, Annika,' she said.

'I've still got the same mobile number, so if you ever want to get in touch you only have to—'

Nina clicked to end the call.

What did Ingemar Lerberg know that he shouldn't have known?

Why hadn't he revealed it?

And why had he been left alive?

It was afternoon by the time Annika got back to the newsroom. The southern link road had been blocked and traffic on the Essinge motorway had ground to a halt, as usual. She had spent the time stuck in traffic researching Ingemar Lerberg and putting the material together in her head. She took out her laptop, downloaded the recordings from the video-camera to the server, logged them in slightly haphazardly, then emailed the picture editor to give him the time-codes where he could find usable stills for the print edition. She stood up to fetch a cup of coffee from the machine, then put together a piece for the online

41

news channel, one minute and twenty-five seconds, about Ingemar Lerberg. The pictures weren't particularly good. Too dark and grainy, just as they had been throughout this miserable spring. The wind meant that the frame swayed during her to-camera piece, and she looked greasy and hollow-eyed, but there was nothing unusual about that. The angle she was putting on the story was a bit tenuous, but she thought it just about held together.

'The police are facing a total mystery after the attempted murder of former MP Ingemar Lerberg,' she began. 'There are currently no credible motives for the brutal assault. No threats had been received, and it isn't clear how the perpetrator got into the house. According to the *Evening Post*'s sources, police haven't found any signs of a break-in at the scene, which is located in the fashionable suburb of Solsidan in Saltsjöbaden . . .'

'He's still alive, then?' Nilsson said above her.

'Sorry,' Annika said. 'Shall we send someone to the hospital to finish him off?'

He sat down on her desk. 'We've had a call from the Christian Democrats. They're going to be making a statement about their colleague at their headquarters in half an hour. Can you take it?'

She looked at her watch. 'Sure.'

'Has the prosecutor confirmed that the crime's being classified as attempted murder?'

'I called her from the car.'

'Are you dealing with the dog?'

She looked at him uncomprehendingly.

'Stefan, four years old,' Nilsson said. 'Found dead in the hall, according to the main news agency. Can you do an overview of his background as well?'

'The dog's?'

'Was Lerberg controversial? Any threats? Maybe a list of possible motives? And check out why he was forced to resign, even if we'll probably have to wait and see if he's going to survive before we publish it.'

Annika did a quick search for ingemar lerberg politician.

Nilsson leaned in front of her screen. 'And call him a leading politician throughout. After all, he was in the running to be party leader at one point.'

'Yes,' Annika said. 'For a whole afternoon, long enough to warrant a leader column in the *Evening Post* . . .'

'Don't be like that,' Nilsson said, and stalked back to the newsdesk.

She glanced through the list of headings on the screen. How quickly things were forgotten. She knew she'd read about Ingemar Lerberg in the days when he was newsworthy but, apart from a few hazy memories of a tax scandal, she really didn't know anything about him. And why should she?

She clicked on the link that looked the most interesting.

The Christian Democrat had certainly been a colourful character on the political scene eight or ten years ago. He had arrived in Parliament with the sort of political beliefs that could probably best be compared to those of the American Tea Party movement: dismantling the state, individual freedom, unquestioning faith in God and capitalism. Among other things, he had suggested re-organizing regional councils and privatizing social services.

Ingemar Lerberg believed that Christianity should be made an obligatory subject in school, and taxes halved. State benefits should be automatically tied to some sort of 'service to society', an idea described by his critics as 'unpaid slave labour'. He backed up this proposal with a quote from the Book of Genesis: *In the sweat of thy face shalt thou eat bread.*

The Bible turned out to be a recurring theme in Lerberg's politics. That some people were richer than others was perfectly acceptable, according to Matthew: *For whosoever hath, to him shall be given, and he shall have more abundance.*

He must have missed the bit about the camel and the eye of a needle, Annika thought.

She saw the time on her laptop. The Christian Democrats' headquarters were in Gamla stan, in the centre of Stockholm where it was impossible to park: she'd have to get a taxi if she was going to get there in time.

'Annika, one more thing.' Nilsson was back at her desk. 'What's the Ministry of Justice saying about this case? They're bound to be keeping informed. Can you look into it?'

'Do you think I should call the under-secretary of state?' she asked blithely.

'Yes, why not?'

Annika sighed and opened her notes. Her partner, Jimmy Halenius, was under-secretary of state at the Ministry of Justice and the minister's closest associate.

Nilsson would know full well that she wasn't going to call him to ask about a work-related matter. He tilted his head and looked at her slyly. 'You place a lot of importance on ethics, facts and relevance, don't you?'

Annika arched an eyebrow. What was he up to now?

He waved his right hand expressively. 'I mean, you're always going on about that sort of thing, telling us not to devalue words, to show all sides of an issue, take responsibility for the people we interview, not try to act as prosecutor, judge and executioner all at the same time . . .'

44

'You make me sound like some sort of union boss pontificating on national radio.'

'Yeah, but I'm right, aren't I?'

She shrugged. Jimmy would be home around six, and he'd offered to make elk stew.

Nilsson stood up and waved to someone at the newsdesk. 'Valter, come over here.'

Annika craned her neck and saw a young man heading towards them.

'Annika, this is Valter Wennergren. He's on placement from the College of Journalism and will be with us over the summer. It's really important that the younger generation gets a firm grasp of ethics right from the start, so I was thinking that you could look after him, show him the ropes, let him follow you in your day-to-day work . . .'

Nilsson was smiling at her. Looking after trainees was a form of punishment. It took time, energy and engagement, without any professional compensation.

The young man shook her hand and introduced himself politely. He was dark, tall and thin, almost skinny, with spiky black hair and a little goatee beard. 'Great,' he said. 'I'm really looking forward to seeing how you work here in the newsroom.' He spoke a very pronounced upper-class Stockholm Swedish.

Annika smiled at him. She hated the idea of Nilsson getting the better of her. 'Welcome,' she said. 'You're not related to the Wennergren family that owns the paper, are you?'

He gave her a wry smile. 'Son of Albert,' he said.

Ah, the new chairman of the board.

'But I'm adopted,' he added quickly, as if that somehow made him less culpable. 'From Iran.'

'Well, we don't choose our parents,' Annika said.

Valter unbuttoned his jacket. 'I hope I won't be too much of a nuisance.'

'Not at all,' Annika said. 'It's always great to meet new colleagues and have a chance to discuss and analyse what we do. There's far too little of that sort of thing in the newsroom, these days.'

She smiled at Nilsson. His expression was now rather strained.

'Well, then. Valter, from now on you follow Annika wherever she goes. Hope you both get a lot out of your time together.' He went back to the newsdesk.

Now the young man seemed at something of a loss.

'There's no point in sitting down,' Annika said. 'We're going out on a job.' She called for a taxi.

Anders Schyman watched Annika Bengtzon disappear in the direction of the caretakers' office. She seemed so carefree, with her easy stride and messy hair, and that hideous bag slung over her shoulder. For a moment he felt envious. Maybe she was the smart one, having turned down the chance to join the management, choosing instead to stay at the front-line of reporting.

'Hello? Are you still there?' The voice of Albert Wennergren echoed from the speaker-phone.

Schyman coughed. 'I'm quite sure there's no one inside the organization who could take over,' he said. 'We'll have to recruit from outside.'

'And you're still certain you want to go?'

If there was one thing in life he was sure of, it was that. 'The decision's been taken,' he said simply, as if it had been beyond his control.

'What's the position with our competitors? Any unac-knowledged talent that's starting to feel bitter?'

Bound to be. But who wanted to appoint an embittered, unacknowledged competitor to lead the organization? What a uniquely stupid idea. 'Difficult to say,' Schyman said.

'It's going to be tricky finding someone of your calibre,' Albert Wennergren said.

There it was, at last. Recognition. *Tricky. Calibre.* Schyman didn't know what to say.

'That blogger's got me a bit worried,' the chairman went on. 'There've been a number of comments this afternoon. Have you seen them?'

Oh, yes. All twenty-eight of them.

'Have you thought about responding?'

Schyman shifted uncomfortably in his chair, which squeaked and groaned. 'Not at the moment. That would only lend credibility to his claims.'

'We'll have to keep an eye on developments. Have you ever had any contact with her? I mean, did you ever meet her, talk to her face to face?'

Anders Schyman stared at the phone, bewildered. 'Who?'

'Viola Söderland. After the documentary was broadcast, I mean. Since then. Anything confirming that you were right, that she's alive and disappeared of her own volition?'

After it was broadcast? No, he hadn't.

'Well, I can't imagine the story's got legs,' Albert Wennergren said dismissively. 'Can you do me a favour and look through your contacts one more time, see if you can come up with anyone who might be a potential successor?'

He promised he would.

Once they'd hung up he went back to the blog, the Light of Truth. Pretentious name. Still only twenty-eight comments. He breathed out and went back to the official page on planning regulations.

Wind turbines didn't need planning permission if they were less than twenty metres high, or lower than the distance to the boundary of the property. However, there were local rules for the Stockholm archipelago, stipulating that turbines mustn't be erected within a kilometre of the nearest building – perhaps that applied only to bigger turbines of a more industrial nature.

He'd have to call the planning office the following morning and find out.

A young man with floppy hair and narrow glasses was sitting behind the oversized reception desk at the Christian Democrats' headquarters, smiling the pious smile that people of faith sometimes hid behind. Annika walked up to him, trailed by Valter. 'We're from—'

'The *Evening Post*,' the receptionist filled in. 'We're running a little behind schedule. Would you mind waiting a few minutes?'

They were evidently holding court, one appointment after another. The receptionist raised his shoulders apologetically. 'Can I get you some coffee while you wait? We've got freshly baked lemon muffins.'

'Thanks, that would be—' Valter began.

'No, thanks,' Annika said. 'Don't go to any trouble on our account.'

'Some water, perhaps?'

'Thanks, but we're fine,' Annika said.

Valter looked at the floor. The receptionist sat down, effectively disappearing behind the desk.

Offering a journalist something to eat or drink had a calming effect on the subject of the interview, making them feel simultaneously relaxed and occupied. It increased the subject's confidence, which could be good or bad, depending on the situation. Obviously they weren't there to interview the receptionist, but it was difficult to exude any sort of authority while you were eating.

Annika took a pen and notepad from her bag, and dug out her digital recorder. This interview wasn't going to be sufficiently visual for television – old men in offices were banned, unless you were demanding explanations from a real bigwig – so she was aiming for an online audio broadcast.

A moment later a door behind the desk opened and Bosse from the other evening paper stepped out into the foyer with a photographer.

'Have you had a chance to check out the Light of Truth?' Bosse asked, as he passed her.

'Your turn now,' the receptionist said to Annika and Valter. He showed them into a conference room, complete with whiteboard and a modern IT set-up.

The party's management committee, with the exception of the party leader, was grouped around an oval table, made of birch, and stood up as Annika and Valter walked in. The party leader was the opposition's spokesman on international aid and, according to Jimmy, he was making the most of every opportunity to travel to as many exotic places as possible before he lost the next election and had to stand down.

There were three men and one woman. The party secretary, Klas Borsthammar, welcomed them, and introduced his colleagues: Hans Olovsson, Bert Tingström and Marianne Berg-Holmlund. They looked sombre, as befitted the circumstances.

'Please, have a seat,' Klas Borsthammar said.

They sat at the table. Annika started the recorder and put it down on the table.

'Terrible business,' Klas Borsthammar said, looking at Valter. 'Incomprehensible that something like this should happen to one of our politicians, one of our most prominent representatives—'

'Is that how you see Ingemar Lerberg, these days?' Annika interrupted.

The party secretary lost his thread and looked at her in surprise.

'Is Ingemar Lerberg still one of your most prominent representatives?' she asked. 'I thought he'd been a local politician out in Nacka for the past seven years.'

Borsthammar cleared his throat. Marianne Berg-Holmlund gazed at her hands, which were clasped on her lap as if in prayer.

'I saw that he's been a keen advocate of changes to social services in Nacka,' Annika said. 'What does the party leadership think of his opinions?'

Hans Olovsson leaned across the table and looked straight at Valter. 'Ingemar's a great chap. His attitudes can be controversial, but he's very tolerant of people who don't share them. He's never judgemental. I'm from Stockholm as well, and I know that Ingemar is very highly regarded in the area.'

'And he's an excellent businessman,' Bert Tingström added.

'If Sweden had more men like him, we wouldn't have any unemployment in this country,' Klas Borsthammar said.

The other men nodded at the trainee. The woman turned her face to the wall. She seemed to be fighting back tears.

'He was personally responsible for developing the system of coordinating maritime transport,' Bert Tingström said. 'It's unique – there's nothing like it anywhere else in the world, and he's planning to expand it hugely over the next few years.'

'And so tragic for his family,' Hans Olovsson said. 'Ingemar is devoted to his wife and children. This must have hit them incredibly hard.'

The three men nodded again. The woman wiped her nose. Valter glanced at Annika, who was sitting quite still, observing the situation. When she was younger, she occasionally found that she became invisible when she was out on a job, especially if she happened to be accompanied by a male photographer who felt the need to assert himself, but it had been years since that had happened.

'When was the last time any of you spoke to Ingemar Lerberg?' she asked.

The three men turned towards her, then looked at each other questioningly.

'Well,' said Hans Olovsson, 'we're in touch all the time, so it's a bit hard to—'

'Do you see each other regularly?' Annika asked. 'At local meetings, or at party conferences?'

All three nodded, now looking at her and Valter. Yes, at meetings and conferences, definitely.

'What does his wife say? Have you spoken to her?'

'No, presumably she's at the hospital,' Bert Tingström said. 'At her husband's side.'

'So you haven't spoken to her?'

No answer. Annika looked at her notepad. She hadn't written anything. 'Why did you arrange this meeting?' she asked quietly. 'What do you want? Really?'

Silence descended around the table. Valter squirmed.

The ventilation hummed. Klas Borsthammar stared at her – she certainly had his attention now. He straightened his shoulders slightly.

'We know that the media will be interested in the party leadership's comments about what's happened,' he said.

Annika met his eye. He glared back.

'So what has happened?' she said. 'Could you describe it to me?'

The three men glanced at each other, and the woman sniffed loudly.

'Our party colleague has been grievously assaulted in his own home,' the party secretary said, rather uncertainly.

'Yes,' Annika said. 'That much is already clear. But what else? How did it happen? Is he going to pull through? What sort of injuries did he suffer? What can you say that we don't already know?'

There were several seconds of silence. Then Bert Tingström cleared his throat. 'His arms and legs have been dislocated. And he was severely beaten as well.'

Annika's throat contracted. *Arms and legs dislocated?* There was something very odd about this business. 'What are your thoughts on the assault? Could it have been politically motivated?'

The men exchanged glances again.

'Possibly,' Klas Borsthammar said. 'There are so many violent lunatics on the extreme left. One of them could certainly have attacked him. Like that man in Tucson, Arizona, the one who shot that congresswoman in the head . . .'

'You mean the man who shot Gabrielle Giffords?' Annika said. 'He was hardly left-wing, surely.'

'Unless there was a financial motive,' Hans Olovsson said. 'A successful businessman like Ingemar always runs the risk of extortion. Criminals in this country are crossing the line more and more.'

'Was there anything in his political activities in recent years that was controversial enough to provoke an attack of this nature?' Annika asked.

'How controversial were the young people on Utøya?' Bert Tingström wondered.

He had her there, Annika thought.

'Has anything happened to his business recently? Anything that could have prompted the assault?'

They all looked at Bert Tingström. 'Well,' he said, 'I don't know if the expansion of the company was imminent, but Ingemar had talked about it . . .'

The woman hadn't said a word. Annika wondered what she was doing there if she didn't have anything to contribute. She glanced at her watch. 'Well, thanks for taking the time to see us,' she said, reaching for the recorder.

'Can I ask something of you?' Hans Olovsson said.

Annika stopped, and the three men stared at her.

'What you did to Ingemar seven years ago was deeply dishonourable,' Hans Olovsson said. 'He was entirely innocent, and you in the media destroyed his political career. Bear that in mind when you write about him now.'

They were addressing her personally, of course. Eve enticing Adam to commit sin. Even though he was the one who had bitten into the apple, it was all her fault. Annika looked the man in the eye. 'I observe the law regarding the confidentiality of sources,' she said. 'I never go digging into the sources of our stories. So I don't know how that information reached us at the paper.' She had the impression that Hans Olovsson blushed slightly.

She picked up her belongings, shook their hands and left the room, Valter trailing after her.

They got onto a bus outside the Palace of Nobility. Valter ended up standing next to a pushchair while she squeezed into a seat at the back. She pulled out her mobile and called the prosecutor in Nacka, Diana Rosenberg. (Making professional calls from a taxi was out of the question: in the past she had read the contents of her conversations in trade magazines and on gossip sites. Buses, on the other hand, worked fine.)

The prosecutor answered on the fourth ring, sounding abrupt and stressed. She couldn't comment on the victim's injuries and she asked for a degree of reticence in any information that was published.

'Is it true that his arms and legs had been dislocated?' Annika asked, glancing at the passengers around her. No one was taking any notice but she still took care to speak quietly.

The prosecutor fell silent. 'I can't confirm anything,' she said eventually.

'What does his wife say?' Annika asked, holding her digital recorder close to the phone.

'We haven't managed to get hold of her yet,' Diana Rosenberg said.

'No? Where is she?'

The prosecutor didn't answer, and Annika was struck by a flash of realization. 'You don't know where she is. She's disappeared. Could the perpetrator have taken her? Has there been any ransom demand?'

Now the young man on the seat next to her was staring at her.

'Not as far as I'm aware,' the prosecutor said.

Her phone started to vibrate in her hand – another call waiting. She glanced at the screen: Thomas, her ex-husband. The prosecutor hung up and Annika clicked to answer him.

'Hello, Thomas,' she said. 'How are you?'

Since he had got back from Somalia where he had been kidnapped, he hadn't been in very good shape. She felt guilt wrench at her stomach. The kidnappers had amputated his left hand, and when he was finally discharged from hospital she had left him and moved in with his boss.

'I'm in a lot of pain,' Thomas said, 'and I've got loads to do at work. Can you have the children this week?'

She closed her eyes and clenched her teeth. 'You know I can, but they'll be disappointed. Especially Kalle.'

'I doubt it.'

'Thomas, we've talked about this before . . .'

'Can you or can't you?'

She swallowed. 'Sure. But that'll mean they're with me this week, then all next as well.'

'It's probably for the best.'

They hung up before she could say anything stupid.

The newsdesk staff, plus sport and entertainment, had gathered in Schyman's office for the usual 'six meeting' (it started at five o'clock, these days, but was still called the 'six meeting', which could sound rude to infantile ears) so the newsroom looked empty and abandoned in the greyish-white light of the computer screens.

Valter followed her.

'Berit's on a job in Norway,' Annika said, 'so you can sit in her place.'

'I didn't think you had your own desks,' Valter said, peering rather suspiciously at the desk and chair.

'We don't, but that one is Berit's. Have you got a user-ID and password yet?'

He put his rucksack on the desk and sat down tentatively. 'Yes . . .'

'Good. Call the Ministry of Justice and ask for their opinion on the Ingemar Lerberg case. There's always some new investigation into threats against politicians to refer to. They won't say anything, but check the statistics from the latest investigation and do your best to squeeze a general comment out of them. Make sure you call Lerberg either a "top politician" or a "national figure", seeing as our leader column mentioned him in the speculation about the Christian Democrats getting a new party leader about a hundred years ago. And keep it under eighteen hundred keystrokes, including spaces.'

The young man took off his jacket, ran his hands through his hair, pulled a laptop from his rucksack and hooked it up to the network. He seemed to pick things up quickly.

She got her own computer out, logged in and wrote a short summary of Ingemar Lerberg's political career. She described his passions and beliefs as honestly as she could, without leaving herself open to accusations of slander, and explained that in recent years he had concentrated on his family and business, as well as local politics in Nacka. She put together a piece for the online radio service, one minute and ten seconds, using some quotes from the party leadership.

That left her with the most controversial part of her task: how to deal with Lerberg's arms and legs, which, according to Bert Tingström – a not particularly impressive source – had been dislocated. And where was Nora, the victim's wife?

She called the press spokesperson at Nacka Police, followed by the head of media at National Crime. They talked to her in person and were very professional, but neither would confirm either a missing person or any specific type of injury. Not that she had expected them to. After a moment's hesitation she decided to call Commissioner Q, now head of the Criminal Intelligence Unit at National Crime.

'Annika,' he said, 'I'm disappointed in you. I was expecting you to ring this morning.'

'I'm a big girl now,' she said. 'I can manage fine without you. Besides, you're so important, these days, that it takes me a while to pluck up the courage to disturb you.'

'Spare me,' he said. 'What do you want?'

'Is Nora missing?' she asked.

'We don't know where she is, but "missing" is too strong a word.'

'Are you trying to find her?'

'Negative. Not in an organized way.'

'But you have been looking for her? To tell her what's happened to her husband?'

Q sighed. She had manoeuvred him into the position where she wanted him.

'Yes, we have been looking for her. No, we haven't found her.'

She swallowed. 'I've heard that Ingemar Lerberg's arms and legs were dislocated. Have I been correctly informed?'

'To be honest, I don't know precisely what his injuries are,' the commissioner said. 'We've had someone up at Intensive Care, but I haven't spoken to her yet.'

'Is Nina Hoffman working for you now?' Annika asked. 'I saw her out at Solsidan.'

Q sighed again. 'If you're so smart,' he said, 'I'm sure you can put together this article without my help.'

He hung up. She bit her lip. It would have been good to get the information confirmed, but at least she had a

57

named source to refer to. Bert Tingström hadn't asked to remain anonymous, and his remarks were recorded.

She pulled up her video clip from Solsidan and reworked it. It would have been useful to have video footage of the people inside the room, but there was nothing she could do about that now. She dug out an archive photograph of Tingström and played the quote of him describing the injuries over it, taking care to make clear that this was his information rather than the paper's. It was a little clumsy, but it worked. Then she updated the news report, adding a few more details, and made sure she included the dog's age. Finally she wrote a short piece about Nora Lerberg, who appeared to have vanished without a trace. She quoted Q, the prosecutor and the press spokesperson in Nacka as saying they had tried without success to get hold of her, but that she wasn't the subject of an official search. It wasn't great, but it would do.

She let out a silent sigh. 'Valter Wennergren,' she said. 'Has anyone ever called you VW? Volkswagen?'

He rolled his eyes.

'Have you finished?'

He pressed his keyboard and an email with the heading threatened politicians appeared on her screen: 1,780 characters, including spaces. The press spokesperson at the Ministry of Justice couldn't comment on the specific case of Ingemar Lerberg, but said that the minister was following developments closely, and expressed regret at the increasing level of violence against elected representatives. That was followed by a summary of the current situation, using figures from the latest government investigation, as well as some slightly less-up-to-date statistics in the most recent report from the National Council for Crime Prevention.

'Excellent,' Annika said.

When she had sent the whole lot off – the new video piece, the online radio item and the three articles – she stood up, pulled on her coat and packed away her laptop.

She waved at Schyman in his glass box on the way out.

Thomas Samuelsson stared at the computer screen in front of him. The Light of Truth. What pretentious irony. But whoever was behind it was good at expressing himself. (Why did he assume that the writer was male? He just did. The turn of phrase felt masculine.)

He took a deep breath.

Schyman deserved it. Thomas had only met him a few times, even though he worked so closely with Annika. Presumably he thought he was too important to associate with the families of his staff.

Thomas got up and walked the short distance to the kitchen. His legs were heavy and his back felt stiff. His hand ached – the phantom hand that was no longer there. The prosthesis (the hook!) was heavy and unwieldy. He hadn't made up his mind what sort he wanted yet. This latest version certainly wasn't in the running, he knew that much.

They had all lied to him. Not just Annika, although she was obviously the worst, but everyone else as well. His employers, not to mention the people in the health service.

Oh, there are brilliant prosthetics, these days. Just wait till you see them! In a lot of ways a prosthetic hand actually works better than an ordinary hand. Have you ever considered that? You can open tins without an opener, lift hot things directly off the stove or barbecue. You can use it as a hammer, you don't have to worry about

corrosive acids, and you can hold a match until it's burned
right down . . .

He opened the fridge door. There were chicken fillets
and steak but he wasn't particularly hungry.

Telling Annika he had a lot to do at work hadn't been
quite true: he'd taken the week off sick. He just felt that
things were getting on top of him, and his bosses in the
Ministry of Justice were very *understanding* because they
were conscious of the *trauma* he had suffered. Take all the
time you *neeeed*, your job will be waiting for you when you
feel like . . .

That was the least they could do, Thomas thought, as he
shut the fridge. He had risked life and limb for his work,
and was now crippled for life and had lost his family. The
least he could expect of his employers was that he should
be allowed to keep his job. It would look bad if they tried
to fire him. He could see the headline: 'GOVERNMENT
FIRES MUTILATED HERO' . . .

No, they'd never dare. They'd rather leave him mould-
ering in a corner at the taxpayers' expense, somewhere in
the main government offices at Rosenbad where no one else
wanted to be, perhaps on the ground floor with a view of a
brick wall on Fredsgatan.

They had put him to work on money-laundering.

Of all the dull, pointless areas of responsibility, Cramne,
his hypocritical boss, had tasked him with looking into international financial crime. Again. He could still recall the
man's forced smile on his first day back at the department,
before he knew that Annika had been fucking the under-
secretary of state, and when he still believed the lies of the
prosthetics industry, the claims that he would eventually be
able to control the prosthesis *by thought alone* – Sweden
was actually a *world-leader* in that area of research . . .

'You're the perfect choice,' Cramne had said, 'with your experience. Finance, international trade and security, great!'

And when they had stood up and were about to shake hands afterwards, Cramne had hesitated: he hadn't wanted to get it wrong and touch the metal fake, the hook.

No one expected him to achieve anything. No one had said anything, but he could feel it. They clearly thought his intelligence had been based in his left hand, not to mention his desire to participate in human conversation and boules tournaments. No one invited him along any more. Not just because of the terrible weather and the fact that no boules matches had been arranged: even if they had been, he knew they wouldn't have asked him. They stared at him in the corridor and whispered behind his back. The skinny female secretaries who used to give him the come-on now concentrated on their computer screens whenever he walked past.

He contemplated making himself a sandwich. But he would have to hold the bread with his hook, and he didn't like using it.

He walked back into the living room and stared at the meagre furnishings: the sofa, the computer desk, the rug. All of it from Ikea. Cheap and lacking in style. They had belonged to Annika. He hated the flat. It was cramped, just two bedrooms, and far too light. It was on the top floor of a corner building on Kungsholmen – Annika had got hold of it through her contact in the police force when she and Thomas had been living apart. After she had let him down (deceived him, tricked him, abandoned him), she had transferred the tenancy to him and moved out, dumping the worthless contents of the flat on him, not just the furniture but the crockery, books and DVDs as well. And he no longer had any savings. Annika had given all their money to the bastards who had kidnapped him in Somalia, so now he was sitting in a birdcage near the sky, hating every minute of it.

He sat down at the computer. The Light of Truth was actually very interesting.

He refreshed the page. Eight new comments had been added since he'd last looked.

He leaned back in his chair.

Might it be possible to have that arsehole at the *Evening Post* fired? That would be brilliant.

His spirits lifted. He felt light and fluid again, his breathing quickening. He hunched over the keyboard, hesitated for just a moment, then logged in under his usual alias: 'Gregorius', after the tragic character in Hjalmar Söderberg's novel *Doctor Glas* (cuckolded by his wife, murdered by his doctor). He never deployed Gregorius at work, oh, no. He might not be a computer genius, but he wasn't a fool either. After all, he had lived with a tabloid bitch for ten years, so he'd learned a thing or two about how the media worked. No one would be able to trace Gregorius to an IP address at Rosenbad.

The site's administrator hadn't opted to moderate comments, so they appeared immediately. He took a deep breath, and felt a glow of satisfaction spread out from his midriff.

Gregorius:
Anders Schyman is a hypocrite!!

He stretched his back contentedly. Maybe he should make that sandwich after all.

*

Annika still wasn't used to living on Södermalm. Coming home from work was still an intoxicating rush, from Medborgarplatsen Underground station, along Götgatan and Katarina Bangata to Södermannagatan to Jimmy's – no, their *shared* flat. She breathed in the scent of tarmac and admired the façades of the buildings as she passed, hundred-year-old brick, with ochre stucco, and the trees. It had almost stopped raining now.

Jimmy's – *their* – rented apartment was on the third floor of a house built in 1897, six rooms plus kitchen, which he had acquired through his contacts in the trade-union movement. (Yes, a clear case of corruption, definitely worth a front-page exclusive in the *Evening Post*.) As he had added her name to the lease, which was as good as marriage without a prenuptial agreement, she was now an accomplice.

The lights in the stairwell went on with a humming sound that spread up through the building. She ran up the steps, past the leaded windows looking out onto the courtyard, her heart thudding. Suddenly she was in front of the brass nameplate, shimmering in the glow of the low energy bulb:

HALENIUS SISULU
BENGTZON SAMUELSSON

Their surnames, and those of their children. The sight of it always made her pulse quicken. She unlocked the door and stepped into the hall, removed her jacket and kicked off her shoes. 'Hello, everyone!'

Kalle and Ellen came running out of the living room, gave her a quick hug, then disappeared back to their video game.

Then Jimmy was there, his brown hair on end, wearing

63

an apron and a pair of running shoes, holding a wooden spoon. She put her hands to his face. felt his unshaven cheek under her fingers as she kissed him on the lips. 'Hello,' she murmured.

'Hello, you.'

She pressed up to him.

'You'll mess up your clothes,' he muttered into her mouth. 'I've spilled some sauce on the apron.' But he put a hand to the base of her spine and drew her to him.

She kissed him again.

'When's food ready?'

Jimmy let go of her abruptly. His daughter, Serena, was standing right next to them. Her eyes were cold and black. 'In a quarter of an hour. Do you want to help Annika lay the table?'

She turned away and went back to her room.

Jimmy disappeared into the kitchen. Annika followed him and put the things she had bought on the way home in the freezer, then laid the table in the dining room, six places.

'Could you get the water?' Jimmy said, as he brought in the casserole dish and a frying-pan.

She carried two jugs to the table.

'Will you call the kids?' she asked, feeling a pang of cowardice.

Serena and her twin brother Jacob lived with Jimmy all the time. Their mother, Angela Sisulu, worked for the South African government and lived in Johannesburg. She had been awarded her PhD while she was working part-time as a model, and was the cause of Annika's huge inferiority complex.

Kalle and Ellen came into the dining room, and Kalle hovered close to Annika so he could be next to her. She sat at the table and started to ladle the stew onto the children's plates. Neither Serena nor Jacob looked at her as they took their seats. Serena identified strongly with her mother: she had the same cornrow plaits, and wore the same colourful cotton blouses. She was chatty and talkative with everyone but Annika. Annika wasn't allowed to touch her, help with her hair, do her coat up or give her a goodnight hug. Jacob looked a lot like Jimmy, and his hair was an unruly mess, just like his dad's. He was quieter, more uncertain than his sister and a little easier to reach.

Jimmy sat down opposite Annika and spooned some of the stew onto his own plate. 'Okay,' he said. 'Good and bad things about today. Kalle, you start.'

Kalle took his time chewing the food in his mouth, then put his knife and fork down. 'I scored a goal when we played football during the lunch break. But Adam in 5B tackled me and pushed me over in the mud.'

Kalle's accounts of school life always revolved around his friends and what they had done or not done to him, around arguments and confessions, and how others perceived him.

'The next Zlatan,' Jimmy said, giving the boy a high five. 'Jacob?'

'We got our maths tests back, and I got them all right. In geography we had to write an essay about the different ways people live and the conditions of life in different parts of the world, but I'd already done that so I was allowed to have a go on Google Earth instead.'

Annika kept her expression neutral: it seemed so odd to hear a ten-year-old express himself like that. He never presented any bad experiences at the dinner table, just validation-seeking successes. He and Jimmy high-fived as well.

Serena dabbed the corners of her mouth with her napkin. 'We did a dress rehearsal of the musical. Neo hasn't learned his lines and Liam messed up the guitar part.' She sighed.

Ellen thought for a moment before she spoke. 'We had a lovely lunch – pancakes and strawberry jam.'

Ellen rarely had anything negative to report, but Annika was fairly sure that wasn't because she was fishing for praise. She knew that the glass was half full while Kalle and Serena assumed it would soon be empty.

'We managed to get a new piece of proposed legislation through Parliament, to increase control of the financial sector,' Jimmy said. 'And on the way home I stepped in a puddle and one of my shoes got soaked through.'

Ellen giggled.

Annika wasn't sure if she approved of Jimmy's bureaucratic accounts of government work at the dinner table. Maybe it was good for the children to become acquainted with the vocabulary so they grasped that working life was complicated and full of responsibility, but there was also the possibility that it would make them arrogant. She didn't know which was more likely.

Jimmy looked at her encouragingly. She put down her knife and fork. 'The good thing is that I got a new work colleague today. He's a young man who's going to be doing practical experience on the paper over the summer, and I'm going to be his supervisor. The bad bit was getting stuck in a traffic jam inside a tunnel for almost an hour.'

'You sound like you're a lorry driver,' Serena muttered.

To her dismay, Annika's eyes filled with tears. Why did the girl have to be so unkind to her?

'Annika got some ice-cream on the way home,' Jimmy said. 'Would anyone like any?'

'*Yeees!*' Kalle, Ellen and Jacob cried.

Serena tossed her hair back. 'No, thanks.'

Annika cleared the table while Kalle got the ice-cream out of the freezer.

Once the sprinkles, the caramel sauce and the Belgian strawberries were on the table, Serena changed her mind and helped herself to a big dishful.

After dinner Jimmy disappeared into the combined office and library. Ellen and Annika filled the dishwasher. The other children slumped in front of the television.

'Aren't we supposed to be with Daddy this week?' Ellen said, as she put the forks in their own compartment in the cutlery tray.

Annika wiped the worktop. 'Yes, you are, but Daddy isn't feeling very well, and he's got such a lot to do at work . . .'

'Don't you and Jimmy have a lot to do at work?'

Annika put the dishcloth down, sat on a chair at the kitchen table and pulled her daughter onto her lap. 'I'm just pleased I get to have you with me,' she whispered, kissing Ellen's ear.

'Can't you move home again? To Daddy?'

Annika's arms stiffened. 'Daddy and I don't love each other any more. I live here now, with Jimmy.'

'But Daddy loves you. He said so.'

She put the child down. 'Thanks for helping,' she said. 'Off you go and play now.'

She was left sitting in the kitchen, alone.

*

I still don't understand where they come from, how they can be so complete, so contained. Sometimes I can see myself in them, and maybe Ingemar, but they're unique. The combination of

67

potential inherited traits is exactly the same in all three of them but they're still so different. You can't even see that they're related.

They're part of me. I created, carried and gave birth to them, but ever since they began to breathe they've been entirely themselves. I'm replaceable, just like their father. The thought makes me feel breathless. Could I live without them?

*

The man shifted position among the low fir-trees at the edge of the forest. There were still forensics officers working inside the house. At least three, possibly four, he could see their shadows move behind the net curtains. He actually felt great respect for the methodical way they went about their work, the pride they took in it. By extension, it was a reflection of the value of his own contribution, and their regard for his professionalism.

He was patient. There was no hurry. Sooner or later she would appear. As he waited he focused on his breathing. He liked to live each moment consciously, and breathing anchored him in the here and now.

But in his mind he wasn't there at all.

He was in a restaurant in Stockholm. He had invited a work colleague to dinner and was discussing the purchase of some forest in Hälsingland. They had come to the conclusion that the amount of timber available was considerably higher than the survey had indicated – it had probably been carried out during the winter, the depth of the snow not taken into account.

He moved deeper among the trees.

He was aware that he was leaving footprints in the soft snow, but the cheap trainers he was wearing could never be traced back to him, or to his mirror-image. He would get rid of them as soon as he left Solsidan.

He looked upwards, peering through the branches of the firs. The rain had stopped, but the wind was tugging at the branches, and dark clouds were scudding across the sky. He regretted not being able to hear the rustling of the treetops. Tomorrow would be another cold, wet day. That would make things more difficult, considering what he was probably going to have to do. Not insurmountable, just slightly more complicated.

But he wasn't the sort of person to dwell on negatives. He saw possibilities where other people focused on problems. Maybe she was on her way. Maybe she was just waiting for the forensics team to pack up and leave. He was patient. There was no hurry. He saw one of the forensics officers inside the house straighten his back and yawn.

Maybe it was almost time.

Sooner or later she would come.

TUESDAY, 14 MAY

The meeting room was at the end of the corridor on the eighth floor. Nina stepped through the door at nine o'clock sharp, not sure whether she should have been a little early or a few minutes late. The room was large and light, with windows on both sides, and was crowded with furniture. Straight ahead, a blank wall acted as a huge noticeboard. It was covered with information about ongoing cases she knew nothing about, one of them apparently called PLAYA.

The others had already arrived, three of them – evidently the recently convened investigative team. Commissioner Q was one of them, today dressed in a pink Hawaiian shirt. A large man, with a bald head and serious sideburns, introduced himself to her as Johansson, the group's secretary. He looked mournful. Nina shook his hand. The Barbie doll from yesterday, who had supplied her with a passcard and a computer and had shown her to her desk, was also there. Her name was Lamia Regnard, and she worked as an investigator and researcher. Her face was lit up like a sunrise.

'Have you had coffee?' Q asked, passing Nina a mug. She took it and sat down. The others were at neighbouring desks, surrounded by pads and sheets of paper, which they leafed through and read as they drank from similar mugs. Lamia was staring intently at a laptop.

'Why do you think Turkey are going to win?' she asked. 'They haven't won since Sertab represented them in 2003.'

'It's the final on Saturday,' Johansson explained, glancing at Nina.

The Eurovision Song Contest.

He handed out copies of the forensic report from the crime scene, then leafed back through his notepad. Nina looked through the seven-page report, trying to block out Lamia's singing.

'Who wants to start?' Q asked, leaning back in his desk chair.

Lamia put down her mug and pushed back her laptop. She adjusted her hair, then began to speak from memory.

'We've had a reply from the mobile operator. According to them, it was the wife, Nora Lerberg, who alerted the emergency services. The trace indicates that she was in the vicinity of Solsidan station at the time. That's about four hundred metres from the house.'

Nina's mind instantly flew back to the crime scene, and she saw Solsidan from above, the house at the end of the narrow road, the forest, the footpaths. That was where the wife had called from. Why? Why did she go to the station before sounding the alarm? It must have taken something like five minutes – five minutes that might have been critically important. She must have had an extremely good reason. Clearly she wanted to stay out of the way. Unless she'd thought he was dead.

'Is there a recording of the call?' Q asked.

Lamia poured herself some more coffee from a flask. 'It wasn't a call – she sent a text message.'

Nina opened her mouth to protest: it wasn't possible to text the emergency services.

Lamia went on: 'You can do that if you register your

74

number in advance on the internet. Nora Lerberg registered both her mobile phones about six months ago.' She gabbled off the numbers.

Johansson was writing quickly. Nina wondered why the woman had memorized them.

'Why does she have two mobiles?' Q asked.

Lamia fiddled with her hair.

'I've got two as well,' Johansson said. 'One for work, and a private one.'

'What did the text message say?' Q asked.

Lamia tilted her head to one side. 'Help. And then the address.'

'And Nora Lerberg hasn't turned up overnight?'

'Negative.'

'What do we know about her?'

'Nora Maria Andersson Lerberg, born on the ninth of September, twenty-seven this year, married to Ingemar for eight years. Gave up studying economics at Stockholm University. Housewife.'

Why would she have a work mobile if she was a house-wife? Nina wondered.

'Okay,' Q said. 'Obvious possibilities. Is she dead? Injured? Could the perpetrators have taken her with them? Has there been any sort of ransom demand?'

Lamia shook her head.

'What about the children?'

'They've been with their aunt, Kristine Lerberg, since Thursday. Ingemar's sister lives at Grusvägen fifteen in Vikingshill.'

'Okay. We'll be treating Nora Lerberg's disappearance as a separate investigation from now on. Can you put out an alert, Lamia?'

She nodded, blonde curls bouncing. She pulled her

laptop towards her and began to feed the command into the system. 'The risk factor is high,' she said, still typing. 'Hospitals and mortuaries were checked yesterday. Nora Lerberg's computer and one of her mobiles were still in the house. The computer's with forensics, and we've requested the call histories of both mobiles.'

Nina looked at the blonde doll-woman for a moment, then down at her own papers. She leafed through them intently: where was all this information?

'We've requested credit-card records, information from her bank and passenger lists,' Lamia went on. 'Our colleagues in Nacka are talking to the neighbours.'

'We should get their report today,' Q said, then turned to Johansson. 'Forensics?'

Johansson finished writing something, which took almost a minute. They all waited in silence. Nina's hands felt as if they were growing in her lap. Then the man cleared his throat.

'The upper floor of the house, where the victim was found, is probably also where the assault was carried out. There are traces of blood and saliva in several locations up there, on the landing, in the bedroom, on the stairs, and possibly also in the children's rooms.'

Johansson got a paper handkerchief out of his pocket and blew his nose. Nina thought it almost looked like he was wiping a tear from the corner of his eye.

'We've found prints from six individuals all over the house,' he continued. 'Three adults and three children.'

'In the parents' bedroom as well?' Q asked.

'Yes.'

'Did they have a home-help? A cleaner, an au pair?'

'Not known at present.'

Johansson turned a page of his pad. 'We haven't found

any evidence on the outside of the property. No sign of a break-in. All the doors were locked when the patrol arrived, so the perpetrator locked up afterwards when he or she left. It's difficult to determine whether anything has been stolen, but items that are usually of interest to thieves, such as passports, computers, iPads, mobiles and so on, all seem to have been left. Obviously some individual items may have been taken, but that can't be confirmed right now.'

'Lerberg's business?'

Johansson bent over a different bundle of papers and looked through them slowly. 'The company has three main clients who account for ninety per cent of the turnover – a shipping company in Panama, another in the Philippines, and a transport business in Spain.'

'Can you check them out?' Q said to Lamia.

Johansson glanced up at them over his glasses. 'Forensics were finished by three o'clock this morning, but we're keeping the cordon in place for the time being.'

'What about his political activities?'

Johansson coughed. 'Lerberg was a member of the Committee for Social Services and Care of the Elderly, which is responsible for funding youth and children's services, financial support, refugee centres, psychiatric and addiction issues, as well as care of the elderly and disabled.'

'Quite a few loaded issues there, then,' Q said. 'Distribution of money, refugees, not to mention drug addicts, alcoholics and the mentally ill. Any specific threats against Lerberg?'

'Nothing the Security Police are aware of,' Lamia said.

'Was he in favour of any particularly controversial policies? Open-door immigration? Slashed benefit payments?'

'Our colleagues in Nacka are looking into that.'

Q turned to Nina. 'How's the victim doing this morning?'

'I spoke to his doctor a little while ago. His condition is unchanged. He's still sedated after the operation.'

'Can you give us an account of his injuries?'

Nina looked through her notes, then at Lamia. The woman was peeling an orange. She pulled out a segment and offered it to Nina with a smile.

'Er, no, thanks,' Nina said. 'The assault appears to have taken place between Thursday evening and Friday morning last week. It looks as if the perpetrators – there were probably at least two – stuck to tried and tested torture methods. How much detail should I . . . ?'

'Go for it,' the commissioner said.

She straightened her back.

'*Falaka*, or foot whipping, is one of the oldest torture methods we know of . . . Blows with batons or sticks cause extreme pain that starts in the soles of the feet and travels all the way up to the head.'

Johansson took notes, shaking his head. Lamia ate her orange, licking her fingers. Q was watching Nina intently.

'Ingemar Lerberg was beaten on the soles of his feet with a hard, thin object, probably a whip or a telescopic baton . . . Well, that's just my supposition. Both his arms were out of their sockets, so he could have been subjected to a spread-eagle . . .'

Johansson's shoulders began to shake. If she didn't know better, she would have thought he was crying.

'That means the victim's hands are tied behind his back, then he's lifted up by his wrists. The strain on the shoulders is immense, and the victim soon passes out from the pain.'

'Where at the crime scene could that have been carried out?' Q asked.

Nina visualized the interior of the house. There were lamp-hooks in the ceilings, but nothing strong enough to hold the weight of a grown man. And she couldn't recall any items of furniture solid enough. 'Possibly the upstairs landing. There's a wrought-iron railing at the top of the stairs. It seemed a bit loose – they could have fastened the rope there.'

Nina looked at Q, who nodded for her to continue. 'He was also subjected to a *cheera*, or tearing, as it's also known. That means that the legs are pulled apart until the muscles tear. Lerberg had suffered severe bleeding in his groin.'

The secretary blew his nose again. Yes, he really did seem to be crying. Nina glanced at Lamia and Q, but neither of them seemed to have noticed the man's emotional state. She picked up the third page of the forensics report. 'The plastic bag that was found in the children's room could have been used for a dry Submarino. That's an asphyxiation technique – Lerberg showed signs of oxygen deprivation. He had also been severely beaten, primarily in the face – one eyeball had split.' She was feeling slightly sick.

Q nodded in encouragement. 'What does this tell us about our perpetrators? Is it possible to trace their methods to a particular geographic area?'

'*Falaka* is especially popular in the Middle East. *Cheera* is used in India and Pakistan, among other places, and the spread-eagle is also known as Palestinian hanging. It's used in Turkey and Iran, for instance.'

Johansson made more notes.

Q stood up. 'So a relatively uneducated guess would suggest that we're dealing with an area south-east of Sweden?'

'Not necessarily,' Nina said. 'These are tried and tested methods everywhere. The Submarino is also known as La

79

Bañera, which suggests south-west rather than south-east.'

'Unpleasant,' the commissioner said. 'What business was Lerberg in? Something to do with shipping?'

'Coordination of maritime transport,' Lamia said.

'What the hell could he have been shipping that would have warranted such an excess of violence? Drugs? Money? Children? Nuclear weapons?'

'He didn't ship anything himself, just arranged the loading of different vessels and made sure they weren't travelling empty between harbours,' Lamia said.

Q looked at the rain-streaked windows and sighed. 'This is getting ridiculous. How the hell can there be so much water up there?' He turned back to Nina. 'I want you to find out what this is all about,' he said. 'You're right, there must have been at least two perpetrators, but what drove them to this insane torture? Lamia, put in a request to see his accounts. And where on earth is the wife? Did they take her with them? If so, where, and why?'

Nina quickly noted down what the commissioner was saying. When she looked up Lamia was typing again. Johansson blew his nose. Q was on his way out through the door.

Nina assumed that the meeting was over. It had lasted exactly twenty-two minutes.

The newsroom was suffused with the same grey light that had characterized it all year. Not just because of the climatic conditions outside the windows. Since the centre of journalistic activity had slipped from print to the online edition, the sharp edges of the newsroom had faded and dissolved. The daily cycle had disappeared – the room seemed to have stopped breathing. There were no longer any deadlines – or, rather, every moment was a new deadline.

Annika put a plastic mug of coffee from the machine on her desk and caught sight of her reflection in the rain-streaked glass.

Back in the Stone Age, when Annika had first been taken on at the *Evening Post*, two editions had been published on normal days: the early one, commonly known as the backwoods edition, and a later version, which reached the suburbs and areas around major cities. Under extreme circumstances an even later updated edition was occasionally published, but only for central Stockholm. The entire editorial machinery had lived and worked according to those deadlines. Mornings were a time for staff to catch their breath, for contemplation, planning and, hopefully, reflection. The noise began to rise in the afternoons. Chair legs scraped across the linoleum floor. What to lead with? Was there anything from the regions? What did the news agencies have? And the mix! The mix had to be right! Entertainment? Sport? And something funny! Any amusing animals for page sixteen? A cat that had walked a hundred and eighty kilometres to get home? Pictures! The name and age of the cat!

When darkness fell and the daytime staff had gone home, the light would shrink to islands around the newsdesk, the sports desk and the entertainment section. The noise was lower, more intense and focused. Heartbeats rose, the pace of activity increased and everyone was focused. As the clock approached 04.45, the deadline for deliveries to the Norrland flight, the atmosphere was tense. Hair on end, shirt-tails flapping, howls of rage at crashing computers, crisis calls from the print-works, always about the failure

81

of the yellow plate to arrive on time, and could they try sending it again? Then, as the deadline passed, the sense of release once the night-editor had sent the last colour file and the message arrived telling them that the presses had started to roll in Akalla. Shoulders slumped and keyboards were pushed away. All of that was ancient history, these days. She didn't understand why she even remembered it.

Annika dropped her bag and raincoat on the floor and hooked her laptop into the wireless network. Her homepage was set to the *Evening Post*'s online edition: the paper's surveillance of modern society was governed now by clicks. Not that that was anything to complain about. Active participation by the country's citizens in its ultimate form. Give the people what the people want. Want to know who slept with whom in the *Big Brother* house last night? Click here! Watch grainy footage of a cheap duvet bouncing up and down in one corner, and remember to like us on Facebook! Or watch the car-chase right up to the crash! Watch an Indian man pop his eyeballs out! Must read – RIGHT NOW!

The online updates happened in a constant, arrhythmic torrent, made up of every conceivable colour, all mixed together, meaning that the end result was inevitably brown. There was no day, no night. Just a constant howl of stress.

She looked over at Schyman's glass bunker. He was reading something on his computer, something very important from the look of it. It was ironic, really. He had turned the *Evening Post* into the biggest printed newspaper in Sweden just as that had ceased to matter, when the printed edition was merely an advertisement for the digital edition. The internet was what mattered, and online they were hopelessly outclassed in spite of all the infrastructure projects, high-tech digital solutions and android-based platforms. Their competitors owned the internet, not as a result of their journalism but because of their flashy adverts, street pictures and traffic information.

'Good morning.'

Annika looked up. Valter was disgracefully alert.

'Can I sit here?' He had already put his rucksack in Berit's place.

'Of course,' she said. 'Welcome to another day in the citadel of free speech.'

Valter Wennergren put a copy of the declining print edition of the paper on the desk, took off his jacket, laid it on top of his briefcase and sat down. 'What are you doing today?' he asked, sounding genuinely interested.

'The Lerbergs,' Annika said. 'We'll have to keep an eye on Ingemar. Whether he dies or not, it's a story. And there's an alert out for his wife now. "Where is Nora?" You know the sort of thing . . . If anyone releases pictures of the kids, we'll change that to "Where's Mummy?" Or, even better, "Mummy, where are you?"'

She handed him a copy of the picture of Nora that the police had issued, a portrait from the family album, with a description attached: 'Nora Maria Andersson Lerberg, twenty-seven years old, 1 metre 68 centimetres tall, long, ash-blonde hair, grey-blue eyes, normal build, weight approximately 65 kilos. Probably wearing a crucifix round her neck, plus wedding and engagement rings, plain, eighteen-carat gold. Clothing at time of disappearance: unknown. Healthy skin, doesn't use makeup. Takes Levaxin for thyroid problems. No other medication, no allergies.'

'I'd be happy to tag along,' he said, taking the picture and studying it for a moment. 'I've just got one question first.'

Annika logged into Facebook. At the top of her newsfeed

she read that Sjölander, a colleague who was sitting on the other side of the partition, had eaten breakfast with a secret source at the Sheraton. (If you really wanted to describe a source as secret, why write on Facebook where and when you met them?)

Valter Wennergren opened the paper again. 'On page thirteen.'

Annika looked away from the screen.

'It's about Gustaf Holmerud,' Valter said.

She pushed the laptop away and grabbed a copy of the paper. Entire mornings could pass now without her ever leafing through it. 'What is it you're wondering about?' she asked, turning to pages twelve and thirteen. Twelve was an advert for a new type of scratch-card. Thirteen was dominated by two pictures. One showed a man smiling, wearing a crayfish-party hat and bib, and the other a young woman in a school-graduation cap.

I KILLED JOSEFIN
Serial killer confesses new crime

Annika looked at the photograph of the blonde girl, Hanna Josefin Liljeberg, from Täby kyrkby, nineteen years old when she was found murdered on Kungsholmen in Stockholm. Suddenly the past fifteen years vanished and Annika was back there, her first summer temping job at the *Evening Post*, that scorching Saturday afternoon at the end of July, peering in at the crime scene through black iron railings. Josefin's eyes staring straight into hers, clouded and grey, her head thrown back, mouth open in a silent scream. The bruise on her right breast, the green tinge to her stomach. The blunt grey of the stone behind her, the muted vegetation, the shadow play of the foliage, the closeness and heat, the nauseating smell.

'Why isn't anyone else writing about this?' the young man wondered.

Annika put her hand on the girl's smiling face. 'Maybe we've got better sources,' she said quietly.

Sjölander had written the article. The bulk of the text was an ecstatic account of the fantastic breakthrough in the hunt for Josefin's unknown killer: at last, the mystery surrounding the young woman's murder could be solved after fifteen years of uncertainty!

Annika looked at the rain streaming down the window. 'It was that scorching hot summer,' she said. 'You know, when Sweden was a banana republic: forty degrees centigrade, ridiculously high interest rates, and we were really good at football . . .'

Valter Wennergren blinked, totally uncomprehending. He had probably still been at nursery school then.

'Josefin was found behind a gravestone in the little Jewish cemetery in Kronoberg Park. She was naked, strangled . . . Her boyfriend had done it. His name was Joachim. He was never convicted.'

'But now Gustaf Holmerud has claimed responsibility. Will it go to trial?'

She closed the paper, finished her coffee and stood up, still holding the plastic cup. 'Probably not. There's a new prosecutor looking after Holmerud, now that the last one's been promoted. I'm going to get some more. Do you want any?'

She waved her cup, and he looked horrified. 'Do you really drink that stuff?'

Her intercom crackled. It was Anders Schyman. 'Annika, can you pop into my office?'

*

85

He watched Annika Bengtzon stride towards the coffee machine. He really ought to follow through on his idea of introducing a dress code for the newsroom – he couldn't have reporters looking like that when they were representing the newspaper in the city. She was wearing some sort of jacket, jeans and a creased top, and she obviously hadn't washed her hair that morning.

Annika pulled open the sliding door and poked her head into the room. 'What?'

'Come in and close the door behind you.'

She stepped into his cubicle, shut the door and faced him. Now he came to think about it, there wasn't much wrong with her clothes. They just looked a bit odd on her, as if she hadn't put them on properly that morning. And the jeans were definitely too big for her.

'How's it going?' he asked, trying to look relaxed.

'The police have put out an alert for Nora Lerberg now,' Annika said. 'It's a really weird case. I'm heading out there again in a while.'

'I know Ingemar Lerberg pretty well. Or knew him, at least. We don't have much contact any more. He's a nice man.'

'Really?'

'Well, his political ideas might be a bit radical—'

'That people with a BMI of over thirty should no longer be treated by the national health service, you mean? Or that libraries should stock only "authorized" books?'

He stood up irritably. 'Have you seen this?' he asked, twisting his computer so she could read it.

She came over to his desk. 'The Light of Truth. What is it?'

'A blog,' Schyman said, and pointed at his chair. 'Sit down.'

She did so, pulled herself close to the desk and read.

'This is the second post,' Schyman said. 'He wrote one yesterday as well.'

'So I see,' she said.

'He's claiming that Viola Söderland is dead,' Schyman said. 'His sources are two of Viola's former business partners. They were convicted of false accounting and defrauding creditors when Golden Spire went bankrupt, Linette Pettersson and Sven-Olof Witterfeldt, two really reliable witnesses . . . He claims I tricked my way to those two journalism awards, that I produced the documentary about Viola Söderland as a freelance commission for the insurance company so they wouldn't have to pay out on her life insurance policy to the children. He writes that—'

'Yes, I can see,' she interrupted.

'All the evidence suggested she was alive,' he said. 'Alive at the time, anyway. When I made the documentary. Perhaps she's dead now, I don't know . . .' He reached for a printout of that day's blog-post. There was a photograph taken from the hill on Vikingavägen, not of his house but only a few hundred metres away.

'This is what Bosse was talking about,' she said.

He narrowed his eyes. 'Who?'

'On the other paper. Covers crime. He mentioned it yesterday, out at the crime scene in Solsidan.'

Schyman felt anger rising: that was precisely the sort of thing he needed to know. He had to put a stop to it, and find out how far it was spreading. 'Why didn't you say something?'

She brushed a strand of hair off her forehead. 'Like what? That someone said something nasty about you?' She turned her attention to the text again. 'There must be something wrong with whoever wrote this. "Without culture, morals,

87

or any other lasting values, he infects our planet, using up air and space . . ." So your resignation isn't enough for him. He thinks you ought to die?'

His mouth dried. 'I presume so.'

'Why do you think it's a man? The worst idiots can actually be women. Like Anne Snapphane, to take just one striking example.'

She sounded very matter-of-fact, as if the blunt attacks on her in the media by her former best friend had had no effect on her at all. Schyman was fairly certain that they had.

'What does he want?' Annika asked, looking up at him. 'What's the point, assuming that there is one? Do you know? Or is this just another case of plain old envy?'

He sank down on the visitor's chair. 'I don't know. I don't understand what's so controversial about what I did. I made a television documentary eighteen years ago about a missing billionairess, in which I listed all the evidence that suggested she was still alive. I didn't claim she was, though.'

'Oh,' Annika said. 'I remember that programme – they used to use it as course material at the College of Journalism. You did claim she was alive, didn't you?'

'I said that everything pointed towards the *likelihood* that she was alive,' Schyman said.

'It doesn't sound like the Light of Truth is interested in linguistic niceties,' Annika said. '"He has intentionally lied and deceived the entire Swedish people, this self-appointed crusader for honour—"'

'Yes, yes,' he interrupted. 'How should I deal with it?'

'Seriously?' Annika said. 'Ignore it. After all, there isn't anything you can do about it.' She stood up.

The editor-in-chief's shoulders tightened in frustration.

'He claims I was bribed by the insurance company, and that I bought my "luxury villa" in Saltsjöbaden with the money! That's insane. It used to belong to my wife's parents and we bought it more than thirty years ago, twelve years before I made that documentary!'

'If you start to fight him, you'll only make him look legitimate,' Annika said.

'But he's wrong! I can prove it – I've still got the deed of purchase and—'

'"Speak in anger and you will deliver the greatest speech you will ever live to regret."'

He closed his eyes. Dear God, she was quoting Churchill at him. 'You have a very low opinion of my ability to express myself,' he said.

'As long as the established media don't jump on the story, there's no need for you to worry,' she said. She walked out of his office, closing the door behind her. He watched her go across to the desk where Albert Wennergren's boy was waiting. Why on earth did the lad want to become a journalist when he had every opportunity to pick a well-paid, respected profession with a decent future?

He sighed and decided to check the weather in the Rödlöga archipelago.

Nina's room was cramped, with thin, bluish-grey curtains, pale wood furniture from Kinnarp, and a window facing an internal courtyard and the brown panelling of the building opposite. She shared it with a man called Jesper Wou, whom she hadn't met yet – he was away on international business in Asia.

She put her gym-bag on the floor next to the bookshelf,

on her side of the shared desk. Even if her colleague was away, she wasn't about to start invading his space – that sort of thing quickly became a habit, and she'd soon find herself thinking that all his things belonged to her, that he was in the way, even when he was just sitting on his own chair.

Her thoughts were going in circles. The violence to which Lerberg had been subjected was so precise, the torture methods used so specific that they had to mean something. She had seen violence at close quarters as a child, had grown up with it: violence as an instrument of power, a way to crack helplessness and frustration, to claim territory. But this was something different.

She opened the most recent working document on her computer.

'Nina Hoffman?' Another colleague was looking in at the doorway, keen to say hello. This one was very tall and thin, and was wearing a baseball cap. They shook hands. 'Welcome to National Crime.'

His name was Oscar Gyllensköld, a police investigator with an office three doors down on the left.

Lovely to meet you, yes, she was sure she was going to enjoy working there.

When he shuffled away in his Birkenstocks she contemplated closing the door, but decided against it. She'd just have to put up with the introductions for a while.

She went back to her notes, and the collection of documents, search results and extracts in the digital folder.

Looking for answers about Lerberg's attackers using an analytical approach was pointless. People were capable of doing anything to each other – she knew that from both theory and practice. *She had shot and killed her elder brother, Filip, whom she had worshipped. Yes, she had*

90

been afraid of him, but she'd still adored him.

Out of the window she studied the building on the far side of the courtyard. Everything was earth-coloured in Sweden, grey and beige and brown. She wondered if other people reacted to that. Somewhere inside her she carried the colours of her childhood, sharp and pungent, solid green, bright blue sea, blinding white light from a sun high in the sky.

She looked away from the brown and the contrast inside her.

The nature of the violence spoke volumes. It was important – of crucial importance. In the past twenty-four hours she had read more than she'd ever wanted to about torture, and had examined every component part of its brutality. In rare cases it could be the result of pure evil, a delight in inflicting pain, but that was unusual. Usually it was an expression of power, ordered or at least sanctioned by a state. Torture had been around as long as civilization, and was still used in three-quarters of the countries in the world.

Most people would be capable of inflicting a degree of torture if they were ordered to and the conditions were right. She remembered how surprised some on her course had been when they read about the Milgram experiment, and how upset they were by the results. They had tried to come up with explanations in their bright seminar rooms, in their course literature, something to say, *There's no way I would ever do that.*

The experiment, which had been conducted at Yale in the 1960s, had never been refuted. Forty volunteers, all empathic, well-balanced and mentally stable, had been given the role of 'teacher' in a piece of scientific research led by an 'experimenter'. The 'teacher' was to ask questions and punish or reward a 'learner', another man in the next room, using electric shocks.

Fairly soon the learners began to scream with pain on the other side of the wall. They shouted that they had heart problems, that they feared for their lives. All the teachers were unsettled by this, but the experimenters in charge of the study encouraged them to carry on, using four degrees of verbal prompt:

'Please continue.'

'The experiment requires that you continue.'

'It is absolutely essential that you continue.'

'You have no choice. You must go on.'

Sixty-five per cent of the teachers went on tormenting their learners until the maximum dose of shock had been administered three times, 450 volts each time. (In fact, the learners were actors and there were no electric shocks, but the teachers didn't know that.)

Other similar experiments had followed, conducted all round the world. The number of individuals who were prepared to go all the way was constant: between 61 and 66 per cent of the population. Women were just as likely as men to give the maximum dose of electricity, but felt worse about it when they did so.

Nina looked out of the window again. An expression of power, but whose? The torture had been too thorough, too professional, to have been an accident or inflicted by a madman. A state? An intelligence agency? Who would attack a Swedish citizen in a democratic country? Or had it been someone with ambitions to act like a state, perhaps with supranational ambitions, the sort of power that didn't acknowledge any borders?

She pushed away her computer, stood up and walked round to Jesper Wou's side. His part of the desk was completely clear, not so much as a pen left out. Lovely. She didn't like disorder. His bookcase contained just the usual factual literature, a copy of the Murder Bible (or *The Police Handbook for the Investigation of Serious Violent Crime*, to give it its proper title), a few official investigations into organized international crime, and a dozen volumes in some sort of Asian script – she thought it might be Chinese but it could just as easily have been something else. Jesper Wou: the name undoubtedly suggested two diverse cultural backgrounds. She wondered how long he would be away, how long she would have the office to herself.

She would have liked an office of her own, but perhaps that would come in time.

Her eyes rested on one of the investigations in the bookcase. She listened out for any noise in the corridor before reaching for the file: *Organized Crime Around the World*, published by the European Institute for Crime Prevention and Control, affiliated with the United Nations (HEUNI), Helsinki.

Slowly, she walked back to her chair.

It was considerably more likely that Lerberg had been the victim of violent thugs than some foreign intelligence agency, and there were certainly plenty of crime syndicates. She opened the file, and found the names of the Italian gangs, the largest of which was currently 'Ndrangheta, as well as Solntsevskaya Bratva, 'the Brotherhood', the biggest and most powerful criminal organization in Russia, D-Company in the United Arab Emirates, the Zeta and Sinaloa cartels in Mexico, the Colombians, and the Five Families in the USA: big, powerful, ambitious.

She leafed through the file and stopped when she reached the section about Chinese Triad gangs. Some passages had been underlined, and there was some illegible scribbling in the margins, things Jesper Wou had found worth following up. Maybe this was what he was working on at the moment. Perhaps he was in China. Stationed there for a while?

She was beginning to find the room cramped, even without him on the other side of the desk.

'Welcome to National Crime.'

Nina jumped and quickly closed Jesper Wou's file. A woman with big brown hair and a broad smile was standing in the doorway. Nina got to her feet and went over to introduce herself. The woman's name was Maria Johansson, she was an operational analyst, and had been working on PLAYA for the past three years – she said it was driving her mad. Nina made an effort to smile naturally.

Once Maria had gone she put the report back in Wou's bookcase. Then she slumped in front of her computer. Was she going to end up sitting there until she, too, went mad?

She had been on leave of absence from the Södermalm Police for the past four years. The plan was that she should return to her post as an inspector in the Katarina district when she had completed her studies, but she had conveniently managed to suppress that. When a woman from HR had called in February to discuss what date she would return to duty, Nina had been caught off-guard. The thought of sitting in a patrol car made her feel physically sick.

She had handed in her notice the following day, then applied for and got a job with an international security company, a good job with a decent salary, in their unit for crime prevention and the investigation of internal crime. Their offices were ultra-modern, glass, steel and black granite, and she had shivered every time she walked in. When the HR woman had called again to ask if she would be interested in working at National Crime, she had said yes without hesitation. The bosses of the security company were angry, not that she was bothered by that. But she had given a lot of thought to her own decisions: how considered had they been?

She woke her computer again.

Why had Lerberg been tortured? Because of something he knew? Why not shoot him?

She looked through an outline of torture during the Inquisition, then under Pol Pot and Pinochet, and eventually came to the United Nations' definition of torture: 'Any act by which severe pain or suffering, whether physical or mental, is intentionally inflicted on a person for such purposes as obtaining from him or a third person information or a confession, punishing him for an act he or a third person has committed or is suspected of having committed . . .'

Punishment, information, confession.

Three motives for the use of torture rather than ordinary violent brutality. On the victim or 'a third person'. Possibly the cruellest form of torture: tormenting a man's wife or child to get him to talk, confess and be punished.

Outside, it had started to rain again.

As a source of information, torture was hopeless. People who were seriously motivated held out the longest but the innocent went to pieces almost immediately and would say anything to avoid further pain.

Why had the perpetrators carried on for so long? Because Lerberg was motivated and held out or because he genuinely didn't know what they were trying to find out?

And where was Nora?

*

He had never been to Orminge shopping centre before. That was hardly a disadvantage – quite the contrary, in fact. Every suburban shopping centre in Sweden was constructed according to the same principles, and he regarded the idiosyncrasies of this particular example as an interesting challenge.

There was a footbridge above the entire car-park, an offset suspension bridge, the cables of which didn't hang vertically but stretched out from the pylons towards the ground. Most peculiar! He stopped to study the construction for a while, trying to discern its origins and the reason for its use there. Then he strode quickly onto it, taking pleasure from being in the here and now.

The shop signs screamed at him. They were large and garish, which told him that the customer profile wasn't the most sophisticated in Sweden. The possibilities on offer included food and makeup, dentists and hairdressers, chemists, florists and gymnasiums. People could live their entire lives in Orminge shopping centre without ever going short of anything vital.

He could hear a rumble in the distance, presumably from the motorway into Stockholm, or perhaps from some air-conditioning unit. He couldn't tell the difference between such sounds any more – his hearing had suffered too many traumas over the years. He couldn't see any benches, or any representatives from the shadier side of society, which prompted him to leave the footbridge.

He walked inside the temple of shopping. Food, makeup and hair-care on the ground floor, a beautiful glass dome above. He took the escalator to the next floor. There he found pale-wood benches, occupied only by a young mother, her pushchair and mobile phone. She pretended not to see him. He was unfamiliar and uninteresting, the sort of person young mothers avoided.

The man looked dutifully around the shops, his gaze passing over shoes and watches, vitamins and fried food. On the way down a different escalator he read: 'So much to experience! Two floors full of shopping and personal service.' He nodded. Experiencing things was important. And he always went for personal service, if he had a choice.

He stopped for a moment, focused on his breathing, his anchor to the here and now.

But, naturally, he wasn't actually there.

At that moment he, or rather his mirror-image, was evaluating a forestry project up in Storuman, where rather too many young trees had been stripped out when the area was cleared. There were four witnesses who could attest to his presence, as well as a debit card receipt for coffee, mineral water and five freshly baked Danish pastries.

He stopped outside the Orminge Grill for a few seconds, momentarily at something of a loss. The smell of food turned his stomach. He hurried up the concrete steps leading to the local parish hall of the Swedish Church, without any great expectation of finding what he was looking for, but he rarely left any stone unturned.

Lo and behold, the parish hall was right next door to the state-run alcohol store, and on the benches provided by the faithful, out in the Lord's lovely fresh air, sat a whole gang of them. So practical! They didn't have to go more than a few metres before they could start drinking.

He walked over to them, pulled a full bottle of Koskenkorva vodka from his inside pocket, and asked, in a singsong Norrland accent, if anyone would like a drink.

Thirty seconds later he was a member of the gang.

*

Annika had her feet on the desk and was eating a pre-packed salad containing vegetables that had been shipped halfway round the planet and tasted accordingly. Valter had gone out to get a hamburger, so she took the opportunity to Skype Berit, who was sitting in her hotel room in Norway, writing something as they talked. The camera on her computer was slightly crooked and all Annika could see was one wall and a bit of Berit's hair.

'Today I interviewed a girl from Norrköping, a literary scholar, who moved to Oslo six months ago,' Berit said. 'She spends eight hours a day sitting in a fruit factory peeling bananas.'

At least a hundred thousand Swedes worked in Norway, most of them doing jobs that the Norwegians refused to do. Berit was writing a series of articles about the new Swedish underclass.

'My brother-in-law is there this week trying to find a job,' Annika said. 'I doubt he's even going to get one peeling bananas.'

'Maybe I should talk to him about his dreams and ambitions,' Berit said.

'It would be a very short interview,' Annika said.

Tore, one of the caretakers, appeared beside her desk, evidently keen to talk to her. He seemed so cross that Annika wondered if he was personally acquainted with Steven, her hopeless brother-in-law. 'You've got a visitor,' he said.

'Who is it, and what do they want?'

'A Marianne Berg-Something. Says she wants to talk to you.'

Berit adjusted her camera so Annika could see her chin, hands and chest.

'She's the CD woman from yesterday,' Annika told

Berit, but at that moment she realized that Marianne Berg-Holmlund had followed Tore into the newsroom and was standing right behind him.

'I've got to go,' Annika said, clicking to close the connection with Berit and standing up to greet the woman.

Tore wandered back to the caretaker's desk.

'The seedy woman,' Marianne Berg-Holmlund repeated. Annika felt herself blush.

She had looked her up after their meeting: the woman was a member of the Christian Democratic Party committee, their International Council, and the executive board of Stockholm City Council. 'You did seem rather isolated among all those seedy men,' Annika said, gesturing her to Berit's chair. 'What can I do for you?'

The woman sat down cautiously and fiddled with her handbag. It was a multi-coloured Louis Vuitton, so vulgar that it was probably genuine.

'I'd like to talk to you about Ingemar. Lots of us feel really desperate about what's happened.'

Annika looked at her thoughtfully. She was clearly very uneasy. 'What do you mean? Weren't your colleagues telling the truth during yesterday's interview?'

Marianne Berg-Holmlund took a handkerchief out of her bag and twisted it between her fingers. 'I don't know how to say this . . . My friends in the party, they don't know Ingemar . . .'

Annika picked up a pen and notepad.

'They talk about what happened as if they knew him,' the woman said, her eyes filling with tears. 'As if they cared. They've got no idea, and they can't imagine . . .' She blew her nose loudly.

'Are you referring to Ingemar's resignation?' Annika wondered.

She nodded. 'Among other things. Do you have to tell anyone that I've been here? Can I be anonymous?'

Annika glanced around. Marianne Berg-Holmlund was sitting in the middle of the newsroom of the largest evening paper in Sweden (if you were counting printed copies, of course), talking to a reporter, and she thought no one would notice? 'If you want to give me information anonymously, then that's your prerogative. I'll never tell anyone what you've told me, if you don't want me to. On the other hand, I can't guarantee that I'll be able to publish anything.'

Berg-Holmlund nodded eagerly and took a deep breath. 'They make out that they're supporting Ingemar now, but I know they called the papers. Ingemar's a brilliant politician, he's got a natural flair for it, and he was a threat to the party leadership. They wanted to get rid of him, I know. Hypocrisy, that's what it is. It's immoral. Stabbing someone in the back and then not taking responsibility for it.'

Annika studied her. 'Do you know this for certain, or is it just a suspicion?'

She clasped her handbag tighter. 'The party leadership knows nothing at all about Ingemar. It's all getting rather ridiculous . . .' All of a sudden she seemed almost amused. 'Like that bit about him being such a good businessman. Ingemar was a wonderful person and a brilliant politician, but he's always been a terrible businessman. How he manages to keep that company going is beyond me.'

As Annika was taking notes, she saw from the corner of her eye that Valter had appeared. He stopped about ten metres away, unsure of where to sit.

Marianne Berg-Holmlund sighed and wiped her eyes. 'I'd say that Ingemar is the only person who is capable of

100

steering this party's policies in the right direction,' she said.

Annika rocked gently on her chair. 'So your sympathies are with him, as far as politics are concerned?' she asked.

The woman nodded vigorously. 'Absolutely. There's a small but close-knit group of us who rate his political opinions very highly.'

'So, you think homosexuality is an abomination?'

Marianne Berg-Holmlund stiffened. 'That's not my opinion. It's in the Bible.'

Annika put down her pen and notepad and pulled her laptop towards her, searched the internet and read the results. Then she looked up. 'It's an abomination to eat shellfish too. It says so in Leviticus chapter eleven, verse ten. Which do you think is worse? Homosexuality or prawns?'

The woman sighed.

'Sorry if I seem to be labouring the point,' Annika said, 'but I find political Biblical references fascinating. In Leviticus twenty-five, verse forty-four, it says that you can own both male and female slaves from neighbouring countries. Tell me, how do you interpret "neighbouring country"? Norway and Finland, or would it have to be somewhere outside the European Economic Area?'

'It's easy to make fun of the Bible,' Marianne Berg-Holmlund said. 'You're not the first to do it.'

Annika smiled briefly and pushed away her laptop. 'So, you think Ingemar was treated badly by your colleagues in the party?'

The woman was wary now. 'You wrote terrible headlines about the accusations, but nothing when he was found not guilty.'

Annika raised her eyebrows. 'Not guilty?' she said. 'I haven't read about that.'

101

'That's exactly what I mean.'

'But if he was completely innocent, why did he resign?'

Marianne Berg-Holmlund jerked her head back. 'It isn't easy to resist when there's a mob demanding you go.'

'What do you want me to do?' Annika asked. 'Write that we were wrong? That Ingemar was the victim of a conspiracy among his party comrades?'

The woman glared at her. 'You crushed his political ambitions. Now someone's crushed him physically. I just wish that one or other of you could be held responsible for what you've done.'

She stood up and made for the door.

Valter stared at her as she passed him. 'What was all that about?' he asked, looking rather unsettled.

Annika watched the woman leave. 'Internal political intrigue inside the Christian Democratic Party,' she said. 'She just sold out her friends in the party because they sold out her friend in the party. And she's angry that we wrote about his tax fiddle.'

Valter sat down. 'What about all the Bible stuff? Are you a Christian?'

Annika turned her laptop so Valter could see the screen. 'A classic argument,' she said. 'There are loads of different versions of it online. Aaron Sorkin used it in an episode of *The West Wing*, but there are plenty of examples in social media.'

She pulled the laptop back towards her. 'According to Exodus thirty-five, verse two, we should kill everyone who works on a Sunday. And Deuteronomy twenty-one, verse eighteen onwards tells us what to do when a child is disobedient – they're to be stoned to death outside the gates of the city.' She looked up at him. 'Do you think it has to be the gates of the city? Wouldn't outside in the garden do just as well?'

Valter chortled.

'There are loads of them,' Annika said. 'If you go to the barber and get your hair and beard trimmed, you're committing a sin, according to Leviticus nineteen, verse twenty-seven. If you swear, the whole congregation has to stone you to death, Leviticus twenty-four, verses fifteen and sixteen. And this one's my favourite – listen. "When a man sells his daughter into slavery, she shall not go out as a male slave may."' She gazed at him thoughtfully. 'Mind you, she did say a few things that are worth checking up . . . Do you know how to get hold of information on Swedish companies?'

While Valter looked for details of Ingemar Lerberg's business activities, Annika read up about his resignation. What if the woman was right? She scrolled down the list of search results for ingemar lerberg tax.

The first articles about his dodgy tax affairs had appeared on a Tuesday morning in November seven and a half years ago. Several of the big media companies seemed to have gained access to the information simultaneously: the big tabloids, the main morning paper and Swedish Television. Sjölander had dealt with the story for the *Evening Post*. The headline was stark and loud:

TAX RAID ON SENIOR POLITICIAN
Party secretary: 'We take all forms
of criminality very seriously'

She skimmed the article, trying to read between the lines and see through the fanciful phrasing. 'Tax raid' meant that the tax office had requested Lerberg's accounts for investigation. It happened to most limited companies at regular intervals.

The party secretary's quote was accurate, no doubt, but he had been talking about the party's attitude towards crime in general, not Ingemar Lerberg. How else could he have replied to the journalist's question? 'We are relaxed about all forms of criminality'?

No one in the party leadership appeared to have expressed an opinion about Lerberg, either for or against.

Day two had seen the media coverage escalate in the expected manner:

Senior Politician Reported to Police Prosecutor Examining Tax Fraud

To the average newspaper reader, Ingemar Lerberg's fate was now sealed. The police had been brought in, a prosecutor was looking into the case, and all that remained was a severe custodial sentence. The fact that he hadn't already resigned as a Member of Parliament seemed incomprehensible.

But when Annika took a metaphorical step back from the text, it was obvious that Lerberg had been reported to the police by some concerned citizen with no particular insight into the case, an Angry Taxpayer, who thought it was disgraceful that well-known people cheated at the expense of ordinary citizens. The prosecutor would have had to weigh up the evidence to see whether it was worth setting up so much as a preliminary investigation.

She did another search.

104

Day three: the dramaturgically correct third act:

Senior Politician Writes Exclusively About Tax Fraud

Ingemar Lerberg had met the criticism head-on in a self-penned piece published in the *Evening Post*. Like most people under pressure, he had written too much, almost to the point of jeopardizing his legal case, and the ultimate effect was to make him look guilty. He explained various points in so much detail that they became baffling and dull, and all his arguments came across as excuses.

On day four, the story of Ingemar Lerberg's 'tax fraud' concluded as expected: the politician resigned and stepped down from his parliamentary seat with immediate effect.

Annika sighed. Why did people in positions of power never learn how to handle the media? She leaned back in her chair and watched Valter staring at his computer screen.

For the following day's paper she needed a more in-depth angle on the politician's missing wife, Nora. The articles about the search for her and an update on her husband's condition were already finished and online (Ingemar Lerberg was still unconscious, and Nora was still missing without trace) – she had to update them before she went home – but she should really try to find something more substantial for tomorrow's print edition. The Lerbergs' children were being cared for by a relative, Ingemar's sister Kristine Lerberg, but she was refusing to talk. Annika had called twice and had been sent packing in no uncertain terms on the second occasion: didn't she realize that Kristine was waiting for news about Ingemar and Nora? She couldn't switch her phone off and Annika was taking up time and energy in the midst of her grief –

she might even be stopping important information reaching her.

Annika had put together a short piece about the anguish of the relatives, quoting Kristine Lerberg, but hadn't got much further than that. The problem was that there was very little public information about Nora. She was mentioned a few times in various media in connection with Ingemar Lerberg's election campaign eight years ago, but since then she evidently hadn't participated in her husband's political life. She didn't appear to have a job, she wasn't active in any organizations, and she wasn't on Facebook. She didn't blog or tweet under her own name, and hadn't taken part in any digital debates.

So, what did she spend all her time doing?

She had three children, of course, aged one, three and five, and, considering her husband's religious and political preferences, Annika assumed that state childcare was out of the question. She had at least registered a mobile phone number, and Annika tried calling it for a third time. The phone was still switched off.

Annika looked at her computer screen. Silvervägen 63. Nice address. Maybe she was friendly with the neighbours. Went for walks with a triple-seat buggy and the now murdered dog, chatting about the weather and house prices across wooden fences and lilac hedges, gossiping about the other women in the local mothers' group, the latest books and films?

Annika brought up a street view of Solsidan and took a slow walk along the virtual Silvervägen. The pictures must have been taken last summer: the weather seemed rather grey but the trees were in leaf. When the road wasn't full of police cars and media it looked much classier. Annika clicked along the somewhat distorted perspective, scanning the edge of the screen, then saw what she was looking for.

There, on the lawn in front of Silvervägen 48, was a colourful plastic tractor next to a little inflatable paddling pool. She typed the address into the online population database, and two seconds later she had the full names and ages of everyone who was registered as living there.

Just as she'd thought.

The Lindenstolphe family had two children, aged five and three. She had found the Lerberg children's little playmates.

The phone numbers were all in the public domain, landline, work and mobile, for Therese and Johan. Annika cleared her throat and picked up her mobile.

Therese answered on the landline – she was at home, then. She was rather taken aback when Annika introduced herself as a reporter from the *Evening Post*, but she didn't hang up.

'Obviously it was a huge shock. That sort of thing isn't supposed to happen on our road,' she said.

'Do you know the Lerberg family?' Annika asked.

'Yes, of course. Nora and I belong to the same mums' group – our boys are the same age.'

Bingo.

'I'm trying to get a clearer picture of the family,' Annika said, 'so I can give an idea of them as something more than just victims of crime. And, of course, I'd like to hear how this has affected you, as their closest neighbours.'

Therese paused. 'I don't know, there are other people who know them much better . . .'

'We're not after family secrets or anything like that,' Annika said. 'We're just trying to get a bit closer to this tragic occurrence.'

Therese thought for a moment, then gave in. The children

107

had to have their lunch, and then a nap, but Annika was welcome to visit in an hour's time.

Annika breathed a sigh of relief. No matter what Therese had to say, the story was safe. It would almost be enough just to print a picture of the anxious neighbours accompanied by the caption, 'We never imagined that something like this could happen on our road!'

'Do you fancy coming on an outing to the real world?' she asked Valter.

He looked up from his computer. 'What about Ingemar Lerberg's company?'

She put her feet on the desk and looked at her watch. 'What have you found?'

He held up a printout and read from it: '"International Transport Consultancy was set up seven years ago, has three employees, and a turnover of six point eight million kronor. Main activities: consultancy in management, administration, transport and business development . . ."'

'I get it,' Annika said. 'And no doubt it ends with a statement that the company isn't permitted to be involved in anything that could be legally interpreted as banking or the provision of credit. Those are just the standard phrases. Who's on the board?'

He raised the printout again. 'Ingemar Lerberg is MD, chairman of the board and sole shareholder. Kristine Lerberg is on the board, and Nora Lerberg is listed as a director.'

The sister who was taking care of the children, and his wife. Typical family business.

'Their accountant is Robert Moberg, of Moberg & Moberg Accounting Services in Saltsjöbaden,' Valter said. 'The company's profit margin is around five per cent.'

As far as Annika understood, that was pretty reasonable.

She wondered how well informed the CD woman really was. 'Does he have any dormant businesses?'

'Four,' Valter said. 'Lerberg Investment, TL Investment Consulting, TL Consult Expert, and Lerberg Consulting.'

Annika raised her eyebrows. 'What does it say at the end of the report?'

Valter picked up the next sheet and read out, '"Self-employed tax status withdrawn. Bankruptcy discharged."'

Maybe Marianne Berg-Holmlund had known what she was talking about after all.

'When did the last company collapse?'

Valter looked through the printouts as Annika stood up and pulled on her jacket. 'Seven years ago,' he said.

'Let me see,' Annika said, reaching for the sheets of paper.

The officers of the bankrupt companies were exactly the same as those of the active business, with the exception of Lerberg's wife. Even the accountant was the same, Robert Moberg. She went back to her desk, looked up Moberg & Moberg on the internet, and found office and mobile phone numbers for the two accountants, Robert and Henrik.

'What are you doing?' Valter watched Annika write the numbers on her notepad.

'If the bankruptcy has been discharged and there's no suspicion of tax fraud or other impropriety, the company's financial records will be publicly available. They have to be kept for ten years. They'll be stored somewhere, and Robert and Henrik will know where. Besides . . .' Annika switched off her computer '. . . I'll be damned if they don't remember what happened when Ingemar Lerberg's businesses collapsed. Oops, I just swore. Leviticus twenty-four, verses fifteen and sixteen.'

'Do you reckon the newsroom would do as the whole congregation?' Valter wondered.

'Let's go,' Annika said.

*

I can't breathe on my own: I can't get enough oxygen without help. Space ended when my mum died – her last breath drained the world of life-giving air. I was left alone in the void, falling and falling with no hope of avoiding the wild beast at the bottom. I have to keep hold of myself all the time to stop myself slipping. The scream inside me is silent and boundless. I'll do anything – *absolutely anything* – to escape. Freedom is nothing: give me boundaries, any boundaries – I'll pay. *I'm happy to pay.*

*

Annika turned off towards Solsidan. The coarse winter grit crunched under the tyres. Presumably whatever private company had won the contract for road maintenance hadn't had time to get out there and take care of it.

Valter was gazing intently through the window. 'I thought there'd be loads of massive luxurious houses out here,' he said, sounding rather disappointed.

The houses lining the road were mostly villas built in the seventies, with outsize roofs that were the result of a strange glitch in government construction grants, meaning that roofs had expanded briefly to absurd proportions when Annika was a child.

'Don't worry, Valter,' she said. 'They're coming up soon.'

A minute or so later they reached the really fancy ones, with bay windows, leaded glass, hedges, little brick walls, gravel paths and raked lawns. The Church of the Epiphany and the school, the Sea Scouts' hut and the beach at Erstaviken.

'The one with the most money when he dies is the winner,' Valter said.

'Says the young heir to the Wennergren fortune,' Annika said.

Forest took over. Silvervägen clung to the Saltsjöbanan railway line like a pair of figure-skaters. The villas weren't as impressive there, mostly small wooden houses from the thirties and others built of large pale bricks. They passed the station, a colourful building that reminded Annika of the Tyrol, with a bistro and a fast-food kiosk. A little blue train was waiting at the platform.

Silvervägen 48 was a recently built, white-stuccoed villa, a modern design. Annika got out of the car and turned her face into the wind. She squinted and could just make out the Lerbergs' small house by the turning circle at the end of the road.

'Can you get the tripod from the back seat?' she asked Valter, and headed towards the Lindenstolphes' home.

Ignoring the doorbell, she knocked cautiously on the outer door – the children were supposed to be having a nap. Therese opened the door a couple of seconds later: she must have been waiting just inside.

'Welcome,' she said in a low voice, and shook Annika's hand, a firm, dry touch. 'Kids are funny, aren't they? They can tell when something's going on. It was almost impossible to get Sebastian off to sleep.'

Annika stepped inside and found that the house didn't have a hallway. The entire ground floor consisted of a single space: the ultimate in open-plan living. There was nowhere to hang coats. She took off her muddy shoes, put them by

111

the wall and walked across the polished stone floor. The cold went straight through her damp cotton socks, sending little shockwaves up her calves. She looked around, trying not to seem too obviously inquisitive. A staircase over by the kitchen area led up to the floor above and she could hear the Disney Channel coming from that direction. Next to the staircase there was an oak dining table, minimalist, oiled wood, the middle-class ideal. Oddly shaped bookcases without any books on them were arranged along the walls – Annika recognized them from some design magazine she'd flicked through.

'I called a couple of friends,' Therese said. 'People who know the Lerbergs a bit better . . .' She gestured towards a group of sofas at the other end of the room. Two women stood up and came towards them. 'Sabine and Lovisa . . .'

Annika felt a pang of annoyance. Group interviews were always harder than individual conversations. The participants always took more notice of each other than the questions. She gave them a strained smile.

Sabine and Lovisa shook hands. They had both had a French manicure. All three women were wearing indoor shoes; she and Valter were the only ones in their socks.

'The whole thing feels unreal,' Sabine said. 'It seems impossible that something like this could happen here, in Solsidan . . .'

The friends were confusingly similar, all conforming to the restricted uniform of a well-to-do thirty-something woman: glossy bleached hair, gym-toned body, dark clothes of good quality.

'Let's go and sit on the sofas,' Therese said. 'Would you like coffee?'

'I'm fine, thanks,' Valter said.

'That would be great,' Annika said. 'And Valter would like some as well.'

Therese smiled and went off towards the kitchen area at the other end of the room.

Two gently curved sofas were positioned on either side of an oiled oak coffee-table, with two more formal armchairs at each end.

'Is it okay if we film this?' Annika asked. 'It's for the website.'

Sabine straightened and adjusted her hair, but Lovisa seemed uncertain. 'I don't really know,' she said, glancing at Therese, who was busy with the coffee-machine.

'We can't promise that we'll definitely put anything up. That depends on how the rest of the news looks,' Annika told her, and Lovisa said no more.

'It's horrible when it comes this close to you,' Sabine said, checking that her graphite-grey cashmere cardigan was buttoned properly. 'I mean, we're neighbours – we were in the same mums' group when the children were younger, and that creates a bond. You've got something in common, which sort of ties you together.'

Annika passed the camera to Valter. 'Do you want to do the filming?'

Valter looked horrified. 'But I've never . . .'

'Just hold it still and the autofocus will keep the picture sharp. Don't move it around too much, and never use the zoom – that makes it impossible to edit smoothly.'

Together they set up the tripod and fixed the camera to it. As they finished Therese appeared with a tray of coffee. 'The buns are from this morning, but I think they're still edible.'

Their hostess set out cups and plates for the buns. The

113

coffee was strong, thick as tar and extremely good – real espresso.

'I can understand your reaction,' Annika said, putting down her empty cup and looking at Sabine. 'Your neighbours have been the victims of an extremely unpleasant crime, and there doesn't seem to be any obvious explanation. How is that affecting the way you and your family think, seeing as you live so close?'

Annika hoped she'd say what she had said before the camera was switched on, and Sabine evidently understood what was expected of her. She fluttered her eyelashes and couldn't help glancing at the lens. 'It all feels unreal,' she repeated. 'It seems impossible that something like this could happen here, in Solsidan . . . It's horrible when it comes so close to you. We were in the same mums' group when the children were younger, and that creates a bond – you've got something in common, which sort of ties you together.'

Annika couldn't help smiling. She must have practised her lines in front of the mirror.

'We had our boys at the same time, my Leopold and her Isak, just a few weeks apart . . .' Sabine embarked upon a detailed account of her first delivery. Annika waited for her to finish.

'Could you describe the Lerberg family, how well you know them?'

Sabine ran a hand over her hair, adjusting a few stray strands. 'They're very . . . particular. Like when they have people round, for instance. Everything's so well organized. Everything matches, from the invitations to the table decorations and place-cards. Nora always has a theme, maybe a colour or a season, a song or a particular style of dress.'

'Do they often have people round?'

'Well, maybe not that often . . . They tend to keep to

114

themselves. Nora's so incredibly busy with her home. She bakes, makes jam and knits – she always has so much to do.'

'Where could she be? Do you think she left of her own accord?'

The atmosphere in the room changed. Sabine's eyes widened: the thought that something serious might have happened to Nora evidently hadn't struck her before.

'I . . . It's terrible.' She said no more.

Annika looked at Therese. 'What do you think?'

Therese sat completely still. 'I don't know,' she said. 'I've been thinking about Nora since I heard about it yesterday morning. She's . . . a very serious person. Shy, perhaps. We usually see each other at the children's morning playgroup at the church. None of our children goes to nursery . . .'

Annika was taking notes. 'What do you usually talk about?'

Therese swallowed. 'I don't think Nora usually talks much with any of the other mums. She's mostly preoccupied with her children and her audio books.'

'Audio books?' Annika said.

Therese put down her cup. 'It's actually a bit odd,' she said. 'Nora's always listening to audio books. Streamed through her mobile. I once asked her if she'd like to join our book group, but she said she didn't have time to read . . .'

Annika stopped writing.

Sabine had found her tongue again. 'I know!' she said. 'Nora says such strange things. I asked if she'd like to join our cookery club on Wednesday evenings, but she said she went to yoga at the Studio then . . . but she doesn't. My friend Bettan is the yoga leader for that class.'

Silence descended around the table again. Annika could hear the whirr of the little fan in the video-camera. This

115

wasn't going very well. She turned to Lovisa. 'How do you know the Lerberg family?'

The young woman tucked her hair behind one ear in an automatic gesture. 'I don't know Ingemar, but Nora was in the same class at school as my younger sister, out in Gustavsberg. She used to come round to ours sometimes.'

Her hair fell forward again, and she tucked it back. 'I used to feel sorry for her,' she said quietly.

'Why?' Annika asked, writing again.

Lovisa hesitated for a moment. 'She had a stammer.'

'Did she?' Sabine was surprised.

Lovisa picked up a bun and took a little bite. 'She learned to hide it. The stammer, I mean. You can't hear it now.'

Sabine looked genuinely concerned. 'But why haven't you mentioned it before?'

'We moved to Saltsjöbaden and I didn't see her again until we ended up in the same mothers' group.' Lovisa leaned back in the sofa and crossed her arms and legs, evidently done with being interviewed and talking.

Annika studied the young woman thoughtfully. She was just as blonde and thin as the others, with a big diamond on her left ring finger and a Rolex on her wrist, but she was pale, and her eyes were evasive. 'Do you still see each other?'

'No, not much.'

'Where do you think she might be?'

She twisted a lock of hair between her fingers, an obvious sign of stress. 'No idea. What do we ever really know about anyone?'

Sabine shifted uncomfortably, possibly unsettled by the idea that she had no real control over her neighbours.

Annika decided to try another angle. 'Do any of you know how she met her husband, Ingemar?'

116

'There's a big age gap, obviously,' Sabine said. 'He's – what? – twenty years older?'

'Eighteen,' Therese said, biting into a bun.

'Nora was young when they got married, wasn't she?' Annika said. 'Just a teenager?'

No one said anything.

It was a rhetorical question: Annika already knew the answer. Nora and Ingemar had got married the year Nora turned nineteen, on 25 May, just in time for Ingemar's campaign for election to Parliament.

'So the Lerbergs' children don't go to nursery?' she tried instead. 'Does Nora have a job?'

'No,' Sabine said. 'Her husband's a politician, after all, a Christian Democrat. He thinks women should be chained to the stove, have children and devote themselves to keeping their husbands happy and healthy.'

Therese stiffened. 'It can actually be a conscious choice to stay at home with your children,' she said.

Sabine stretched her back. 'Of course,' she said. 'I'm all in favour of choice in family life. I just think it's odd that a modern individual would choose to ignore all aspects of personal development.'

Therese's cheeks had turned bright red. 'We don't all have two Filipinas in the basement to do the washing and cleaning,' she said.

Now it was Sabine's turn to look upset. 'Is there something you'd like to say about the way I live my life?'

Annika felt it was definitely time to round things off. 'Valter,' she said, 'can you take some close-ups of everyone so I've got something to use in the editing?'

The women remained on the sofa for a few more minutes while Valter filmed them.

Then Annika stood up. 'I won't take up any more of

117

your time,' she said. 'Thanks very much for letting us intrude.'

Valter switched off the camera.

Sabine got to her feet. 'It's a shame you didn't get a chance to meet our kids,' she said. 'But perhaps there'll be a chance for that another time.'

Annika quickly packed away her pen and notebook, then the video-camera and tripod, and shook their hands. They left the women standing by the door. Annika could feel their eyes on her back as they walked towards the car.

'Christ,' Valter said, as they set off along Silvervägen. 'What are we going to do with that?'

'There are some decent quotes we can edit together.'

'You mean the clichés? "How could something like this happen?"'

She gave him a wan smile. 'You're a quick learner.' She fished her notebook out of her bag and handed it to him. 'Moberg & Moberg's office is on the way back. Can you look up the address?'

Valter set about the task with great energy, but not even his youthful enthusiasm had any effect on the car's complicated satnav system. Eventually Annika parked at a bus-stop and Googled the address on her mobile.

She called the office, found out that it was open until five o'clock, then drove off towards the motorway.

'Why are we going there?' Valter wondered. 'To look at Ingemar Lerberg's old accounts?'

'Not just that,' Annika said. 'I want to know if Ingemar really was fiddling his tax.'

It had stopped raining, but the brown sludge from the tyres of the cars in front kept splattering the windscreen. Annika switched on the wipers. The cleansing fluid had run out, and the brown sludge smeared messily across the windscreen. She slowed down.

'You shouldn't underestimate the value of old accounts. Lerberg ran that last bankrupt company while he was an MP for almost a year. If he was doing business with Saudi oil sheiks at the same time as pushing for a trade embargo against Saudi Arabia, that's kind of exciting, isn't it?'

Valter Wennergren stared out through the windscreen. 'We'd still have to give him the chance to comment before we published, though, surely.'

'Of course,' Annika said.

'If he survives,' Valter said.

The roadside was now lined with scrub, scrawny birches and hazels that should have been in leaf for several weeks now. Big out-of-town stores, car-repair workshops, plant nurseries, power lines. They passed Fisksätra, endless rows of concrete apartment blocks, a viaduct bearing a poster for an art exhibition in a gallery in Saltsjöbaden. Valter sat and stared out of the passenger window for a long while, then turned to Annika.

'Shouldn't the relatives be informed before we publish the name of a victim of crime?' he asked. 'His wife hasn't been told, has she, seeing as no one knows where she is?'

Annika glanced in the rear-view mirror, then pulled into the right-hand lane. 'Every situation is different,' she said. 'There's no fixed template, sadly. It would be much easier if there was.'

'But this case isn't that complicated, is it?' Valter said. 'The wife doesn't know anything, but we're still publishing the victim's name and picture. Isn't that in breach of press ethics?'

She was overtaken by a lorry that threw a cascade of

water across the windscreen, washing off the worst of the sludge.

'The local press in Nacka published Lerberg's name and picture on their websites the moment the ambulance drove off,' Annika said. 'His neighbours and employees began to make statements. Practically everyone close to him already knew what had happened by the time we went public. It would have looked very odd if we had concealed his name under those circumstances, as if there were something dodgy about the whole situation.'

Annika indicated right and turned off onto the main motorway towards Stockholm.

'But there is something dodgy about it,' Valter said. 'I mean, the bloke was almost killed.'

The motorway, blasted through rock, ran past cliff-faces and noise-dampening barriers. Annika thought back to the women in Solsidan, to the big house with its ice-cold stone floor, all the effort that went into hair-colouring, bun-baking and finding the right curtains to match the sofas. Some time ago she had read an article about scientific research that showed it was possible to shop your way to a better quality of life, but only in three specific areas: food; travel and new experiences; charity and gifts. Eating, doing new things, and giving things away. So how come everyone put so much effort into the rest of it? Were the researchers wrong? How else could sofas and fingernails be so important?

'Do you think the evening papers are obsolete?' Valter asked out of the blue.

Annika glanced at him. 'Do you mean the print media in general or . . .?'

'Investigative journalism used to balance out the gossip, but that's pretty much been taken over now by documentaries and books.'

'But we're the ones who draw attention to the documentaries and books. Their message only gets across because of the established media.'

'Impoverished freelancers and underpaid film-makers spend years working on a story, then the evening papers write one article and appropriate the glory for themselves. Talk about getting a free ride!'

Annika couldn't help smiling. 'Are you sure you've chosen the right place to do your work placement?'

The young man glared through the windscreen. Annika slowed down and turned off towards Hammarbyhamnen, leaning forward to peer through the filthy windscreen. 'So, are you ready for this?'

The office was in Södra Hammarbyhamnen, not the fashionable new residential area, but next to the old light-bulb factory in the industrial district. The accountancy firm of Moberg & Moberg was located on the ground floor of a three-storey apartment block from the seventies.

The door was opened by a woman with lipstick on her teeth. 'I'm afraid Robert isn't here,' she said, and was about to close the door again, but Annika walked into the office, forcing her to stand aside.

'We'd be just as happy to see Henrik,' she said.

The office was based in an ordinary three-room apartment. It was very obvious that Moberg & Moberg didn't spend their profits on interior design. The bookcases and desks looked as if they had come from Ikea's starter range at the time the place was built.

'Have you booked an appointment?'

Annika smiled. 'I called from the car, Annika Bengtzon. We're from the *Evening Post* newspaper, and we've got a few questions for either Robert or Henrik Moberg.'

The assistant glanced uncertainly behind her. 'I don't know if he's got time to—'

At that moment Henrik stepped out from what would once have been a bedroom. He was tall and heavy, dressed in a jacket and shirt that was open at the collar. He didn't seem particularly pleased to see them. 'What can I do for you?' he said curtly, as he shook their hands.

'We've got a few questions about one of your clients, Ingemar Lerberg, and his businesses,' Annika said.

'And we're governed by the law of confidentiality, as I'm sure you're aware,' the accountant said.

He was clearly finding the situation extremely uncomfortable, Annika thought. His face was dark and he had a fixed set to his mouth.

'First and foremost, I'd like to know what happened with the tax-office investigation into Ingemar Lerberg's business seven and a half years ago,' she said.

The man's eyes widened slightly – that clearly wasn't the question he had been expecting. 'Why?' he asked.

'I couldn't find any details in the media archives,' she said breezily.

'That's not particularly strange,' Henrik Moberg said. 'Nothing was ever written about it. I told Ingemar he ought to release a press statement after the investigation was over, but he didn't want to. He said, "They'll still twist it to make me look like the tax offender of the century."'

'So they found him innocent?'

'He was late with his VAT return on two occasions, and was given a fine totalling one thousand kronor.'

A thousand kronor, less than two parking tickets outside her front door on Södermalm would cost her. But that wouldn't have made any difference. Ingemar had been right: the media would indeed have turned it into a crime comparable to high treason. Annika nodded and smiled. 'We'd also like to look at the accounts of his older companies, the ones that went bankrupt,' she said.

Henrik's face closed. 'What for?'

Annika continued to smile. 'I don't have to tell you that. Those documents are public files.'

The assistant shuffled anxiously in the background.

'We don't have the resources to look through the archive right now,' Henrik said. 'But if you could specify exactly what you're after, we'll see if we get a chance next week.'

Annika's smile was still firmly in place. 'No need. We can go through the archive ourselves. Where is it?'

The accountant exchanged a quick glance with his assistant. 'In the basement. But . . .'

'Excellent,' Annika said. She walked out into the stairwell and began to go down the stairs.

Henrik and his assistant hurried after her.

'The accounts from Ingemar's first two companies have been destroyed,' Henrik said, 'so we can't help you with those.'

Annika tilted her head to one side. 'We'll take the other two then, please.'

Henrik nodded to his assistant, who disappeared into a dimly lit corridor. 'The media has become an arena for gladiatorial combat,' he said. 'You send people out into the spotlight, cheer and applaud them, then shoot them down and watch them bleed to death.'

Annika looked at him calmly. 'The gladiators were the big celebrities of the Roman empire. It wasn't just slaves and Christians who were forced to fight in the ring. Upperclass boys would apply to get in too. Things went so far that they had to impose a lower age-limit for gladiators . . .'

Henrik turned on his heel and disappeared back upstairs.

Valter was looking round, wide-eyed, his ethical doubts seeming to have dispersed in the dry basement air. 'What a strange place to keep an archive of bankruptcies,' he whispered.

Annika peered into the darkness of the corridor. It reminded her of the basement in the block of flats on Tattarbacken in Hälleforsnäs where she had grown up, a three-storey brick block like this one, with a communal laundry and drying rooms, and storage areas divided by chicken wire. Proximity to Stockholm meant that properties like this one had aged considerably more gracefully than their cousins in the backwaters of Södermanland. The stairwell had been painted recently, and the stone floor was polished to a shine. At the end of the corridor there was a small desk, with a chair and a reading lamp.

The assistant wheeled out a trolley with the files balanced on top. There weren't many: four covering one bankruptcy, and three the other. 'Just leave them here when you're finished,' she said. She still had lipstick on her front teeth.

'Which ones relate to Lerberg Consulting?'

She pointed to the files on the left of the trolley. Then she trotted back upstairs, her heels clicking on the stone steps. Valter looked at the files with a degree of horror.

'Have a seat,' Annika said, pointing to the chair by the little desk. Then she took off her jacket, folded it and laid it on the stairs. She grabbed three of the files and sat down.

'Why do you want to look at those in particular?' Valter asked.

'This is the company that was investigated by the tax office,' she said, opening the first page.

Valter sat down warily on the old office chair. 'Where shall I start?'

'At the beginning, perhaps?'

Valter read the labels on the back of the files and opened one. He checked each page before moving on. 'Lerberg Investment,' he said. 'Offices on Strandvägen in Saltsjöbaden. Three employees, Ingemar Lerberg and two secretaries.' He let out a whistle. 'Ingemar was paying himself a quarter of a million kronor a month, while the secretaries got twenty thousand.'

'A generous employer,' Annika said. 'At least towards himself.'

She flipped through receipts and invoices, sorted by date. Each receipt was stapled to a sheet of A4 and categorized according to strict criteria. They included office supplies, office furnishings, entertaining, IT equipment, taxis, parking costs, travel, expenses, wages, pension . . .

She paused over a large bill from the Operakällaren restaurant in Stockholm: 7,900 kronor. Carefully she lifted the receipt, and the names of those in attendance were written on the back. None meant anything to her.

Valter read out: 'Conference trip to Monaco, five nights at the Hôtel de Paris.' He looked up at Annika. 'Isn't that . . . ?'

'The casino in Monte Carlo? Yep. Carry on.'

He turned a page. 'Yacht hire. Lease of helicopter for transport between Monaco and the airport in Nice.'

Annika moved on to the next file. The documents rustled. She came to another bill for entertaining at Operakällaren, no names she recognized. Christmas lunch at the Grand Hotel. This time there were several old acquaintances: Kristine Lerberg, Nora Andersson and Helmer Andersson, among others. Ingemar's elder sister, his future wife and possibly her father. A little family dinner at the company's expense.

'Stage costumes, twelve thousand five hundred and

ninety kronor,' Valter said, and looked up at Annika. 'Can you really claim for that as a consultant?'

'Have you come across any income?' Annika asked.

Valter leafed back and forth. 'There are records of payments into the company account,' he said. 'Capital injections from investors.'

Annika had similar bank records of in-payments from customers. The company names meant nothing to her: Lindberg Investment, Sollentuna Entrepreneurs, Viceroy Investment Inc. She opened the last file. Now she was approaching the dates mentioned in the articles in the media. The first receipt was another huge bill, this time from a restaurant, Edsbacka krog, out in Sollentuna, dating from October seven and a half years ago. At the time Edsbacka krog was the only restaurant in Sweden with two Michelin stars. Two people had eaten the tasting menu, and had drunk some astonishingly expensive wines. She turned the thin sheet of paper over. The guests had been Ingemar Lerberg and Anders Schyman.

Her hand froze in mid-air.

Anders Schyman?

'Do you think,' Valter said, 'that it might have been one of the investors who did it? Someone who had lost all his money?'

Annika stared at the names on the back of the restaurant bill, then turned back and checked the date: 28 October. Barely two weeks before the torrent of articles had begun to appear. She closed the file. 'Seems a bit of a long shot,' Annika said. 'After all, his company has been doing well recently.'

'So what does this mean? Can we write about it? The bankruptcies? Or the restaurant bills?'

Annika stared at the wall. 'Not right now, at any rate,'

she said. 'We can't very well portray him as dodgy while he's lying at death's door.'

'But if he gets better? We can write about it then? That would be okay?'

All of a sudden Annika felt very clearly that she'd had enough press ethics for one day. She stood up, shook her jacket and put it on. 'Maybe,' she said. 'Let's go.'

Anders Schyman bent down and pulled open the bottom drawer of the filing cabinet that stood against the far wall. Hanging folders inside, plenty of papers. Documents. Notes, in alphabetical order, from government crises and defence cutbacks to primary-school policy.

He groaned.

It must be there somewhere. He was absolutely certain that he'd kept it. Surely he would have done.

He shut the drawer with his foot and sat down at his desk. The first place he had looked was the little filing cabinet on wheels, but without any great expectation of finding the old video-cassette there. He had a reasonable idea of what was in his desk drawers. But the old dresser by the glass wall, the bookshelves and the archive cupboard had been a trip down Memory Lane. God, he'd covered so many storms in teacups, politics, power games and corruption at every level, but he hadn't managed to find the old VHS tape containing a recording of his prize-winning documentary. It wasn't at home, he was sure of that, because his wife had cleared out everything like it several years ago, and had asked him if there was anything he wanted to keep. He'd told her he'd look through it all a bit later but had never got round to it, and in the end she'd just got rid of it all. He hadn't been bothered at the time. Anything that was at all relevant to work was kept in his office at the paper anyway. Or so he'd thought.

Where the hell had the documentary got to?

He'd looked among the classics on Swedish Television's open online archive, but it evidently wasn't regarded as such. Obviously his former employers would have a copy in their archive but they would have finished for the day, and if he wanted to buy a copy it would probably take several weeks to get hold of it and cost a fortune. Above all, though, he didn't want to alert anyone at the national broadcaster that something was going on and that the subject was suddenly relevant again.

Let sleeping dogs lie, he thought, although the real issue at the moment was just how soundly the dog was actually sleeping. The latest post on the Light of Truth had already attracted 590 comments. Everyone hated him, with just ten exceptions. He had read each and every one.

He had come to realize that the level of detailed knowledge about Viola Söderland's life was practically limitless. The 580 expert commentators all knew with absolute certainty that he had lied through his teeth in his documentary and that the old billionairess was dead and buried, and had been for twenty years. The question was whether she had been dead during those years when she had been running her company into the ground. Golden Spire: the property company that had been in the vanguard for the new deregulated capitalism of the late 1980s, when the banks' lending cap was abolished and the grab-what-you-can attitude was celebrating its greatest triumphs. Viola Söderland borrowed money and bought properties, which she then mortgaged, and with that money she bought more properties, which she mortgaged, eagerly cheered on by, among others, her colleagues, Linette Pettersson and Sven-Olof Witterfeldt. It had carried on like that until the bubble had burst and Golden Spire collapsed like a pack of cards.

He still had the notebook, though, where he had scribbled down information about her disappearance. Viola Söderland had vanished from her villa in Djursholm on the night between 22 and 23 September almost twenty years ago. Her bag, passport and wallet were still in the house; the front door was unlocked. There was a broken vase on the hall floor, but apart from that, there was no sign of disorder in the house.

Where on earth could he have put the video tape?

He remembered recording the programme. The editorial team had gathered at work to watch it, but he had chosen to watch it at home with his wife, and had even taped the announcer's remarks before and after the programme as well. It had been broadcast on 13 April. The nominations for the Best Journalism Award were made public on 8 November that year. He hadn't been surprised when he won. Everyone who had seen the programme had been convinced that Viola Söderland was alive. He'd had no interview with her so he couldn't show footage of her in front of a newspaper with the day's date on it, but he had provided practically everything else. How she had planned her flight in advance, how she had fled one night through a pitch-black Sweden and left the country over the border to Finland at Haparanda.

He even knew where she had stopped to refill her car: a Mobil petrol station in Håkansö, forty kilometres south of Luleå on the E4. He might not have had current footage of her, but the logical conclusion was that Viola Söderland had taken refuge in the recently resuscitated state of Russia. She would hardly have stayed in Finland after

driving through Customs in Torneå, on the Finnish side of
the border, and could have reached Russia before anyone
had even noticed she was missing back home in Sweden.
It was harder to predict where she might have settled. By
the Black Sea, perhaps, or in one of the resorts along the
shore of the Caspian, if she was after sun. In Moscow or St
Petersburg if she wanted culture and metropolitan life. He
had travelled to all four places and had filmed interior and
exterior shots so that viewers would have an idea of the
sort of life Viola might be living now. By that point viewers
would be so convinced of the elements of Viola's dramatic
flight that they would confidently expect to see her in the
next shot.

It was a very good documentary. He had always been
pleased with it, the crowning glory of his career.

Now it existed as nothing more than a lie on the internet.

*

I've never seen him cry before.

Silence falls. We cease to exist.

I'm here, I say, everything can be as it was, but he doesn't
reply. I'm not getting through: his eyes shy away, his back is
angular and pale.

The world becomes completely grey, dense as concrete.
You can't breathe concrete.

And I make up my mind.

*

Kristine Lerberg lived in a brown brick villa surrounded
by woodland, not far from the water. Not that she actually
had a sea view. Nina parked her car in the drive. The house

lay dark and silent. The curtains were closed, but Miss Lerberg had said she'd be at home.

Nina got out of the car and locked it with the remote. The gravel path had been raked, and last year's leaves were gone from the lawn. A few cowslips were poking up by the walls of the house. A row of half-dead plants lined the path – Nina thought she recognized the leaves as tulips. The flowers were gone, the stalks nipped off halfway down. Deer, probably.

The porch was made of well-oiled pinewood. The bell set off a three-tone ringing that echoed inside the house. The door opened a crack as someone inside shouted: 'Isak, no, don't open it!'

A little boy was standing in the doorway, looking up at her with big eyes, a bubble of snot hanging from one nostril.

'Hello,' Nina said. 'My name's Nina. Is your auntie at home?'

The door flew open. Kristine Lerberg grabbed the child's arm, wrenching his shoulder, and he stumbled backwards, his face contorting into a sob. She held him behind her and gave Nina a hostile glare. 'Are you from the press as well? No comment!'

'Nina Hoffman, National Crime Unit,' Nina said, as calmly as she could, holding up her ID.

Kristine Lerberg hesitated for a few seconds, then took a step back. 'I'm so sorry,' she said. 'Come in.'

They shook hands. The child howled. Nina shut the door behind her. The hallway was very dark. Two more children were visible further along the gloomy corridor, a younger boy and a toddler. The toddler started to cry in sympathy with her elder brother. Nina took her shoes off and hung her jacket on a hook under the hat-rack.

'There, there,' Kristine Lerberg said, picking up the toddler. 'Boys, go and play in the nursery. There, now.'

The older boy sniffed a few times and wiped his tears.

'Can we watch *Bamse*?' he asked.

'All right,' the woman said. 'Do you know how to turn it on?'

The two boys disappeared into one of the rooms further along the corridor. The woman put a dummy into the toddler's mouth and led the way into a dark, stuffy room.

'I wasn't supposed to be looking after them for so long,' she said, sinking into a plush floral-patterned sofa. 'Ingemar brought them over on Thursday evening and asked me to have them for the weekend. Do you have any idea how much longer they're going to have to stay?'

She rocked the toddler frenetically on one knee. The little girl sucked at her dummy.

'I can't answer that,' Nina said, pressing to start the digital recorder on her phone. This wasn't a regular police interview, so there was no need to state the time, date and location.

'Have you got hold of Nora?' the woman asked.

'Not yet.'

'Can you believe it – abandoning your children like that? Have social services been informed? Don't they have people on call any more? I've got a job to do.'

The theme-tune to *Bamse*, the little cartoon bear, echoed faintly from deeper inside the house. Nina studied the woman. She was Ingemar's elder sister, fifty-two, never married. She wore her hair in a neat bob, greying naturally. She worked part-time as the financial manager of a construction company in Gustavsberg.

'What did Ingemar say when he dropped the children off?' Nina asked.

'I've already spoken to one of your officers,' the woman said. 'Yesterday afternoon. Inspector Danielsson from the Nacka Police.'

Nina hadn't known that: there was no record of it in the notes. Bloody amateurs. 'I'm sorry that we have to keep disturbing you like this,' she said. 'This probably won't be the last time that the police want to talk to you. Large investigations get a lot of resources, but I'm afraid they also make a lot of demands of witnesses and relatives.'

Kristine Lerberg nodded, apparently satisfied with this response. 'Ingemar asked if I could look after them,' she said. 'I wasn't sure, I thought it was all a bit last-minute. But that's what happens when you live alone. No one thinks your time matters . . .'

'How did he seem?'

The toddler dropped the dummy and started to cry again. Kristine got up impatiently, picked up the dummy, then, holding the child, carried her out of the room. Nina heard her heels click towards the sound of *Bamse*. The crying stopped.

'I'm sorry,' she said, as she returned to the sofa. She sat down again and ran her hands over her knees to get the creases out of her skirt.

'Was he happy? Tired? Upset?'

The woman's eyes slid across the bookcase, as though she were looking for a memory among the ornaments. 'He was rather short with me,' she said. 'When I tried to explain that I was thinking of going to a lecture at the Rotary Club on Saturday afternoon, about entrepreneurial spirit in Africa, he was annoyed. Asked when I'd suddenly become so interested in starting businesses abroad. I tried to tell him it wasn't like that, and that if you're a member, then—'

Nina put her hand on Kristine's. 'I understand it must be hard to talk about it,' she said.

Kristine's eyes filled with tears. 'Is he going to be all right?' she whispered, glancing hastily towards the corridor. 'What am I going to do with the children if he doesn't make it? And why hasn't Nora come home? Where can she be?'

Nina looked hard at her. 'When did Nora leave?' she asked in a low voice.

The woman started to pick at the hem of her skirt. 'Leave?'

'Ingemar told you Nora had gone away when he left the children, didn't he, and that's why you agreed to look after them, in spite of the Rotary Club? When did she disappear?'

Kristine Lerberg cleared her throat. 'On Wednesday evening,' she said, once again looking towards the sound of *Bamse*. 'They'd had a row. The children don't know anything. When do you think I ought to tell them?'

'What was the row about?'

Kristine Lerberg stood up. 'Goodness, look at me, sitting here and forgetting my manners! Can I get you a cup of coffee?'

'Sit down,' Nina said.

She sat. Nina studied her hair, her slender hands, with their neatly manicured nails, her slim figure.

'It was Ascension Day on Thursday, of course,' Kristine Lerberg said blankly. 'I had the day off. I'd been to church and then I went to the Liljevalch Gallery, and I'd only just got home and poured myself a glass of Chablis when Ingemar arrived – it must have been around half past four.' She glanced at Nina as if that were an unsuitable time for a glass of wine. Nina didn't say anything. 'His eyes were red, as if he'd been crying. Well, that or drinking. The children were playing up. They do that when Nora isn't around. She

134

spoils them. "Nora's left me," he said. I didn't believe him. Nora isn't the sort who leaves anyone – she hasn't got it in her.'

She pulled a paper handkerchief from her skirt pocket and blew her nose. 'He said they'd had a row. On Wednesday. Nora had picked up her coat and walked out. She didn't take her handbag, or her umbrella. She just walked out and closed the door. Do you remember how hard it was raining on Wednesday? She didn't come home all night. Ingemar was beside himself with worry, said something must have happened to her. And then this terrible assault! When can I visit him? And what am I going to tell the children?'

She put her hands over her face and wept.

Nina let her cry, and waited until the sobs had died down. 'How was Nora?' she asked. 'Was she depressed?'

Kristine's eyes roamed round the room. 'I don't really know her that well. She always has so much to do with the children, and that house, and Ingemar's always so busy . . . There's that business with her thyroid, but depression? No, I don't think so. What did she have to be depressed about?' She ran a hand through her hair and pursed her lips.

Nina realized that she was jealous of Nora. 'Where do you think she might be? A holiday home? Do she and Ingemar have some place they usually go to?'

Kristine shook her head.

'What sort of coat was it?'

Kristine Lerberg wiped her face with the handkerchief. Her eye makeup had run. 'What sort of coat?'

'You said that Nora took her coat and walked out. When she left home. What sort of coat was it?'

Kristine screwed up her eyes. 'I – I don't know. Probably the one she always wears. An oilskin. Water resistant, I suppose. Dark grey-brown, maybe.'

'Would you happen to have a picture of her wearing it?'

Kristine glanced round the room, as if a photograph might be lying there somewhere. 'No one has albums any more. On the computer, perhaps.'

'Could you take a look and see if you've got a picture of Nora wearing that coat, and send it to me?'

She handed over one of the business cards Lamia had printed for her, and Kristine took it without looking at it.

'Do you know what the row was about? Did he mention that?'

Kristine blew her nose again and shook her head. 'No. And I didn't ask.'

Nina racked her brain for questions. 'Did Ingemar and Nora have any help in the house? Anyone to help with the washing and cleaning, maybe watch the children sometimes?'

Kristine straightened her back and massaged her neck. 'Definitely not. Nora took great pride in looking after her home herself. I helped out and watched the children whenever she had to go in for check-ups on her thyroid.'

'Auntie Tine, why are you sad?'

The eldest boy, Isak, was standing in the doorway, arms hanging by his sides, eyes full of anxiety.

'I think you should tell the children,' Nina said. 'Who else is going to?' She picked up her phone and switched off the recorder, then got to her feet.

Isak watched her as she put her shoes and coat on and walked out.

The newsroom was almost deserted, standing empty and grey in the dull afternoon light. A few individuals sat around the open-plan office, enclosed in some sort of digital reality. The photographers had been rationalized away long ago and, these days, Picture-Pelle was alone, his face computer-blue over at the picture desk as he bought in amusing pictures from international agencies – *A kangaroo hopping about on a landing strip*, and other similarly important subjects. The website staff sat behind their screens updating the site, but almost all the reporters were out on jobs. The new demands for moving pictures meant that editors could no longer make a quick phone-call to get a quote: they had to send someone out in the rain to meet people who would speak in front of a camera.

Annika shook out her raincoat, then hung it on the back of her chair.

'Shouldn't we write something about this weird weather?' Valter Wennergren said, wiping the rain from his face. 'I mean, this isn't normal.'

'We've published so much about the weather this spring that it no longer sells,' Annika said.

She glanced at Anders Schyman's glass cubicle. Had he really enjoyed a slap-up meal at Ingemar Lerberg's expense ten days before the paper had made the politician out to be a tax dodger on its front cover? Or had Lerberg just written a name on the receipt, any name, even though he was actually dining with someone else? But why choose Schyman's? Okay, so they knew each other. But other than that?

And what was he up to now? Annika could see his big backside sticking up above the units by the glass wall while his desk was piled high with boxes and heaps of papers.

'What do we do now?' Valter asked.

Annika took the video-camera out of her bag and sat down. 'Put together a minute or so about Nora's friends,' she said. 'You need to edit out all my leading questions. And mark one bit so that Picture-Pelle can print a still.'

Valter was clearly stunned. 'But I've never edited a news item before.'

'You've done four terms at the College of Journalism?' she said.

'Five,' Valter said, sitting down. 'Mind you, it's called the Journalism, Media and Communication Programme these days.'

'There's no way you can fail,' Annika said. 'The editing program is designed for digital morons. Load it up, edit, compose. Use my pictures of the crime scene if you need to do a voiceover – they're on the server. One minute thirty, maximum, it's not worth more than that.'

Now the editor-in-chief was sitting down and talking on the phone.

She reached for her own phone and called Södermalm Hospital, the National Crime Unit and the Nacka Police. There was nothing new to add about the Lerbergs. She wrote a short piece with the suggested heading 'The Shadow Over Solsidan', where she described Nora and Ingemar's life with the children and neighbours (parties, audiobooks, church playgroup), how upset their friends were, and how the brutal crime had affected the entire community.

She stood up and pulled on her coat, put her shoes back on, zipped up her bag and slung it over her shoulder. 'I'm going home to make a chicken casserole,' she said. 'See you tomorrow.'

She headed for the exit without looking back.

The children had installed themselves in different parts of the apartment when she got home. Ellen came rushing out from her room, and Kalle from the television room, where he was evidently in the middle of a car race with Jacob. 'I keep losing,' he said, pressing his face to her stomach.

She ruffled his hair. That was the way it was: Kalle always lost to Jacob, and not only in video games.

'Crash into him from behind,' Annika said. 'At least that would annoy him.'

Kalle looked up at her with big eyes. 'But you're not allowed to do that,' he said.

'Nonsense,' Annika said, giving Ellen a hug. 'It's only a game.'

'But what if he doesn't want to play with me again?'

Annika smiled at him. 'Okay. Overtake him instead. Then you'll win.'

He trudged back to the television and Annika turned her attention to her daughter. 'I've done a drawing,' Ellen said. 'Do you want to see it?'

'Definitely,' Annika said. 'Then would you like to help me make mango chicken?'

'Yes!' Ellen cried, and disappeared into her room to get the drawing.

She could hear Serena talking on the phone somewhere further inside the apartment. She was speaking English, possibly to her mother. Annika felt tiredness sweep over her, like a chill wind. Violence and ethical dilemmas were nothing compared to this.

'Here. It's *The Dying Dandy*.'

Annika took the sheet of paper. It showed several figures grouped around a sofa on which lay a very tired-looking man. 'Wow,' she said.

'It's a painting,' Ellen said. 'By Nils Dardel. We had to copy it. Do you think he's really going to die?' The little girl looked concerned.

Annika had to smile again. 'No,' she said. 'I don't think

so. But I think he likes being the centre of attention, with everyone fussing round him. What do you think?'

Ellen giggled.

'Come on,' Annika said. 'Let's go and do some cooking.'

Mango chicken was Kalle's invention. He loved savoury dishes with fruit, and always wanted pineapple on his pizza, or apple with pork chops, but most of all he wanted mangoes in everything. The original recipe, which had simply been a variation on her long-standing stir-fried chicken, contained cashew nuts but Serena was allergic to them so she had swapped them for peanuts.

'Your cousin's coming over for dinner tonight,' Annika said, as she got out the chicken fillets, mangoes, coconut milk, onions and fish sauce.

Ellen blinked in surprise.

'Destiny, you remember her,' Annika said. 'Auntie Birgitta's daughter. Birgitta's coming as well – they're going to eat with us.'

Ellen lit up. 'Destiny's really pretty!'

She was like a little doll, a carbon copy of her mother as a child. Birgitta was the fair, pretty, cheerful, kind sister. Annika had always been the dark, difficult, smart, tough one.

'Birgitta asked if Destiny could stay with us for a few nights. What do you think?'

'She can come in my bed! We can sleep top-to-tail!'

Darling Ellen. She hugged her daughter, feeling her tiredness wash away.

Serena came into the kitchen, then stood in the doorway with her arms folded. 'Dad's going to be late,' she said. 'He messaged me on Facebook.'

Annika went on smiling, even though her cheeks stiffened. 'Thanks,' she said, 'I know. He'll just have to eat whenever he gets home. Do you want to help me with the cooking? We're having mango chicken.'

Serena turned on her heel, her plaits swirling, and went back to her room.

Annika watched her disappear along the corridor. Beyond her sense of inadequacy she felt a flash of fury. Surely the girl could have the decency to reply when spoken to.

'Can I measure the rice?'

She took three deep breaths with her mouth open, then turned back to Ellen. 'Sure.' She got out the rice and the decilitre measure while Ellen fetched a pan from the cupboard.

'Mummy, why don't you like Serena?'

The room swayed and she had to grab hold of the gas stove to stop herself falling. She looked at Ellen, aghast. 'Why do you say that? I like Serena a lot.'

Ellen turned away and concentrated on measuring out the rice. 'Eight people, that's four decilitres,' she said confidently.

'Why do you think I don't like Serena?'

Ellen took the pan over to the sink to fill it with water. 'Your eyes are angry when you look at her.'

Annika gulped. 'I'm not angry at all,' she said. 'Do you want me to help you with the water?'

'No, I can do it. Eight decilitres?'

'Seven will be enough.'

As the rice began to boil, Ellen disappeared into the television room. Annika stir-fried the onions and chicken, added some fish sauce and a bit of coriander, then finally the mangoes and peanuts. She laid the table in the dining room, pausing when she got to Destiny's place: did she eat with a spoon? Did she drink from a normal glass, or did she have one of those plastic beakers? It seemed a lifetime since she'd had a two-year-old.

She sat down at the empty table and took a deep breath. She didn't want to be on bad terms with Birgitta. She had always felt a sense of her own inferiority in comparison with her sister but it should have gone by now. Yes, Mum loved Birgitta more, but she couldn't change that: it was just something she had to live with. Annika had done much better as an adult, to put it mildly, but she didn't need to ram it down Birgitta's throat every time they met.

She looked at the time. Birgitta was supposed to be there at six. It was five past.

It would be good for their children to get to know each other, so that the cousins could be friends.

No question.

At a quarter to seven, when Kalle and Jacob had managed to fall out in the television room, Annika decided it was supper-time, whether her sister was there or not.

They had eaten, cleared up afterwards and parked themselves in front of the television before Birgitta finally showed up. It was twenty past eight when the doorbell rang. Annika was seething with irritation, but she forced herself to smile as she opened the door.

Birgitta was neatly made-up and dressed very smartly. Destiny was hiding behind her mother's flared skirt, and looked exhausted.

'Hello,' Birgitta said, with a smile. 'Sorry we're a bit late.' She stepped into the hall and pulled off their dripping coats. A little puddle quickly formed on the floor.

'Not to worry,' Annika said, crouching beside the little girl, who was still clutching her mother's skirt. 'Hello,

Destiny. My name's Annika, I'm your auntie. Do you remember me?'

The child pressed her face into the skirt. Annika noticed that she left a trail of snot on it.

'Come on, Diny, say hello to your auntie,' Birgitta said, pulling the child by her arm and making her trip over her own feet. Annika caught her before she fell. The little face contorted and she began to cry. Birgitta sighed. 'It's like this all the time,' she said, picking her up. 'We're going to have her checked out to see if there's something wrong with her. She's always crying.'

Annika could see how tightly the child was clinging to Birgitta's neck. All the irritation drained out of her and she, too, was suddenly on the verge of tears. She gulped them back. 'Come in,' she said, leading them into the dining room.

Birgitta and Destiny's dishes were the only ones left on the table.

'Oh, we've already eaten,' Birgitta said. 'We went to McDonald's, and Diny had Chicken McNuggets – you like those, don't you?' She bounced her daughter up and down.

'Coffee?' Annika asked, aware that her voice was trembling.

'No, thanks, we're fine. We won't stay long.'

She put Destiny on the floor and sank onto a chair. Annika crouched beside the child again. 'I've got a little girl called Ellen. She's got lots of nice toys. Would you like to go and see them?'

Destiny stared at her open-mouthed. Annika met her gaze. She felt uneasy. Perhaps Birgitta was right. Perhaps there was something wrong with the child.

But then Destiny nodded, little polite nods. She wiped her nose on her jumper and took Annika's hand. Annika led her along the corridor to Kalle and Ellen's room.

Ellen was sitting in there, drawing. She beamed and dropped her crayon when Annika and the little girl came into the room.

'Destiny! Hello! Oh, you're so pretty!' She ran over and gave the child a hug. The little girl stiffened, then hugged her back.

'Serena!' Ellen called. 'Come and see who's here! Destiny's arrived!'

The little girl blinked her long eyelashes. Annika was afraid she was about to start howling again, and held out a protective hand. 'Maybe you should be a bit careful with her.'

Serena came in and, to Annika's surprise, she looked happy. 'Oh, isn't she sweet!' She knelt down beside her.

Destiny looked at the bundle of plaits in astonishment.

'Is it okay for her to be in here with you for a bit?' Annika asked. Neither of the older girls answered, which she took as agreement, so she went back to the dining room. Birgitta was standing by the window, looking out. 'The weather's just as bad in Norway,' she said. 'Nothing but rain there too.'

Annika sat at the table. There was something sad and restless about Birgitta that she hadn't seen before, a hint of darkness that had appeared over the past few years. She ought to ask her how she was. How their mother was. She ought to ask after Steven and their old friends in Hälleforsnäs, but when she tried to formulate the question her throat felt oddly constricted.

Birgitta glanced at the art on the walls, modern and abstract (charitable purchases from local party groups, Jimmy had explained), the crystal chandelier above the table, the hand-woven rug on the floor (from a women's

144

cooperative in Turkey, a great idea, the sort of thing that really deserved support). 'You've got a very smart home.'

There was a hint of acid in the remark.

'We might be moving soon,' Annika said. She bit the inside of her cheek. Why, why, *why* did she feel the need to be so superior with her sister?

Birgitta raised her eyebrows in curiosity, exactly the same gesture that Annika knew she herself used. She smiled to counteract the effect of her words. 'Jimmy's been offered a new job,' she said. 'It's not official yet, but if he takes it, we'll be moving to Norrköping.'

'Norrköping?' Birgitta said. 'Do people actually live there?'

Asks the woman who lives in a rented three-room flat in Hälleforsnäs . . .

'Jimmy grew up on Himmelstalundsvägen. It would be like going home for him.'

'What about your job? Are you going to commute?'

Annika looked out of the window. She could just make out the stone façade of the building opposite and the grey sky through the rain-soaked glass.

'I've been at the *Evening Post* all my working life. I've written every article so many times now that I no longer have to interview people to write them.'

'I thought you lived and breathed for that paper.'

There was definitely envy, and a hint of malice, in Birgitta's tone.

'It's not a bad job, but there's nothing magical about it now. I've reached the same stage as my colleague Berit. She goes to work and does what she has to, then hurries home to her husband and grandchildren, and that's enough.'

Birgitta's smile became cruel. 'Clever Annika and her lovely job, and now she's got the perfect home-life too.'

The anger in those words hit Annika in the gut with such force that it knocked the air out of her. She stood up and gathered together the last remaining dishes from the table. 'What was it you wanted help with?' she asked.

Birgitta smiled. 'Steven's in Oslo, looking for work.'

'Yes, so you said.'

'There's loads of places to try in Norway. We're thinking of moving there – he wants me to go as well. We're going to see if we can find somewhere to live.'

Annika looked at her. 'And you're wondering if I can look after your daughter?'

Birgitta's smile faded.

'When are you going?'

Birgitta sat down, as if all the energy had drained out of her. 'Friday afternoon.'

'So you're going to be looking for a flat and applying for jobs on Norway's National Day and over the weekend?' Annika said, aware of how sharp she sounded.

Birgitta stood up hastily. 'You don't have to if you don't want to.'

'Why can't Mum have her? Or is she going through one of her phases?'

A shadow crossed Birgitta's face and she brushed her hair back. 'What do you mean?'

'Is she drinking again? Is that why she can't look after Destiny?'

Birgitta didn't answer. She was standing nailed to the parquet floor, staring blankly ahead of her. Annika could hear the girls laughing in Ellen's room. Suddenly she felt close to tears again. 'Of course she can stay here,' Annika said quietly. 'Bring her round on Friday afternoon. I'll make sure I'm home.'

*

In my dreams I am dancing across a grassy heath in a lacy dress. It's thin and white, and swirls around me in the breeze. I'm light as a feather, clear as glass.

On the heavy soil of Silvervägen I am solid and clumsy. My movements feel wrong inside those rooms. The people around me are thin and cold, their lips narrow and sharp, their voices brittle and out of reach.

The best place in their home is the bathroom – I flee there when the air gets too heavy, and I breathe: I catch my breath in their fragility. I open the bathroom cabinet and take in all their weaknesses: medication, dental floss, lubricant. I lift the toilet seat and see the yellow urine stains on the porcelain. I notice the hairs in the plughole of the shower.

And once, when there was no toilet paper, I used a bath towel to wipe myself.

*

Annika was sitting in front of the television, half asleep, when Jimmy came home. The children were all in bed, either sleeping or surfing on one of their electronic gadgets. He walked quietly over to her in the living room, slipped onto the sofa and pulled her into his arms. She wrapped hers round his shoulders, put her nose against his neck and breathed in his scent: salt and old aftershave.

'Hello,' he whispered.

She kissed his chin, and his hand slid inside the waist of her trousers. He smelt of beer. She blew against his Adam's apple.

He sighed. 'Sorry I'm so late.'

'No problem,' she mumbled. 'Birgitta was here, my sister . . . She's asked if we can babysit over the weekend – she's going drinking in Norway with her husband.'

147

'That pale kid with the name ending in *y*?'

'People in glasshouses . . .' Annika said.

'What's her name – Chastity?'

'Destiny. Instead of arriving on time and eating with us, like we'd agreed, they stopped at McDonald's . . .'

He sighed again.

'What is it?'

He scratched his head. 'That assault,' he said. 'Lerberg. It's a really messy business.' He let go of her and sat up. 'Q briefed us this morning, I've just been for a drink with the minister to talk things through.'

Annika waited patiently, and noticed the dark rings round his eyes.

'We're probably going to have to issue some sort of statement tomorrow, although there isn't much to say. The police are fumbling in the dark.'

'But they're going to have to come up with something, surely. Nothing from Forensics?'

'Well, obviously there are plenty of lines of inquiry, but none of them leads anywhere. Yet.'

Annika leaned against him and listened to his breathing. 'I went through the accounts of his old businesses today, the ones that went bankrupt,' she said. 'His reputation as a successful businessman is considerably exaggerated. The only thing he seems to have been really good at is wasting money.'

Jimmy looked at her in surprise. 'Really?'

Annika nodded. 'He had four bankruptcies in seven years. Nothing improper, just too many outgoings and too little income. His wife, Nora, wasn't much liked among the neighbours. She kept to herself, didn't want to join the cookery club or reading group.'

'Have they set up an emergency therapy circle yet?'

'More or less. I met her friends at Therese Lindenstolphe's – she was bound to have a fancy name like that, obviously. We ate freshly baked buns.'

Jimmy whistled.

'The leader of the group is called Sabine. We heard about her children, husband and the first time she gave birth. I'd put money on her having applied to all those posh reality shows several times. Not *Big Brother*, the ones where people get to show off what they've already got . . .'

He chuckled and pulled her closer to him.

'And Ingemar Lerberg knows Anders Schyman,' she mumbled. 'They had dinner together at Edsbacka krog a few weeks before he resigned.'

She unbuttoned his shirt and slipped her hands round his waist. Jimmy's body was broad and rough, still enough of a miracle to make her feel giddy.

'The minister wants to know . . .' he said into her hair.

Her hands stopped. 'What did you say?'

The rumour that Jimmy had been asked to take over the Migration Board wasn't true. He had been offered the Prison and Probation Service, which was also based in Norrköping, and which, if possible, was an even riskier post.

'That we haven't decided.'

'When does he need to know?'

Jimmy kissed her.

WEDNESDAY, 15 MAY

At 04:46 Anders Schyman gave up. He had been lying there staring at the glowing red numbers on the clock-radio for more than an hour, and knew he wasn't going to get any more sleep. He turned his head and looked at his sleeping wife, her lips parted, eyelashes resting on her cheeks, chest rising and falling under the duvet.

She was right: a self-righteous blogger making aggressive and sweeping accusations about something he'd done eighteen years ago wasn't worth getting upset about.

He disentangled himself from the damp bedsheets and got out of bed, naked, and with cold feet. He ignored his dressing-gown and pulled on the previous day's clothes without showering, then crept out of the bedroom and closed the door as quietly as he could. Not that it was really necessary: his wife could have slept through a nuclear war.

Down in the kitchen he brewed some coffee, a whole jug, strong. It wasn't good for him, but just then he didn't give a damn about his health.

He ended up sitting at the kitchen table, staring at the wall of the house next door. He had never had a sea view, no matter what the Light of Truth claimed.

There was a cold draught over the floor and his feet were frozen – he'd never got used to it. He had sat there with his

153

morning coffee for thirty years, and for at least nine months out of twelve he had to rub his feet against each other to warm them up. Adding extra insulation would mean pulling up the pine floor that dated back to 1912, and his wife was opposed to that. The house, in spite of everything, was mostly hers. She had grown up there, and had only ever lived in one other place: his two-room flat, the bathroom on the other side of the courtyard, in the outer reaches of Södermalm, for a few years in the early 1980s before they had bought her parents' place and installed themselves in Saltsjöbaden for good. She wanted their children to grow up there, so they could have the same peaceful childhood she had had, as the only child of two ageing parents (they had been forty and forty-eight when she was born: ancient in those days). His eyes came to rest on the built-in kitchen cabinets – as much of the original furnishings as possible had been kept during the renovation.

They had never had any children. Today they might have tried IVF or considered adoption, maybe even surrogacy, but it had never really felt terribly important. Not to him, anyway. They had each other, he had always been very focused on his work, she had her job at the health centre and all her friends from childhood, the cultural association, the theatre group, the book club and her Pilates class on Tuesday evenings.

They had had a good life, a fantastic life, together.

His salary from the Wennergren family had been the icing on the cake. He had to admit that the Light of Truth was correct on that point: he had sold his soul to buy the house on the island.

Well, maybe not sold: he still had his soul (or part of it), and just rented it out to make the best of things at the *Evening Post*. He believed in democracy and freedom of expression, because what was the alternative? State-produced media definitely had its place, and he had done good, respectable work during his many years at Swedish Television, but without commercial competition all state-run media soon succumbed to the tyranny of power.

He had done Sweden a favour when he'd taken up his post as legally accountable publisher on behalf of the Wennergren family.

He cautiously drank the dregs of his coffee. His stomach was burning ominously. Maybe he should try to eat something.

He glanced towards the alcove behind the staircase, his study.

Should he take a look now, or wait until he got to the office?

He had received a few requests for interviews the previous day, all of which he had ignored. Hopefully, that would stop his colleagues publishing anything, although it was no guarantee. He hesitated for a moment, then pushed his chair back and went over to the computer. His hands were shaking as he typed in his password, a pulse throbbing in his neck. The office chair nestled snugly at the base of his spine. He went onto the Light of Truth and read the heading of the latest post. The same as yesterday evening. Nothing had happened during the night.

He breathed out, and felt his shoulders relax.

Then he leaned forward again and did a search of the established media. The other evening paper was at the top of the list. The result hit him like a punch in the stomach.

New allegations:
SCHYMAN LIED HIS WAY TO JOURNALISM PRIZE
Took bribes to make documentary

He couldn't breathe. He got to his feet, staring at the screen. Linette Pettersson and Sven-Olof Witterfeldt, Viola's embittered business partners, were quoted as reliable and objective experts, not as the interested parties they were. That they had served prison sentences for financial offences was described as an unfortunate consequence of their employment.

The second result was the professional journal, *Noted*. They didn't even bother to hide behind the alibi of 'new allegations', and had no hesitation in declaring that the Light of Truth was right:

Blogger reveals
SCHYMAN'S BLUFF
Faked story about missing woman

The aggrieved faces of Pettersson and Witterfeldt glared out at him from the screen. They claimed they had been 'waiting twenty years for justice', although it wasn't immediately apparent why.

And then there was the gossip site, mediatime, whose opening page was adorned with a large portrait of him, and the heading:

BRIBED AND LIED
Rank hypocrisy laid bare

He stumbled backwards towards the door and made his way through the hall, stubbing his big toe on the step before he threw up the coffee in the guest toilet.

*

Thomas walked with easy strides to Rosenbad's main entrance. The bag containing his packed lunch hung from his hook, carefully tied on, while his right hand swung slightly with each step he took. Anyone who noticed him would see a civil servant on his way to work in the government chancellery, one of the select few who shaped society, a powerful man who made history every day.

Unfortunately there weren't many people to see him at that hour. From the corner of his eye he caught sight of a man in a small vehicle cleaning the streets, someone delivering papers, and a few losers in raincoats pushing shopping trolleys. This was the drawback of sneaking in to work before everyone else, but he still preferred it. His number-one nightmare was bumping into Jimmy Halenius, but he couldn't bear sitting in that horrible flat any longer. This way he could avoid both the under-secretary of state and the sympathetic glances of his colleagues as he passed their doors in the corridor.

He always kept his own door closed. Maybe that made his colleagues think he was working on something strictly confidential, but he was well aware that he wasn't fooling anyone. His crap investigation into international financial crime would be stuffed into some archive somewhere and would never see the light of day. On the one hand, it was obviously a huge waste of taxpayers' money, but on the other the government was getting off lightly.

He reached the highly polished chancellery door, fished his passcard out of his right coat pocket with his right hand, slipped it through the reader and tapped in his code. The lock opened with a little click, he took a step backwards, tucked away the card and waited for the door to swing open.

No one could see he had a hook in place of his left hand.

He had pulled a leather glove over the prosthesis, and was wearing the matching glove on his right hand. It hadn't been easy putting the right glove on with the hook but he had managed it.

He passed the inner doors, walked up the short flight of steps to the marble foyer, greeting the guard with a light wave of his right hand, then repeated the manoeuvre with the card and code to get to the lifts.

His own office was on the ground floor, but he always stopped briefly by the lifts. Anyone who saw him standing there would assume he was going up in the building, up to floor five or six, where the minister was based, or even all the way up to the Cabinet Office and the prime minister's domain at the very top of the building.

Then he quickly slipped into his own corridor.

No one else had arrived, just as he had predicted.

His room was cramped and sparsely furnished. As was everyone else's, but that was no excuse.

He put his packed lunch in the little kitchen area he had had installed in one corner: fridge, a small freezer, microwave and coffee machine. It was a practical arrangement. He didn't have to eat or have coffee out in the communal area, and the cleaner took care of the washing up. After a moment's hesitation, he decided to have some Roma, one of the stronger coffee capsules.

With his cup in front of him (on the right, so he could hold and lift it), he sat down at his computer. He used to be pretty good at typing, fast, and his lying bastard of a doctor had said he could learn to do it with the hook, but it was utterly hopeless.

International financial crime, under investigation for the umpteenth time.

Yeah, yeah, he knew it was important, a cornerstone in

the fight against organized crime. The criminals' problem wasn't smuggling drugs/dealing weapons/selling young girls into prostitution (delete as applicable), but making their money legitimate. They couldn't just walk into a bank with a sack of money and imagine it could be deposited in an account of their choosing: the depositor had to be able to prove that he had acquired the money legally. Every bank and financial institution had now agreed to report suspicious behaviour, even in the Cayman Islands.

Everyone knew that, and everyone knew how the criminals got round it. (He wasn't thinking of the simple practice of sending so-called smurfs to pay five hundred dollars at a time into different bank accounts.) Using companies protected by legislation on business confidentiality in various tax havens, such as the aforementioned Cayman Islands or the considerably more convenient Gibraltar, the money was circulated via fake invoices and phoney companies until eventually genuine accounts showed actual money and real profits, possibly some properties built using unregistered labour, the materials bought for cash (the cement supplier had no trouble proving that he had acquired the money in an honest, legal way, because he really had been paid for his cement). Then the properties could be sold and the business would make a profit and, hey presto, the drug smuggler had an account containing money that was pure as the driven snow.

His task this time was to investigate the best way for police authorities in different countries to communicate in order to stop cross-border financial crime.

As if that was going to take eighteen months!

'Send an email, for fuck's sake!' he felt like shouting. 'Or pick up the phone and call them!' If the lazy fuckers learned to speak English, that would be an end to the problem.

He chuckled to himself – it really was very straightforward. He drank the last of the coffee, then pulled a face: it wasn't hot enough. He would have to replace the coffee machine: it clearly wasn't up to the job.

Then he made himself more comfortable on his chair and surfed the net, checking sites he usually followed, reading up on what had happened in his favourite debates overnight. The thread 'Gossip about media bitch Annika Bengtzon' was his favourite site and where he always started. It was on one of the shadier discussion forums, not as well trafficked as the more established ones. And he hadn't started the thread, which meant that there really were people out there who hated her. Sadly, there wasn't much activity in it, nothing for at least a week now, even though he had written several posts saying that she was having an affair with an overweight Member of Parliament. No one had picked it up and run with it. That evening he would come up with something juicier, something that would make people react.

Sophia Grenborg's Facebook profile had already been updated twice that morning – his former lover seemed to live the whole of her pathetic little life on Facebook. He clicked to like both posts, just to keep her simmering: he could have her back whenever he wanted. She had shown up at the hospital, crying and cradling him and kissing his cheeks until he had pushed her away. He hadn't wanted her sympathy.

He checked a few dreary feminist sites, but when he got to the Light of Truth he found reason to pause. The crazy blogger had put together an ambitious summary of that morning's reactions to his revelations about newspaper editor Anders Schyman, and it was a pretty impressive list. Even the traditional media had jumped on the story now.

160

They were hiding behind phrases like 'it is being claimed online' and 'one critical blog suggests', but the meaning was clear enough. The most recurrent accusations were that Schyman was a hypocrite, a liar and open to bribes.

Thomas clicked his way quickly through the list of links. He had to make a real effort not to turn into Gregorius and join in with the discussions, but that would have to wait until he got home. Now that he actually thought about it, it seemed very likely that he might be feeling unwell after lunch.

There was movement in the corridor as his colleagues began to arrive. He opened his work on the investigation and kept it in the background as he went through the websites.

The most interesting comments weren't anonymous, but signed 'Anne Snapphane', Annika's arch-enemy and former friend who was now an editor at mediatime. She had written an account of the editor-in-chief's hypocrisy that was magnificently sharp and to the point. She described what it was like working at the *Evening Post*, how reporters were pressured to exaggerate and lie (misrepresentation and distortion were described as 'stylistic matters'), how Schyman had ruled the newsroom using nepotism and an iron fist. She also took the chance to give Annika a passing kicking, describing her as Schyman's most prominent henchperson, the one most slavishly devoted to the *Evening Post*'s rancid policies . . .

There was a knock on his door, and Thomas jumped so hard that his hook hit the keyboard. He quickly clicked to hide Snapphane's embittered rant and leaned over his work on the investigation. 'Come in!'

Cramne, his boss, put his head round the door. He probably didn't dare come in – perhaps he thought disability was contagious.

'Hello, old man, how are you?'

Thomas smiled weakly. 'Thanks,' he said. 'Well, things are moving forward. I'm waiting for a response from the Spaniards . . .'

Cramne opened the door a little wider. 'I mean with you . . . You were off sick for a few days?'

He forced himself to swallow the angry retort that was on the tip of his tongue. 'Just a cold,' he said. 'Nothing serious.'

'Do you fancy lunch today? Fairly early? A few of us are thinking of heading to the Opera Bar.'

Ah, so they'd decided to make a collective show of sympathy towards the cripple. He shrugged his shoulders. 'That sounds really great, but I've got a conference call booked with the Greeks at half past eleven and then . . .'

Cramne raised his hands in a gesture that showed he was both disappointed and disingenuously impressed. 'Okay,' he said. 'Just say the word if it gets postponed or something. Those Greeks do have a tendency not to come up with the goods . . .'

Thomas laughed politely at the lame witticism until the door was closed. Then he sighed. Now he was going to have to organize a bloody conference call. What could they discuss this time?

'I don't want to wear this. It's horrid.' Ellen tugged at the zip of the raincoat.

'I know you don't like it,' Annika said, 'but you'll be soaked before you get to school if you wear the other one.'

Kalle tutted by the door. Frustration bubbled inside Annika. Kalle was always ready on time, and ended up

162

all sweaty and annoyed while Ellen made a fuss about insignificant things.

'It's got a scratchy zip,' Ellen said.

Annika pulled it down a few centimetres so it wasn't touching the little girl's chin. 'Would you rather have to sit in school all day when you're wet and cold? And then get ill and not be able to go riding?' She guided the child towards the door. 'If you don't catch the next bus you're going to be late.'

The children still went to school on Kungsholmen, the one they had attended before she and Thomas separated, but they had to spend half an hour getting there when they were living with Annika. Ellen gave her a wounded look as she closed the front door. Annika heard their footsteps disappear down the stairwell.

She breathed out.

Jimmy had set off for work early that morning, so it was up to her to see that Jacob and Serena left home on time. They went to a school just a few blocks away, so didn't need to leave for another quarter of an hour.

'Jacob?' she called down the corridor. 'Serena? Are you nearly ready?'

No answer.

She went back into the kitchen and made another cup of coffee, got out her mobile and went onto the other evening paper's website. While the coffee was filtering through the machine into the mug, she skimmed through their coverage of the Lerberg case. They were pushing hard with the missing wife, probably because they had managed to get hold of a genuinely charming picture of Nora and two of the children.

The machine fell silent, the signal that the coffee was ready. Jimmy had a machine that made coffee from small, coloured aluminium capsules, ridiculously expensive and presumably anything but environmentally friendly, but the coffee was good. (Mind you, who was she to judge that? She liked the tar that came out of the machine in the newsroom.) Once Jimmy had asked her to buy more capsules from the company's concept store on Kungsgatan, which had been something of an otherworldly experience. The shop was like an aircraft hangar. When she'd stepped through the doors she'd been greeted by three young people with ambition to be models, dressed in Armani suits, competing to see who could give her the biggest smile. They were standing behind a counter made of metal and dark hardwood, and welcomed her in chorus. One handed her a queue ticket, with the sort of gesture that suggested she was being given a Fabergé egg. Then she was let into the shop itself – and gawped. To say that it was high-concept design was an understatement: marble floor, dark wood, large television screens on which George Clooney wandered about drinking coffee. Another twenty or so models in similar suits were standing behind a kilometre-long counter selling those little capsules at astonishing prices. All of a sudden she became aware of how wet and greasy her hair was, and how much mud she had on her shoes. She had walked out, unable to bring herself to buy their coffee, but drinking it was no problem at all.

'Nora would never leave her children,' she read in a headline on the other paper's website. Bosse had written the article: he had managed to dig out a few other 'friends', similar to Annika's group of mums. Bosse's women – four in total, smartly dressed, neatly coiffed, holding pretty children in their arms – declared that Nora was very popular in the area, an example to them all in her devotion to her husband, children and housework. She had

164

lived a quiet, unostentatious family life when she wasn't
socializing with neighbours and friends . . . Naturally they,
like Annika's mums, hoped that Nora would soon be home,
and that Ingemar would recover, so that their community
could settle down again and life could return to normal.

Annika couldn't recall ever having lived a 'normal' life.
As for calm, where on earth could she find that?

'Jacob, can you come here?' she heard Serena call from
the bedroom corridor.

She lowered her mobile, hesitated, then put her cup down
and went to Serena's room.

The girl had chosen a patterned cotton dress with
buttons up the back, and she couldn't reach the two top
ones.

'Hang on, I'll give you a hand,' Annika said, forcing herself to sound cheerful.

Serena spun round and took a step back. 'Get out,' she
said.

Annika stopped. 'I just want to—'

'Jacob can help me. We don't need you.'

Annika felt all the air go out of her lungs. She gasped.
She ought to say something, but what? She bit her lip and
moved aside to let Jacob into the room. Serena turned
round and Jacob fastened the two top buttons. 'Thanks,
Jacob,' she said airily, then pushed past Annika and headed
for the hall.

Annika stayed in the room until she heard the front door
close. She shut her eyes for a few seconds, waiting for the
pressure in her chest to ease, but it didn't.

What have I ever done to you, you little bitch?

That thought eased the pressure slightly, and made it
easier to breathe again.

Then she started to cry.

*

Ingemar Lerberg was lying in an ordinary hospital bed, slightly raised at the head, his arms lying slightly away from his body, elbows bent. Nina looked at him through the glass panel in the hospital door. The ventilator had been disconnected, but there were a number of tubes leading from his body to a drip and various monitoring devices. He was dressed in a white hospital gown, no socks. A white blanket covered his legs and torso, but his feet were bare. She couldn't help staring at the soles of his feet. They were badly swollen and discoloured blue, yellow and green, criss-crossed with wounds and covered with thick, black scabs. He had a dark patch over one eye.

Senior consultant Kararei came hurrying along the corridor.

'Is he awake?' Nina asked.

'He regained consciousness intermittently during the night. He's had some sleep this morning, but he was awake a short while ago.'

Nina studied his body. 'He's not bandaged,' she said.

'Only over the scars from his operation,' the doctor said. 'You can't bandage ribs, and the soles of the feet heal best if they're left uncovered.'

'Can he talk?'

'He understands what we say, but he's been intubated and had a tracheotomy in his throat for the ventilator, so his larynx is badly swollen. You can have a few minutes with him, but no more than that.'

'Why is the patch black?'

The doctor looked at her quizzically.

'Everything else is white,' Nina said. 'Why is the patch over his eye black?'

Dr Kararei blinked. 'I honestly don't know,' he said, pushing the door open and walking into the room.

Nina followed him. A cool breeze swept past her out into the corridor.

'Ingemar,' the doctor said, walking over to the man. 'I've got a police officer here who'd like to talk to you. They're trying to find whoever did this to you. Do you feel up to seeing her?'

The man in the bed turned his head slightly and his single eye, hazy and bloodshot, focused on Nina.

'My name's Nina Hoffman,' she said. 'I'm from the National Crime Unit.'

The eye stared at her.

'I understand that it's hard to speak,' she said. 'Can you nod your head?'

The man didn't move.

'Can you blink?'

The man blinked his swollen eyelid. She breathed out, suddenly conscious that she had been holding her breath.

'Blink once for yes, and shut your eye completely for a few seconds if you want to say no,' Nina said. 'Can you do that?'

The man blinked once.

'Do you feel up to answering some questions?'

Another blink.

Nina straightened her back. She had only a few minutes so she would take her own theories as a starting point. 'Were you assaulted by two men?'

The man blinked.

'Did you recognize them?'

He closed his eye. Nina waited. No. He'd never seen them before.

'Did they want information from you?'

167

A blink.

'Were you able to give it to them?'

The eye closed, and remained shut. A tear trickled out and ran down past his ear.

They had asked for information Ingemar hadn't been able to give them, something concerning him or a third person, someone close, possibly someone who was missing.

'Do you know where Nora is?'

The man's entire body arched up, the eye widened and stared at her in terror. A noise emerged from his throat – it sounded like a moan. Dr Kararei hurried over to him and Nina took a step back in alarm.

'Ooooh!' Ingemar Lerberg's arms jerked uncontrollably, his legs cramping.

Dr Kararei pressed the alarm button: a red light began to flash outside the room and a siren sounded. Two nurses came rushing in and Nina took several more steps back.

'Nooooo,' Ingemar Lerberg shouted. 'Noooohhhaaa . . .'

She stared at the man, frozen to the spot in horror. The door behind her flew open and hit her hard in the shoulder as another doctor ran into the room. She stumbled to one side, then rushed out into the corridor, away from the ward, away from the hoarse screams. She didn't catch her breath until she reached the lift area. She took the stairs down from the fourth floor and hurried through the large glazed lobby and out into the rain.

She got back to her sterile room at National Crime. She closed the door – she'd had quite enough introductions. As an operational analyst she was a resource, someone who was supposed to help structure a great deal of information, and to do that she needed peace in which to think. According to her job description, she was expected to present the results of her analysis to the group both verbally and in writing, so she ought to be given the space in which to come up with them.

She sank gently onto her chair, let out a deep breath, then took out a bottle of mineral water and an apple and put them on a napkin on her desk. The documents from that morning's group meeting were spread out in front of her. Someone must know something – someone must have seen something. The surveillance footage from Solsidan station hadn't revealed anything. No Nora caught on camera at the entrance or on the platform. She could have passed the station on foot, outside the range of the cameras, or left by car. But not in one of the two cars at the family's disposal, a Mercedes registered to Ingemar Lerberg's company, or the Nissan Micra that he owned privately.

There was a knock at the door, hard and rapid. Before Nina had time to react Lamia had entered the room and made herself comfortable on her desk. 'Were you able to talk to him?'

She was sitting on the documents. Nina took hold of the papers and tried to pull them out. Lamia raised one buttock to release them.

'He was conscious,' Nina said, 'but his larynx is swollen and he's got a hole in his throat for the ventilator.'

'What did he say?'

Lamia reached for the bottle of water, unscrewed it and took a deep gulp. Nina glanced at the Barbie woman: she was swinging one foot and beaming like the sun.

'He communicated by blinking,' Nina said. 'He was assaulted by two men. He'd never seen them before. They wanted information from him – something he didn't know. He reacted extremely strongly to the question of where Nora might be, had convulsions and screamed her name.'

169

'Do you want that apple?' Lamia was pointing at it.

'Er, yes,' Nina said.

The woman reached for the apple and took a big bite, then put it back on the napkin. 'The passenger manifests have arrived,' she said, with her mouth full. 'There's a result for Nora.' Then she picked up the water-bottle, opened it and drank some.

Nina felt the hairs on the back of her neck stand up. Why the hell couldn't she have said that at once? 'Where is she?'

'We don't know where she is, but we know where she's been. She flew to Switzerland two weeks ago, to Zürich with Swiss Air, just for the day.'

Nina was struggling against various impulses that struck her one after the other: to throw the woman out of her room, to move the bottle of water away from her, and get her to explain what had happened.

'Switzerland?' she said, almost under her breath. 'What was she doing there?'

'The people at Ingemar's company knew nothing about it – I've called and asked. They don't have an office in Zürich, or any clients. And there's nothing to indicate any business connections with Switzerland, or any secret bank accounts, not in any computer or files or financial records. The Lerbergs never declared any capital income abroad.'

She smiled cheerily.

'These days it's actually possible to get hold of information about Swiss bank accounts,' she said, screwing the lid back on the bottle and putting it down on the desk.

'Nora's passport was found in the house, wasn't it?' Nina said, leafing through the forensics report.

'In a drawer in the bedroom,' Lamia said. 'Issued on the thirteenth of December last year. Her previous passport was reported stolen to Nacka Police at the end of November. It

170

disappeared at the same time as her purse, along with her driving licence, credit cards, ID card, car and house keys, when her handbag was stolen in a café in Nacka shopping centre while she was doing some Christmas shopping.'

Nina stared at her. There was something really odd about the woman. 'Have you got a photographic memory?' she asked.

'There's no such thing,' Lamia said. 'But I have got an eidetic memory, from the Greek *eidos*, to see.' She tilted her head to one side.

Nina didn't understand her answer and wasn't sure what to say.

'Ingemar Lerberg wasn't working for the security services, by the way. At least not as far as the people working for him know,' Lamia went on, untroubled.

'If the work was secret, then presumably his staff wouldn't tell you about it anyway,' Nina said.

Lamia wasn't about to be put off. 'They're not aware of any couriers or deliveries of secret material, and they look after all the administration and invoicing—'

'Why did Nora have her passport in her handbag?' she interrupted.

Lamia blinked her long eyelashes.

'You don't need your passport for Christmas shopping,' Nina said. 'And she had her driving licence and ID card with her.'

Lamia smiled. 'Ingemar Lerberg's company has three big customers who make up ninety per cent of the business's turnover: Panama General Cargo, Philippines Shipping Lines, and Cargo International España . . .' She went on to provide figures for turnover and profit, but Nina wasn't listening.

The only time you needed a passport was if you were

171

planning to cross a border outside the Schengen Area. And she thought that some airlines required a passport as ID, even if a Swedish ID card worked practically everywhere in Europe, apart from the United Kingdom.

'Where did Nina's handbag go missing? Exactly, I mean,' Nina asked, cutting off Lamia mid-sentence.

'At Hot Spot Coffee. It's on the ground floor.' The answer came without a moment's hesitation.

'Were there any witnesses?'

'That wasn't clear from the report.'

Nina tugged at her ponytail. 'Do you think you could move a bit?' She reached for the phone, which was hidden behind Lamia's backside.

'Oops, of course,' the blonde said, and jumped onto the floor.

'Can you shut the door after you?' Nina said.

'Sure,' Lamia said, and trotted out of the room on her high heels.

Nina picked up the receiver. Slowly she dialled the number of her colleagues out in Nacka: this was definitely a long shot. When the receptionist answered, she explained that she was calling from the National Crime Unit, even if the words still felt odd in her mouth. She asked for Superintendent Lundqvist, the officer in charge of the local investigation into the Lerberg case. The receptionist put her through without any questions.

Lundqvist sounded very stressed when he eventually answered. 'Nora Lerberg's handbag? I don't know anything about a stolen handbag. When's it supposed to have gone missing?'

'Her passport was inside the bag. She had a new one issued on the thirteenth of December last year.'

'That's six months ago!'

172

Nina looked at the closed door, glad that no one could hear her. 'I'd like to know the circumstances surrounding the disappearance of her handbag and what she said when she reported it missing.'

There was a noise in the background, and someone shouted something.

'Listen, Hoffman, things are a bit hectic right now.'

'Anything we ought to know?'

The superintendent let out a loud sigh. 'This morning one of our local talents was found hanging from the branch of a tree out near Kråkträsken, naked and smeared with honey, a plastic bag over his head.'

Nina's head was buzzing.

'Local talents?'

'One of society's lost sheep. They hang around in Orminge shopping centre.'

'Is he dead?'

'As a doornail. So if you'll excuse me . . .'

Naked, smeared with honey, and asphyxiated with a plastic bag?

Hanging from a branch?

Hanging from a branch?

Images ran through Nina's head, names, methods. 'Was he hanging from his knees, with his wrists tied below his knees?'

Lundqvist lost his thread. There was silence on the line. Then he cleared his throat. 'How . . . ?'

La Barra.

'I'm coming out to you,' she said. 'Right away. Kråkträsken, you said?'

'What—'

She hung up and looked at Jesper's bookcase.

The method has several names: apart from La Barra it is

also known as El Pollo (the chicken) or Pau de Arara (the parrot's perch).

She pulled on her jacket, put her mobile into her pocket and headed for the exit.

Lovisa Olsson lived in one of the really showy old villas in Saltsjöbaden, on Vikingavägen, with lots of decorative carving, a three-car garage and a big glazed veranda facing the sea. Annika parked on the road in front of the house, locked the car and looked about her in the pouring rain. The lawn had been raked clear of leaves, and there were tulips growing along the front of the house. She could make out a swing behind the garage, and a tarpaulin on the ground, presumably covering a swimming-pool.

The porch had two ornate wooden doors, with both a doorbell and a brass knocker. She hesitated, then decided to use the bell. It rang inside, the sound echoing between the rooms. She was almost expecting a maid in uniform and lace cap to answer the door, but in the end a little boy with a runny nose opened it. He stared at her. He had curly black hair and a comfort blanket in one hand.

'Is your mummy at home?' Annika asked.

The boy looked up at her warily. 'What's your name?' he asked.

'Annika,' Annika said. 'What's yours?'

'Come in!' Lovisa called, from somewhere inside the house.

'Mark,' the child said, and ran off.

Annika went in and closed the door behind her.

Lovisa hurried into the hall, without any make-up, her hair loosely tied up. In her arms she held a little girl, her head covered with cornrow plaits, just like Serena's.

'Welcome,' she said, shaking Annika's hand. 'I've got the children at home today. I hope that isn't a problem – they can't seem to shake off their colds in all this rain.'

Annika hung up her coat. The water dripped onto the hall floor. Lovisa turned and led her into a vast sitting room.

'I was rather surprised when you called,' she said, glancing over her shoulder. 'Wasn't yesterday enough, at Therese's?'

'Almost,' Annika said.

Lovisa was clearly agitated. She went into the kitchen. 'I've got a doctor's appointment with Mark in a little while.'

The kitchen was enormous, with black and white chequered tiles on the floor, and custom-made fittings, no wall cabinets, just shelves. Multi-coloured LED lights were set into the ceiling. There was a black granite island containing a glass hob and griddle, and a bar with inbuilt lighting. Annika had never seen anything like it outside interior-design magazines.

'You seemed to be the one who knew the Lerberg family best out of the mums' group,' Annika said, sitting on a tall bar stool. There were crispbread crumbs on the granite worktop.

'Is this going to be in the paper?' She sounded worried.

'Probably,' Annika said. 'Is that a problem?'

Lovisa put the little girl in a child's chair. 'I'm just going to put a film on for Mark,' she said, and went off into the house.

Annika was left sitting with the little girl beside her. The child stared fixedly at her, wide-eyed and wary, on the verge of crying at the slightest provocation. One of the lights in the ceiling cast a bright blue spot on the granite between them. Annika tried to focus on the spot, but her eyes kept meeting the child's. She realized it was Serena's silent anger that she was seeing in them.

'Hello,' she said. 'My name's Annika. What's yours?'

The toddler's face crumpled into tears and she tried to get out of her chair. Annika glanced around desperately for something to distract her, but before she could find anything Lovisa ran in and picked up her daughter.

Annika brushed her hair from her face, discreetly swept the crispbread crumbs onto the floor, took out her pen and notepad and put them down in front of her. 'You've got a lovely home,' she said.

'Thanks,' Lovisa said.

'Have you lived here long?'

'We bought it when I was expecting Mark.'

Annika smiled and tried to relax her shoulders. So Lovisa and her husband were loaded. She felt curiosity simmering inside her. She tilted her head, then wrote the date and time on the pad, concentrating, as if it was important.

'What line of work is your husband in?' she asked lightly.

'He's with the IMF,' Lovisa said.

Annika blinked.

'The International Monetary Fund,' Lovisa said. 'At their offices in Geneva. But that's not where we got the money. My dad owns a number of ICA supermarkets.'

Annika looked down at her notepad. Lovisa had seen through her question, and she blushed.

'My husband was born in Sweden,' Lovisa went on, in a clearer, drier voice than before. 'His parents are from Nairobi, both doctors. Samuel's dad is head of Intensive Care at Södermalm Hospital. He's looking after Ingemar.'

Annika did her best to maintain a neutral expression. Lovisa gave her daughter a beaker containing a red liquid.

'How is he getting on?' Annika asked.

176

Lovisa gave her a look that seemed almost amused. 'Samuel's dad? Oh, he's fine, thanks. We read that he was Ingemar's doctor in the *Evening Post*. He never tells us anything.'

Annika tried to smile but failed. She decided to stop stomping about in Lovisa's family background. 'You said you've known Nora since you were children,' she said. 'Were you in the same class?'

Lovisa mashed a banana that she tried to feed to her daughter, but without much success. 'She was in the same class as Marika, my little sister, two years below me. Nora was a bit . . . sad, when she was younger. Partly because she stammered, and partly because of her mother. She was always sick, and then she died.'

'Oh dear,' Annika said.

'Breast cancer,' Lovisa said, trying to push the mashed banana into the child's mouth. 'She had no hair, I remember . . . She died when Nora and Marika were in year four. How old would that make them? Ten?'

'Did Nora have any brothers and sisters? She grew up with her dad?'

'He was head of the porcelain factory,' Lovisa said. 'He's dead now, too – he went a year or so ago.'

'Does your sister still see Nora?'

The little girl spat out the banana. Lovisa sighed and gave up. 'No, my sister lives in London.' She wiped the child's mouth, and the little girl protested loudly.

'So you wouldn't say they were close friends?' Annika asked.

Lovisa shook her head. 'Nora isn't close to anyone,' she said.

She glanced at her watch, the Rolex.

'How do you mean?' Annika asked.

Lovisa stood up, suddenly irritated. 'Nora doesn't want friends, she wants admirers. She fusses and makes jam and juice and knits and everything matches, you know, the perfect politician's wife. The fact that Ingemar used to be an MP is made out to be as big a deal as if he'd been the American president, and she keeps going on about how bloody unfair it was that he was forced to resign . . . She even got a dog because it fitted the image. The only thing she's never managed to do is lose weight.'

Annika thought about Ingemar Lerberg's multiple bankruptcies. 'Do you know if the Lerbergs had any financial problems?'

Lovisa laughed. 'If they did, do you think Nora would have told anyone?' She picked the child up from her chair. 'She was fond of reminding people that she'd studied economics at Stockholm University, like it was as good as the School of Economics or something. As far as I know, she never graduated.'

Lovisa handled her daughter confidently and comfortably. She was a very wealthy woman, but she looked after her own children, and didn't seem to have a Filipina in the basement, even though she had the money and the space for one. And she clearly didn't like Nora Lerberg.

'Can I quote you on this?'

Lovisa looked horrified. 'No! God, no, you mustn't! Whatever would people think of me?'

Annika smiled. She could use the quotes indirectly, and say they were from an anonymous source.

Lovisa was visibly nervous now. 'I don't think they were short of money, though. Samuel's seen Nora on the plane to Geneva several times, and once when she was having lunch at Domaine de Châteauvieux – you know the one, two Michelin stars, down by the river?'

Annika wasn't personally familiar with fancy restaurants in Switzerland. She stood up and gathered her things together, all of a sudden tired of marble and LED lighting.

'And she's very good at playing the piano,' Lovisa went on, with a strained smile. 'She got onto some sort of music course up in Norrland – Piteå, I think it was.'

Annika's mobile rang. She smiled apologetically and had to dig about in the bottom of her bag before she found it.

It was Anders Schyman. He sounded stressed. 'Where are you?'

Annika glanced at Lovisa. She was rinsing the child's hands under the tap. The little girl was shrieking. 'Out on a job.'

She left the kitchen and walked towards the hall.

'Can you come to the office? Straight away.'

'Has something happened?'

'I want to talk to you. Albert Wennergren is coming as well. Can you be back before lunch?'

Her thoughts slowed and came to a complete stop. What had she done wrong this time? 'Is this something I need to prepare for?'

'No. Just come as soon as you can.' He hung up.

Lovisa came out into the hall. 'I don't want to rush you, but the doctor's appointment . . .'

'Of course,' Annika said.

Schyman had never called her like that before. Ever.

Lovisa looked close to tears. 'Please don't print any of that. I didn't mean it. And I have to go on living here. Please.'

*

179

His heart was pounding, rhythmic and heavy, like a bass line. His feet splashed with each step he took in the mud, and his breathing sounded rough. He wasn't in top form, but he could still pass as an ordinary jogger. The few people he encountered saw a middle-aged man in a shabby tracksuit and the right sort of shoes, defying the rain to postpone his heart attack, if they paid him any attention at all. His hair was slicked back, in contrast to the previous day when it had been wild and bushy, his stubble unkempt.

No one from Orminge shopping centre would recognize him.

He had parked the car by the harbour at the far end of Skarpövägen, then jogged along the waterlogged footpaths in the direction of Saltsjö-Boo. His internal compass told him he was about five hundred metres north-east of Mariedal, and almost exactly a kilometre south of Hamndalen.

He slowed and breathed the dampness into his lungs. The effect was almost intoxicating. He really did love this, the smell of moss and decomposition, the sound of branches rubbing against each other. You didn't have to be Sigmund Freud to grasp that this was where he was from, brought up in pine forests and marshes, himself and his twin brother, in the district of Älvsbyn in the woods of Norrbotten, outside the village of Vidsel in the very northernmost part of Scandinavia. The extensive forests outside their childhood home formed part of what used to be known as Robotförsöksplats Norrland, the Norrland Missile Test Site, now shortened to the more manageable Vidsel Test Site. It was an area the size of the southern province of Blekinge, used exclusively for testing new weapons of mass destruction, bombs and advanced drones. Explosive power was measured, the effect on nature and materials observed. He knew they had once built a large bridge spanning

180

nothing at all simply because the Swiss wanted to blow one up. Countries all round the world tested their weapons there. They had developed more than forty different types of guided missile there, including the RB40, which was used by such stable and uncorrupt countries as Iran, Pakistan, Bahrain, the United Arab Emirates, Indonesia, Singapore, Thailand and Venezuela.

Suddenly Mother and Father appeared in his mind, his mother's nervous hands, his father's closed face. His parents, God rest their souls, had been forcibly evacuated from Nausta; the village was apparently still there, or part of it at least, abandoned and decaying, a ghost town in the middle of the test area. Father used to apply for permission to return each year, but was always turned down, which made him angry and bitter, and far too ready to seek solace in the bottle. Perhaps that was why he and his mirror-image didn't drink spirits . . .

He liked forest. He was used to moving about in it.

They should have found the man by now. If not, he'd have to make sure that they did or the animals would get to him.

He speeded up again. He was wet through and didn't want to cool down and start to freeze. He thought he could hear noises from the east, voices talking, car engines, but it was hard to be sure in the rain, with his terrible hearing.

His feet drummed rhythmically, his heart thudding its bass line. He did a thorough check of his body as he ran, focusing on his breathing as he tried to experience every aspect of the different parts of his body. He started from the bottom: toes and feet, calves and knees, twinges – pain, perhaps – chill or heat, up through his thighs, heavy muscle and bone, then his abdomen, chest, arms and shoulders, head. He liked to take care of himself, to give his body the attention it deserved.

As he approached Kråkträsken he stopped by a tree-stump and stretched. With a suitably pained expression, he massaged his calves and thigh muscles.

Chalk-white police lights were dancing among the tree-trunks.

They had found him. Excellent.

His choice of location had been correct. No further action was required on his part.

He pushed his chest out slightly, then turned and jogged back towards the car.

*

The magic was enough to start with, the fact that he saw me, that he existed. Every touch was electric, tightening the strings inside me, making me heavy and wet. Being able to share his body was like passing a boundary, being let into a room that was his, and his alone. His lips might have been too dry and too thin, but the enchantment was more than enough to make up for that.

It wasn't his hands that stopped, it was his eyes. His interest. They looked away, didn't want to make the effort, focused else-where, on other goals. Recognition. Publicity. Adventure. His desires became an irritant. To deflect his withdrawal I turned my gaze inward, focused on myself, used him as I would any other crutch. It's destructive in the long run, I know that, not sharing each other's space, but I haven't got space to take care of my longing right now.

So I wait.

*

Nina turned off the motorway towards Orminge, passed a shopping centre, carried on along Mensättravägen for a few hundred metres, then turned left towards Hasseludden. She was holding the wheel in the twenty-past-eight grip so beloved of the police, a habit from all those years in patrol cars, her foot resting lightly on the accelerator pedal as she paid careful attention to her surroundings. The area was heavily built up in places, and fairly representative of Swedish suburbs in general. She passed a row of four-storey apartment blocks made of modular grey concrete.

La Barra. That can't be a coincidence, there has to be a connection.

On Valövägen the character of the buildings changed to mainly single-storey houses of a very basic design. It ought to be somewhere around here.

She parked next to a path that led into the forest, got out and locked the car.

It was still raining hard.

She looked around. There was no sign of anyone on the road. A few cars were parked some distance away on one of the side-streets.

If she'd read the map correctly, she should be a couple of hundred metres south-east of Kråkträsken.

She climbed down into the ditch and up onto the path. At first it was solid, but as soon as she left the grey daylight behind and the treetops had closed above her, her feet sank into wet earth. The vegetation consisted mainly of low pines and feeble birches; the ground was covered with brown pine needles and last year's scrub. The winter storms had taken their toll on the forest – one birch had snapped off completely, and there were plenty of broken branches.

A jogger ran past her without saying hello, a young woman with a ponytail wearing a turquoise tracksuit. She

183

seemed to be struggling. An elderly man with a dog came towards her from the other direction, and nodded to her as he passed.

This must be a popular path for joggers and dog-owners, during the day at least. She couldn't see any lights, so it wasn't illuminated at night. Maybe it was used as a ski-trail during the winter.

She stopped and listened.

The main sound was of dripping water, but there was a bird of some sort, she didn't know which. She could make out a rushing sound, possibly the treetops, or perhaps from the motorway leading to Stockholm.

She kept going carefully along the path. Pine cones crunched under her feet. A minute or so later she could see water between the tree-trunks, the first of the two small lakes known as Kråksträsken.

She knew from the map that the path passed between the lakes. She carried on for another hundred metres or so until she reached a footbridge that was submerged in water, brown with algae.

There was no way she could get across, not without thick-heeled wellington boots.

Instead she went round it and headed towards the second lake, then heard voices somewhere off to the north. She left the path and headed through the heather. A bright white light soon became visible between the trees.

The pine tree stood in isolation on a rocky outcrop, with a thick trunk and stubby crown. The lower branches were as thick as a man's thigh and the bark was gone; the wood had taken on the colour and structure of driftwood, grey and silky smooth.

The scene was harshly lit by lamps powered with huge batteries. Several plain-clothes officers were busy behind a large rock. Two uniformed police were stationed by the cordon, and one nodded to her – she recognized him from the crime scene on Silvervägen.

The dead man was hanging from the lowest branch, close to the trunk. Its thickness meant that his legs were bent at a ninety-degree angle at the knees, and his wrists were fastened to his ankles with duct tape. His head was hanging down, thrown back. *La Barra. The parrot's perch.* He was naked. The plastic bag that had been tied round his head had been removed. His eyes were wide-open and badly bloodshot, and his face was red with blood that had settled there. There was a grey film over the irises, but the eyes were probably blue. His mouth was covered with duct tape. His whole body, including his hair and face, was covered with honey, which had solidified in the cold. Ants had made a path up the tree-trunk and out onto the branch, and were crawling over the body, creeping in and out of the nose and ears.

'Is Lundqvist here?' she asked the uniformed officer she had recognized.

'He's with Henriksson from Forensics,' the man said, nodding towards the detectives behind the rock. Taking a wide detour around the pine, Nina went over to them.

Lundqvist came to meet her. 'I have to say, I'm a bit surprised to see you here,' he said.

'What do you know about him?' Nina asked, glancing towards the dead man.

Lundqvist took a deep breath, hesitated for a moment, then decided not to play games about jurisdiction. 'He's known as Kag,' he said. 'Karl Gustaf Evert Ekblad. Born on the west coast of Finland, in Vaasa, in the autumn of 1962. He moved to Sweden when he was three, with his parents, four brothers and sisters. He's spent the past decade sitting on various benches in Orminge shopping centre.'

'His clothes?'

'Assuming he wasn't running about naked in the forest, the perpetrator took them with him.'

'How long has he been hanging here?'

'His associates at the shopping centre say he was with them yesterday, so he must have ended up here some time during the night.'

Nina looked up at the treetops. She thought the rain had eased slightly. 'Was he one of your regulars?'

'No, actually,' Lundqvist said. 'Kag kept himself together. The last time we had to get involved was when he went on a serious bender eight years ago. He drank, but he wasn't a thief or a drug addict, and he wasn't violent.'

She turned back to the man hanging in the tree, a well-behaved tramp. 'Where did he live?'

'This is where it gets a bit odd,' Lundqvist said. 'Kag doesn't actually have any connection with Orminge. According to the files, he emigrated to Spain seven years ago.'

Nina spun round and stared at him.

'There hasn't been any official record of him in Sweden since then. He doesn't get sickness benefit, no social support, no pension,' Lundqvist went on.

'But he used to hang around Orminge shopping centre. You're sure about that?'

'Apparently he rented a room somewhere, as a lodger, but his friends don't know where. He bought his drink from the state-run off-licence, no moonshine or ethanol, and he got his lunch from the Orminge Grill every day. A thinbread roll with two hotdogs, dressing and prawn salad.'

'So he's got money,' Nina said.

Lundqvist sighed. 'Whatever it was he did, he did it to

the wrong people. They must have tortured him really badly. His nails have been pulled out, and this business with the ants is monstrous, isn't it?'

Nina raised her chin. 'Yes, it is,' she said.

Smearing torture victims with honey and putting them on anthills was a tried and tested method in Africa, especially Angola. Apart from the fact that it was incredibly painful, La Barra also meant that the blood circulation to the legs was cut off. If the victim survived, their injuries often led to gangrene and amputation.

'Lundqvist,' Henriksson called, from beside the body. 'Have you seen this?'

The police chief walked towards the pine tree and Nina followed him. They went round it to stand next to the forensics officer.

Something was sticking out of the victim's rectum, something pale, difficult to see.

'Shall I . . . ?'

Lundqvist nodded.

The forensics officer took hold of the object with his gloved hand and pulled.

It was a sheet of paper, folded and rolled up. A few ants were running across its sticky surface. Henriksson unfolded it. A yellow sun in a blue sky, flowers on the ground, an animal, two large figures and three small ones, all smiling, the children holding lollipops.

'A child's drawing,' Lundqvist said, bemused.

Mummy, Daddy, two brothers, a little sister, and a black dog.

'It's the Lerberg family,' Nina said.

*

'Are you quite sure that this is the reporter you want to involve in the matter?'

Chairman of the board Albert Wennergren was sitting in the visitor's chair, his body language demonstrating extreme scepticism. Anders Schyman couldn't tell if this was to do with the chair, the reporter, or perhaps the situation. 'If you have any better suggestions, I'm all ears,' he said.

That was unnecessary, but he couldn't help himself.

And Wennergren's doubts weren't without a certain justification, not least if you could see Annika Bengtzon trudging towards the glass box they were sitting in, her hair in a messy plait down her back, her trousers wet with rain. She stopped and knocked on the door, even though they were staring right at her.

'Come in,' Schyman said, then gestured towards the sofa in the corner.

He walked round the desk and sat down in the armchair. Albert Wennergren stayed where he was, looking uncomfortable, as Annika shut the door behind her and remained standing in the middle of the floor. 'What's happened?' she asked.

'Do you know Albert Wennergren?' Schyman asked.

The chairman of the board stood up and held out his hand. 'I heard that you're Valter's mentor,' he said, smiling slightly hesitantly.

Say something nice, now, for God's sake, Schyman thought, but, of course, she didn't.

'Is this going to take long? I've got a lot to do.'

'Have you read this morning's papers?' Schyman asked, trying to sound calm and business-like.

Annika turned to him. 'Are you referring to Lerberg or the Light of Truth?'

He gulped. 'The latter. And this is going to take a while. You're welcome to have a seat.'

She sat on the sofa, as Albert Wennergren turned his chair to face the little coffee-table.

'The blogger's managed to break through into the established media,' she said. 'You need to make some sort of comment.'

Schyman nodded. 'I've dug out the documents about the house purchase, my tax returns for the years in question, my contract of employment with Swedish Television . . .'

She twisted on the sofa and held up a hand to stop him, but he raised his voice and went on.

'. . . and I'm prepared to counter any accusation of bribery and lies. I can prove that—'

'Schyman,' she said. 'I said a comment, not a declaration of war.'

He fell silent. The chairman of the board folded his arms and turned to her. 'So what do you think he should say?'

Wonderful. Now they were talking about him in the third person, as if he wasn't actually there. As if he were a problem that needed to be solved, a puppet to be jerked into action and set loose in the columns of other papers.

'Think about it,' she said, actually turning to look at him. 'Don't make the same mistake politicians do when they're under pressure. You can't defend yourself point by point – you'll get bogged down in a mass of detail that will only give rise to more accusations and speculation.'

'That's not a bad point,' Albert Wennergren said. 'You can discuss the matter in more general terms, say that the accusations are entirely without foundation, then throw in the idea that the really interesting thing is the responsibility of publishers and the lawlessness of the internet.'

They couldn't be serious, Schyman thought. His life was

in danger, maybe not literally but metaphorically at least: someone was out to crush him and his professional reputation, and they thought he ought to enter an abstract debate about responsible publishing?

'After all, we often hide behind phrases like "it has been claimed in social media" and "such and such a blogger says", then write about personal attacks and rumours and cruel gossip all without so much as the blink of an eye,' Annika said. 'You could discuss that, couldn't you?'

Was she having him on?

'The point of any comment has to be to exonerate me,' he said.

The reporter looked at him and bit her lip. 'Do you remember Daniel Lee?' she said. 'The South Korean pop star?'

Schyman blinked several times. 'The one who did "Gangnam Style"?'

Annika half closed her eyes, the way she did when she heard something really stupid. 'This may come as a shock, but there's more than one musician in Korea. "Gangnam Style" was by Psy.'

Albert Wennergren leaned towards the coffee-table, suddenly animated. 'Daniel Lee, he was the singer in Epiq High, wasn't he?'

Annika nodded. 'The first Korean group to break the USA and have a number-one single.'

'I've read about him,' Wennergren said. 'He's extremely talented.'

'That's putting it mildly,' she said, turning to Schyman. 'In three and a half years he got a BA and an MA in English at Stanford University. He wrote short stories in English and Korean that became bestsellers, and he married a Korean film star.'

'That's right,' Wennergren said enthusiastically. 'And

then there was that rumour, what was it again? That he'd lied about his education?'

'A fifty-eight-year-old Korean in Chicago claimed that Daniel Lee's qualifications were fake, using pretty much the same strategy as the Light of Truth. His hate blog attracted loads of followers.'

Schyman kept his expression neutral: how the hell did Wennergren know all this? Was everyone else really listening to Korean pop music?

Annika looked right at him. 'Daniel Lee produced all his diplomas. His tutors and classmates all swore he was telling the truth, but none of it made any difference. Whenever he produced a document, they just said he'd forged it or stolen someone else's identity.'

'Exactly,' Wennergren said. 'The vilification was completely bizarre.'

'Daniel Lee couldn't go out without being attacked. He left his record company, his brother got fired from his job, his mother was called a whore and told to leave Korea.' She fell silent.

Schyman cleared his throat. 'I'm sorry,' he said. 'I – I don't remember Daniel Lee.'

'How about Barack Obama? Heard of him? There's still a huge group on the internet who claim he's not American. It doesn't matter how much proof of his birth he provides.'

He felt his chest getting tighter.

'You can't beat conspiracy theorists,' she said, in a low voice. 'Unless you can produce Viola Söderland, alive and kicking, on some live-broadcast news programme.'

Schyman nodded. 'That's what I wanted to talk to you about.'

She raised her eyebrows.

191

'I want to move you from normal reporting for a while so you can devote your time to investigating Viola Söderland,' he said.

She stared at him blankly. 'You mean find her? Alive? To prove that you were right?'

That wasn't quite how he would have put it but . . .

'You didn't manage to get hold of her at the time, when it all happened, but you think I can find her? Now? Eighteen years later?'

He could hear that it sounded a little . . . difficult.

She turned to Wennergren. 'What do you think of this idea?'

'It could be worth a try.'

Her eyes narrowed again. Wennergren looked at his watch and squirmed on his chair.

'So you think this is okay?' she said. 'Using the paper's resources in this way?'

Schyman's heart sank.

Wennergren smiled rather warily, then put his hands on the armrests and stood up. 'I'm very sorry,' he said, 'but I've got a meeting, so I shall have to leave you.' He turned to Schyman. 'Let's talk again this evening, shall we?' He faced Annika.

'I've heard so much about you – it was very nice to meet you,' he said.

She stood up and shook his hand, seeming surprised.

Schyman shut his eyes and rested his head on his hands.

Annika looked at her editor-in-chief and tried to figure out what was going on. He was hunched up with his head in his hands, and he looked terrible, scruffy and unshaven.

192

She thought she remembered him wearing the same clothes yesterday.

'What was Wennergren doing here?' she asked. 'One crazy blogger is hardly a matter for the board, is it?'

Schyman let out a deep sigh. He sat up and leaned back in his chair. 'We were supposed to be announcing my retirement as editor-in-chief on Friday,' he said. 'But that's out of the question now. The mob would think they'd won, and that would be my legacy. That I had to resign because of an accusation on a blog.'

'Retirement? Why would you want to do that? You've got several years left until you collect your pension, surely?'

He looked close to tears. 'I honestly don't think I can bear much more of this,' he said.

He shut his eyes. She gazed at him, in his dirty shirt, the most important boss in the Swedish media (well, print-media, anyway). He had huge power in the mass media but that didn't mean he was immune to his own weapons. Quite the reverse, perhaps. She'd seen it plenty of times: journalists were the most sensitive professional group going when it came to being called into question publicly, and the tougher the reporter, the more touchy they were. Criticizing a critic led to a chorus of indignation. Accusing an editor of impropriety was a thousand times worse than accusing a politician or a bank director of the same thing.

She shifted uncomfortably. He wanted to use her as a tool to clear his name, and evidently he had the blessing of the board to do so. When she thought about it, it was probably a sensible idea: allowing him to resign in disgrace would have had ominous consequences for the *Evening Post* as a brand.

She cleared her throat quietly. 'I've seen the documentary twice,' she said. 'First when it was broadcast on SVT –

I must have been in my late teens – and again at the College of Journalism. Have you got a copy of it?'

He sighed again. 'Sorry,' he said. 'I've looked, but I can't find it.'

She waited, but he didn't say any more. In the end she got up and fetched a pen from his desk, took a sheet of paper from his printer, put the paper on the coffee-table and sat on the edge of the sofa.

'Let's take it from the beginning,' she said. 'In the programme you declared that Viola Söderland disappeared of her own free will, didn't you? What was that based on? I want every last detail.'

He shrugged his shoulders reluctantly. '"Declared" is probably putting it too strongly . . .'

She decided to be patient.

'It was all incredibly well planned,' he said eventually. 'Viola spent at least a year preparing her flight.'

'How do you know that?'

'She changed her surname to her mother's maiden name a year before she disappeared, and started to use her middle name. Viola Söderland became Harriet Johansson.'

She wrote *Viola Söderland – Harriet Johansson*. 'That could have been just a coincidence?'

Schyman sat up straighter on his chair and shook his head. 'No,' he said. 'She started using her new identity. Among other things, she bought a used car, privately, as Harriet Johansson from a man in Skärholmen. She paid cash and offered to send in the change-of-ownership forms, but never did. That meant the purchase was never registered, the former owner still listed as the official owner of the vehicle.'

Annika made notes. 'I don't remember that. Was the original owner in the television programme?'

194

Schyman stroked his stubble. 'I met him three times and he stuck to his story. But he didn't want to be filmed. An actor read his statement.'

A shiver ran through her. 'An actor? You used actors in your documentary?' *Dear God, as long as the Light of Truth never finds out about that!*

'We filmed him from behind and had him speak in voiceover. It wasn't as if we were fabricating anything.'

No?

'Have you got his name? The seller, I mean.'

He sighed. 'Yes, somewhere. I can dig it out. I'll email it to you.'

She looked at him. His eyes were red-rimmed. 'What else?' she asked.

'She reported her passport lost at the same time as she changed her name. It was never actually destroyed, which meant that when she got hold of a new one, she had access to two passports. The old one looked valid as long as no one checked it against the Swedish Police Authority database . . .'

She made more notes, then looked up again at Schyman. He was scratching his stubble.

'She made a short visit to the Cayman Islands three weeks before she disappeared,' he said. 'The purpose of the trip was to bring back a large amount of cash in US dollars.'

'And how do we know that?'

'Her passport was stamped.'

'The real one?'

'Affirmative.'

'And how do you know what she was doing there?'

'What do you do in four hours in George Town?'

She stopped taking notes and sat there in silence, staring

at the sheet of paper. Something didn't make sense.

'She had a tailor alter the lining of her coat,' Schyman went on. 'He sewed in a number of pockets, sealed with zips. They were measured very carefully, four pockets measuring sixteen by seven centimetres, one fourteen by ten, and one seven by three.'

Annika wrote down the measurements. 'American dollar bills,' she said. 'They're almost sixteen centimetres by seven.'

Schyman nodded, slightly brighter now. 'Plus passport and car keys,' he said. 'She'd hidden a bag containing the rest of the cash in the luggage compartment of the car.'

'How deep were the pockets?' Annika asked.

'I don't know.'

Annika jotted down some quick calculations: if a dollar bill was 0.1 millimetres thick, and the highest value note one hundred dollars, then a one-millimetre thick bundle of notes was a thousand dollars. Four pockets could probably hold a bundle about ten centimetres thick.

She put the pen down and studied what she had written. 'So Viola had a car that no one knew was hers. She had a name that no one knew about. She had two passports and a tailor-made coat containing about a hundred thousand dollars.'

'Correct.'

She picked up the pen again and tapped it against her front teeth. 'And that car is the one captured in the picture,' she said.

The picture from an illegal surveillance camera at the petrol station outside Piteå was the only real evidence that Viola Söderland had fled, and that she was alive. Annika remembered it clearly: it had been reprinted everywhere in the aftermath of the TV documentary.

196

'It was that car, yes,' Schyman said.

Annika could see the photograph in front of her, very clearly, in spite of all the years that had passed: grainy black-and-white, a light-coloured car, a flash hitting the windscreen, a woman in a dark coat in the passenger seat and a fuzzy figure to the right of the picture. There was a pump to the right, slushy snow, and an out-of-focus rubbish bin in the foreground. The number-plate was clearly visible in the light of the flash.

'Critics claimed it wasn't Viola Söderland in the picture,' she said.

Schyman nodded. 'It was her.'

She looked at him carefully. There was definitely something that didn't make sense, something he wasn't telling her. 'What makes you say that?'

'I'm quite sure.'

'How did you get hold of the picture?'

'It's in the public domain. It was taken at that petrol station on the E4 in Norrbotten. The owner had got fed up of people driving off without paying and had set up his own surveillance camera overlooking the pump, without putting up any signs and without permission or a licence . . . He was prosecuted and convicted for breaking the law on camera surveillance, and that picture formed part of the evidence.'

She nodded. 'I remember the story, but how did you find the picture?'

'Like I said, it's in the public domain.'

She fixed him with her gaze. 'And how did you know where to look?'

He reached for a bottle of water on the table, poured himself a glass and drank it. 'How do you mean?'

'This picture was buried in the evidence of a humdrum

case in – what? – Luleå district court? And you just happened to stumble across it?'

He put the glass down. 'Piteå had its own court in those days. The petrol station was on the E4 in Håkansö, on the way to Luleå.'

She chewed the inside of her cheek. 'I'm sure you were a very talented reporter back in the day,' she said, 'but there's no way you could have found this on your own. You had a source. Someone who put you on the trail, sent you in the right direction . . .'

He didn't answer.

She looked at her notes. There wasn't much to go on. 'Names,' she said. 'The name of the man who sold the car to Harriet Johansson, and the names of the tailor and the owner of the petrol station?'

'You'll get them,' he said.

'And you aren't willing to let me have your source?'

She waited for him to reply.

'If it is the case,' he said eventually, 'that I have a source I've never revealed, then there's probably a very good reason why I've kept quiet.'

She nodded. 'Viola's colleagues, Pettersson and Witterfeldt, why are they so angry with you?'

Schyman let out a deep sigh. 'They were prosecuted in Viola's place. They've probably been waiting to have their revenge for years and, of course, Viola isn't around.'

'And there was never anything to suggest that Viola was the victim of any sort of crime?'

'The police found a broken vase by the front door in her home, apparently, and there was some footprint or fingerprint or strand of hair, something along those lines, which could never be traced. A neighbour had seen a man outside, but that never led anywhere.'

198

'What do I do about the Lerberg case?'

He seemed not to understand what she was talking about. Then he stood up. 'Write up what you've got. Berit will have to come back from Oslo a day early – she can take over. I'll tell Patrik that you're working on a special project from now on.'

'What about the trainee, Valter?'

'I'll have a word with him about confidentiality,' Schyman said.

'No need,' Annika said. 'I can do that.'

She stood up, clutching the sheet of notes, then moved to the desk and replaced Schyman's pen.

At the glass door she stopped. 'By the way,' she said, 'did you have dinner with Ingemar Lerberg at Edsbacka krog a couple of weeks before he resigned?'

Anders Schyman stared at her, eyes wide. 'What do you mean by that?'

She kept her gaze on him. 'Speaking of information in the public domain, if I managed to find the receipt, there's a chance that other people will too.'

All of a sudden he was angry. 'So what? We had dinner, he offered to pay, we were fellow Rotarians.' He sat down on the desk, hands on his thighs, combative now.

'Was that why we were the worst?' she asked. 'To prove that we weren't making any special allowances for him?'

'We were worst at everything in those days.'

She turned to leave.

'What happened to him?' she heard Schyman say behind her back. 'What happened to Daniel Lee?'

She stopped at the sliding door. 'He made a solo album that got to number two on the *Billboard* chart, and number one on iTunes in Canada and the USA. According to MTV, it was one of the five best debut albums in the world that year. And his detractors still claim that he's lying.' She closed the door behind her.

All children drew pictures, didn't they?

Lundqvist hadn't been impressed. He wanted to find out if the child's drawing had been produced by one of the Lerberg children before he linked the investigation on Silvervägen with the one at Kråkträsken. Nina couldn't recall seeing any children's drawings in the house, but they could have been tucked out of the way somewhere.

She made herself more comfortable at her desk. If she wanted information about Kag from the Spanish police, the protocol was clear: she needed to contact Interpol and get them to pass on any questions she wanted answered. She clicked her ballpoint pen. It was a long time since she had lived in Spain, but the years hadn't done anything to shrink Spanish bureaucracy, she was sure. If she went the formal route she could probably expect some sort of answer next month, possibly next year. And how should she formulate the question? What was she after? Her palms itched: picking up drunks and cleaning police cars had been much easier.

She pulled her laptop towards her, went onto Google and searched for 'karl gustaf evert ekblad', and got almost thirty thousand hits. A bit too broad, clearly . . . She limited the search to the exact name, and got no results at all.

She pushed the laptop away, got up and went to stand at the end of the desk, looking out at the courtyard. Had he been tortured where he was found? Henriksson couldn't say anything definite before he had conducted a thorough search of the site, but it didn't seem improbable. Regardless

200

of where the abuse and murder had taken place, the victim must have screamed with pain – might someone have heard something? The site was in the middle of the forest, and Ekblad's mouth was covered with duct tape, so it was unlikely that anyone would have been able to hear muffled cries at a distance of half a kilometre or so, over by the residential area. If their preliminary guesses were correct, Ekblad had died during the night, when it was pitch black and pouring with rain, so no one would have been out running. The scene was also a hundred metres from the path, which also happened to be waterlogged and impassable.

So how had Ekblad got there? Was he tricked into entering the forest, or was he forced?

And why?

She had to start by finding out who he was.

Nina went back to her chair, pulled her laptop towards her again, then tried 'buscar gente España' (search people Spain). There were a number of possibilities, most of them dating sites. She tried 'paginasblancas.es', the Spanish telephone book, and searched for 'karl gustaf evert ekblad' in every possible combination and in every province. No results.

He didn't appear to have been particularly visible in Spain either.

But where had he got his money from? He had been lodging somewhere for several years, he drank every day, and bought food from the Orminge Grill. He must have had some sort of income, and his fellow alcoholics had said he had a mobile phone.

She went onto another search site, einforma.com, which listed individuals and companies, typed the murdered man's name into yet another search box and pressed 'buscar'. The page took ages to load.

201

Empresas y Autónomos (5) Ejecutivos (1)
Karl Gustaf Evert Ekblad
Coicidencia por denominación principal
Provincia: Málaga

Her arms goose-pimpled.
Hello there, Kag.
She clicked the first result.

Denominación:	Karl Gustaf Evert Ekblad
Domicilio Social:	AVENIDA D . . .
Localidad:	29660 MARBELLA (Malága)
Forma Júridica:	Sociedad limitida
CIF:	B924
Actividad Informa:	Servicios relativos a la propiedad immobiliaria y a la propiedad industrial
CNAE 2009:	6810 Compraventa de bienes immobiliarios por cuenta propia
Objeto Social:	EL COMERCIO IMMOBILIARIO SIN LIMITACIÓN, Y EN SU CONSECUENCIA, LA ADQUISICIÓN, USO, ARRENDAMIENTO, VENTA, ENAJENACIÓN TRANSFORMACIÓN POR CUALQUIER TÍTULO DE BIENES INMUEBLES Y DERECHOS REALES SOBRE LOS MISMOS, ASÍ COMO . . .

It was a business. Kag had a business in Spain. Something to do with property and industrial rights of ownership, the acquisition of property, unlimited trade and acquisition, leasing, sales and rental . . .

An estate agency.

She clicked the address and found herself confronted

with a new form. To find out the details of Kag's business she had to register on the site and fill in all the marked fields.

No problem, she thought. As she filled in her name, telephone number and email address, the white boxes turned green until she reached the one labelled NIF/CIF, which required a Spanish ID number. She thought for a moment, then made one up that looked like it might be genuine, starting with a capital L followed by seven numbers, then a final letter. The box turned red. She tried a different number. Red. Another letter. Still red. She could feel frustration creeping in: she wasn't going to get hold of the information without a correct ID number.

She clicked back and looked at one of the other five results.

La importación y exportación de suelos de piedra y madera . . .

Import and export of stone and wooden flooring, sales and installation of kitchens and bathrooms, interior design and architectural services . . .

A building company.

She went back and checked the other results. They were presented in the same way, and gave her fragments of information. There were another two construction companies, and a building-supplies wholesale business.

So Kag ran five companies in Marbella while he was sitting on a bench in Orminge shopping centre.

She wasn't able to find out exactly where the companies were based. The only thing she could see was the postcode, which told her that all five were in the area inland from Puerto Banús on the Costa del Sol, in *el barrio* known as Nueva Andalucía. She couldn't get any further details about the ownership structure, nothing about the composition of the boards, or any detailed information about turnover and level of activity.

But all of this could be uncovered by the Spanish police in the blink of an eye.

She Googled 'policia nacional marbella', reached for her phone and dialled the number. She peered at her watch and hoped it wasn't siesta time. Mind you, the Spaniards had *aire acondicionado* these days. She had read somewhere that it had fundamentally changed Spanish society, more than any other single phenomenon. For the first time in the history of civilization they no longer took four-hour lunch breaks during the afternoon when the sun was at its hottest. Instead they switched on *el aire frío* and carried on working.

'*Policia nacional, buenas tardes. Cómo puedo ayudarle?*'

Nina shut her eyes and asked for the duty superintendent, the words pouring out of somewhere inside her brain that she hadn't known existed: her voice and intonation changed, assuming a lower tone. She had missed Spain: she missed the smells, the heat, the greenery.

The superintendent came on the line and she introduced herself, explained who she was and why she was calling. The police officer sounded surprised and rather sceptical.

'I know I'm not following official procedures here,' Nina said, 'but this is a very unpleasant case, extremely brutal, and it would be a huge help if I could have some assistance getting hold of information about the murder victim's businesses.'

She could hear a radio in the background, a jingle, *radio ora, tam-ta-dam, la lejor selection de música* . . .

'Excuse me,' the superintendent said, at the other end of the line. 'This might sound like a strange question, but are you from the Canary Islands?'

She took a deep breath and, to her astonishment, felt tears spring to her eyes. '*Si, señor, nací en Tenerife* . . .'

'Well, then,' the police chief said, 'why didn't you say so straight away? What was it you wanted help with?'

She gave him Kag's details and the names of the companies, and heard the superintendent's pen scratch as he made notes.

'No problem,' he said. 'I'll get back to you before the weekend. *Hasta pronto*.'

The dog had been killed using 'unusual methods'. That was what it said. It was an article in the local paper. I remember it well – it was at the bottom of the page on the left-hand side. It described how the perpetrators, two 'young boys', had caught the dog and bound its paws together. Then they had put fireworks in the dog's anus and ears, and set light to them.

I can still feel the boundless terror I experienced as I read those words. I can conjure it up at any moment, the incomprehensible disgust, the nausea, the disbelief: how could it be true?

The picture that illustrated the article showed a solemn uniformed police officer, Stefan Westermark. He was the officer who had caught the 'young boys'.

'You just can't understand how normal lads could do something like this,' he said in the caption.

The boys' excuse was that the dog was only a stray that hung around outside the blocks of flats in Fisksätra, shitting in sandpits.

When Ingemar finally agreed to get a pet, I knew exactly what sort of dog I wanted. Not some inbred puppy with a family tree, but a stray from a dogs' home. I wanted to do good – I wanted to make amends, make a difference.

But the dog I rescued from suffering and being put down doesn't like me.

It doesn't understand that I mean it well.

THURSDAY, 16 MAY

Suddenly Annika was lying awake and staring at the wall, fragments of the nightmare already dissolving into fog.

She had been back in Hälleforsnäs, the small town where she'd grown up, by the stream below the old works. Midges were buzzing about. Birgitta had been there, and Sven, her first boyfriend. He looked so sad.

'Can't you sleep?' Jimmy said.

She turned her head. He was half sitting up, reading his iPad. She realized she was thirsty and needed a pee. The disquiet of the dream faded and she took a deep breath, hearing the rain beat against the windowpane. Through the open bedroom door she thought she could make out the children's breathing as a chorus of warm gasps, but that must have been her imagination.

Birgitta still lived in Hälleforsnäs. She passed the stream by the works every day – she had walked those streets all her life, and now her daughter was doing the same. They visited Mum up at Tattarbacken and bought pizza from Maestro on Friday evenings. Then she saw the women of Solsidan in her mind's eye, with their coffee-machines and polished stone floors.

'What is normal life, really?' Annika whispered. 'The

calm, happy, normal thing that everyone else has, where is it?'

Jimmy lowered his iPad, which lit his face from below, and smiled. 'Every life is abnormal, an endless process of crisis management. If it's not something to do with the kids, it's health or work. The rest is just the gaps in between.'

She hauled herself up into a sitting position beside him, plumping up the pillows behind her back. 'Are you happy?'

He switched the pad off, his face vanished and his head became a dark silhouette against the pale wallpaper. He pulled her closer to him. 'Is it important? Are you?'

She snuggled up beside him, and noticed that he was a bit sweaty between the legs. She breathed in his scent. 'I don't know,' she said. 'I don't know if it's important. You're important, and the children, and belonging somewhere . . .'

He ran his hand over her taut stomach and kissed her.

'I need to pee,' she whispered, and disentangled herself from his arms.

By the time she got back to the bedroom he was already asleep.

*

I went looking for Mum.

Naturally I heard what the grown-ups said, that she was gone, that she'd gone home to God, but I thought she must have left me something, that she would find a way to communicate with me, to let me know that everything was all right, that it was just a terrible mistake. The bird on the windowsill looked at me with Mum's bright eyes. Perhaps it flew between the sky and Heaven. (The bird version of Mum didn't have her tired, dead eyes after the chemotherapy, but the real ones, the ones she had when she still had hair.) Maybe she was hiding among the weeds in the field down towards the porcelain factory . . . Maybe she was in the wind.

But she never spoke.

I waited and waited and waited. I was so clever and alert and focused. I really was prepared: at night I would look out of the window until dawn to make sure I didn't miss her, but she let me down, night after night after night.

In the end I turned my back and stopped longing.

I burned the photograph album containing all the pictures from her youth on a mound of stones at the edge of the forest.

*

Johansson was sitting in the meeting room on the eighth floor, crying, when Nina got there. No one else had arrived, and she stopped in the doorway, unsure whether to step inside or walk away. He noticed her presence, coughed and blew his nose. 'Come in,' he said. 'I didn't mean to startle you.'

She stayed where she was. 'How are you doing?' she asked cautiously.

He shrugged his broad shoulders. 'I'm not too bad,' he said shakily. 'Coffee?' He held up a flask and a mug.

She didn't really drink much coffee – at home she always made tea – but she stepped into the room and nodded. 'Thanks, I'd love some.'

He poured her a mug and passed it to her. 'Sugar and milk?'

'Thanks, it's fine as it is.'

Silence descended. Nina sat on a chair a suitable distance

away from him and let the mug warm her hands. 'Why are you so sad?' she asked quietly.

He sat and thought for a while. 'Is it possible to be anything else?' he said eventually. 'Considering the way the world looks?'

'Do you mean in general terms, or from our perspective here at work?' Nina asked warily. She heard how bureaucratic the question sounded. The chair suddenly felt uncomfortable, and she shifted position.

Johansson evidently took the question seriously because his brow furrowed as he pondered his response. 'Both, actually,' he replied. 'Or, rather, they're connected, aren't they, our work and the reality of the world out there? They're two aspects of the same thing, the whole, and the splinters that we work with.' He blew his nose again. 'But of course it feels good to make a contribution. That's why I joined the police. Well, I'm sure you understand that – you're a police officer too.'

Nina drank some coffee. How much did he really know about her? How much were people told when a new member of staff was employed? 'Have you always worked at National Crime?' she asked, hoping she didn't sound too nosy.

He shook his head. 'I was transferred here after the accident.' He reached for a bundle of papers and began to sort through them.

Nina took a few deep breaths. 'The accident?'

Johansson looked surprised, as if the whole world had been kept updated about his life story. 'Yes, I got shot in the leg during a training exercise. Just a flesh wound. I was in the rapid response unit back then, but it went horribly wrong. The bullet hit me in the thigh and it looked like I was going to bleed to death, but one of the guys in the group had medical training. He tied a tourniquet, and, well . . .' He carried on sorting his documents. 'I got a bit sensitive after that. Over-sensitive, according to my kids, but that's not the sort of thing doctors diagnose.'

Lamia trotted into the room with her laptop in her arms. 'Yep, that's the way it is,' she said. 'Johansson's a former tough guy who got shot and lost his edge.' She went over to the big man and kissed his cheek. Johansson smiled shyly at her, and she turned to Nina. 'How are you getting on? Do you feel at home here yet?'

Nina had never felt at home anywhere, and refrained from answering.

The blonde smiled and patted her arm, then sat down in her usual place and opened her computer. 'Q's got an important visitor from Rosenbad so we're going to have to look after ourselves today. They might call in a bit later.'

Nina's skin burned where Lamia had touched it, and she rubbed her arm.

Lamia looked up at them. 'How are we going to do this? Who wants to start?'

Johansson distributed his papers: printouts of the report from the Nacka Police. It included an interview with Ingemar Lerberg's staff: two secretaries, Märta Hillevi Brynolfsson and Solana Nikita Levinsky, the results of their door-to-door inquiries and a thorough analysis of Lerberg's political activities. It also contained an account of the as yet fruitless search for the person who had notified the emergency services.

Nina handed round a summary of the murder at Kråkträsken. Lamia was clutching some printouts, but hadn't made copies of them.

'The cordon at the crime scene on Silvervägen has been lifted,' Johansson said. 'We've got access to a set of keys

213

if anyone wants to go and take a look. The second round of door-to-door inquiries in the area didn't come up with anything. There's no post-mortem report for the victim at Kråkträsken yet, but they've found fragments of skin under one fingernail so it might be possible to get some DNA. The staff at Lerberg's business, Hillevi and Solana, have been questioned several times. But you can read that for yourselves.'

Nina picked up the papers eagerly. She liked transcriptions of interviews, the spontaneous and fragmentary dialogue – they became film scenes in her head. She could sense the anxiety of the two employees.

> *Lead interviewer*: This new client, what was the name again? Ah, here it is, ASCL . . .
> *Solana*: Asia Shipping Container Lines.
> *LI*: Yes, Asia Shipping.
> *S*: Ingemar negotiated the contract. It's only a trial to begin with, but it'll give us one hell of a boost . . .
> *LI*: Have you met the client?
> *S*: Who, me? God, no! I look after the invoices. But once the contract is up and running we usually get a free-lancer to do the invoices and I become office manager. I've been doing this for ages now.

Nina leafed through the document, reading random extracts.

> *Lead interviewer*: Have any threats been received?
> *Hillevi*: Threats?
> *LI*: Towards Ingemar or the company, anything you're aware of?
> *H*: No. Not . . . no.

214

LI: The three big clients, the shipping companies from Panama and those other countries, do you have any contact with them?

H: Me? No, not me.

LI: Have they ever expressed any dissatisfaction with the way your company has managed things?

H: How do you mean?

The text woke memories of the monotonous routine of work in Katarina District, all the interviews she had conducted and typed up, all the weapon-cleaning and reports to fill in. The nights in patrol car 1617 with its hard suspension, the people she took in for questioning, who didn't want to talk, the smells at the bottom of the food chain, bad coffee and acid reflux.

Lead interviewer: Have you noticed any change in mood recently?

Solana: In Ingemar, you mean? No. Should I have?

LI: I was wondering if you might.

S: I mean, I've been with him so long, ages really. I was working for him back when he was in Parliament, when Ingemar was a Member of Parliament, I mean, and . . . well, he's been the same cheerful person the whole time. Well, maybe not when those horrible things were being written about him, that was really awful.

LI: Has anything happened that . . . ?

S: He didn't talk so much after all those articles, actually. He seemed a bit more cagey around strangers. Not towards me, of course, we go way back. But he got more cautious. Different. Towards other people, I mean.

215

'One question,' Lamia said, waving one of Nina's printouts.

Nina straightened her back, ready to answer.

'Why was he called Kag?'

Nina blinked. Lamia waited expectantly for a reply.

'I don't actually know. Karl Gustav, KG, that probably ended up as Kag . . .'

Lamia made a note.

'This child's drawing,' Johansson said, hunched over a different printout. 'Was it done by one of the Lerbergs?'

'That hasn't been confirmed,' Nina said. 'The crayons don't match those found in the house, but it could have been drawn at a friend's or at school.'

Nina was aware that the connection between the crimes was tenuous. One happened indoors, the other outside. In one the victim had died, in the other he survived. One was dressed, the other naked. The methods were different. Lerberg was an establishment figure, Kag a down-and-out.

'The excessive violence is the connection between the crimes,' she said. 'And it's not subtle. We're supposed to know. Both the acts themselves and the drawing are messages.'

'Who for? Us?' Lamia asked.

'Not necessarily,' Nina said.

Lamia looked at both her and Johansson. 'Is it my turn now?' She didn't wait for confirmation, just sat up straight and started. 'There haven't been any transactions in any known bank accounts since Wednesday last week. No matches at any passport checks or on any passenger lists in the past twenty-four hours, and no ransom demand.'

'Are we talking about Nora now?' Nina wondered.

'She adopted her maiden name a year ago. Until then she was just Lerberg. Mrs Andersson Lerberg has a personal Visa card, and a Mastercard from her husband's company. Statements from her personal account show repeat purchases. Every Thursday she goes shopping at ICA Maxi on Per Hallströms väg in Nacka. The Maxi shops are those really big ones. Then there's ICA Kvantum, which sounds like it ought to be bigger but isn't. Then there's ICA Supermarket and ICA Nära as well . . .'

'Perhaps we could skip the size of ICA's various stores,' Johansson said amiably.

Lamia smiled. 'Okay. Nora used to top up with eggs and milk and other fresh groceries at the ICA Supermarket on Torggatan in Saltsjöbaden twice a week on average – that's the smaller sort of store, but not the smallest. She gets petrol from Statoil on Solsidevägen and at weekends she buys fresh bread from Kringelgården bakery up in Igelboda. She uses Classic Dry-cleaning and Tailoring on Laxgatan in Saltsjöbaden – they repair shoes and cut keys as well – apart from a couple of occasions when she went to Royal Tailoring on Östermalmstorg in the centre of Stockholm. A piano-tuner from Vaxholm takes care of her piano each spring and autumn. She goes to Ikea before Christmas, Easter and midsummer, and on her last visit she spent a hundred and ninety-two kronor—'

'No plane tickets?' Nina asked.

'No travel at all. Apart from petrol. For the car.'

'Nothing to Switzerland on the third of May, then?'

Commissioner Q walked into the meeting room, accompanied by a blond man so handsome that Nina caught her breath.

'So,' Q said, 'this is the group working on the Lerberg case – Arne Johansson, Lamia Regnard and Nina Hoffman.' He gestured towards each of them as he introduced them. Lamia's eyes twinkled like stars at the blond man.

'This is Thomas Samuelsson, the government's special investigator into money-laundering and economic crime.'

Nina gasped. Dear God! He must be Annika Bengtzon's husband, or were they actually divorced now? Nina had never met him, but Annika had talked about him. He worked for the government as a researcher – at least, he had four years ago: could there be two with the same name?

The man walked straight over to Nina and introduced himself. His handshake was warm and strong. 'Nice to meet you,' he said. His eyes looked right into hers: they were pale, almost translucent.

'Bearing in mind our victim out at Kråkträsken, I thought it would be in order for us to get an update on the situation down on the Costa del Sol in Spain,' Q went on.

Lamia fluttered her eyelashes when the blond man shook her hand. Even Johansson looked happier.

But Annika Bengtzon's husband had had one hand chopped off when he was kidnapped in Somalia, and this man had two. She had just shaken the right, and the left held a coat and an expensive leather briefcase.

'I assume you're aware of the basics of how money-laundering works,' Thomas Samuelsson said, sitting down on one of the desks with his briefcase beside him, one foot firmly on the floor, the other dangling in the air. He was wearing an expensive suit with a simple T-shirt underneath, which gave him a casual but sophisticated air.

Nina saw both Lamia and Johansson nod: yes, they were very familiar with money-laundering.

'The problem for international crime syndicates isn't manufacturing weapons or drugs, smuggling goods or finding a market for them. It's cleaning up the dirty money so that it can be used. Building a network, or smurfing, as it's known in bank jargon, is the big bottleneck in the flow

218

of illegal money. A good smurf is worth his weight in gold to a crime syndicate.'

He smiled at Nina.

'As far as Spain is concerned, there's been a noticeable deterioration in the conditions for international crime syndicates in recent years, specifically on the Costa del Sol,' he went on. 'The Spanish government has taken a number of steps to put a stop to such transactions. On the thirty-first of October 2012, for instance, new fraud legislation came into force, limiting cash payments between companies to two and a half thousand euros. And early in 2013 they finally permitted greater scrutiny of financial institutions, under a law that has existed since 2010 but which hadn't previously been implemented.'

Lamia shifted in her chair, making her skirt slide up her thigh, but apparently Thomas Samuelsson didn't notice.

'Of course, we have to remember that the financial crisis has hit everyone. Spain's economic development since the millennium was based upon rapid expansion of the construction sector. That was also where a lot of the laundered money was processed, so when the industry suffered a total collapse, the criminal machinery developed problems.'

Nina got it. The euro crisis meant Kag had run into trouble – or, rather, the companies he fronted had.

Johansson leaned forward. 'What other effects has the crisis had? Has drug use in Spain gone down, for instance?' He sounded genuinely interested. Nina had never heard him sound so enthusiastic before.

Samuelsson adjusted the creases in his trousers. 'It's still the biggest market in Europe, but it's a very good question. It is possible to detect a slight reduction and . . .'

Q stepped in front of her, blocking her view of the man. Nina had to stop herself craning her neck to look over his shoulder. 'Nacka have found Kag's landlord,' he said quietly. 'I thought perhaps you might like to drive out there and have a word with him.'

'I'll go as soon as we're finished here,' she said.

Q cast a glance at the blond man and smiled.

Anders Schyman had decided to hit back, hard and with force. He devoted six pages of the print edition of the paper to his own defence, with photographs, facsimiles and detailed explanations, countering the accusations on the Light of Truth, or the Lie of Truth as the headline writer so cleverly called it.

Engage in some sort of debate about responsible publishing?

Yeah, right!

This was how bullies, online trolls and conspiracy theorists should be dealt with, full blast: hit them with their own arguments, ram their so-called facts down their throats.

He had published his contract of employment with Swedish Television (he most certainly wasn't freelance!), his tax returns for the years when the documentary was broadcast, its original screening and the repeat (he hadn't earned millions in those years when he was a television reporter on state wages), and his thirty-one-year-old contract for the house. All his other tax returns were available for download as a PDF for anyone who was interested. There was also a picture of their house (luxury villa?), the view from their terrace (not a glimpse of sea as far as the eye could see!), and, just to be sure, pictures of his and his wife's cars (an ordinary Saab and a Volvo).

220

The intercom burst into life. It was from Reception. 'Anders? Can you take a call from a news agency? It's about the reports filed with the police.'

He stared at the intercom. 'Reports filed with the police?'

The loudspeaker clicked.

'Anders Schyman?'

It was a male voice. He picked up the receiver.

'What's this about?' he asked curtly.

'Hello, I'm Anders Burtner, from the TT news agency. I was wondering if you wanted to comment on the accusations filed against you with the police?'

He stared at his shelves, the reference books he kept going back to, again and again, his lodestars in the murky world of tabloid journalism: a dog-eared copy of Günter Wallraff's *Lowest of the Low* from 1985, Jan Guillou and Göran Skytte's *Stories from the New World*, and many editions of the Publicists' Association yearbook.

'What accusations?' he said.

'You haven't heard about—'

'No,' he interrupted.

Show strength and solidity. The one who stands firmest wins.

The agency reporter took a deep breath. 'You've been reported to the police for fraud and document forgery because the contract for your house is a fake,' the reporter said. 'The tax office will be investigating your tax returns for the past ten years. My source tells me that unfortunately they can't go back any further than that. Also, you've been reported to the National Board for Consumer Complaints . . .'

Schyman sank onto his chair and stared at the wall in front of him.

'. . . the Broadcasting Commission, and the Parliamentary Ombudsman . . .'

'What a colossal waste of taxpayers' money,' he said. 'This is all bollocks.'

'Bollocks?'

'None of this is going to lead anywhere – anyone can see that.'

'So your comment is that this is bollocks?'

'You bet it fucking is,' he said, and hung up.

He got up and walked round the room three times.

That had told him, the bastard.

Then he stopped and stared at his bookshelves. Günter Wallraff had faced huge criticism and hostility throughout his career. He had been tortured by the Greek police, then imprisoned and falsely accused of being a Stasi collaborator. Jan Guillou had uncovered the Social Democrats' policy of spying on their own, and was also imprisoned and falsely accused of being a KGB agent. That was the sort of thing that happened to controversial reporters. They had to stand up to the blows of the establishment. It went with the job.

A feeling of calm spread through him.

The Light of Truth was hardly representative of the establishment. Online trolls were insignificant, after all, people with no voice, the people he was supposed to protect.

Anxiety and self-doubt followed.

Perhaps he hadn't handled that interview with the news-agency reporter particularly well.

He looked at the phone, hesitated for a moment, then lifted the receiver and dialled zero for Reception. 'I won't be taking any more calls today.'

Despair struck.

What had he done?

'Bollocks'?

Oh, God, he'd have hell to pay for that.

Kag's landlord was a Hans Larsén, resident at Valövägen 73, just a few hundred metres from the patch of forest that led to Kråkträsken. Nina parked on the road in front of the house, got out of her car and locked it. She couldn't see the footpath from there.

The building that had been Kag's home was characteristic of the area: small, one storey, with a flat roof. Several of the neighbouring houses had been extended or modernized over the decades, and had acquired sloping roofs or concrete cladding, but not number seventy-three. The dark wooden panelling needed varnishing, the mailbox was crooked, and there were no flowerbeds. A pair of greyish-white curtains hung in the big picture window, stopping anyone seeing in.

Hans Larsén lacked either the interest or the money to bother with home maintenance and decoration.

He opened the front door as soon as Nina got out of the car. 'Are you from National Crime?'

She shook his hand and introduced herself. The man nodded: he was a former fireman, which practically made them colleagues, he said. Nina didn't agree, but let it go.

'Your colleagues from Nacka have been here and emptied his room,' Hans Larsén said. 'They've put a no-entry sign on the door. How long will that have to stay there?'

'I'm sure they'll let you know,' Nina said.

He had prepared coffee, put shop-bought buns in a basket on the table, and pottered about between the stove and the kitchen table, getting out napkins and sugar-lumps.

'It's a terrible business,' he said, glancing at Nina.

His hands shook slightly as he poured the coffee. Nina studied him discreetly. He was in his seventies, clean-shaven, well dressed.

'All those years you serve other people,' Hans Larsén said. 'You get up in the middle of the night and risk your life to save other people from burning buildings, you move gas canisters out of harm's way at huge personal risk, you pull people out of crashed cars, dear God, all the things you do, but you never for a minute believe that your own tenant will be murdered.'

'Had Karl Gustaf lived here long?' Nina asked.

Hans Larsén turned his back on her and fiddled with something on the worktop. 'Not very,' he said evasively.

Nina sat in silence for a while. 'There's no need to worry,' she said eventually. 'I don't care what sort of arrangement you and Kag had, I just want to find out who killed him.'

Hans Larsén swung round and glared at her. 'You surely don't think that – that Kag and I . . .'

Nina couldn't help smiling.

The man reddened. 'No, well . . . It wasn't like that.'

She leaned across the table. 'Hans,' she said, 'I'm not going to report you to the tax office. I don't care if you didn't declare the income from the rent in your tax return.'

Hans Larsén exhaled on a long sigh of relief. He sat down at the table, dropped two lumps of sugar into his cup of coffee and stirred hard. 'I'm grateful to you,' he said. 'Kag was my lodger. He's lived here for several years, with his own entrance and bathroom. He never disturbed me. He wasn't allowed to bring his drinking buddies back here, and he never did.'

'Several years, you said. How many?'

Hans Larsén looked up at the ceiling. 'Let's see now, time really does fly – it'll be seven years this summer.'

'How much rent did he pay you?'

A hesitant glance. 'Four thousand five hundred, but that included heat and water, and internet access.'

'Did he use the internet much?'

Hans Larsén became defensive again. 'Not really. He didn't have a computer of his own. But he had a new phone, one of those smart ones, and could surf the net on that. I've got wireless, of course.'

This last remark was made with a degree of pride.

'Did you get the impression that he had a lot of money?'

Hans Larsén nodded. 'Oh, yes – well, I don't know about a lot. Who has a lot of money these days, apart from bankers? But he always paid the rent on time, and he had a fridge of his own in his room where he kept bread and butter, beer and tomatoes. Do you want to see it?'

Evidently Hans Larsén had made a habit of visiting his lodger's room and checking the contents of his fridge.

'Is there anything left to look at?'

'The bed and the chest of drawers.'

'I'll respect my colleagues' no-entry sign,' she said.

The man seemed suddenly anxious. 'It's going to be tricky making ends meet now – it's a big loss of income. Is there any sort of social security that covers things like this, do you know?'

He was pushing his luck now, Nina thought. He hadn't declared seven years' worth of rental income to the tax office, and now he wanted compensation because his illegal funds had dried up.

Her mobile started to vibrate in her inside pocket. 'That would be tricky,' she said, pulling her phone out. 'You'll probably have to find another lodger.' She looked at the screen: Södermalm Hospital. 'I'm afraid I've got to take this call,' she said, standing up.

She hurried out onto the front step, closing the door behind her. 'Thanks for calling,' she said to Dr Kararei.

'It's not good news,' the doctor said. 'There's been a rapid deterioration in Ingemar Lerberg's condition overnight. He's suffered a massive embolism caused by septicaemia, which probably stems from the infections in the soles of his feet. It's taken hold of his lungs and he's back on the ventilator.'

Nina glanced down the street. In the background she could see the forest. Deep among the trees lay Kråkträsken. 'What does the embolism mean?'

'His blood coagulation system has collapsed. He's got microscopic blood clots all over his body. We can probably deal with the infection, and we're giving him anticoagulation treatment to deal with the embolism, but we don't know if his brain has been affected.'

Hans Larsén opened the curtains and peered at her through the window. She turned her back on him pointedly. 'What's the prognosis? When do you think we'll be able to question him again?'

There was silence for a few seconds.

'Perhaps I'm not expressing myself clearly enough,' Dr Kararei said. 'We can't be sure that he's going to regain consciousness again, ever.'

She felt a chill in her gut, spreading slowly through her chest. The wind grabbed at her hair and made her eyes water. 'Did he say anything else yesterday? Anything about the perpetrators, or his wife?'

'He's been unconscious since you left the ward yesterday morning.'

Nina thanked him and ended the call, then went back in

226

to Hans Larsén. She stopped in the kitchen doorway. 'It's very important that you think about this carefully and tell me the truth,' she said. 'Did Karl Gustaf ever mention a man called Ingemar? Ingemar Lerberg?'

Hans Larsén stared at her with alarm. 'Ingemar? No, that's the sort of name you'd remember.'

'Are you quite sure? You've never heard Kag talk about an Ingemar Lerberg?'

Hans Larsén's eyes widened. 'Isn't that the politician who got beaten up?'

'What about Nora? Nora Lerberg?'

The man shook his head. 'Never.'

'Where did Kag get his money from?'

Hans Larsén sank down at the table. 'You don't ask people that sort of thing.'

'How did he pay the rent?'

'Cash. He didn't have a bank account.'

'And you're quite sure about that?'

He nodded.

She put her mobile back into her pocket, which also contained the keys to the Lerberg family's home on Silvervägen.

She thanked him for the coffee and hurried out to the car.

'Seriously?' Valter said dubiously. 'She's been gone twenty years, and Anders Schyman wants us to find her?'

'Seriously,' Annika said. She understood his scepticism. To Valter, Viola Söderland's disappearance might as well have happened in the Middle Ages. He had been a baby when she'd gone missing – he had no way of relating to the event, and had never heard of Golden Spire. He had

227

dutifully written down the facts she had presented to him: the change of name, the passport, the trip to the Cayman Islands, the car, the tailor, the picture from the petrol station.

'But how's this going to work?' he asked. 'After all, no one's seen her since she vanished.'

'If she's alive, there'll be people who see her every day,' Annika said.

They were sitting in their usual places in the newsroom. Patrik Nilsson hadn't tried to send them out on some pointless task all morning so Schyman must have told him they were engaged in an important project.

'I think we should work backwards,' Annika said. 'Take the last lead first.'

'The owner of the petrol station,' Valter said.

'There were several petrol stations in Håkansö, outside Piteå, in the early 1990s,' Annika said. 'This one was a Mobil but it closed down ages ago. The owner wasn't named in the documentary, but his name is Ulf Hedström. Can you look him up while I deal with the tailor?'

Valter pulled his laptop towards him and began typing.

The shop that had made the special lining for Viola's coat was called Västgård's Dry-cleaning and Key-cutting, and was based in Solna, just outside Stockholm. The owner, Björn Västgård, had done the work himself. He had appeared in the programme – Annika remembered a cheerful, red-haired man with a broad chest and strong arms. He was clearly excited about being on television, and – with an appropriately conspiratorial air – went into great detail about the peculiar job, actually the most peculiar he had ever had, sewing hidden pockets into the lining of an ordinary coat.

He couldn't have led a particularly exciting life, Annika

228

mused, as she typed into Google. 'Västgård's Dry-cleaning and Key-cutting' didn't come up with anything – it had probably changed name and owner. 'Björn Västgård' gave 412 results, but none had anything to do with dry-cleaning or tailoring. She went into the database covering the population of the whole country and restricted the search criteria: four matches, much more manageable. The red-haired Björn Västgård ought to be in his sixties now, which fitted two of the men on the list, one in Spånga and one in Järfalla.

She called the one in Spånga first and his wife answered. 'Björn's working in Norway at the moment,' she said. 'He'll be home next Friday.' No, he had never worked as a tailor in Solna.

She moved on and tried the mobile number of Björn Västgård in Järfalla. He answered on the second ring, and sounded loud and enthusiastic. Yes, he had run a dry-cleaning business in Solna in the 1990s. He was happy to talk to the *Evening Post*. He was working as a delivery driver, these days. Maybe they could meet for a coffee somewhere. He suggested the café next to the metro station out in Mälarhöjden in three-quarters of an hour.

Annika hung up and wondered how Valter was getting on. He looked slightly manic: his hair was sticking straight up and he had sweat on his forehead.

'There are loads of Ulf Hedströms,' he said.

'If you try the population register you can see where in Sweden they are. Focus on the ones up in Norrbotten. When you click the names you'll be able to see how old the person is.'

'Brilliant.'

She sighed: what did they teach them at college?

'There's a man who's going to be sixty-six on Monday,'

he said. 'Lives on Ankarskatavägen in Piteå. Could he be the one?'

'Why don't you call him and ask?' Annika said.

He hesitated. 'What shall I say? That we're looking for Viola Söderland?'

'Maybe not directly,' Annika said. 'Do you want me to try?'

He clicked at his computer and a phone number appeared on Annika's screen. She dialled the number and a woman answered, 'Hedström,' in a weak voice.

'Good morning,' Annika said cheerfully. 'My name's Annika Bengtzon, and I'm calling from the *Evening Post*. I was wondering if I could speak to the Ulf Hedström who ran the Mobil petrol station in Håkansö in the 1990s. Have I got the right number?'

Annika could hear the woman's strained breathing as a recurrent crackle on the line. 'I know it's his birthday on Monday,' she said, 'so it's probably not too early to wish him many happy returns, but if he's not too busy doing—'

The woman started to cry. 'Why can't you just leave us alone?' she shouted.

Annika held the phone away from her ear. 'Sorry?' she said.

'Ulf's dead, and you keep phoning and phoning,' she wailed. 'What do you want?'

Valter leaned forward.

'Oh,' Annika said, 'I'm so sorry. I didn't know that he was dead. When did it happen?'

Valter slapped a hand to his forehead.

'Last month,' the woman sobbed. 'What do you want?'

'I haven't called before,' Annika said. 'There must be some misunderstanding. What did he die of?'

'It was his prostate. So you're not the one who's been

230

calling? From that blog?' She blew her nose.

'No,' Annika said. 'I'm calling from the *Evening Post*, the newspaper. Has a blogger been trying to contact Ulf?'

'Several times, while he was in the hospice in Sunderbyn. Is it about that picture? The one of that rich bitch?'

Yes, Annika had to admit that it was.

The woman sounded angry now. 'He dismantled the camera and took his punishment. What more could he have done?'

Annika closed her eyes. This was the crux of the story: how could Schyman have known about that picture? A tiny fragment of evidence in a preliminary investigation that had led to a trial and conviction in a little district court in Norrbotten? And how had the picture ended up with the police?

'How did Ulf get caught for setting up that camera?' she said.

The woman on the phone let out a deep sigh. 'Someone grassed. Ulf thought it was one of the people who used to steal petrol, but I have my own theories. It was one of the other petrol-station owners, someone who wanted to get rid of the competition.'

'So someone called the police and tipped them off about the camera?' Annika said. 'And you don't know who?'

'No. They said it was anonymous.'

'Do you know when they received the tip-off?'

'In September that year. The rich bitch drove past in the middle of the night, and the police were there the next morning. She was on the last picture.'

'Have you heard from Viola Söderland at all since that picture was taken?' Annika asked. 'Do you know if she visited the petrol station on any other occasion?'

'Never,' the woman said. They hadn't heard a thing,

apart from that blogger who wouldn't stop ringing. Annika thanked her, expressed her condolences once more, and apologized for intruding at such a difficult time.

'Bloody hell, that was rough,' Valter said, once she'd hung up.

'That's just what happens sometimes,' Annika said. 'There's always a bit of a delay with official records so we had no way of knowing he was dead.' She stood up and put on her coat. 'Do you fancy coming out to the suburbs for coffee?'

They picked up one of the paper's cars and headed south on the E4. It wasn't raining hard enough for Annika to have the windscreen wipers on, but too much for her not to use them. She left them on, and had to put up with the squeak of rubber on glass.

'I've been thinking about Gustaf Holmerud,' Valter said.

Annika glanced at him. 'Having trouble letting go?'

'I checked the archive. The rest of the media wrote about him for a while, and quoted us, but then they stopped. Why?'

Annika noted that he said 'us' when referring to the *Evening Post*, and took that as a good sign. 'We launched him,' she said. 'He was our creation.'

Valter goggled at her.

'Last autumn five women were stabbed to death in the Stockholm region over a fairly short period of time,' she said. 'Murders of women by their partners aren't regarded as proper murders in the media, often only referred to in passing, pretty much like deaths from drink-driving or genocide in Africa. But I started to tease Nilsson. "Maybe it wasn't their partners. What if you're missing a serial killer?" He took me at my word. He started to push the theory of a psychopathic serial killer in the Stockholm suburbs as hard news, and soon the police were forced to comment. Then that nutter turned up and claimed responsibility for everything.'

'But he's been convicted of five murders,' Valter said. 'Are you saying he's innocent?'

'Not entirely. He probably murdered Lena, a forty-two-year-old mother of two from Sätra. They'd had a brief relationship last summer, until she ended it. I think the rest of the media have figured out that Holmerud is a mythomaniac. They're trying to distance themselves from the whole story, but the *Evening Post* can't do that because that would mean admitting our mistake.'

Valter was clearly bewildered. 'But,' he said, 'why didn't Holmerud's lawyer do anything?'

'The lawyer wasn't there to get his client off, he was there to speak for him.'

'But how could the court fall for it if he wasn't guilty?'

'He had detailed knowledge of one of the murders – Lena's. He read up about the others – all the facts were in the media, after all. The police and the court put together reconstructions of the crime scenes, and our man was very convincing. Maybe not worth an Oscar, but pretty close. He was convicted on the basis of his own confession, plus the knife he used to kill Lena. Okay, where's this café?'

Valter tapped on his mobile. 'Number one Slättgårdsvägen. You need to turn off at the next junction.'

Annika left the motorway and entered a grey suburban paradise of cramped plots and mix-and-match houses typical of the era they were built, much like Silvervägen in Saltsjöbaden: 1920s villas with hipped roofs and boxy outbuildings, 1940s houses with panelled façades, breeze-block constructions from the turn of the century.

Suddenly she heard Anne Snapphane's voice inside her head. *This is where happiness has made its home.* Her reaction was almost physical, a kick in the gut. Where on earth had that come from? She brushed the hair off her face and took a deep breath. Sometimes she really did miss Anne, her pungent view of life and the world, her refreshing disregard for convention. Annika had always known that she was a bit unhinged – her intense ambition to become famous had been just one of the symptoms, but in the end their friendship had stopped working. Anne had embarked on a sort of vendetta against Annika on the internet. From her new position as a reporter for the gossip website mediatime, Anne had taken every opportunity to snipe at her.

She shook off the unsettling feeling of loneliness and parked in front of the entrance to Mälarhöjden metro station.

The café was on the ground floor of a block of 1940s flats, selling a classic Swedish-café menu of salads, pies and calorie-loaded pastries. Björn Västgård wasn't there yet. Annika and Valter decided to have an early lunch while they waited. People came and went, some eating, others buying sandwiches or cake to take away. Everyone seemed to know everyone else. Annika felt as if she was back in Maestro in Hälleforsnäs.

They were having coffee by the time a van emblazoned with the name 'Hot Shots' pulled up outside. Annika looked at her watch – he was only forty minutes late, which should probably be regarded as a success (it was almost impossible to pin delivery companies down to a particular date).

A bearded man, extremely overweight, struggled out of the van and headed towards the café. The door squeaked and the bell rang as he came in. His face cracked into a broad smile when he caught sight of Annika. 'There you are,' he said, shaking her hand firmly. Annika could never get used to the fact that people recognized her – which version of her had they seen? The reporter, the wife of the kidnapped government official?

Björn Västgård got a cup of coffee and a Danish pastry, which Annika paid for. He settled onto a chair that creaked under his weight. 'Oh, yes,' he said, sighing happily. 'I ran that shop for seventeen years, seventeen years full of all sorts of weird jobs, I can tell you. It wasn't all replacing the zip on a pair of favourite jeans or adding darts to old dears' Chanel rip-offs, oh, no. I had to put hidden pockets in attaché cases and sew vibrators into latex underwear. But the lining of that coat really was the weirdest of the lot.'

'Why?' Annika asked.

He took a large bite of the pastry and chewed. 'The first thing that struck me was that she was dressed in such a peculiar outfit,' he said, once he'd swallowed his mouthful. 'When she came into the shop I thought she was a Muslim – she was wearing a hijab with all her hair tucked away and one of those long skirts that they go about in. When the shop was quiet, though, and she was the only one in there, she took the headscarf off and I recognized her at once.'

'You could tell she was Viola Söderland?'

His whole face was beaming. 'As true as I'm sitting here. It struck me that someone really rich had just wandered into my humble little shop. I'd thought birds like her had servants who sorted their dirty washing out, and I suppose she did, because this was something completely different.' He leaned across the table and lowered his voice. 'This was something altogether out of the ordinary.'

235

Annika noticed a couple sitting at the next table stop talking to listen to the former tailor. He took a deep gulp of coffee and another bite of his pastry, scattering crumbs on the floor.

'She'd brought a coat with her in a paper bag from ICA, a grey woollen coat, good quality. She wanted the lining changed, she said, and she had very particular specifications for what she wanted the new one to look like.'

Annika read from her notepad. 'Four pockets measuring sixteen by seven centimetres, one fourteen by nine, and one seven by three.'

The tailor was astonished. He had flakes of pastry in his beard.

'My boss still has his notes,' she said. 'Anders Schyman, the man who interviewed—'

'Of course I know who Anders Schyman is. He's having a very hard time in social media at the moment, under attack from all sides.'

'Yes,' Annika said. 'Was there anything else special about that lining?'

The man stared at her with surprise, as if the measurements ought to be special enough. 'The zips,' he said. 'They had to be concealed. The pockets mustn't be visible, and they had to be watertight.'

'Watertight? Why?'

Björn Västgård leaned even closer. 'Who knows?' he whispered.

Annika scribbled some notes. 'So you agreed to do the work? How long did you have to do it in?'

He finished his coffee. 'Two days. She was in a hurry. I explained I'd have to charge more if I was going to have to do it so quickly, an express fee, and she agreed to that.'

'How did she pay? By card?'

'No, cash.'

'Did she show you any ID?'

Again he looked surprised. 'No, why would she have done that?'

'So it might not have been Viola Söderland in your shop at all?'

The man just smiled.

Annika cleared her throat. 'And when did this happen? In relation to her disappearance?'

'Two weeks before she went.'

'Did she pick the coat up herself?'

'Oh, yes, wearing the same Muslim outfit. She was very happy with the work, extremely pleased, actually . . .'

'Have you ever heard from Viola again since then?'

He let out a deep sigh. 'Not a peep,' he said. 'I don't think she's in Sweden. If she had been, she would have come back to me, I'm sure of that, because she was so happy with my work.'

Annika looked down at her notes. It wasn't much to go on. The urgency to get the lining changed suggested she was planning her flight and running out of time. The question was: why? And why did the pockets have to be watertight? Was she planning to go swimming with the coat on? Or was it raining as much that autumn as it had been this spring?

She gave him a rather strained smile. 'Thank you very much,' she said. 'We really appreciate you taking the time—'

The man put a large hand over hers. 'I've got to ask – how's your husband?'

Embarrassed, Annika pulled away her hand. 'How do you mean?'

'After the kidnapping in Somalia. That was such a terrible business.'

He certainly had a memory for faces, and an eye for detail, she had to admit. She put her notebook back into her bag.

'I hope that blogger comes to his senses soon,' Björn Västgård said.

'Has he contacted you?' Annika asked.

'Several times. Unpleasant type, if you ask me.'

'Have you met him? Do you know who he is?'

He shook his head. 'We've talked on the phone and he says his name is Lars. I told him what I'm telling you now, that Viola Söderland wasn't planning to die, she was planning to live.'

He stood up and brushed the crumbs from his trousers. 'It was nice to meet you. Give my best to your old man.'

The Hot Shots delivery van pulled away with a roar.

'Why was she going round dressed as a Muslim?' Valter said, as he watched the vehicle drive off.

'Muslim women are invisible in Sweden,' Annika said. 'People don't see them, they look right past them. Schyman mentioned that in his documentary.' She got to her feet. 'Right. Let's go to Skärholmen and find the man who sold her the car.'

Nina moved carefully around the furniture, scared of touching anything, which was irrational – the forensics team had completed their work.

The Lerberg family's living room was cosy, thoughtfully decorated. Slightly over-furnished, perhaps. A sofa and two armchairs – Nina thought she recognized the design from Ikea – that had been created for people with more traditional homes: slightly bulging arms, soft cushions, chocolate-coloured.

She was standing on the wooden floor in her stockinged feet, and the cold crept up between her toes.

She had never been part of a family that had a home and didn't really know what they were supposed to look like. She had grown up in various collectives where adults (*men*) with different languages and backgrounds came and went, and by the time she was a bit older, her mum was ill (*crazy*) and they moved to Södermanland, it was already too late. There was never any safe haven, just a chilly storage location. God, she had been frozen during those first years in Sweden – it was cold almost ten months of the year – but on Tenerife (back *home* on Tenerife?) it was always nice and warm, with occasional rain but mild winds. She had lived beneath fig trees and among thickets of mint, in a shower of orange blossom and on beaches made of lava. The coarse sand between her toes, the smell of the sea.

She looked around the cramped living room. There was an old circular teak coffee-table, probably from the fifties. Inherited, or from a flea market. No pot-plants. A fairly small flat-screen television on a low shelf along one wall, twenty-eight inches, maybe, and a DVD player with small speakers. A few children's films, cartoons, Astrid Lindgren classics. Paintings of traditional subjects on the walls, clumsily produced in oil or acrylic, boats and landscapes.

Why did Nora disappear?

She created this home, then left it. Somewhere there had to be a hint of an explanation.

An open fire with birch logs, no ashes. A bookcase containing bestsellers and a few ornaments, a blue bird, a gold-coloured deer that functioned as a thermometer. An old rocking chair by the window, some knitting in a basket next to it. A piano against one wall.

Nina went over to it and carefully sat down on the stool.

239

The first time she had tried playing a real piano was in Julia's home, her childhood friend in Södermanland. Victor, one of her mother's boyfriends, had played the guitar, but she'd never seen any other musical instruments before she'd stepped into Julia's living room. She remembered the concentration as she pressed the keys, how fragile and beautiful the notes had sounded. Julia had been able to play several pieces, she remembered: 'The Entertainer', by Scott Joplin, from *The Sting*, and Beethoven's 'Moonlight Sonata', but Nina had never managed more than a very basic children's song. She pressed a few keys up to the right of the keyboard where the notes were high, then down to the left where they ought to be lower, but there was no sound at all. She pressed the bass keys a bit harder, soft little thuds – nothing.

She straightened her back. She listened hard. The house was completely silent. She closed her eyes. Everything was still. There ought to have been some hint of movement, a draught from a loose window, a sigh from the hundred-year-old floorboards, but the rooms had stopped breathing.

Where was the life in this house?

She didn't know what the norm was so she wasn't sure what was bothering her. She opened her eyes and took a deep breath. The air was slightly damp and a bit chilly. The cadaverous smell from the dog hadn't quite gone.

She went over to the window. The curtains were light, with an abstract floral pattern. They were supposed to look as if they came from Svenskt Tenn, but they, too, were actually from Ikea, the label still attached. She drew them smoothly. They moved easily, didn't catch anywhere. So the curtains were practical, not just aesthetic: they were used, put there as a protection and defence, if need be.

The daylight outside was heavy and grey. It tumbled

240

in through squeaky-clean windows – the glass must have been washed no more than a week ago. She watched a train rattle past on the Saltsjöbanan track on the other side of Silvervägen. Even though it had stopped raining, she could see the moisture sparkling on her car on the road.

She turned her back to the window and went out into the hallway. It was narrow and fairly dark. There had been a Persian-style rug the first time she visited, but it had been taken away for analysis now, leaving a pale rectangle on the wooden floor to show where it had been. The hat-rack was still there, but the outdoor clothing that had hung on it had also been removed.

She looked up at the staircase, trying to imagine Ingemar Lerberg hanging there, tied to the wrought-iron railing above. He must have screamed. Even if he had tape over his mouth there would have been an awful lot of noise. She went to the small hall window, which was square, fairly high up, and looked out onto the front steps and the garden below. The house had been dark and unlit during the night between Thursday and Friday. No one had seen anyone arrive or leave the house during the evening, through the night or the following morning. There hadn't been any unfamiliar cars parked in the neighbourhood.

The kitchen was bright and airy. Lime-washed pine floor, mass-produced rag-rugs, oiled beech-wood surfaces. A toaster on the worktop. A stainless-steel fridge and freezer, both from Ikea. She leaned against the sink. The sense of silence and emptiness grew stronger.

She bent to open the cupboard under the sink. Containers for rubbish and recycling. Dishwasher tablets, ecological drain cleaner, steel wool, all neatly lined up. She wondered if the forensics officers had left them like that. She closed the cupboard door and opened one of the glass-fronted cabinets. Wine glasses from Orrefors, a dozen. A wedding present, perhaps. She held one of the glasses up to the light. No marks at all. She replaced it and shut the door.

She didn't know what a home was, but something was telling her that this wasn't right. There was something strained about it, the curtains, the furniture and window-panes. It wasn't organic – it had no life, no pulse.

She wondered if that meant anything.

She went out into the utility room, where the built-in cupboards were less smart. Washing-machine, tumble-drier, airing-cupboard, a hook on the back door . . .

Her eyes stopped. She crouched.

A pair of slippers, light brown, worn, made of a blanket-like material. They were positioned beside the back door, neatly lined up next to a bucket containing a mop.

She went back to the kitchen, tore off a piece of kitchen roll, then returned to the utility room.

She picked up the right slipper with the paper and turned it upside down.

Size 34.

Nora wore size 38 or 39. At least, that was the size of all the shoes in her wardrobe.

She crouched there for a while. Then she replaced the slipper and called Lamia, and asked her to send a couple of forensics officers to Silvervägen with an evidence bag big enough for a pair of slippers, then to get hold of surveil-lance footage from every station along the Saltsjöbanan line for the morning of Monday, 13 May.

Annika turned into the multi-storey car-park at Skärholmen shopping centre, a huge concrete structure stretching as far

242

as the eye could see. She drove to the back of the second floor and found a spot fairly close to the entrance, five hours' free parking.

'This Light of Truth,' Valter said. 'Have you read the blog?'

'Some of it,' Annika said, switching the engine off. 'Why?'

'I've read just about all of it,' he said thoughtfully. 'Not the comments, there are thousands of those now, but he hasn't written anything about interviewing Björn Västgård.'

She took the key out of the ignition and grabbed her bag from the back seat. 'Björn Västgård's version of events doesn't fit the blogger's, so he's just pretending it doesn't exist.'

They got out of the car.

'Can you make a point of remembering where we parked, or we'll never find our way back here,' Annika said. She had a hopeless sense of direction.

They took the escalator up to the shopping centre, a classic suburban mall with a glass roof and all the obligatory chain-stores. Outside there was a large concrete square. Annika stopped at the doors and squinted as she peered out at the blustery scene. 'He's supposed to sell vegetables here,' she said, nodding towards some market stalls in front of a brown brick edifice, which, according to a sign next to the wooden door, was Skärholmen Church.

A dozen men, all from somewhere outside Scandinavia, were gathered beneath the canvas awnings covering the stalls. A few women in headscarves and full-length skirts were picking at the lettuces and turnips.

Annika went over to the first stall. 'Excuse me,' she said. 'I'm trying to find Abdullah Mustafa. Is he here today?'

The man gave her a brief sideways glance as he carried

on putting out a tray of yellow peppers. 'We've got lovely strawberries today,' he said. 'Extra lovely, extra sweet.'

'Abdullah Mustafa,' Annika said. 'He's supposed to work at one of these stalls?'

The man shook his head. 'Cucumber?' he suggested. 'We've got lovely cucumbers.'

Either the man didn't know who Abdullah Mustafa was, or he didn't want to say. Annika moved on to the next stall. 'Hi, excuse me, but I'm looking for someone,' she said. 'Abdullah Mustafa?'

'Don't know him,' the man at the second stall said, and turned his back on her.

Valter grasped Annika's arm and pulled her away. 'How about I give it a try? They might find it easier to talk to someone like them.' He turned his collar up against the wind.

She blinked, taken aback. 'What do you mean?'

'You know, another immigrant.'

'I think these guys are Kurds. You're not Kurdish, are you?'

'No, Iranian, but I can pass as all manner of things . . . Kurdish, Arabic, South American . . .'

'With that accent? From the very smartest bit of Östermalm?'

He clenched his teeth and looked at the ground, visibly hurt.

'Sorry,' she said, 'I didn't mean . . .' She took a step back. 'Go ahead, I'll follow you.'

They walked back in among the stalls, passing the two men Annika had already spoken to and moving further in. Valter stopped a man selling knitted children's clothes with garish patterns, and asked for Abdullah Mustafa. The man pointed at a man in a cap who was busy unloading boxes of French beans from the back of a Volvo van.

Valter walked up to him. 'Abdullah Mustafa?'

The man in the cap put his box down and looked up.

'My name's Valter Wennergren,' Valter said, in his drawling Stockholm accent, holding out his hand. 'Sorry to disturb you when you're working, I'm from the *Evening Post* newspaper and I was wondering if I could have a few words with you. Can I get you a cup of coffee?'

The man shook Valter's hand, wary but not dismissive. 'A few words about what?'

'The same thing everyone else has been asking you about recently,' Valter said. 'That car you sold to a rich woman a hundred years ago.'

Amusement flashed across Abdullah Mustafa's face, then he turned away. 'I've got nothing to say.'

Annika watched Valter. He clearly wasn't about to let Abdullah Mustafa go now that he'd found him.

'I understand,' Valter said. 'It was such a long time ago.'

The man spun round and looked straight at him. 'I remember,' he said. 'I just don't want to talk.'

Valter shrugged. 'OK,' he said. 'You don't want to talk. What are you afraid of?'

'I'm not afraid.'

'No?'

The men stared at each other for a moment.

'I need to unload these,' Abdullah Mustafa said, nodding towards the van.

'I can wait,' Valter said, taking a step back.

Abdullah Mustafa turned towards the boxes. A few minutes later he had finished. He closed the door and looked at Valter. 'I need to get the van out of the way. I'll see you at Kahramane in ten minutes,' he said.

'Sure.'

'Kahramane?' Annika said, but Abdullah Mustafa had already driven off.

Valter gave her a slightly desperate look. 'We can find it, can't we? There can't be that many places called Kahra . . . Kama . . .'

Annika took her mobile out, Googled 'karamane' and got 40,600 results. She added 'skärholmen' and got one: *Welcome to Kahramane Restaurant on Bredholmsgatan, just outside the shopping centre!*

'It's often a good idea to ask for the address,' Annika said. 'This way.'

Valter trudged after her as she headed back into the mall. They passed chemists, clothes stores and a hobby shop – a man tried to get them to sign up to a cheap and completely useless mobile operator – and then they were out the other side. In front of them was the Kahramane restaurant. Above the door a sign showed a beautiful sunset, and some Arabic or Kurdish writing, Annika couldn't tell which. Valter pulled the door open, walked straight up to the counter and ordered a chicken shawarma with fries and all the trimmings.

'We've only just eaten,' Annika pointed out.

'Yeah, salad,' Valter snorted, popping a piece of chicken into his mouth.

They sat down at one of the little tables. There were a few men in the far corner, talking quietly with their heads close together, but otherwise the place was empty. A television on the wall above their heads was blaring out an Iraqi music channel. Beautiful men and women sang pop songs in an unfamiliar key – it was evidently some sort of chart run-down.

Valter had already managed to eat most of his chicken by the time Abdullah Mustafa came in. He greeted the staff behind the counter and got himself a cup of coffee without paying. 'So what do you want to know?' he said, glancing suspiciously at Annika.

'This is my colleague,' Valter said, nodding towards her. 'We'd like to talk about the woman who bought your car.'

The man took his cap off, smoothed his hair down and took a seat opposite them. 'There was nothing unusual about it. I put an advert in the paper saying I wanted to sell my Volvo 245. She rang up. She was actually the only person who called. It was pretty old, three hundred thousand kilometres on the clock – I have to drive a lot for work, get vegetables for the stall . . . She said her name was Harriet Johansson. She showed me her driving licence. It said Harriet Johansson and a couple of other names, but it checked out. It was her.'

Valter wasn't taking any notes, and Annika wondered for a moment if she should get her pen and pad out, but decided against it.

'Then there was loads of stuff in the papers when Viola Söderland disappeared,' Valter said. 'You didn't recognize her as the woman who had bought your car?'

The man shook his head. 'I don't read the papers much, just the *Metro* occasionally. I didn't really think about it.'

'So she bought the car straight away?'

'She took it for a test drive, then bought it. It was very quick. She paid cash, five thousand. I was very happy. It was a good car but the mileage was high, and it was pretty rusty.'

'And when was this?'

'In the summer, June. I wanted to get rid of it during the summer because the winter tyres were worn out.'

So Viola Söderland had bought the car three months before she disappeared, Annika thought.

'I filled in the form about a change of ownership and she signed it, then said she'd post it. I didn't think any more about it. I bought a new car, a Ford, but it was nowhere near as good as the Volvo so now I only drive Volvos.'

'When was the next time you heard about the car?' Valter asked. 'When Anders Schyman contacted you?'

'No, no,' he said. 'When the police called me.'

'The police?'

'The Finnish police. The car was left parked outside Kuusamo, on the Russian border, with the keys in the ignition.'

Annika wished she could write all this down: it was new.

Abdullah Mustafa nodded to himself. 'It had been there for a fortnight. That was when I realized she hadn't sent off the change-of-ownership form. The car was still mine.'

'What happened to it?'

'I got it back.'

Annika and Valter stared at him.

'Have you still got it?' Valter asked.

The man shuffled on his chair. 'No,' he said. 'I sold it at once. I only got three thousand the second time, but that was still good. It didn't have any winter tyres.'

'What condition was it in? Had it been knocked about, dented?'

'No, it was the same as when I sold it. Nice and clean, just rusty.'

Why hadn't he mentioned this before? Or had he?

Annika hesitated. Should she intervene in the conversation? Ask if he'd seen the documentary about Viola? Or would she only spoil things?

'When you got the car back,' Valter said, 'was it empty?'

'Empty?'

248

'Was there anything inside the car that wasn't there when you sold it?'

The man seemed to slump. The chart show above their heads started from the beginning again.

'It was empty. Well, almost empty. There was one thing. A case.'

Valter and Annika sat without speaking, waiting for him to go on.

'In the boot,' Abdullah Mustafa said. 'There was a compartment at the back of the car, under the floor, for storing the jack and spanners . . . It was in there, under a blanket.'

'A case?' Valter said.

'A little one – a briefcase. Leather. Thin.'

Annika felt the hair stand up on the back of her neck. Anders Schyman hadn't heard about this, she was sure. 'Did you look inside it?'

The man hesitated. 'There was nothing valuable. Just old stuff. I put it back inside.'

'What did you do with the case?'

The man took a deep breath. 'I thought she might have left it there by accident, Harriet Johansson, so I kept it. But she never called.'

'Where is it now?'

He thought for a moment. 'In the garage, I think.'

'You've still got it?'

'I don't think I ever got rid of it.'

'Could we take a look at it?'

The man peered at his watch. 'I've got to take a delivery out to Botkyrka, but we should have time.'

*

Mum taught me to knit. First casting on, then pulling the wool through the back loop, one after another, until the row was finished and I could turn it round and start again. Plain knitting, ribbing, then crochet, it was completely magical, the way the long thread from the ball of wool could become something so completely different, and I was responsible for the change. I was the one creating it all.

It was almost like being God, I said.

Mum laughed at me. It was back when she still laughed – but then she stopped laughing, and I stopped being God.

*

'Under the jack?'

Schyman looked suspiciously at the leather briefcase Annika Bengtzon had placed on his desk: light brown and dusty, smelling of engine oil.

'It was Valter who persuaded Abdullah Mustafa to let us take it,' she said.

He glanced through his glass wall: the trainee was sitting in Berit Hamrin's place, his attention focused on his mobile phone. 'And it's been kept in a garage?'

'For almost twenty years,' Annika said.

'What's inside it?'

'You're welcome to open it and take a look,' she said.

He clenched his fists, feeling his fingernails dig into his palms. Then he reached for the case, undid the brass lock and opened the lid. Carefully he put his hand inside and pulled out the first thing he found: a thin folder. His fingers were trembling as he opened it at the first page.

It was a wedding photograph.

God, it was her – it really was Viola, a smiling young woman with sixties hair and a short white wedding dress, the bridegroom in a trendy suit with impressive sideburns. He swallowed hard.

'I presume that's Viola and her husband,' Annika Bengtzon said.

Schyman blew his nose. 'Olof Söderland,' he said, sounding choked. 'They married young, both in their teens.' He leafed through the album slowly, almost respectfully.

On the next page were studio pictures of two babies laughing at the camera: a blond boy in knitted dungarees and a red-haired girl with a bow in her hair and a lace dress.

He took a deep breath and coughed. 'Henrik and Linda,' he said.

Viola Söderland's children had been born just a year apart – they must be around forty-five now.

He turned another page. More pictures of the two children, at the beach, next to Christmas trees, school photographs, the girl on a horse, the boy with swimming goggles standing on a podium, school graduation pictures. In all there were twenty or so photographs in the album.

'The pictures were carefully chosen,' Annika said.

He nodded. 'She took the children with her when she left.'

He felt for the next item in the case, more confident now.

A pair of child's shoes, white, with pink laces.

The girl's, no doubt. She was the eldest: the first child's first pair of shoes.

Next: a bundle of letters, tied with a red ribbon.

'I read a few,' Annika said. 'They're love letters from Olof to Viola when she was training to be a teacher.'

He ran his fingers over them, then put them down.

A plastic bag containing two locks of hair, one blond, the other ginger. He felt them through the plastic and they slipped out of his fingers. He looked at the items spread out on his desk. What would you rescue from a burning house?

'There's one more thing,' the reporter said.

He turned the case upside down. A discoloured leather wallet fell onto the desk. He shook the briefcase, looked inside it, felt all round the lining. There was an internal pocket but it was empty.

He felt a pang of disappointment – was that all?

He picket up the wallet and sniffed it. What had he been expecting? A recent photograph and a note of her current address?

'That must have been in water or a fire or something,' Annika said.

He inspected the wallet. The leather was stained with something brown and dried-in, definitely a man's. There was still money inside, five-kronor notes, with Gustav Vasa on one side and a capercaillie on the other, ten-kronor notes, with Gustav VI Adolf on them, a hundred-kronor note, with Gustav II Adolf, all long since obsolete, and all discoloured along the top edge. In another pocket a black sleeve contained a driving licence from the 1970s, with a red stamp to the value of thirty-five kronor, and a photograph of a handsome young man with shoulder-length hair. It had been issued in the name of Olof Söderland.

'Viola was a widow,' Schyman said. 'Did you know that?'

Annika shook her head. Schyman looked at the picture of the young man, the bottom left corner covered with a red stamp that hid part of his chin.

'Her husband died in a car crash when the children were small. This must be his wallet.'

'She never remarried?'

Olof Söderland had a fringe and full lips. His eyes

252

weren't looking at the camera but at something to one side. Perhaps he had had his wallet in his inside pocket when he died.

'No.'

'You realize what this points to?' Annika said. 'All the things in this case that was left in that car?'

He closed the driving licence and put it back in the wallet, then gathered the things together and returned them to the briefcase.

'This briefcase says several things,' Schyman said, closing the brass lock. 'Viola prepared for her flight and wasn't planning to come back. She took her dearest memories with her and hid them in the car where no one would find them.'

Annika nodded. 'True. But she didn't take them with her when she abandoned the car.'

He put the case in the middle of the desk and didn't respond.

'She was planning to live, but I don't think she succeeded,' Annika added.

His whirring mind came to an abrupt halt. What if he had been wrong? What if everything had been a huge mistake, and she had been dead all along?

She shifted on her chair. 'It's difficult trying to work on this when I'm not being given all the facts.'

His mouth had dried. 'What do you mean?'

Her eyes narrowed, the way they sometimes did. 'You don't have to tell me who the source was,' she said, 'just how you came to have the information.'

He shut his eyes and could see the man in front of him: his thin, dark-blond hair, his rather uneven front teeth, his bulging stomach. 'I honestly don't know his name,' he said. 'He never told me. He gave me the information on the condition that I never revealed I had got it from someone else.'

'And you promised.'

He sighed. 'I promised. And now I'm breaking that promise.'

'And what did he tell you?'

'Everything. The car, the coat lining, the Cayman Islands – the lot.'

'And the picture from the petrol station?'

He looked at the floor. 'And the picture from the petrol station,' he conceded.

'There's someone standing to the right of the picture, in a pale jacket. Was that him?'

'I don't know. Possibly.'

'Did you know that the car had been found at the Russian border?' she said.

'I did,' Schyman said, 'but I never got it confirmed. The car had been scrapped by the time I made the programme. Abdullah Mustafa claimed he didn't know what had happened to it, so I left that detail out.'

'He sold the car twice,' Annika said. 'He was terrified he'd done something wrong and was going to be thrown out of Sweden.'

He could feel her eyes drilling into him.

'You realize you could have been the victim of a planted story,' she said. It was a statement of fact.

'There was a very active search for Viola Söderland in those first few years, wasn't there?' she went on. 'After all, she owed the state loads of tax. Could the police have been getting close to the truth? Was there someone who didn't like that? Could your television programme have been a way to get the authorities to look in the wrong place?'

The possibility had occurred to him – he wasn't born yesterday. But the logical conclusion had reassured him: if someone wanted to stop the authorities looking for Viola

Söderland, they would have tried to persuade him that she was dead, not that she was still alive.

Annika stood up and put her hand on the briefcase. 'What are we going to do with this?'

He remained seated, clutching the arms of his chair with his hands. 'What do you think?'

'I think we should contact Viola's children and ask if they want it. Unless we should give it to the police?'

Both options made his brain short-circuit, and he flew up from his chair. 'Not the police, and not Viola's children!' he shouted. 'All of this is their fault! They're saying I made the programme to stop them getting their inheritance! Have you seen what they've said today? That I caused Linda to have a miscarriage – that I killed her baby!'

She was staring at him again, with those narrowed eyes. 'I haven't seen them make any statement anywhere,' she said. 'Maybe they aren't behind this at all. Maybe it's all the invention of that lunatic. His name's Lars, by the way.'

Schyman lost his train of thought and realized he was quite breathless. 'His name's Lars? How the hell do you know that?'

Annika leaned across the desk. 'He's calling round all your sources and introducing himself. Is what you said to the TT news agency true, by the way? That it's all bollocks?'

He closed his eyes for a moment, then opened them. 'I know I should have managed that a bit more professionally.'

She shoved Viola Söderland's briefcase across the desk. 'You decide what to do with it!'

She walked out through the glass door, closing it hard behind her.

*

255

Annika sat down at her desk, grabbed her notepad and pen and called Commissioner Q's direct line.

'Bengtzon,' he said, when he answered. 'It's been several days since you last called. I thought you'd broken up with me.'

'I like to play hard to get,' she said. 'Have you got much going on?'

'I'm not going to say a thing about Nora,' he said.

'I don't give a damn about Nora,' she replied. 'I'm after another missing woman now. Do you remember Viola Söderland?'

'Golden Spire? What about her?'

'Were you involved in the search for her?'

He chuckled. 'Your faith in me is so great it's almost touching. No, Bengtzon. Twenty years ago I was a duty officer in the Southern District. I never had anything to do with Viola Söderland.'

She made her voice bright and cheerful. 'I was thinking that maybe you could look up what happened in the case? If you haven't already got too much to do, of course . . .'

He laughed again. She could imagine him shaking his head and scratching his navel. 'I thought your boss told the nation where she'd gone?' he said. 'Didn't she run away to Russia?'

'It looked like it,' Annika said. 'She planned her escape very carefully, bought a car without anyone's knowledge, changed her name a year before she disappeared, managed to get hold of two passports, picked up a load of cash from the Cayman Islands, sewed the money into her clothes, packed a case with her dearest memories . . . She must have ended up somewhere. You lot must have something after all these years. Haven't you?'

Q was quiet at the other end. She could hear him breathing. 'She changed her name?' he said at last.

Annika looked back through her notes. 'She added her mother's maiden name and started using her middle name. Viola Söderland became Harriet Johansson.'

'What did you say about her having two passports?'

'She reported the first one stolen and got a new one. She left the new one in the house when she fled, but the old one would still have worked as long as no one checked it with the official Swedish register.'

She heard Q tapping at his computer.

'Okay, Bengtzon,' he said. 'Could you tell one of our operational analysts what you've just told me, about Viola Söderland, and I'll see if I can't find some way to help you?'

Annika was lost for words: this was too good to be true.

'What are you up to now?'

'Who, me?' She straightened in her chair. 'You never give in this easily.'

'One of our analysts will call you later this afternoon.'

Then he hung up.

Annika was left holding the receiver, astonished.

Nina had been waiting in the road outside the villa in Vikingshill for twenty minutes when Kristine Lerberg finally drove up in her Nissan Micra and turned into the drive. The woman got out with jerky, abrupt movements, her mouth set.

'Thanks for seeing me at such short notice,' Nina said, as she walked over and shook hands. 'I could have come to your workplace.'

'We're busy with the budget,' Kristine Lerberg said curtly. She dug in her handbag for her keys as she walked towards the house with short, quick steps. Her neatly cut hair bounced against her collar each time her heels hit the ground. 'Can I get you anything?' she asked, without looking at Nina. She turned on the light in the hall, hung her coat on a hanger, brushed off the shoulders, then took off her boots and put on a pair of indoor shoes. She went into the kitchen.

'Don't go to any trouble on my account,' Nina said, taking her shoes off.

'Well, I'm going to have a glass of wine,' Kristine Lerberg said, filling a long-stemmed glass from a box in the fridge. She sat at the kitchen table and took a large sip. Nina sat down opposite her and discreetly put her mobile on the tablecloth with the recording app switched on.

'I heard that social services are looking after the children now,' she said, checking that their conversation was being recorded.

Kristine Lerberg smoothed a crease from the cloth. 'I can't have them,' she said. 'I've got a job to go to.'

Nina wasn't sure if the woman meant short- or long-term, so she didn't respond.

'Ingemar's got worse,' Kristine went on. 'They don't know if he's ever going to wake up again.'

'So I heard,' Nina said.

Kristine nodded to herself. 'You never know what plans the Lord has,' she said. 'Have you found him?'

Nina was unsure what she meant.

Kristine gestured with her hand. 'The man who did it?'

'Not yet, but we're exploring a number of lines of inquiry. That's why I wanted to talk to you again.'

Nina took a small notebook from her inside pocket and

read out loud from it. 'Friday, the third of May,' she said. 'Do you remember what you were doing that day?'

The woman sat perfectly still and shut her eyes. She hadn't touched her glass of wine since the first sip. 'I have Fridays off,' she said, in a toneless voice, 'so I must have been at home . . .' She seemed to slump in her chair. 'The third of May . . . That's, what, last week? I was looking after the children. Ingemar was away on business and Nora had one of her thyroid appointments at Södermalm Hospital.'

Nina studied her carefully. She seemed to be telling the truth. She certainly appeared to believe what she was saying. 'Do you often look after the children at times like that?'

She nodded again, then swallowed. 'I try to help whenever I can. And I like the children, I really do.'

'How often would you say it happens?'

'Me looking after them? Once a month, something like that, and sometimes in the afternoon if Nora has to do the accounts . . . She does the bookkeeping for Ingemar's company, and she's very particular about it. It takes a lot of her time.'

'Is she often busy all day?'

'Thyroid treatment isn't an easy procedure, Nora usually wants to rest afterwards, which can make the days rather long, but obviously . . .'

'You told me before that Nora put a lot of effort into her family, looking after the children and the house.'

Kristine Lerberg put her face into her hands, then sat up and looked at Nina defiantly. 'We all do the best we can, don't we?'

She had taken the question as criticism. Nina concentrated on keeping her face expressionless and tried not to feel irritated. 'Are you sure Nora didn't have any help in the house?'

'Absolutely,' Kristine said. 'Ingemar would never have allowed it. I don't have any help with the cleaning either – it's unnecessary. It's a privilege to have a home to take care of.' She lifted the glass, but took only a small sip.

Nina turned a page in her notebook. 'So the children spend quite a lot of time with you,' she said. 'What do they usually do when they're here? Do they like drawing?'

Kristine Lerberg nodded. 'Oh, yes, especially Isak. He's very talented.'

'Could I see some of his drawings?'

The woman looked at her. 'What for?'

'Unless you don't keep them?'

Kristine stood up. 'Of course I do,' she said, and marched out of the kitchen. Nina followed her into the dark corridor leading to the bedrooms.

The room on the far left was furnished with a bunk-bed and a cot. There was a red-painted child-sized table and chairs in the middle of the floor, and beneath the window an old desk with a chest of drawers and a laminated top.

'What do you want to see? Isak's latest drawings?'

'And his crayons as well, if I could,' Nina said.

Kristine went over to the desk and pulled out the top drawer. She took out a box of crayons and a small sheaf of drawings and laid them on the desktop.

Nina picked up the box: Winsor & Newton Oil Bars, fifty millilitres. 'Did you buy these crayons, or did Nora?'

Kristine looked at the cot. 'I did.'

Nina put the box back and picked up the top drawing. It was a picture of three children and a little angel. Kristine moved to stand beside Nina and smiled. 'He's got a wonderful imagination – he talks the whole time while he's drawing. That's him and his brother and sister and their guardian angel.'

She reached for another drawing. 'This is me,' she said, pointing to a cheerful figure in a dress and high heels.

'The guardian angel,' Nina said, looking at the first picture again. 'Who's that?'

Kristine's smile widened. 'Isak's faith is very strong and clear, even though he's so young. He has an angel who looks after him, his brother and sister. He says she watches over them when they sleep.'

'Does he ever take his drawings home?'

The woman's eyes filled with tears. 'He's so desperate for his mother's approval that he's always taking little presents home for her.'

Nina smiled cautiously. 'Thanks for letting me take up your time again.' She indicated the picture in her hand. 'May I keep this?'

When she got back to the car she did a quick Google search for Winsor & Newton Oil Bars on her mobile phone. Then she cast a last glance at the brown brick house. She could see Kristine Lerberg moving about behind the kitchen curtains. Nina started the engine and drove off.

She had reached the motorway back to Stockholm when her mobile rang. She put her ear-piece in and answered. It was Commissioner Q. 'How's it all going out in the real world?' he asked.

Nina kept both hands on the wheel, staring straight ahead. 'The child's drawing that was found on the victim in Kråkträsken could have been produced in Kristine Lerberg's home,' she said. 'The crayons might well match. She bought them some very high-quality oil-based ones, the same as Forensics identified from the drawing found at the crime scene. They cost seven hundred kronor online for a box of twelve . . .'

'Wow,' Q said. 'Have you got a sample we can analyse?'

Yes, she had.

'Anything else?' Q asked.

'Nora fooled her sister-in-law into thinking she's been having monthly treatment for her thyroid at Södermalm Hospital.'

'Fooled?'

'There's no such treatment. There's something called a TRH stimulation test, which is indirectly to do with the thyroid, but it's not a treatment as such, and certainly isn't administered regularly . . . Nora had one of these "treatments" last Friday.'

'When we know she flew to Zürich for the day,' Q said. 'Very interesting. While I've got you on the phone, there's something else I'd like you to do. You know Annika Bengtzon from the *Evening Post*, don't you?'

Nina clutched the wheel more tightly. Yes, she did.

'I'd like you to call her,' Q said. 'She's got some interesting information about a twenty-year-old case that might be worth taking a closer look at.'

Nina felt a cold shiver run up her spine. What had she done wrong? Why was she being taken off the Lerberg case? Disappointment rose into her throat and she had to cough. Oh, well, she wasn't in charge of the way their work was allocated.

'Who should I hand over the Lerberg case to?' she asked curtly.

The head of Criminal Intelligence chuckled. 'Nina,' he said, 'don't be so negative. You're not being taken off the case. You have my permission to divulge information about the preliminary investigation to Bengtzon. She may be a hack, but she knows how to keep her mouth shut. Use your own judgement, tell her what you have to about the Lerberg case.'

Then he hung up.

As Thomas looked at the weather website, anxiety rose inside him. Just in time for the weekend the weather was going to change: the rain was going to stop, and it would be sunny, twenty degrees. Everyone in the city would be out in the streets and parks, turning their faces to the sun, smiling at each other and swinging their bare arms, without gloves.

He couldn't wear his hook without sleeves. How could he sit on a rug in the park with a long-sleeved top on (he couldn't button shirts with one hand, so had to wear T-shirts under his jacket) when everyone else had theirs off?

He'd have to sit indoors until September, when the cold and rain set in again, hiding himself and his mutilated body away from the light and warmth, away from all the hypocrites and morons.

Mind you, it did get cold in the evenings, properly cold, even in July and August. It would be okay to wear a sports jacket then. And a sweater.

He clicked away from the site and stared at the background to his desktop, drowning in its blue until his vision clouded and he realized he was crying. There was no point in trying to resist – he had learned that. It was better to let the pain pass through him until it dissolved.

He hadn't gone back to work after that meeting at National Crime. He'd felt exhausted, having those women staring at him. The blonde bombshell and the model with chestnut-brown hair. He had noticed the brunette staring at his hook – they hadn't been expecting that.

He wiped away the tears with his right hand. His hook lay useless in his lap.

Slowly he got up from the computer and went into the kitchen, his shabby, poorly laid-out kitchen. Once the pain had passed, it left a vacuum that slowly filled with gnawing irritation. It was lucky he never did any cooking – it would have been impossible in this dump. When he had lived here with Annika, she had attempted to cook her basic kindergarten recipes on the gas stove in the evenings, and they had tasted pretty much as expected. He particularly remembered the mango chicken – God, the crap he'd had to stomach for the sake of domestic harmony over the years. These days he bought delicacies that were either already cooked or could be heated in the microwave. That was one of the great advantages of being in charge of his own life: the quality of cuisine had gone up by about a thousand per cent in the past six months.

He opened the fridge. Serrano ham, strawberries, vendace caviar, prawn salad – the very finest food. But he wasn't very hungry – he could easily wait a while for dinner.

He went back to his computer and refreshed the weather website. No cold front had appeared during his excursion to the kitchen, and the weekend was still predicted to be warm and sunny.

He went onto the *Evening Post*'s website. He usually avoided it, didn't want to risk coming across Annika when he wasn't expecting it, but it was okay as long as he was prepared. Sometimes he even watched her dreadful video reports. She'd aged since she'd left him, all wrinkled and hollow-eyed.

At least she wasn't the lead item on the website today,

which was something. Instead the editor-in-chief was deemed the most important story of the day.

THE LIE OF TRUTH
All the facts about Viola Söderland's disappearance

Anders Schyman had written a long, rambling piece in which he dismissed the accusations online. He was using the paper to promote his own personal cause, with page after page of pointless documents that were supposed to provide proof of his innocence.

Irritating. Men in positions of power never took responsibility for their actions. Whenever someone yanked their trousers down they just stood there whining and complaining. Curious, he moved on to the Light of Truth to see how the blogger had responded to the attack. It was a hotbed of activity. So far that day the Light of Truth had published forty-eight new posts, with references and links to various media, and a torrent of comments was pouring in. He (or, rather, Gregorius) read a few of the comments posted by other readers, and gave them his approval by awarding them five stars, to show his active appreciation.

Then he looked at his own comment from two days ago:

Gregorius:
Anders Schyman is a hypocrite!

No one had given him any stars. Not a single one. No one had left a comment.

Bile rose in his throat.

Schyman and Annika and all the other powerful, influential people in society were seen and heard all over the place while he was completely ignored. He rubbed his nose to stop it running.

Then he went back to the most recent post on the Light of Truth and wrote a short, incisive comment inspired by the blogger's argument:

Gregorius:
Anders Schyman should be fucked up the arse with a baseball bat. Hope the splinters form a bleeding wreath around his anus.

The comment appeared on the site at once. He felt his breathing speed up, and his anxiety melted away as his scalp began to itch.

Was it too much? Too childish? Was 'anus' the right word in this sort of context? Should he have said 'arsehole' instead?

After just ten seconds his contribution to the debate flashed.

Five stars.

His breathing got even faster.

There was a ping, a response to his comment:

hahaha, way to go man! U butfuck him real good

Okay, 'butt-fuck' was spelled wrong, but the feeling was undeniable.

He was starting to get hard.

Annika was standing in a carriage on the Underground, squashed between a hundred-and-fifty-kilo woman and a

266

teenage immigrant when her mobile rang. She apologized and dragged her phone out, accidentally hitting an elderly man's head with her elbow. He glared at her as she managed to answer.

'Yes, hello, this is Nina Hoffman,' the woman at the other end said.

A flash of warm clarity shot through Annika and her senses sharpened. 'Hello,' she said, into the face of the young immigrant. He tried to turn away to avoid her breath.

'I've been asked by Commissioner Q, the head of the Criminal Intelligence Unit at National Crime, to get in touch with you.'

Annika couldn't help noting that Nina didn't sound over-enthusiastic about having to talk to her. 'Now isn't a good time,' she said, trying to turn away from the young man.

The carriage lurched. All the passengers were pushed towards the corner where Annika was standing, and the hundred-and-fifty-kilo woman trod on her foot.

'Is there somewhere we could meet for a quiet chat?' Nina Hoffman asked.

Annika tried to pull her foot free as she held the phone away from her ear. She managed a glance at her watch. She was already late. 'I've got to cook dinner,' she said. 'You'd be very welcome to come to the flat.'

Nina Hoffman hesitated. 'I'd rather . . .'

Annika freed her foot. 'Södermannagatan 40B,' she said. 'I'll be there in a quarter of an hour.'

She waited until Nina Hoffman said, 'OK,' before clicking to end the call. Carefully she moved her foot and wiggled her toes. Nothing felt broken.

She liked Nina. There was something brittle and tragic about her, but she was rock-solid inside.

She found herself staring at a teenage girl squashed against the door at the end of the carriage. She was clutching a rucksack out of which stuck the arm or leg of a cuddly toy. Her eyes kept flitting between the people around her. She didn't seem to have an adult with her. Maybe she was on her way home from school to one of her parents – one had left the other and taken a flat, or a new partner, some distance from her school. Now here she was, like a sardine in a tin, shunted from one place to the other for her parents to fulfil their vision of A Perfect Life: love, passion, freedom, recognition, security . . .

Who did she think she was kidding?

Annika looked away from her. Her own children were shaking and rattling in a carriage just like this one because of her life choices. She had denied them a stable upbringing with two parents, a proper home, and now Jimmy wanted to move to Norrköping. He hadn't said so in as many words – he had actually said remarkably little about the invitation to take charge of the Prison and Probation Service but she knew he wanted to accept. What would that mean for her? She couldn't move to Norrköping with the children: she and Thomas shared custody and he'd never agree to let them move to another city (the fact that he often shirked his parental responsibilities had no impact on his need to exert control), so where did that leave her?

The huge woman trod on her foot again.

'Ow!' Annika said loudly.

The woman, who was already sweaty and red-faced, turned an even deeper shade of puce. 'Sorry,' she said, looking down and lifting her foot slightly.

Annika took a deep breath. Her family circumstances were hardly the fault of this poor woman. She would end up alone in Jimmy's apartment (no, *her and Jimmy's*

268

apartment), without the children every other week, and without Jimmy every week. Maybe they'd see each other at weekends – Jimmy could come up to Stockholm or she could go down to Norrköping. It wasn't that far, after all, a hundred and seventy kilometres, maybe, almost commuting distance, and Serena would be there all the time, with her cold, dark eyes and stiff body.

The train braked and she almost fell on top of the poor old man whose head she had hit. The doors opened onto Medborgarplatsen station and people tumbled out. She went with the flow even though the next station, Skanstull, was actually closer to home, but she was desperate for fresh air.

What if she moved to Norrköping with Jimmy? And let the children live with Thomas full-time? Let them escape these horrible rush-hour journeys so that they could walk to school, maybe go home for lunch and during free periods . . .

And only see them every other weekend? Out of the question.

So whose best did she really want?

She hoisted her bag onto her shoulder and quickened her steps.

Nina stood outside the front door looking at the nameplate. Four surnames, a mixture of Swedish and foreign. These people had clearly chosen to live together (well, maybe not the children). Families didn't necessarily have to be tied together by blood (*families = blood*), but could be like this one: responsible, conscious choices by individuals who didn't even have to come from the same corner of the world.

She rang the bell. A girl with blonde hair and bright eyes opened the door. Nina immediately recognized the handsome government official from that morning in the little face.

'Hello,' Nina said. 'My name's Nina. I'm here to see your mummy.'

The child took a step back and called, 'Mummy! Your operational analyst is here!'

Then she vanished, quick as a flash, into a room off to the left, from which Nina could hear electronic bleeping noises.

Annika Bengtzon came out into the hall, wiping her hands on a tea-towel. 'Welcome,' she said, shaking Nina's hand. 'I've got something in the oven, so maybe we could . . .'

Nina took off her jacket and shoes and looked around discreetly. It was an impressive apartment: mirrored doors, high ceilings with ornate plasterwork, and in the living room ahead she caught a glimpse of an old-fashioned tiled stove and a balcony. She followed Annika Bengtzon into a rather cramped, impractical kitchen. A small table with three chairs was squeezed up against one wall, covered with a red and white checked tablecloth.

'Would you like coffee?' Annika asked.

'No, thanks.'

She sat down at the table. Annika crouched and looked through the window in the door of the old-fashioned gas oven. Inside was a large piece of fish – Nina thought it looked like salmon – with a thermometer sticking out of the fleshiest part.

'I was rather surprised when you called,' Annika said. 'And pleased.' She smiled at Nina. Nina looked at the table. Annika sat down opposite her. 'I spoke to Q this afternoon,' she said. 'He was remarkably accommodating, and said someone would contact me. Do you know what he's after?'

Nina looked up in surprise. 'The way I understood it, you were the one who wanted to see us because you've got new information about some old case.'

Annika didn't reply, just looked at her with narrowing eyes. Nina waited for her to say something.

'I don't talk about things that shouldn't be talked about,' Annika said, in a low voice. 'If anything's supposed to be made public I shout about it. If not, it stays with me.'

Nina knew that was true.

'I really only had one question when I contacted Q,' Annika said. 'About Viola Söderland. Are you in charge of her case?'

Viola Söderland? An absurdly wealthy woman who vanished years ago, laden with debt? 'Me? No. Should I be?'

'My editor-in-chief has asked me to track her down.'

Nina looked at her, stony-faced. 'That sounds . . . complicated,' she said.

Annika scratched her head. 'I wanted to know if there had been any developments in the case during the last twenty years or so, and that was when Q said he'd get someone to call me.'

Nina took a deep breath. The kitchen smelt of dill and fish. 'Exactly what did you say to Q?'

There was a ping from the oven. Annika got to her feet and hurried over to it. Moments later the front door opened and a man called, 'Hello!' Children's feet drummed on the parquet floor.

'Dinner's ready,' Annika said. 'Have you eaten?'

Nina's back stiffened. 'I really don't want to intrude.'

271

'You're not intruding,' Annika said, getting the dish out of the oven. The top of the fish was covered with dill and slices of lemon. She sprinkled some sea salt over it, followed by a drizzle of honey.

The man came into the kitchen: Jimmy Halenius, under-secretary of state at the Justice Ministry. He was fairly short, quite thick-set, with brown hair. Not half as handsome as Thomas Samuelsson.

'Hi,' he said, leaning over to shake her hand. 'Jimmy.'

She stood up – she was taller than him. 'Nina,' she said curtly.

'Nina's at National Crime,' Annika said, kissing him on the lips. 'We're going to have a chat later. Can you get another plate out?'

He reached for another glass and plate, then some cutlery. In passing he pressed against Annika, who pretended not to notice, but Nina spotted it.

The little blonde girl came into the kitchen. 'What are we having?'

'You can tell from the smell,' a boy said from the hall.

'Kalle doesn't like salmon,' the girl said to Nina.

'Right, let's eat,' Annika said, nudging the child out of the kitchen with her knee. In one hand she was holding a dish of roasted vegetables, and in the other she was balancing the ovenproof dish containing the fish.

'Let me take that,' Nina said, grabbing some oven gloves.

Annika picked up a jug of iced water from the worktop instead and led the way into the dining room.

An antique table laid for seven, with napkins, side-plates and stemmed glasses. There was some sort of salad on the side-plates. A dark girl, her head covered with little plaits, was lighting the candles in a huge wrought-iron candelabrum.

'I recognize that,' Nina said. 'It's from the old works in Hälleforsnäs.'

Annika gave her a broad smile, rather surprised. 'Wow,' she said. 'Local knowledge. My dad worked there – he was a blacksmith and the union rep. He made this one.'

The dark girl snorted derisively, then blew out the match and put it on the table.

'Don't leave it there,' Annika said. 'It'll mark the wood.'

'It's not your table, is it?' she said, but she picked up the match and took it out to the kitchen.

Nina saw Annika's mouth set. That hadn't been the first time the girl had challenged her.

Two boys came into the room, Annika's son, dark-haired and green-eyed, like his mother, and a mixed-race boy with curly black hair. The children didn't seem to have fixed places, and there was a bit of squabbling about who was going to sit where. Nina ended up next to Annika.

The starter was a classic goat's cheese salad with rocket, cherry tomatoes and pine nuts, topped with honey and balsamic vinegar. It didn't last long, everyone seemed hungry, and then they set about the fish. The family had a tradition of talking about what had happened during the day, so the under-secretary said something about government business, Annika said she'd phoned a man who had turned out to be dead, and the children talked about classmates and school lunches.

'How about you, Nina?' Jimmy Halenius said. 'Good and bad things about today?'

Everyone looked at her, the children with bright eyes, Annika rather amused. She put her knife and fork down. 'I'm a police officer,' she said, then remembered that that wasn't quite true now. 'Well, more an operational analyst,' she corrected. 'I help police officers catch thieves and murderers.'

The children's eyes got bigger.

'Have you caught anyone today?' the blonde girl asked.

Nina felt a smile develop inside her head and crack open on her face. 'I've tried,' she said. 'It's not easy. They're good at hiding, all the bad guys and bandits.'

The children had put their cutlery down and were looking at her, their mouths half open.

'Who's the nastiest murderer you've ever caught?' the darker boy asked.

She reflected. The children seemed used to dealing with complicated words and concepts. They didn't seem bothered by stories about death and tragic events – Annika's description of her conversation with the dead man's wife had made them listen carefully, not recoil in horror.

'Murderers aren't always nasty,' she said. 'Often they're just lonely and sad and angry.'

'So tell us about one who wasn't so nasty, then,' Annika's son said.

Nina smiled at him. He really was a lot like his mother. 'Once I caught a murderer, a young man, only twenty years old. He had killed his best friend with a knife. They were both very drunk, and they had an argument about something, and this young man got angry and grabbed a knife and stabbed his best friend with it. It hit him in the heart and the friend died. The murderer was very sad and really regretted what he had done afterwards.'

'You shouldn't drink so much that you lose your judgement,' the dark girl said.

'What's for dessert?' Annika's daughter asked.

'Ice-lollies,' Annika told her.

This evidently signalled that the meal was over. The

274

children got up at the same time, scraping their chairs, and cleared the dirty dishes into the kitchen.

'I can deal with this,' Jimmy said, opening the dish-washer.

'Let's go and sit in the study,' Annika said to Nina. She went into the hall, then a little room behind the kitchen – presumably it had once been for a maid. The walls were covered with shelves laden with books, folders and reports. A Super Elliptical table took up most of the space, with two laptops facing each other. Annika pulled out one of the office chairs and sat down. 'So, what exactly did I say to Q?' She brushed the hair off her face.

Her shoulders slumped slightly, but Nina didn't think that was anything to do with Q or work.

'Yes, what did I say?' Annika went on. 'I asked if he'd been involved in the search for Viola Söderland. He hadn't, but he knew my editor-in-chief had made a documentary about her, in which he concluded that she'd fled to Russia.'

'I've heard of that programme,' Nina said. 'I've never seen it, though.'

Annika nodded. 'You're a bit younger than me, but most people my age remember it, even if they didn't see it. Viola Söderland became almost a *cause célèbre*, like Nine/Eleven, or Abba winning the Eurovision Song Contest. On a much smaller scale, of course . . .'

Nina shifted on her chair. She wouldn't personally have compared either Abba or Viola Söderland with 9/11, but she understood the point. 'Did you mention that analogy to Q?' she couldn't help asking.

Annika smiled. 'I reminded him about the facts of the Viola Söderland case, that she had been planning her departure for a long time, buying a car without anyone's knowledge, changing her name before she left, getting hold of a second passport, cash from the Cayman Islands, sewing the money into her coat, packing a case with her wedding photograph and locks of her children's hair . . .'

Nina held up a hand to stop her. 'Hang on. She changed her name?'

Annika looked at Nina, her eyes narrowing. 'Q asked that as well. Why did you react to it?'

Nina took several shallow breaths. Q must have had good reason to tell her to breach the normal rules about the confidentiality of preliminary investigations. 'Nora Lerberg changed her name before she disappeared,' she said quietly. 'She adopted her maiden name, Andersson, and declared that she would now be using her middle name, Maria.'

The colour drained from Annika's face. 'When did she do that?'

'Almost a year ago. And in December last year she reported her handbag stolen, and with it her passport.'

Annika stood up and closed the door. She remained there, leaning against it. 'Has she been to the Cayman Islands recently?'

'No,' Nina said. 'But she did go to Switzerland. Last Friday, to Zürich, there and back in a day. She'd been lying to her sister-in-law, claiming that she has to keep going to Södermalm Hospital for treatment when she's really doing other things entirely.'

Annika went slowly back to her chair. 'A neighbour who works for the International Monetary Fund in Geneva has seen her on the flight several times, and she eats at expensive restaurants there. She tells her friends that she's doing yoga on Wednesday evenings, but she isn't. And she claims to listen to audio books, but hasn't got any time to read.'

Nina sat in silence.

'Has Nora bought a car recently?' Annika asked eventually.

'Not that we know of,' Nina said.

'Has she been to see a tailor?'

Nina looked at the window, trying to remember what Lamia had said that morning: hadn't there been something about a trip to see a tailor? In Östermalm?

'I think she might have,' Nina said.

'Have you got much idea about Nora's clothes?'

Nina gave her a quizzical look.

'According to the description, she was wearing trousers and an oilskin coat when she disappeared. Is that right?'

'We don't know for certain. That's an assumption.'

'Do you know if she's got any sort of Muslim outfit in her wardrobe?'

Nina's brain stopped working. 'You mean a burka?'

'A headscarf and full-length skirt, maybe a long coat.'

There were plenty of headscarves in Nora's wardrobe, and a long skirt as well, she was fairly sure of that. Maybe a couple of old coats too. Long? Difficult to say.

'What makes you . . . Why do you call it a Muslim outfit?'

'Haven't you ever tried it?' Annika said. 'Wrapping a scarf round your head the way Muslim women do? It makes you instantly invisible.'

No, Nina had never tried.

What did all this mean? Cars, trips, names, passports, lies . . . Thoughts were swirling through Nina's head, making her giddy.

She looked at her watch, a birthday present from Filip, and got to her feet. 'Can you email me the details about

Viola Söderland's disappearance?' she asked. 'Everything you know? I'll check if there's anything else in the police file about the search for her.'

Annika Bengtzon stood up too. 'It was good to see you again,' she said. 'You're welcome to come and have dinner with us any time you like.'

Nina's throat tightened. 'I'd love to,' she heard herself say.

That evening the sky cracked open and there was a hint of blue evening light on the horizon. The children were more unruly than usual, the boys fighting and Serena crying for her mother. Annika and Jimmy had to make emergency checks on the various bedrooms several times.

It was half past ten before the bedroom corridor was quiet at last.

'I need to let them know about the job tomorrow,' Jimmy said.

They were sitting on the sofa, curled up together in one corner. Annika's shoulders were resting against his broad stomach. She felt her chest tighten, and had to make an effort not to become stiff and unresponsive. 'What are you going to say?'

'What do you think?'

'Is this what you want? To be director general?'

'I think so.'

'Why?' she said quietly.

He stroked her hair. 'It's nothing to do with the title or the position, or the salary, actually. We've spent years on the criminal-justice system in the department, and I know exactly what I'd like to do.'

He fell silent.

'Murderers aren't always that nasty,' Annika said. 'Sometimes they're just lonely and sad and angry.'

Jimmy let out a quiet laugh. 'She's nice, Nina. How do you know her?'

Annika gazed out at the almost dark room. 'Just through work,' she said. 'I was doing a story, and was in her patrol car on Södermalm one night, way back when, with Julia Lindholm, and then I wrote about David's murder. Nina found him, so we had quite a bit to do with each other.' She didn't say any more. There were some things that not even Jimmy needed to know.

'What do you think about the job?' Jimmy asked. 'Should I take it?'

Annika took a deep breath. She was on the brink of tears. 'You should do whatever you feel you must,' she said, forcing herself to sound normal.

He took hold of her shoulders and turned her round so he could see her face. 'Why are you sad?'

She started to cry. 'I'm not sad,' she said.

He pulled her to him, stroking her back and kissing her hair.

FRIDAY, 17 MAY

The prestigious morning paper was first with the news.

Anders Schyman sat motionless at his desk with the newspaper spread out in front of him, letting the implications reach the pit of his stomach.

The headline ran:

I Killed Viola

On a professional level, there was only one way of interpreting this: Gustaf Holmerud was fair game once more. Any doubts there might have been about his status as a serial killer were gone now. In a way, the line he and the *Evening Post* had taken had won in the end.

The article was illustrated with a picture of Holmerud smiling, wearing the crayfish-party hat that had become the trademark of Sweden's Worst Ever Serial Killer. (He wasn't at all, even if he was telling the truth. The worst was still a teenager from Malmö who had killed twenty-seven old people in the late 1970s by making them drink disinfectant.) Alongside was the official photograph of Viola Söderland from the company report presenting the final year of accounts from her business empire, Golden Spire.

The bulk of the text was an interview with Holmerud's lawyer, in which he said his client had now also confessed to the murder of the long-missing billionairess, Viola Söderland. The murder was said to have taken place the night she disappeared from her home in Djursholm.

'This act has tormented my client for almost two decades,' the lawyer said. 'He is extremely relieved to be able to tell the truth at last.'

Below the article was some boxed text listing the other women whose murders Holmerud had confessed to: Sandra, Nalina, Eva, Linnea, Lena and Josefin. The prestigious morning paper naturally maintained a neutral position regarding the veracity of the confessions, but they were presented differently from before. The information was treated seriously, with reference made to police sources and detectives, prosecutors and lawyers, in much the same way that Sjölander had in their own coverage.

Then, on the following double-page spread, there was the article that had elevated Holmerud to credible-witness status. The headline wasn't in a particularly large font, or even especially bold, but it sealed Schyman's fate.

Schyman Documentary Untrue

claimed the headline. A senior judge had reached the relatively simple conclusion that editor-in-chief Anders Schyman and convicted serial killer Gustaf Holmerud could not both be telling the truth, and if Holmerud was right, then Schyman was obviously wrong.

Obviously.

And, these days, Holmerud was a credible source.

Schyman looked at his own photograph. His sense of unreality made the room tilt slightly. The picture was relatively recent. He really had put on weight. Everything was silent around him, except an irritating, high-pitched hum coming from somewhere inside his skull. He looked out through the glass windows at the newsroom. The staff were moving in freeze-frame across the floor, like ants in autumn, talking in small groups, a few glancing in his direction.

The potentially hypocritical journalistic attitude of the prestigious morning paper couldn't really be criticized. News came in varying degrees of significance. Stories balanced each other out. Holmerud's tales hadn't previously been considered interesting enough, and journalistic integrity had weighed more heavily than a spectacular headline, but the consequences of this new confession had tipped the scales in his favour.

The article would also have another effect: the flood-gates were wide open now. Once part of the established media had decided he was guilty, there was no way back. Any hope there might have been of the story miraculously disappearing had now been utterly and mercilessly crushed.

He leafed through the rest of the paper but couldn't be bothered to read anything. Articles about the weather, one about a big cocaine trial under the codename PLAYA that was entering its fifth month, one citing unconfirmed reports that the under-secretary of state at the Ministry of Justice had accepted the post of director general of the Prison and Probation Service, something about disturbances in Thailand with a large number of fatalities.

He let the realization sink in.

All that remained before he reached the edge of the cliff was the bit where he was hounded through the streets.

Just like everyone else who had been 'unmasked' and forced to resign.

His departure into the shadows would lead to a brief moment of triumph for his colleagues. Then there would be a new day and fresh headlines, and he would be branded as the editor who had had to go because of some mistake that no one could remember.

Just like Ingemar Lerberg was remembered as the politician who had fiddled his tax.

Unless he chose to take a completely different path. He couldn't go backwards, this particular story couldn't be rewound, and his flanks were covered by reporters sharpening their machetes.

There was only one other option: upwards.

He would have to acquire wings. Learn to fly. Take the debate to a completely new level. With wings he would be able to sail across the chasm and not fall to his doom in its depths. The altitude would probably give him vertigo, but at least he wouldn't be killed by the fall. He might even be able to land, albeit at the risk of breaking an ankle.

Patrik Nilsson was heading towards the glass cubicle, his gait uncertain and uncomfortable. He opened the door without knocking. 'The staff are unsettled,' he said nervously. 'There's going to be an extraordinary meeting of the union. The representative is calling for your resignation. What do I tell them?'

Schyman studied the young head of news carefully, noting the agitated look in his eyes and the uneasy set of his shoulders. 'Give me half an hour,' he said. 'Then I want a general meeting in the newsroom. It's to be broadcast live on the website. Talk to our video people and get them to rig up lights and cameras. The quality needs to be good enough for the mainstream broadcasters to show. Are the rest of the media calling?'

286

'Constantly. You're not taking calls, so they're being put through to me.'

'Refer them to the live broadcast from now on,' Schyman said, then picked up his phone to indicate that the conversation was over.

'What are we doing about tomorrow's news?' Nilsson asked, with a note of desperation in his voice. 'What's our lead story?'

Schyman put the phone down for a moment as he let the idea dance in his mind. 'Best-selling headline of the year,' he said. '*Heat-wave on its way.*'

Nilsson's face cracked into a relieved smile as he shut the door and headed off towards the web-TV department.

Schyman picked up the phone again and made his first call.

The digital files were arranged numerically on Nina's computer, forty-five of them, all the surveillance recordings from the trains and stations along the Saltsjöbanan line, from its terminus at Solsidan all the way to Slussen in the centre of Stockholm, covering the departures at 09.17, 09.37 and 09.57 on the morning of Monday, 13 May. Lamia had labelled them carefully and clearly: there was no way anyone was going to watch them in the wrong order. That was when the text message alerting the police about the assault on Silvervägen had been sent, from one of Nora's mobile phones. Someone had been in or close to the station at 09.36 on the morning in question, and Nina had a fairly good idea of who she was looking for.

She double-clicked on the first file, and the platform of Solsidan station filled her screen. According to the digital

287

clock in the top left corner, the film sequence began at 09.15.00. There was a train in the station, its doors open, and people were hurrying to board it. The film consisted of a sequence of separate pictures taken approximately one per second. The quality was grainy black-and-white. The sporadic pictures meant that people moved jerkily, like some ancient silent movie, but Nina didn't care. She adjusted the settings so that the film played very slowly. That way she could study each photograph for a few seconds, scrutinizing the new passengers as they appeared before they were swallowed by the train. There weren't many: the morning rush was over. There were no recordings from inside the carriages. Stockholm Local Traffic had camera surveillance in all buses and most Underground trains, but not on the suburban train line out to Saltsjöbaden.

The time on the surveillance footage reached 09.17.00, the doors closed and the train pulled away jerkily. The platform was left deserted in the rain. Presumably the people of Solsidan knew when the next train departed, at 09.37, and the platform remained abandoned for minute after minute.

Nina's mind started to wander as the film jerked forward, second by second. With nothing happening on the screen, it looked almost like a still photograph of tracks and grey vegetation.

In front of her on the desk was a copy of the drawing she had been given by Kristine Lerberg, Isak's picture of himself, his brother and sister, and their 'guardian angel'. The original had been sent to Forensics for comparison with the child's drawing that had been recovered from the crime scene at Kråkträsken.

Isak was good at drawing: the picture had been made with plenty of enthusiasm and an eye for detail. Nina remembered the picture he had drawn of Kristine: her shoes had been the right type and colour, her indoor shoes, the ones she wore when she got home and had taken off her boots.

Nina pulled the copy closer and studied Isak's 'angel'. It was a small figure, fairly broad and squat, with curly black hair, wide dark trousers and a loose top. She was strikingly short, her feet pointed outward slightly, as if she were rather bow-legged, and on her feet she was wearing what could well be a pair of slippers, size 34.

Some youths appeared on the screen in front of her: they seemed to be staring at the same mobile phone. They stopped on the platform, heads close together, for several minutes.

Nina felt her concentration slipping. She had received the autopsy report about Karl Gustaf Ekblad at the morning meeting and reached for it now. He had died from asphyxiation. The injuries to his body were terrible, but not as comprehensive as Ingemar Lerberg's. There was also a DNA sequence from the skin found under his fingernail. It hadn't led anywhere as yet, but somehow it pleased her that Kag had struggled and managed to scratch his killer.

At 09.31 a train arrived from Slussen. A few people got off, collars turned up and umbrellas at the ready. The train remained where it was, standing at the station with its doors open. The youngsters got on. The platform was left deserted once more. Then a young mother appeared with a huge pushchair, which caught in the doorway as she was climbing onto the train – she was visibly upset. She was followed by an elderly couple, the man supporting the woman, then two men in thick overcoats carrying briefcases and talking on their mobiles.

At 09.36.30, just before the train was due to depart, a very short figure hurried onto the platform and got into the rear carriage. Nina stopped the film. Was it a child? She clicked back a few frames. There was the figure once more, extremely short, one metre thirty centimetres tall, maybe one forty, dressed in dark clothing. It definitely wasn't a child – the figure was far too thick-set. Nina could only see her from behind, but she was certain it was a woman. She had curly black hair.

Hello, little angel.

The doors closed and the train pulled away.

Nina clicked away from the film and opened the next file, the recording from the next station on the line, Erstaviksbadet. Two women walked onto the platform separately, seemed to exchange a few words; presumably they knew each other. The train from Solsidan appeared at 09.38 and the women got on together, but no one got off.

Nina switched film.

The next station, Tattby, one minute later.

The elderly couple got off, the man helping his wife.

Next film.

Tippen, 09.40. A group of five youngsters got on; no one got off.

Igelboda, the final stop of the branch line leading to Solsidan, three minutes later. The train emptied, everyone got off and crossed the platform to catch the train from Saltsjöbaden to Slussen. The dumpy angel with curly dark hair was just visible behind the woman with the pushchair. The train set off a minute later.

Nina's fingers trembled as she clicked to start the next film.

Fisksätra, 09.45.

She stared at the middle carriage as if hypnotized. The doors slid open. The dark-haired woman got out and walked quickly towards the exit. Her face wasn't caught on camera.

Disappointment was growing.

Fisksätra.

The woman had travelled to Fisksätra, the most densely populated town in Sweden. How would she be able to find her there? A faceless woman with no name?

Nina clicked to close the media player on her computer, then stared at the blank screen.

Fisksätra was a residential area. People lived there. They didn't go there to shop or have coffee.

So the little woman lived there, the little woman who had sounded the alarm on a mobile phone registered to Nora Lerberg.

Nina felt her shoulders tense. If she was lucky, the flats there would all be rented out by the same landlord or housing association. If she was unlucky, they'd been sold off and there would be hundreds of little housing associations, with no shared database.

She went online to see what the situation was.

All the apartment blocks in Fisksätra were rented, and they all seemed to be owned by the same landlord, a company called Stena Properties.

She breathed out and called the main exchange, explained who she was, and asked to speak to someone responsible for rentals and contracts.

'What area?' the cheery receptionist asked.

Stena was evidently a large company. Nina clarified what she wanted.

'We'll call you back at National Crime. That way we can verify your identity before divulging any information.'

Good, Nina thought.

One minute later her phone rang. The person responsible for the rental of flats in Fisksätra was a man with a pronounced Stockholm accent. 'No, we don't have a Nora

Lerberg among our tenants,' he said. 'Sorry, love.'

Nina took a silent breath. Her luck seemed to have run out. Already? There had to be another way forward, another opening.

'Maria,' she said. 'Have you got a tenant by the name of Maria Andersson?'

'What year was she born?'

'Twenty-six.'

The man whistled to himself as he tapped at his computer.

'Yep,' he said. 'A Maria Andersson, born on the ninth of September, could that be the one?'

Nina closed her eyes. 'Yes,' she said. 'That's her. What's the address of the flat she's renting?'

'Braxengatan twenty-two, fourth floor.'

'How long has she had it?'

The man whistled some more. 'Since July last year.'

Not quite a year.

Nina thanked him for his help and hung up. A moment later her phone rang again – had he forgotten something?

'*Señorita Hoffman? Hola. Buenos días, qué tal? Todo está bien con usted allí en el frío?*'

The Spanish policeman sounded as if they'd known each other all their lives, and Nina's chest filled with warmth. '*Sí, señor,*' she said, smiling at the phone. 'And all the better for hearing your voice.'

The man laughed. 'I've got some information for you,' he said. 'The man you asked about, Karl Gustav Evertere Ekblad, is listed as sole proprietor of the five companies you mentioned.'

Nina swallowed her disappointment. She had been hoping for a minority shareholder somewhere on the periphery.

292

'But it isn't Karl Gustav – how did you pronounce that name?'

'Evert,' Nina said.

'It isn't him who runs the companies, though. Someone else has been authorized to access all the accounts, and looks after the invoices and transactions. Her name is Nora Maria Lerberg.'

Yes! It was her, Nora. No Andersson this time: she'd had the companies in Spain before she adopted her maiden name. Five Spanish companies, for which she paid Kag, an alcoholic from Orminge, to act as a front. Kag was the face of Nora's businesses, and for his trouble received money for drink, rent and thin-bread rolls. Nora was able to launder her money without anyone knowing.

'Do you have an address for the authorized signatory?'

'Yes, she's a *residente* here, and is listed at the same address as the proprietor.'

He gave her the name of a street in Nueva Andalucía, the district where all the companies were registered, and promised to send her an email containing all the details and extracts from official databases.

'Do you go on holiday, Señorita Hoffman?' the policeman asked. 'Have you ever thought about paying us a visit down here in the sun? It's very warm and sunny here, twenty-six degrees in the shade.'

Nina thanked him, hung up, and put her hand down gently on Isak's drawing.

Berit Hamrin was heading towards her usual seat with her suitcase rolling behind her. Annika leaped to her feet and gave her a hug. 'How was Oslo?'

293

'Expensive.'

Valter stood up, looking slightly lost. 'Valter Wennergren, trainee,' he said, shaking Berit's hand. 'I'm sorry, I'm in your place. I'll move at once.'

'No, stay where you are,' Berit said, taking her coat off. 'I can squat at the end of the table for the time being. What's going on here, then?' She nodded towards the newsdesk, where the web-TV team had set up their studio camera, a microphone on a boom, and a large lamp. Bulky cables snaked across half of the room and people kept tripping over them.

'Schyman's about to address the nation,' Annika said.

'About time,' Berit said.

At that moment Schyman strode out of his room with a determined expression. He nodded to Berit. 'We can talk about Norway this afternoon,' he said, as he passed them.

'So he's not thinking of resigning before lunch, then,' Annika said quietly.

The editor-in-chief installed himself in front of the camera. Annika was glad he hadn't decided to stand on the desk. He exchanged a few words with the online editor, then raised his eyes to look out across the newsroom.

'OK, everyone,' he said, in a loud, firm voice. 'If I could just have your attention for a few minutes?'

They fell silent, moving slowly and hesitantly towards the desk, as if the television lamp were dangerous or infectious. Annika, Valter and Berit moved a few steps closer, but stopped at a suitable distance.

'As you are all aware,' Schyman began, 'I am currently the subject of a great deal of scrutiny on the internet and in various other media as a result of a television documentary I made eighteen years ago. There's nothing odd about that.

We scrutinize each other's work far too infrequently in this business, and when it does happen, it is often poorly and uncritically done.'

Annika realized she was holding her breath. She exhaled and forced her shoulders to relax from their hunched posture. Schyman seemed as cool as a cucumber.

'For me, this scrutiny has led to a great deal of self-criticism and reflection,' he went on. 'There are things I could have done differently when I made the programme. But, above all, the criticism has made me think about the way I work now, and how my colleagues and competitors reason when they make decisions about whether or not to publish a story.'

'You can tell he used to be a television presenter,' Berit muttered.

Schyman looked out over the newsroom as he spoke, ignoring the television camera and addressing himself to the people in the room, even if it was abundantly clear that he was focused on the camera the whole time. This speech wasn't aimed primarily at his colleagues on the *Evening Post*, but at the rest of the industry.

'It's a good thing that the rest of the media, in large part, have maintained their sceptical, neutral attitude towards information found on the internet,' he said.

'They've hardly done that, though,' Valter whispered.

'Definitely not,' Annika whispered back. 'But he can't have a go at the rest of the media because they'd get defensive and stop listening to what he's saying. He can't afford to rub them up the wrong way.'

'The internet is an excellent forum for debate and democracy and freedom of speech,' Schyman said. 'But the decision about whether or not to publish any material becomes bigger and more important the more players there are in the arena. There is every reason for me and others to ask ourselves if we are really taking that responsibility seriously.'

'Where's he going with this?' Valter asked.

'Trying to shift the focus of the debate, I assume,' Berit whispered.

'So, as recently as this morning, I have spoken to representatives of the Ministry of Justice about reinforcing the responsibilities inherent in publishing. Power, even power held by the public, has to come with responsibility. We have to be held accountable for anything expressed in the public arena. Individuals need to be protected from threats and slander. Not primarily the editors of large newspapers, but young people on Facebook, Twitter and other social media, female commentators, sports presenters, bloggers of every gender and ethnicity . . . This is a vitally important democratic issue.'

Annika shifted her weight to the other foot. When was he going to get to the point? He couldn't carry on like this much longer, or people would stop listening.

'If I might return to my own situation, I can see that the blogger, the Light of Truth, has put a great deal of work into the rhetoric of denouncing me and the opinions I expressed in an almost twenty-year-old television programme,' Schyman went on, sounding almost amused. 'However, he hasn't been quite as skilful when it comes to his journalism. Later this afternoon, on the *Evening Post* website, we will be releasing a number of previously unknown details that have arisen in the case of Viola Söderland's disappearance. We will also publish interviews with a number of people who were close to Viola Söderland. This involves no risk either to me personally or the *Evening Post* newspaper. We shall take responsibility for what we publish – about that there is no doubt whatsoever.'

He said this in a way that let the assembled staff breathe out, without knowing why.

'One question,' the union representative called. He had once been one of the morning-shift editors, but had been struck by writer's block and now worked full-time as union rep. 'Gustaf Holmerud has claimed responsibility for Viola Söderland's murder. That means you were wrong all along, doesn't it?'

Schyman held his ground with a good-natured expression on his face. 'Yes,' he said. 'I read that too. It is a fact that the *Evening Post* has led the way in the reporting of Gustaf Holmerud's crimes and confession, and of course he has been convicted of no fewer than five murders, both in the Crown Court and the Court of Appeal. But we don't stop our coverage of the case simply because the verdict has been pronounced. We are already investigating the background and circumstances surrounding these, in part, highly questionable judgments. You will be able to read much more about this in the *Evening Post* in the future.'

Annika saw how Sjölander flew up from his relaxed position by the sports desk – he had clearly known nothing about this.

The editor-in-chief got ready to leave the limelight.

'One more question,' the union rep shouted.

Schyman stopped and looked tolerantly at the man, who was obviously plucking up courage to say something.

'Are you going to resign?' he asked.

Schyman blinked as if the question were a joke. 'No,' he said. 'Why would I do that?'

Then he turned away, the light went out and the live broadcast was over. The editor-in-chief strode purposefully

297

through the newsroom. Halfway to his glass box he turned to Annika, pointed at her, then at his office.

'Oh, shit,' Annika said. 'What now?'

'Close the door,' Schyman said, when Annika walked into his room.

He sat behind his desk and studied some documents in front of him. She slid the door shut behind her and stood in the middle of the cramped floor space. 'Nice speech,' she said. 'Do you think it'll be enough?'

'Not by a long shot,' he said, 'but it might do as a start. I've got a job for you.'

She sat down in the visitor's chair. As long as whatever it was didn't take all day – Birgitta was bringing Destiny over that evening: the little girl would be staying at theirs for the weekend. 'Apart from finding Viola Söderland?'

'Viola Söderland's dead,' Schyman said, without looking up. 'At least she is if this fellow's to be believed.'

He handed the documents to Annika. It was a printout of the police interview with Gustaf Holmerud in which he confessed to the murder of the billionairess, a document that most definitely wasn't in the public domain.

'Sjölander's got some good sources,' Annika murmured.

'I want you to go through all the cases Holmerud was convicted of,' Schyman said. 'I want you to rip those verdicts to shreds.'

She looked up sharply. Schyman sighed. 'Yes, yes,' he said, 'I know. You never believed in him. You think those women were killed by their husbands or boyfriends. Well, now's your chance to investigate it properly.'

'So I'm supposed to act like some sort of Don Quixote, going on the attack against the entire justice system all on my own?'

Suddenly he looked very tired. 'I was serious about us taking responsibility,' he said. 'Those verdicts were wrong. We pushed the police and the prosecutor into finding him guilty, and now I've got to try to put things right.'

The bitter light of hindsight, Annika thought, as she returned to the printout.

Holmerud had given a detailed account of how he had kidnapped and murdered Viola, strangling her and dumping her body in a lake he would never be able to find again.

'Have you read the Light of Truth today?' Schyman asked.

She shook her head.

'Linette Pettersson and Sven-Olof Witterfeldt are demanding that I be tried for fraud. Their legal knowledge seems a little limited, to put it mildly. The blogger himself is claiming that the documentary caused Viola's daughter, Linda, to have a miscarriage. I am, in other words, both a fraudster and a child-killer.'

'You've got to sue him,' Annika said. 'He's crossing all sorts of boundaries now.'

The editor-in-chief shrugged his shoulders. 'Several things are slanderous, but that would only play into his hands. He wants a trial, an established platform, and I'm not going to give it to him.'

She felt her frustration growing. 'What do you want me to do? Get Holmerud's convictions quashed against his own wishes?'

Schyman scratched his beard. 'Maybe you could get him to agree with you? Get him to retract his confession?'

'And why would he do that? He probably did murder Lena, so he'd still get a life sentence. He'll end up in Kumla as a wife-killer, way down the food-chain. But if he carries on claiming all those murders, he'll be a legend.'

'So you don't want to do it?'

Annika sighed. Of course she wanted to do it, she really did. Those verdicts needed to be scrutinized: the police investigation had been sloppy and biased and ought to be examined, and the prosecutor who hadn't bothered to look into the case properly should be confronted, the relatives' grief and despair acknowledged.

Schyman's intercom crackled.

'You've got visitors,' Tore said, from the caretaker's desk.

Annika stood up to leave. 'I want you to stay,' Schyman said.

On the other side of the newsroom she could see a confused-looking middle-aged couple.

'Henrik Söderland and his sister Linda,' the editor-in-chief said. 'I thought they should have the briefcase back.'

Braxengatan was on the outskirts of Fisksätra. The area was part of the so-called Million Homes Programme, housing that was erected at the cheapest possible cost on the edges of the big cities between 1965 and 1975, creating a whole raft of social problems.

Nina parked next to a garage door and climbed a flight of steps to get to the entry level. The blocks were brown and white, five storeys high, and hundreds of metres long. Nina walked past door after door until she finally reached number twenty-two.

The stairwell was cool and light and smelt of disinfectant. She went up the stairs, silent in her rubber soles. Various sounds filtered out of the flats she passed, cartoon characters chasing each other, the hum of a fan, a man coughing. On the fourth floor she stopped outside a door marked ANDERSSON. There was no letterbox she could

300

peer through, and no sound of activity inside. She stood there for a minute or so, arms by her sides, then reached out her finger to the doorbell and pressed it.

Nothing happened.

She tried again.

Still no response.

She banged on the door. Hard.

'Open up,' she said loudly. 'This is the police.'

She rang again, three times in succession. The flats around her fell silent, until only the fan was audible.

Shit, shit, shit.

She wasn't going to be defeated now she had found her way here. She would wait until the little woman came home, or until she was on the brink of starvation and had to go out to buy food. Or until the landlord came to evict her because Nora hadn't paid the rent.

'If you don't open the door within ten seconds, we'll break it down,' she shouted.

The lock clicked. The handle was pressed down, and the door opened. The short woman from the train, and from Isak's drawing, was standing before her in the doorway: curly hair, slightly bowed legs. She was in her fifties, dressed in dark trousers and a brown cardigan.

'Please, don't shout on the landing. Come in.'

Her English was perfect, her accent British.

Nina stepped into the flat and looked around the hall: two cupboards, a door that presumably led to the bathroom. She darted quickly over to it and pulled it open. Yes, shower and toilet, empty. She closed the door.

'How can I help you?' the woman asked.

Her face was in deep shadow, but Nina could still tell that she was very frightened. She moved quickly into the larger room: no one. The woman probably lived alone –

she recognized the reflection of her own solitude. Nothing jarred. A narrow bed stood along one wall, with a table and two wooden chairs by the window, and a tiny kitchen area towards the bathroom.

'My name is Nina Hoffman. I'm from the Swedish National Crime Unit,' Nina said, showing her ID. The woman took it and studied it carefully.

'What's your name?' Nina asked.

The woman gave the ID back and looked at the floor. 'Irina,' she said. 'Irina Azarova.'

Maybe that was true, maybe it wasn't.

The woman was making an effort to seem calm and collected, but was fiddling nervously with the buttons of her cardigan. Irina Azarova. She must come from the east, even if it wasn't clear from her accent. Either she had grown up in a Communist dictatorship, or she had fled from one, or had relatives or some other personal connection to the old Soviet bloc. It seemed likely that she would have great respect for the authorities, hopefully rather too great.

'I have a long list of questions for you, Irina Azarova,' Nina said, in a loud, authoritative voice. 'Do you want to answer them here, or do you want to come with me to the National Crime Unit and answer them in an interview room?'

The woman seemed to shrink, and her hands began to shake.

'*Please*,' she said, sounding as if she was about to cry. 'I haven't done anything. Nothing illegal.'

'So where's your work permit?' Nina asked. 'You work for the Lerbergs on Silvervägen in Saltsjöbaden. And you were at a crime scene where a man was found very badly assaulted. You alerted the police by sending a text message from Solsidan railway station . . .'

Irina Azarova sank onto one of the wooden chairs and started to cry. Nina stood where she was, in the middle of the floor. People were always upset to receive an unannounced visit from the police, but this outburst of sobbing was out of all proportion. It had to be a response to something else.

She let the woman cry for a few minutes. When she spoke again, her voice was soft. 'We could talk here for a while,' she said, 'and see if that will do. How does that sound?'

The woman fished a handkerchief out of the pocket of her cardigan, carefully blew her nose and nodded. Nina sat down on the other chair. In the light from the only window she could see some knitting, pink wool.

'What's that going to be?' Nina said, nodding towards it.

Irina Azarova grabbed it and put it into a plastic bag that contained several other balls of wool. 'For the girl,' she said. 'For little Elisabeth.' Nora's youngest child.

'How long have you worked for Nora Lerberg?' Nina asked, putting her mobile phone on the table with its recording device switched on.

'One year,' she said.

'And what have your duties been?'

Irina glanced up at her.

'I know you're there secretly,' Nina said. 'No one knows you work for Nora. She's very careful to say she does everything herself.'

Irina nodded. 'She's a politician's wife, and credibility is important to politicians. Setting a good example to the voters. She wants to be popular among the wives in the area. She wants them to like her, accept her.' She nodded to underline her words.

'So Nora brought you in to take care of her duties as a housewife.'

The woman looked frightened again.

'Can you describe a typical day at work to me?' Nina said gently.

Irina cleared her throat. 'Her husband leaves home to go to work at a quarter to nine. Nora takes the children to the church playgroup at nine o'clock. I arrive on the train that gets into Solsidan just after nine and I take the path through the woods so I can arrive at the house the back way. No one sees me. I let myself in through the kitchen door and work until one o'clock . . .'

'What do you do in the house?'

'Clear breakfast away, clean, do the washing and ironing. I bake cakes and bread, get the evening meal ready so Nora only has to heat it up . . .'

'You fit a lot in.'

The woman blushed. 'Not really. In the afternoons I usually work here, in the flat. Anything that takes a long time to cook I prepare here and take it to Nora the next morning, stews, roast elk, stuffed cabbage, the bread and cakes as well.'

She pronounced the Swedish dishes in an almost perfect Stockholm accent.

'And the knitting?' Nina said.

'Nora thinks handicrafts are important.'

'Do the children know that you work in the house?'

She nodded again. 'Sometimes I stay later, when the children are having their afternoon nap. The boy has seen me several times, the elder one, Isak. He's very bright. Nora said I was an angel who watched over them. He spoke to me, in Swedish, but I never answered. It hurt me, having to lie to the boy. I don't really know what he thinks of me.'

'That you're an angel,' Nina said. 'At least, that's how he refers to you.'

'Has he mentioned me?' she asked anxiously.

Nina studied her carefully. 'Do you know where Nora is?'

The woman's face closed. She didn't answer.

'Do you know anything about her business abroad?'

Still no answer.

'What happened a year ago, when Nora employed you? Something must have happened because until then she managed to look after the house and take care of her husband's accounts on her own. Then all of a sudden she couldn't do it any more. She started to run out of time, began to plan her escape, and got you to help her . . .'

The woman stared at her hands.

'Where are you really from?' Nina asked.

'I don't know if I want to say any more now.'

Nina considered her options. 'Under Swedish law, you've committed a crime by working here without a work permit,' she said. 'You could be fined or spend up to a year in prison for what you've done. And that's if I choose to ignore the fact that you might have assaulted Ingemar Lerberg.'

The woman looked up at Nina and her eyes filled with tears again. 'I never met her husband, not until I saw him lying there on the bed.'

Nina believed her. She wasn't responsible for the assault: she didn't have the physical strength. But she might have been an accomplice, in either word or deed: she could have provided information about the Lerbergs' habits and routines – even unlocked the door.

'If you're honest with me, I won't report you,' she said. 'But for that to work, I need you to tell me everything you know about Nora Lerberg and her business dealings. What do you say?'

The woman nodded.

Nina gulped. She didn't have the authority to make that sort of promise. She would just have to break it if she had to. Or not.

'Where are you from?'

'Ukraine,' Irina Azarova said quietly. 'From Chernobyl. My husband is dead, but my daughters are still there, studying in Kiev. Nadia's going to be a doctor, Juliana a lawyer. I support them.'

Nina checked her mobile phone to make sure their conversation was still being recorded. 'How did you first come into contact with Nora?'

'I put an advert on the internet, saying I could give language tuition. She replied to the advert.'

'Language tuition?'

The woman wiped her nose and tucked her handkerchief back in her pocket. 'Nora wanted to learn Russian. I used to teach Russian and English in Chernobyl, at the high school. It was a good job but very badly paid, and my husband was ill for years, ever since the girls were little. When he died and the girls were going to university, I had to get a different job, a job in the West . . .'

'So Nora wanted to learn Russian?'

Irina Azarova nodded. 'She studied with me, private lessons every Wednesday evening. That was how we started. And she spent a lot of time listening to a Russian-language course on her headphones. She was clever, a quick learner.'

'If you were teaching her Russian, how come you started to do housework for her?'

'Nora had a lot of work to do with the businesses. She was sometimes up all night, and didn't have time for the washing and cleaning.'

'Do you know what those businesses were?'

The woman paused. 'She looked after the accounts of

different companies,' she said. 'I don't know what they were. She never had any meetings with clients in the house.'

'Where did she see them?'

'In Switzerland. I used to have the house to myself on those days. I would change the curtains, clean the place from top to bottom . . .'

'How did she do the accounts? On paper, or on a computer?'

'On computers, two different ones. She spent a lot of time every day working on them.'

Two computers. Two mobile phones. Two passports. Two identities, and at least three addresses: Marbella, Fisksätra, and Silvervägen. Were there any more? Five businesses in Spain. More? She laundered money. Her own? Or someone else's? If so, whose? And where did she get the money from?

'Why?' Nina said quietly. 'Why did she start all this?'

'She once said that she had borrowed money.'

Nina waited. When Irina said nothing, she prompted, 'Borrowed money? Who from? The bank?'

'I don't think so.'

'But why? Ingemar's business was doing well. Did she have expensive tastes? Did she use drugs? Was she a gambler?'

Irina Azarova looked almost insulted on Nora's behalf. 'Definitely not. She was very careful with money, and she barely drank, not even wine. And I never saw her show any interest in betting.'

Nina looked out of the window at a ragged treetop, and behind it an identical brown and white building. Somehow it all fitted together: Nora had borrowed money from the wrong people and was running an international money-laundering operation. Over the past year she had got into financial difficulties.

The Spanish authorities tightened the laws, the construction industry collapsed, and the money-laundering machinery began to break down.

But whose money was she laundering? Hardly her own: she didn't have the resources for that. Was she a smurf for some international syndicate, the people she had borrowed money from, perhaps?

'I don't understand,' Nina said. 'How could she get involved with something like this?'

'She wanted to save his life.'

'Whose life? Ingemar's? He wasn't dying, was he?'

'He needed a platform from which he could influence society, to gain respect.'

'But isn't he afraid of being found out?'

Irina looked horrified. 'Oh, no! Her husband doesn't know anything – he mustn't! He doesn't know that I work in the house. Nora always arranges her meetings in Switzerland for when he's away on business.'

Nina looked out at the treetop again. It had all started seven years ago, after Ingemar's resignation from top-level politics, after all the articles and the supposed tax fraud.

All to gain *respect*.

'Do you know where Nora is now?'

Irina Azarova shook her head.

'She never mentioned that she was planning to flee?'

'No, but she did say she might disappear one day. She was scared and worried. She gave me a mobile phone, told me to send a text message if anything happened to her or her family.'

'Disappear?'

'That's what she said.'

'Die, or flee?'

'I took it to mean that she was frightened.'

'Who of?'

'She never said.'

'Why did she want to learn Russian?'

'I don't know. I asked, but she just said that there were some things it was better not to know.'

'What sort of Russian did Nora study?'

'Ordinary Russian. She used an ordinary language course for beginners.'

'Any special vocabulary? Words or phrases about a particular subject?'

'Nothing like that. Just words and pronunciation and grammar from the course book.'

'Could she have been working for Russians?'

Irina didn't answer.

'There's no office in the house on Silvervägen,' Nina said. 'Where did Nora sit when she did her work?'

'At the kitchen table. She kept the computers in one of the kitchen cupboards.'

That was true. Nora's computer had been found in a compartment next to the cupboard containing the pots and pans, the computer she worked on when she was doing the accounts for Ingemar's company.

'Was there anywhere else she used to keep them?'

The Ukrainian woman stared at her. 'No! There's no office in the house. Ingemar's business was run from a different address.'

Could Nora have taken the other computer with her when she'd left?

According to Kristine Lerberg, Nora had walked out with nothing but her oilskin coat. She didn't even take an umbrella or her handbag. Could she have sewn a laptop into the lining? Perhaps, but that was unlikely – too bulky. Kristine's story of how Nora had left the house had been second-hand, though, filtered through Ingemar. And if Nina and Annika Bengtzon's theory was true, Nora had had a second-hand car parked somewhere in the neighbourhood, a car no one knew belonged to her. She could have hidden the computer in the boot, with her old passport and a bag containing the money. But if she used the computer every day, it would have been impractical to keep it in the car.

'You've still got your key to the house?' Nina asked.

The woman nodded.

'Would you mind giving it to me?'

Irina stood up, went out into the hall and came back with a key that she handed to Nina.

'Have you been back to the house since you found Ingemar?'

'No,' the Ukrainian woman said. 'Can I ask you something?' She was calmer now. 'How did you find me?'

There wasn't really any reason to lie. 'Isak's drawings,' Nina said. 'He drew you in one of his pictures. And then I saw you on surveillance-camera footage from Solsidan.'

The woman slumped on her chair again. 'I stand out in a crowd,' she said. 'It's a genetic mutation, inherited. I was born with too little IGF-1, a growth hormone. The girls haven't got it, thank God.' She smiled fleetingly. 'I can't carry on living here,' she said. 'Where am I going to go? Where am I going to find another job?'

Nina picked up her mobile phone, switched off the recorder and tucked it into her pocket with the key. She gave the woman her card. 'This is my direct line, and my mobile number. I'll need to talk to you again, so call and tell me where you end up.'

Irina nodded.

Nina shook her hand and left the flat.

Irina Azarova would never call her, but that didn't matter.

Ingemar Lerberg had indicated that he had been tortured by two men, not a very short woman.

And a professional torturer, or anyone working with him, would never leave a pair of slippers at the scene of a crime.

Annika had written the text of the article and conducted the web-TV interview. Of course. She always made sure she was the focus of everything, gathering the very worst gossip, making herself out to be incredibly important.

Thomas clicked the symbol to open the video and a blonde woman filled the screen. She was identified as Linda Viljeberg, the daughter of missing billionairess Viola Söderland.

'It doesn't make any difference if my mother is alive,' she said. 'To me she's been dead for twenty years, ever since she chose to walk out on us without a word.'

The video showed a light brown briefcase that was said to contain Viola's 'most cherished memories'. Linda Viljeberg had tears in her eyes as she looked through the old pictures, a pair of baby's shoes . . .

'This feels surprisingly good,' she said. 'Mum took us with her when she left. She didn't leave us behind altogether.'

She wiped away a tear.

A map of northern Finland appeared on the screen, and Annika's hoarse voice croaked that Viola's car had been discovered at the Russian border with the key still in it, two weeks after her disappearance. That was where the brown briefcase had been found.

'What do you think of the Light of Truth?' Annika's voice asked, from somewhere out of shot.

Linda Viljeberg's head snapped back. 'I've never spoken to that blogger. He's never got in touch with either me or my brother. I don't understand where he gets it all from.'

Irritated, Thomas clicked to close the video. Anders Schyman still hadn't resigned, even though the entire internet was howling for him to be sacked. His door was closed, but he listened for noises in the corridor. He heard nothing so he went onto the blog and read the latest comments on the Light of Truth.

Gregorius was now one of the most liked and praised commentators on the whole site: 4.5 out of a possible 5.0 on the star rankings, and more than three hundred people had clicked to like his comment. A warm glow spread through him.

He was itching to add another comment, but he couldn't risk logging in from the government chancellery: that could have horrifying consequences.

A sharp knock at the door made him jump. He clicked to close his browser as Jimmy Halenius walked into the room. 'Hello, Thomas,' he said in a low voice.

Thomas stared at him. What the hell was he doing there?

'What . . . Has something happened?' he asked, as his tongue seemed to swell in his mouth.

The under-secretary of state didn't cut a particularly impressive figure. He was wearing dark blue chinos, a shirt but no tie, and a jacket that was rather too big for him. He ran a hand through his hair, making it even messier than usual.

'I don't know if you've noticed the information that's been circulating in the media this morning?' he said.

Thomas's stomach turned somersaults and he felt dizzy.

He wanted to smash the bastard's face in with his useless bloody hook – what the hell was he talking about? There was so much information circulating – Anders Schyman? Annika's video report?

'Er,' he said. 'What exactly?'

'That I'm to take over as director general of the Prison and Probation Service. It isn't true. I've turned it down.'

Thomas felt sweat trickle down his back. He hadn't seen that. Should he have done? Did that make him a lazy, badly informed employee who didn't keep up with the news?

'Well,' he said, 'of course you can't help wondering . . .'

'Obviously it would have serious personal consequences for you if Annika moved to Norrköping. That's why I wanted to let you know in person that the information is incorrect. So you weren't left wondering why we've been keeping something as important as that from you.'

Thomas ran a hand across his forehead. Halenius came a step closer and Thomas became aware of how clammy his fingers were. He put his hand on his lap next to the hook.

'The Light of Truth,' Halenius said, nodding towards the computer screen. 'Have you seen what that nutter's been writing?'

Thomas turned to the screen and felt his heart stop: he hadn't managed to close the site when Jimmy knocked at his door. The comments glared at him, with Gregorius's contribution glowing bright green:

Anders Schyman should be fucked up the arse with a baseball bat. Hope the splinters form a bleeding wreath around his anus.

Jimmy Halenius scratched his head. 'Christ,' he said. 'You can't help wondering what's going on inside some peo-

ple's heads. "Gregorius". Yeah, that just about sums it up.'
He put his hand on Thomas's shoulder and gave it a brief
squeeze, then turned to leave the room.

'Thanks,' Thomas said, his mouth full of dust. 'Thanks
for . . . well, coming to tell me. In person.'

The under-secretary of state smiled and walked out.

Thomas felt anxiety rise inside him, like a pillar of
smoke, filling him from his knees to his throat. He couldn't
breathe. Oh, God, oh, dear God, what if Halenius knew,
what if he'd realized that Thomas was . . . ?

He closed the site.

There was a computer on the other side of the desk.

Nina froze in the doorway, one foot inside the office, the
other still out in the corridor.

The laptop was the same as hers, with the music app,
Spotify, visible on the screen. Music was playing quietly
from some small speaker somewhere. An open folder lay
alongside the computer, full of printouts covered with
Asian characters.

Jesper Wou was back.

She took a deep breath and made herself walk into the
room. She skirted warily round the desk, keeping a safe
distance from it, then sat down on her chair without taking
her eyes off the new computer. The classical music rose to a
crescendo, then fell silent. Two seconds later another track
started, melodic piano music.

Oh, God. Did he always have Spotify on, or only when
he thought he was alone?

She put the key to the Lerbergs' house on her side of the
desk.

314

Why had Nora needed so much money? What was she borrowing it for? And from whom? Someone she was afraid of, according to Irina. She must have had a very good reason, that much was obvious, or she would hardly have embarked on these crazy international financial transactions.

The piano music changed pace and character and Nina recognized it. It was from some film. Julia used to play the same track, from that film with Holly Hunter in it, the one she got an Oscar for . . .

Would Jesper Wou mind if she switched it off?

No, she couldn't start fiddling with his computer. It would be like helping herself to his lunch.

She adjusted her ponytail.

Nora had been very keen to keep her loans and financial transactions secret. Otherwise she wouldn't have fought so hard to keep them hidden.

Nina leaned back in her chair and closed her eyes. The music swelled and she could see the film in her mind's eye, Holly Hunter playing the piano on a beach while her daughter performed cartwheels in a white dress.

Nora had studied Russian instead of going to yoga classes. She had a Russian-language course on her head-phones instead of the latest Henning Mankell. She flew back and forth to Switzerland instead of getting treatment for her thyroid. She employed someone to knit jumpers for the children and do her cooking. She had a computer that she didn't keep in the kitchen cupboard . . .

'Hi! You must be Nina.'

She opened her eyes with a start. A young man with shoulder-length black hair and a dark suit was looming in front of her. Instinctively she pushed back – he looked like one of the vampires in that film for teenagers, *Twilight*.

315

'Jesper Wou,' he said, holding out his hand.

She got to her feet and shook it. He was the same height as her.

'I've got the other side of your desk,' he said.

'I guessed as much,' she said. 'Nina Hoffman.'

'Welcome to National Crime.'

'Thanks.'

She let go of his hand, and he went round the desk and sat down in front of the computer. 'Sorry about the music, I didn't know you were coming in. I won't make a habit of it.'

'Don't worry,' Nina heard herself say. 'I recognized that bit, from . . .'

At that moment she remembered what the film was called.

The Piano.

*

The keys vibrate beneath my fingers, full of longing. All the hidden music that lives in there and wants to get out, I can hear it calling. Carefully I hit G sharp with my right hand, then G sharp and E, my left hand responds with C sharp, Chopin's waltz no. 7 in C sharp minor, Opus 64/2, so light and ethereal that no one can hear it. It can't be disturbing anyone. The notes emerge tentatively, feeling their way out into the room, pure, unsullied.

The howl comes from behind, a moment before tiny hands pull at my right hand, *Silly, Mummy, stop playing!* I take my fingers off the keys and the lid closes with a muffled thud.

You know Isak doesn't like it when you play. Do you have to provoke him? Ingemar's voice is so weary, and I understand him. So unnecessary. I smile.

Music isn't a career. There's an organ in the parish hall – you can play that, can't you? After the service?

Is this a dream?

I don't know.

*

The piano was tall and black, ornate, with a matt lacquered finish. Two large candleholders made of yellow metal were attached to the front, above the keyboard. Nina touched them cautiously. They were on hinges, adjustable.

It was an old piano, possibly a family heirloom. Nora was a talented pianist – Nina had read that in several newspapers. She had applied and been accepted to do one of the best music courses in Sweden, but had turned it down and chosen to study economics instead, even if she hadn't completed the course.

The piano had been examined by Forensics during their investigation of the crime scene. According to the Lerbergs' bank statements, the instrument was tuned twice a year by a man from Vaxholm. Nina stretched and felt the air fill her lungs. It was now even cooler in the house – someone must have turned the heating down. The silence pressed at her eardrums.

On top of the piano there were some black-and-white photographs: a boy in knitted dungarees and a wedding photograph of a couple with 1950s hairstyles. There was some sheet music, Satie and Grieg. Nina lifted these off and put them on the living-room table, then opened the lid that hid the workings of the piano. A puff of old dust rose up towards her. It was pitch black in there, so she switched on her torch and pointed it into the instrument. The strings stretched across a black-painted steel baseplate, the nails

317

holding them in place arranged in six bowed rows. Further down there were eighty or so small hammers, covered with felt. They were arranged in a long line, like soldiers, shoulder to shoulder, ready to strike the moment the command was given. Nina hit a note in the middle of the keyboard and one hammer came to life, struck its string, and the room filled with the sound. She moved along and hit a bass note down to the left. The hammer hit the string, but there was no clear note. She aimed her torch at the keyboard, then the strings, the nails, the metal plate holding everything together.

Nothing. Nothing out of the ordinary, nothing that shouldn't be there.

So why didn't the bass keys work?

She shone her torch around inside the piano and found two wooden hasps on the inside of the front. She put the torch down and loosened them. The front came away and she managed to lift it off – it was heavier than she'd expected. Carefully she leaned it against the wall next to the bookcase, and one of the candleholders hit the floor.

The piano grinned at her, like a skeleton uncovered. Behind the steel plate holding the strings in place she could make out the back, which formed the soundboard. She shone the torch everywhere.

Nothing.

She crouched down, shifted the piano stool and shone the torch underneath the instrument. There was another wooden hasp: evidently the bottom could be removed as well. She put the torch on the floor as she undid the hasp and removed the rear section.

The strings were fastened to a black steel frame. They crossed in the middle: the tin-coloured treble notes came

318

down to the left and the copper-coloured bass notes went to the right.

She hit the keys again. The high tin-coloured strings vibrated and sang, the copper ones remained silent and dead. Why?

She crawled under the piano, beneath the keyboard, and directed her torch at the bass strings from just a few centimetres away.

Something was pressing against the back of them. She put her finger against the matt black background. Textile. Some sort of felt material, exactly the same colour and appearance as the back of the piano. An object, the size of an A4 envelope, tucked between the bass strings and the black-painted soundboard.

She put her torch down once more and hit her head on the keyboard. The wooden frame pressed against her neck, and she realized she was sweating in spite of the chill in the room. She leaned back and managed to pull a pair of latex gloves from her trouser pocket and put them on. Then she cautiously touched the felt object, which moved under her fingers. Up to the right there was a gap between the black steel frame and the back panel, and she moved the object along with her left hand until she was able to reach it with the right and pull it out through the opening. It was relatively heavy. Her heart was thudding. The envelope was sealed with a strip of Velcro. It made a tearing sound as she opened it and pulled out a MacBook Air.

Well, hello . . .

Nina sat on the floor with the computer on her lap, waiting for her breathing to settle down. The device looked new, but she didn't know anything about Macs – maybe it was actually several years old. She stood up cautiously, one hip aching from the contorted position she had been lying in. She took the computer with her into the kitchen and sat down, putting it on the table in front of her.

That was where Nora used to sit when she was organizing her transactions. Right there, with a view of Silvervägen through the meticulously clean window on one side and the polished horseshoe of white kitchen cupboards on the other.

She opened the lid of the laptop – the screen really was extremely thin. She stared at the black, mute surface. She switched the device on, and held her breath as the programs loaded.

Password?

She breathed out. Nora was careful about protecting her secrets: her other computer had been password-protected as well. Nina closed her eyes. Nora had spent seven years sitting there moving money about and sending invoices – legal and illegal – between various companies, Ingemar's Swedish ones and presumably her own Spanish businesses.

She opened her eyes and looked at the screen thoughtfully. What could the password be?

The most common password in the world was 'password', but in Sweden '123456' was most often used, followed by 'hello' and 'hithere' in third place. Other common passwords were 'abc123' and 'qwerty', the first six letters of a standard keyboard. Forensics would be able to decipher it in an instant, just as they had with the other computer. Even if the hard-disk had been wiped, they would be able to uncover the information that had once been stored on it.

She took a deep breath and tried to relax her shoulders.

A MacBook Air, thin enough to be hidden behind the bass strings inside a piano. The other computer had also been a Mac – it might have been called a Pro. Had Nora sat them next to each other, the small, thin one and the bigger, sturdier one? Did she use them in the same way?

She got her mobile out of her pocket, hesitated for just a moment, then called Lamia's direct line. 'Hi,' she said, the moment her colleague answered. 'Nora Lerberg had a password on her computer, didn't she?'

'Yes,' Lamia said.

Nina stared fixedly at the screen in front of her. 'Can you remember what it was?'

Other colleagues would probably have wondered why she was asking, but Lamia answered straight away: 'Stefan.'

Stefan?

'The dog's name.'

Of course.

'Thanks very much,' Nina said.

'Don't mention it,' Lamia said, and hung up.

Did Nora work on both computers simultaneously? Did she log in at the same time, first one, then the other?

Nina rubbed her hands together for a moment, then typed 'stefan' into the password box.

Welcome, Nora!

Nina's head was buzzing.

She held her hands above the keyboard – she wasn't sure how it worked, but it ought to be similar to a PC.

At the bottom of the screen there was a row of icons for different programs, which expanded as she moved the cursor over them. She clicked on the default email program, and found just one email in the inbox.

Welcome to Mail!

Evidently not a program that Nora had ever used.

She moved the cursor to a folder titled 'Nora's book – memories and reflections', and clicked on it. Another password box appeared: the file was protected. After a moment she typed in 'stefan'. *Wrong password*. She moved on – Forensics would have to sort that out. She opened the web browser instead. The start-page loaded: a Swiss bank with offices in Zürich and Geneva. Nina's pulse quickened and her head began to sing.

Bitte melden Sie sich an.

She wasn't going to get any further without the log-in details. She moved on to the browser's history instead.

Empty, unless she was doing something wrong.

Her eyes roamed across the screen, and she clicked on 'favourites'.

A short list appeared.

At the top, a Spanish bank.

Logical, bearing in mind Kag's five companies.

Next was a bank in the Philippines.

Nina's pulse was hammering now.

Then came a bank in Panama City, and that marked the end of the list.

The three big customers of Ingemar Lerberg's company: shipping companies in Panama and the Philippines, and a transport business in Spain.

She forced her shoulders to relax and pushed her chair back slightly from the table.

Could that be a coincidence?

Unlikely.

She wanted to save his life.

Nina closed her eyes.

Nora had borrowed money that didn't appear anywhere in the family's finances. Was this what she had used it for? Filtering her assets into Ingemar's business? To make him look like a successful businessman rather than a failed politician who had been forced to resign?

One thing was certain: Ingemar knew nothing about it. Hence the computer, the secrecy, Irina . . .

Nora had borrowed money from the wrong people. Had they forced her to launder money in return, or had she entered into that arrangement voluntarily? Maybe she thought she could control the situation. That she would be able to launder enough money for her to repay the debt. Had she ventured deeper and deeper into that world of her own accord, even as her debt grew ever larger?

Nina knew there was no way out of that sort of process. It was a cycle that escalated out of control until nothing but violence was left.

She sank back in her chair and looked around the gleaming white kitchen.

If that was what had happened, Nora had kept everything going for a long while, six years, before it had collapsed around her. She must have panicked.

She had run out of options, once and for all.

*

Ingemar's anger is eating away at me from inside, stealing my oxygen, I'm falling, falling.

He says I'm not fit to look after his children, that I can't be his wife after what I've done.

I try to explain that this isn't about me, it's about him. They want his company now that it's got a major client, a real client, the big Chinese firm, there's real money there now, and

I'm culpable. We are culpable. He can't just close his eyes – there's no way back – but he's refusing. He keeps calling them 'gangsters'.

You can't give in to violence.

I beg and plead impotently, but he refuses to see, refuses to hear.

Ingemar, Ingemar, we have to be rational!

And he turns towards me but he doesn't see me: he sees only my actions, only my mistakes. I'm nothing to him. I'm worth absolutely nothing as an individual. I am a problem, something that could trigger another media avalanche, I am a potential snowstorm of headlines – everything I've done, all my dreams, everything I've tried to achieve . . . His eyes are as cold as a snake's, his hands like daggers pointing at my chest, and my heart freezes to ice. I feel the cold spread through me as the muscles of my heart grow sharp and scrape against each other.

He refuses to listen, and I am nothing.

*

The man was at the back of the crowd of agitated citizens who were screaming and waving their fists at the imposing brick building.

'Child-killer! Child-killer!' the crowd was chanting.

But he said nothing, just stood there with his hands buried in the pockets of his raincoat, watching the mass of people. He had to admit that he found the entire situation breathtakingly comical.

Here he was, surrounded by the mob, unable to deny that Anders Schyman really was true to his word. In complete contrast to what this crowd evidently believed, the editor-in-chief of the *Evening Post* was a man of honour and courage – he would be the first to attest to that.

Not a single word in all these years that there had been a secret source behind his television documentary, not so much as a whisper. Anders Schyman was a good bloke, he could personally vouch for that. He prided himself on being a good judge of character, and he had got better over the years.

The man focused on his breathing for a while, noting the way his stomach tensed when he breathed in, then relaxed when he exhaled, in a constantly repeated process.

It had been when they were doing their obligatory military service that he and his mirror-image had discovered their suitability for their very particular choice of career. They had done very well on their interpreting course in the garrison town of Karlsborg, especially in the simulated torture sessions that later received so much criticism in the press. The two of them had each, entirely unknown to the other, faked breakdowns so as not to stand out from the crowd.

Going back to their ordained careers as forest wardens had felt impossible after that. Instead they had set up their own little forestry company, and had simultaneously embarked upon the considerably more interesting career that now occupied most of their time. They worked as freelancers, primarily in Scandinavia, but they also accepted jobs in other parts of Europe. Their employers were many and various: they would work for anyone who was prepared to pay.

Viola Söderland was their first big case. They had done a few smaller jobs for the Russians, whose own organizations weren't particularly impressive in those days: the post-Soviet nation was very young at the time. Viola Söderland had done business with a lot of them. She had bought forests and land, but then she had tried to defraud them. She had regarded them as Communist amateurs. In the end it was abundantly clear that the money was gone, along with every possibility of recovering it. She was also under investigation by the police, and it was only a matter of time before she started to talk. She was, to put it mildly, a risk-factor that was no longer fit for purpose.

But he and his brother hadn't been very professional in those days. After Viola Söderland, he and his mirror-image had had to do a serious clean-up job. The police were getting closer. He didn't know what the authorities had on them – all they knew was that they had to find some way of dealing with the situation.

The best way to get the police off their tail was obviously to get them to look in a completely different direction. So they had chosen a controversial and risky method: they had contacted a highly regarded television journalist and served him up a watertight story that showed Viola Söderland had fled the country and was now living in luxury in the former Soviet Union. It had been relatively straightforward. Viola had actually been planning to run. She'd told them so entirely of her own accord – they hadn't even had to work very hard on her.

The business with the reporter had been an extraordinary move, but it had succeeded beyond all expectation. The focus of the authorities, including the police, had shifted from the suspicion that Viola Söderland had been murdered to the belief that she was now a tax exile.

After that he and his mirror-image decided that they had to split up. His twin brother – unless, perhaps, it had been himself, it didn't really matter which – had left the country and moved to Spain. They had bought a flat in an anonymous complex on a hillside overlooking Marbella, and one of them had vanished for ever from Swedish statistics. The other went on living a normal, respectable life in the Swedish forestry industry, with a business and an apartment in Täby, just north of Stockholm. They took turns living both lives, under the Spanish sun and in the affluent Swedish suburb, and could always give each other an alibi. That had been necessary a few times – these days it was practically impossible to leave no trace. But usually they moved around entirely unhindered, both in Swedish and Spanish society: a middle-aged man, stocky, not particularly tall, with thinning hair, in a badly fitting jacket and worn shoes. Not even the hookers in Puerto Banús took any notice of them now, him and his mirror-image, two versions of the same man.

The mob around him was busy working itself up into a frenzy. He smiled. This was a bonus he hadn't predicted. It was funny that all these people thought they knew what had become of Viola Söderland.

But Viola Söderland's current whereabouts were totally impossible to ascertain.

He sighed happily.

They had found a bomb-proof site in which to dump their waste. He couldn't help giggling at the thought.

'Bomb-proof' was precisely the right word.

Only in Sweden, he thought. Only in Sweden was there such formidable faith in people's respect for laws and regulations.

The immense tract of land that made up the Vidsel Test Site was obviously out of bounds to the general public, but there wasn't a single fence. Instead there was a sign every thirty metres along the perimeter, informing the public of the inadvisability of entering the area and thereby risking having a missile land on their heads. There was actually a public road running through the whole area. You could use it in any sort of vehicle, as long as you didn't stop to get out and walk. There were cameras mounted in a few places, but it was fairly easy to avoid them.

They had chosen to dispose of their waste there, untroubled by wandering fruit-pickers and people walking their dogs. The only things likely to disturb the results of their work were bombs and grenades. Not a single one had been discovered in all these years.

The whole idea was really very simple. The remains of human bones were very difficult to tell apart from any other mammal's. Only the skull, hands, feet and ribcage were easily identifiable as human to the naked eye. Everything else could belong to a reindeer, a cow, a juvenile elk, or some other medium-sized animal.

So they cut the heads, hands and feet off and buried them carefully, very deep. They broke up the ribcages using a crowbar. Wild animals did the rest. There may not have been any wolves in Norrbotten, but there were enough wolverines, bears, lynx and other predators in the untouched forests for the remains to disappear in a matter of days. They had actually tested the theory using a stolen pig before setting to work with real waste.

After two weeks the pig's bones had been scattered across an area of four square kilometres.

Viola Söderland had been their first real attempt. Where she was today was therefore completely impossible to say. She was probably spread across an area stretching from Vuollerim up to Porjus and down towards Sikfors.

Apart from the skull, hands and feet, of course, which had been safely buried in the moraine some fifty metres from the main road through what had then been called the Norrland Missile Test Site.

But Nora's whereabouts were even more difficult to determine.

Nora had been one of the organization's smarter smurfs. Sadly she had ended up sinking further and further into debt and was no longer meeting her quotas. When the organization had suggested a solution, she had rejected it. Towards the end there were also signs that she had been putting money aside, and that sort of thing was obviously unacceptable. And now she had disappeared, which (from his perspective) was the very worst thing of all. He and his mirror-image had been instructed to get rid of her, but now they couldn't find her. They had no idea where she was, and her husband didn't know either. They had even let the poor bastard live, just to draw Nora out from her hiding place, but it hadn't worked. (The wretched drunk, Ekblad, hadn't had a clue about anything, that much had become apparent very quickly.)

So they had informed Moscow that Nora was gone, because of course she actually was, and that morning's payment for the job had been transferred into the bank account of the forestry company, hosted by the sensible, unimpeachable Swedish Credit Bank.

He shut his eyes and noted the difference in temperature between the air going in and out of his nostrils.

One thing was certain: if their employers found out about their failure and lies, they could count themselves lucky if they escaped with a simple spread-eagle.

The thought prompted him to scrutinize his body, to feel the way the soles of his feet were standing on the ground, the roughness of his jacket under his fingertips.

Their hope was that Nora had gone so deep underground that she would never surface. And if she ever made herself known to anyone around her, he would find out about it, he had made sure of that, and then it wouldn't only be little Nora who disappeared (for good this time!), but her young children too. Nora was well aware of that, because he had told her as much himself.

He relaxed.

The job was finished. He had nothing to fear.

He would have a relaxing Friday evening, watch some television. Treat himself to some nice food. An Indian, perhaps.

The wind that hit Annika as she emerged from the Underground was intoxicatingly mild, and full of exhaust fumes. She stopped at the exit from the metro station for a moment and was elbowed angrily in her back.

These streets were properly hers now, dry and dusty. And they would continue to be hers: she wasn't going to move away from them. That made them feel more solid, and slightly less magical.

Even the sign on the door, the one she and Jimmy shared, was now more of a sign and less of a declaration.

Serena was standing in the hall when she walked into the apartment (*her* apartment!).

'Hello,' Annika said, pulling her boots off. 'Are Kalle and Ellen home yet?'

'No, just me.'

'How was school?'

The girl was wearing one of the sixties-inspired tunics she had been given by her mother. It was tight across the shoulders and a little too short. She glared at Annika with black eyes made of glass. 'Why are you even asking? You don't care.'

330

Annika took her jacket off and hung it up. *Don't lose your temper. Act like a responsible adult.*

'I do care about you, Serena,' she said, forcing herself to sound friendly and understanding. 'I'd like to get to know you better, because we're going to be living with each other for a long time, I hope.'

The girl took a step back, her face full of loathing. 'Long hair and big tits are really lame,' she said. 'And your job's lame, and I don't want to be with you, I want you to *die!*'

Her words took Annika's breath away. The reaction came a second later, shrinking her field of vision until all that was left were lightning flashes of rage.

Fuck you! Standing there in your stupid dress thinking you're something special. You can't be that fucking special if your own mother doesn't want you. I might be disgusting and my job might be crap, but at least I haven't abandoned my kids so I could prance about in some fucking government building in Johannesburg. I'm here! I'm all that's on offer! Maybe you don't deserve any better, you little bitch!

Shame hit her with such force that she had to reach out for support, and found the doorframe. When she caught her breath, it brought with it a howl of guilt and despair. She collapsed onto the hall bench, hid her face in her hands and burst into a flood of tears. Through a haze of snot and tears she saw Serena's feet in front of her by the hat-rack, stubborn and hesitant. Annika screwed her eyes shut and just howled.

'Er . . . sorry,' Serena said. Her feet shuffled. 'I'm sorry, I – I didn't mean it . . .'

She started to cry too. Annika wiped her nose on the sleeve of her jumper (disgusting) and looked up at the little ten-year-old who missed her mum so much she was falling

331

apart, great big tears rolling relentlessly down her soft cheeks.

'I don't want you to die,' she sobbed.

'I miss my mum too,' Annika said, holding her arms out to the child. Serena stepped into her embrace and wrapped her arms around her neck, and wept into Annika's hair.

The doorbell rang, a key was inserted into the lock and the door flew open. Jimmy and Jacob, Ellen and Kalle, Birgitta and Destiny all rolled into the hall with the noise of an invading tank. Annika grabbed Serena's hand and they snuck into the bathroom, locking the door behind them. They wiped each other's tears and look into one another's eyes, laughing tentatively.

'Cold water's the thing,' Annika whispered. 'Then no one can tell you've been crying, but it has to be really cold.'

They let the water run, then bathed their faces. Annika put some more mascara on, and lent Serena her lip-gloss.

'Come on, Serena,' Ellen cried. 'Destiny wants to play with the dolls' house.'

Annika unlocked the door and opened it.

'Coming!' Serena called, and hurried off.

Birgitta was waiting impatiently by the front door. 'Thanks for having her.'

Annika smiled, her heart light. 'Don't worry, she'll be fine with us.' She nodded in the direction of the bedroom corridor, where the girls' voices rose and fell. Birgitta shuffled on the spot and swallowed. 'I need to go if I'm going to catch the plane,' she said.

Annika nodded. Birgitta leaned forward and they gave each other an uncomfortable hug.

The door closed behind her sister. Annika heard the lift start, stop, then set off again. She padded quietly towards Ellen's room. Destiny was laughing, a gurgling toddler's laugh. She stopped in the corridor and peeped into the room. Ellen was holding the mummy doll and walking her through the rooms in the dolls' house, singing a little song. Serena was rearranging the attic, talking to herself. Destiny was cradling the baby doll. All very stereotypical.

The little girl sensed her presence and looked in her direction. Annika smiled and stepped into the room. 'What are you playing?'

Serena looked at her with a degree of trepidation. Annika sat down on the floor next to her and patted her arm.

'The family who live in the house, they're going to go for a picnic in the park,' Serena said. 'Mum, Dad and their children.'

Destiny toddled over to Annika, put an arm round her neck and sank onto her lap. Warmth bubbled up inside her, and for a moment she had trouble breathing. Her vision blurred. 'I need to go and help Daddy in the kitchen,' she said.

Jimmy was standing there with the apron tied round his waist, holding a spatula. The television screen by the little kitchen table showed Anders Schyman being interviewed by a female presenter in a bright blue television studio. Annika stood by the sink and watched him: television makeup made him look smoother.

'No,' Schyman said on screen. 'I'm not going to resign. I'm going to stay and take my responsibility for the development of Sweden's largest daily newspaper.'

He managed to look fairly good-humoured as he said that. Jimmy came over, stood beside her and watched, as fat dripped from the spatula onto the floor.

'Apparently the police had to break up a mob that had gathered outside your home this afternoon,' the presenter said. 'They broke some windows and threw eggs at the building. That must make you feel rather uncomfortable?'

'Of course it does.'

'What's your view of the situation?'

Schyman sighed. Jimmy noticed the dripping fat and swore, put the spatula down and reached for some kitchen roll to wipe it up.

'You're making this crazy online bullying sound like Nine/Eleven, but it's nothing like that. We have to keep a bit of perspective on things . . . Media witch-hunts like this don't happen in dictatorships. They're just a rather unappealing symptom of a functioning democracy.'

'It's quick and easy tonight,' Jimmy said, throwing the kitchen roll in the bin. 'Steak and pre-packed salad from Konsum.'

'Will you be sleeping in the house tonight?' the interviewer asked.

Schyman looked sad. 'Nothing in my life has changed at all,' he replied.

'Are you sure you want yours well done?'

Annika switched off the television and looked out through the window (*her* window!). 'There are lots of things I'm not sure about,' she said, 'but that isn't one of them.'

The lift slowed and pinged, then the door slid open with a sigh. Nina stepped out onto the red landing, took two steps to the left, held her key-card up to the lock and tapped in the code. The door shielding the National Crime Unit from the rest of the world unlocked with an electronic click. She walked quickly and purposefully towards her office, still pumped with adrenalin from her discovery and the forensics officers' brief comments of tacit admiration. They would be spending the whole weekend going through it, dragging out every last trace of digital dust that had ever been stored on the device.

The rooms she passed were empty. Most of her colleagues had already left for the weekend. Music was floating to her from somewhere along the corridor, laughter and voices, and as she got closer she realized it was coming from her room. She straightened her back as she approached, and slowed down.

'The leaders of Solntsevskaya Bratva are utterly obsessed with looking Western and established,' she heard Jesper Wou say. 'Not only has the one known as "the Director" bought himself a French vineyard, but guess what names he's given his new-born twins? William and Kate.'

Nina held her breath and walked through the door, taking in the room as she did when she was securing a crime scene.

Jesper Wou was leaning back in his chair with his feet up on the desk. Johansson was sitting in her place, and Lamia was perched on Jesper's side of the desk. Her skirt had ridden up, exposing almost the whole of her thigh. All three turned towards her, laughing. No one showed any sign of moving.

'Hi, Nina,' Lamia said. 'Q was looking for you earlier. He wanted to talk to you.'

She turned in the doorway and went towards the commissioner's office, her colleagues' laughter ringing in her head.

'Are you coming for a beer later, Nina?' Jesper Wou called after her.

She increased her pace and the length of her stride, and breathed out when she turned the corner at the end of the corridor. The door to the head of the Criminal Intelligence

Unit's office was open, and the commissioner was typing on his laptop.

'Ah, Analyst Hoffman,' he said, as she tapped on the door. 'Come in. You get a gold star for finding that computer. How are you enjoying National Crime?'

He went on writing, not taking his eyes off the screen. She walked into the room and sat on the uncomfortable visitor's chair – had he chosen that one on purpose? Subtle psychological game-playing?

'Fine, thanks,' she said, as she tried to make herself comfortable.

'What do you think of the work? Is it what you expected?'

She sat for a few seconds, silent and uncertain: what *had* she been expecting? The commissioner went on writing.

'Oh,' she said. 'It's very . . . interesting.'

'From what I've understood, you've slotted into the team well.' Her boss tapped a last key with a flourish and pushed the laptop away. 'I pulled out everything we've got on the Viola Söderland case yesterday evening,' he said, leaning forward across the desk. 'After that programme was broadcast on television, it was assumed that she'd fled to Russia. For the first few years the matter was raised at ministerial level, largely as an extradition issue, but the Russians claimed she had never crossed the border, and had never lived in the country. Eventually the case was dropped.'

'Do we believe them?'

Q sighed. 'The Russians didn't really have any reason to lie. In marked contrast to the Bergling case, for instance, where he really had been spying for them – but what had Viola done? Tried to avoid paying tax in Sweden and bought a load of Russian forest. Why would they protect her?'

'Maybe she was living under the radar – they might not have known she was there.'

'Theoretically possible. If you've got enough money you can buy pretty much anything in Russia.'

'Is she dead?'

Q scratched his navel. 'When she disappeared there was some evidence of a struggle in her villa out in Djursholm, a broken vase on the hall floor, and a strand of hair was found among the fragments. What was interesting about the hair was that it didn't belong to Viola, her children, or any of the staff in the house. But that was as far as it went.'

Nina nodded. Twenty years ago it wasn't possible to extract DNA from a strand of hair. The technology was too new, and required a whole bagful. Now, in contrast, mitochondrial DNA could be identified from a single strand. That didn't provide as much evidence as an ordinary DNA sample but it was a start.

'I asked for a mitochondrial DNA test on the hair yesterday evening,' Q said, handing her a rather grainy printout of a biotechnical protocol.

Nina took the paper and looked at it. It was like any other DNA result, and didn't mean anything to her. She put it down. Now it could be checked against various databases: the evidence register that consisted of DNA profiles from unsolved cases, the database of DNA from suspects and, of course, the one containing the DNA of convicted criminals.

'We had a man in for questioning about Viola's case almost twenty years ago,' Q said. 'There was a witness, a neighbour who was out walking his dog when he saw a man getting out of a car outside Viola's house on the night in question. He thought he could remember the registration number, but that turned out not to be the case. The owner of the car he identified had a watertight alibi: he was giving a lecture on the genetic modification of aspen trees up in Sandviken that night . . . He lives out in Täby, so I've asked our colleagues there to go and get a DNA sample from him first thing tomorrow morning.'

Nina nodded. If the man's DNA matched the mitochondrial DNA from the strand of hair, or from any other investigation, ongoing or concluded, it would show up in the search. It didn't necessarily mean anything, but it could be of decisive importance.

'Have you been in touch with Dr Kararei today?' Q asked.

'No,' Nina said, and blushed – she had forgotten.

'I spoke to him this afternoon. Things don't look good for Ingemar Lerberg. He's going to survive, but he's suffered severe brain damage. He could live for years as a vegetable in long-term care.'

'What will happen to the children?' Nina asked, thinking of Isak, the artistic little boy who talked out loud as he drew things.

'There's still a fully functional social-services unit out in Nacka, in spite of Ingemar Lerberg's attempts to get it shut down.'

'But who's going to look after them?'

'Apparently they've been placed in foster-care with a single mother-of-two in a three-room flat in Fisksätra.'

Nina looked out through the window, imagining the cramped space. Five children in two rooms? It might turn out okay. Or it might not.

'That was pretty much the only policy Lerberg managed to get through the social-services committee,' Q said. 'New criteria for the recruitment of foster-parents. Anyone's allowed to make an offer, and whoever bids lowest gets the children.'

Her boss's body language indicated that they were done. Nina cleared her throat. 'Actually,' she said, 'there is one more thing. Would it be possible to have a room of my own? Maybe not straight away, but eventually.'

'Don't you like Jesper?'

She squirmed uncomfortably. 'Yes, but . . .'

He smiled at her. 'Good work on the Lerberg case,' he said. 'And I'm glad you're happy here.' He turned back to his computer, and she went out into the corridor. It was deserted. She walked cautiously back to her room.

Empty. The desk had been wiped clean and the chairs were tucked in.

*

From a short-term perspective, it's incredibly boring to be successful. Monotonous and predictable. Doing the right thing demands so much consideration, anxiety and worry, so much doubt and frustration. Success is a tedious balancing act, walking the high wire without falling, concentrating the whole time, muscles tense, eyes focused straight ahead.

It's so much more fun to let yourself fall, tumble through space, plummet, feel the wind fill your head with freedom all the way down to the ground, swirling, swirling . . .

And then . . .

And then?

EPILOGUE

The residential area lay to the north-east of Moscow. As the crow flew it was only thirty-five kilometres from the Kremlin, but in practice it was many light-years away. The tiles on the façades of the buildings had fallen off in great clumps, exposing the concrete beneath to wind and rain. The buildings stretched from there to eternity, from the railway station all the way to the marshes, identical except for their varying states of dilapidation: fourteen floors, eight entrances, twelve flats on each floor. To begin with she regularly got lost. Her flat was in one of the blocks in the middle of the district: on a couple of occasions she ended up trying to stick her key into the door of the wrong flat before she realized her mistake. Now she couldn't understand how she had ever managed to get lost. Every building was distinctive. By her doorway the tiles had come off entirely, and someone had scrawled Путин навсегда on the cement. *Putin navsegda*, 'Putin for ever'. The name of her street was счастливый улице, Sčastlivy Ulitsa. Happy Street. She'd almost found herself singing the Swedish hit from the sixties when she learned what it meant.

They would look everywhere for her, she knew that. Everywhere, but not here. Not in their own backyard.

The few people who spoke to her knew she came from

Ukraine. She was Irina the piano teacher from Kiev, who made her living giving lessons. She had adopted her old speech defect once more – all those years of hard work to get rid of it actually made that fairly straightforward: she used the same techniques, just in reverse. That kept contact with neighbours and shop assistants to a minimum: she could see people literally squirming as she stammered whenever she tried to speak. No one could bear to talk to her long enough to find out how limited her Russian really was, or detect her hopeless Swedish accent.

Naturally she didn't actually give any lessons. She didn't think the neighbours she had introduced herself to suspected anything – she was so rusty at first that she could well have passed as someone taking lessons. Now she chose harder and harder pieces, a lot of Satie and Boulez, Stravinsky's *Petrushka*. She had bitten off more than she could chew with Maurice Ravel's 'Gaspard de la nuit', but it was a very pleasant torment.

Occasionally she would wake up during the night. She imagined she could hear Ingemar breathing beside her, or smell little Elisabeth. At times like that the pain closed around her, like a coffin, and she would gasp in the darkness with her mouth wide open, panting with her head thrown back until the screaming inside her exploded and died.

She caught sight of herself in the little mirror above the washstand, but she no longer flinched. Instead she stared into the heavily made-up eyes, brown now, the lenses still irritating. The optician had promised the discomfort would pass, but he was wrong. She ran a hand through her short, brownish-red hair – she actually liked it. She examined her firm, slender body. Eating nothing but protein had been easier than she had expected, and the effect had been

344

striking. She had lost fifteen kilos in the months since she had arrived.

A playwright lived in the flat next to hers. He hadn't done very well since *glasnost* and *perestroika*, and these days he mostly wrote melancholy poetry and drank a little too much vodka. He would come round to hers sometimes, putting up with her stammering in return for a free meal.

'When I was a little girl, I saw a television programme about a woman in Sweden who disappeared,' she told him on one occasion. 'It was just after my mother died. She was gone and I was left all alone, and I saw that programme about the woman who had done bad business with the wrong people, and had been forced to disappear for good. The story made a very deep impression on me. She had stashed some money away, assets no one else knew about, and she planned everything very carefully. She changed her name well in advance, and got hold of a new passport. Whenever she wanted to go out without anyone noticing her, she would wrap a scarf round her head, the way Muslim women do. She bought a second-hand car and paid cash for it, but never posted the change of ownership form. She got her money out of the bank before she left, and hid it inside the car. In the middle of the night she left her house and drove the old car across the border at Haparanda, then straight across Finland. She reached the Russian border before anyone had time to notice she was missing. The border guards were tired and hungry, and she had so many dollars with her that she was able to get in without her arrival being recorded anywhere. And then she made her way to Moscow, and left her old life behind without ever looking back. Some people might say she was heartless, that she was letting down everyone close to her, but she had no choice. If she hadn't left, she would have died, over and over again . . .'

'Did she have children?'

She opened her mouth to reply, but found that her voice was breaking. She nodded instead.

'What happened to them? How did it end?'

Irina the piano teacher smiled through a wall of pain. 'She never saw them again.'

Author's Acknowledgements

This is a work of fiction. Any similarities to real people, alive or dead, are purely coincidental. Even if places, times and events in the novel might feel familiar, everything takes place in an alternative reality.

I would like to thank:

Peter Rönnerfalk, head of Södermalm Hospital in Stockholm, for allowing me to bother him with the strangest (i.e. macabre) medical questions.

Varg Gyllander, head of information at the National Criminal Police, for letting me visit National Crime, and for assistance with all manner of questions about police procedure, both sensible and impossible.

Helena Bergström, actor and director, for years of discussion about what happened to Ibsen's Nora after she walked out of the doll's house and slammed the door behind her.

Lawyer Thomas Bodström, for legal expertise and advanced fact-checking.

My daughter Annika Marklund and my husband Mikael Aspeborg for editorial checks.

Niclas Salomonsson, my agent, and his colleagues at the Salomonsson Agency, and of course all the staff at my Swedish publisher, Piratförlaget.

347

And, above all, Tove Alsterdal, author and dramatist, who is always the first to read everything I write, and who discusses and analyses every part of the text, who supports and encourages me, and makes me feel I can carry on. I've said it before, and this time it's more true than ever: without you there would be no books.

The source for the descriptions of the very worst of human atrocities was Amnesty International.

Any eventual errors and peculiarities are entirely intentional.

THE LONG SHADOW
Liza Marklund

A violent robbery has taken place in an affluent area of the Costa Del Sol, in which an entire family are killed.

Annika Bengtzon is assigned to cover the story for the *Evening Post*. But when she arrives in Spain and gains access to the crime scene, she discovers there was a third child – a teenage daughter – who is unaccounted for.

Annika makes it her mission to find the missing girl. But as she delves into the mystery she becomes embroiled in a far darker side of Spanish life than she'd envisioned, as she begins to piece together a terrifying story of violence, abuse and murder.

'Liza Marklund has a knack for building beautifully elaborate and suspenseful plots. One of her greatest surprises is the strength of her heroine, Annika Bengtzon, an astonishing woman and an incredibly complicated character'
KARIN SLAUGHTER

BORDERLINE
Liza Marklund

In the midst of a Swedish winter, a young mother is found murdered behind her son's nursery. Halfway across the world, in the sweltering Kenyan heat, a government official is kidnapped.

As a journalist, Annika Bengtzon is often on the frontline, witness to the darkness humans are capable of. But this time it's different. It's personal.

The official held to ransom is her husband and she must meet the extreme demands of his kidnappers if she is to bring him home. And what of the Swedish mother slain in the snow? Until her killer is found, no one is safe . . .

'In a league of her own'
HENNING MANKELL

dead good

For everyone who finds a crime story irresistible.

Discover the very best **crime and thriller books** and get tailored recommendations to help you choose what to read next.

Read **exclusive interviews with top authors** or join our **live web chats** and speak to them directly.

And it's not just about books. We'll be bringing you **specially commissioned features** on everything criminal, from **TV and film** to **true crime stories**.

We also love a good competition.
Our **monthly contest** offers you the chance to win the latest thrilling fiction, plus there are DVD box sets and devices to be won.

Sign up for our free fortnightly newsletter at www.deadgoodbooks.co.uk/signup

Join the conversation on: